A Rainbow Book

Praise for *The Lhasa Trilogy*—

"In this intriguing book, we are transported on a journey from the dark into the light, a pathway we must all take in our quest for the Ultimate Reality. Highly recommended."

—Larry Dossey, M.D., author of *Healing Words*
and *The Power of Premonitions*

"*The Lhasa Trilogy* is a great story well told. Gary Conrad takes you on a magnificent journey across cultures and across time with scenes so vivid you will think you were there. It is filled with cultural and spiritual insights that will delight you, inform you and inspire you. It is a wonder filled book and worth the read!"

—D. Franklin Schultz, author of *A Language of the Heart*

"Drawing on ancient wisdom, *The Lhasa Trilogy* is a rich, layered tale that takes us on an intriguing adventure. Brilliant and insightful."

—Joan Korenblit, Respect Diversity Foundation

"Gary Conrad has written an imaginative and profoundly wise book. The reader's reward is a feast for both the head and the heart. Enjoy!"

—Dr. Robin R. Meyers, author of *Saving Jesus from the Church*

The Lhasa Trilogy

GARY D. CONRAD

RAINBOW BOOKS, INC.

FLORIDA

Library of Congress Cataloging-In-Publication Data

Conrad, Gary D., 1952-
  The Lhasa trilogy / Gary D. Conrad. — 1st ed.
    p. cm.
  ISBN-10: 1-56825-116-5 (hardcover)
  ISBN-13: 978-1-56825-127-1 (trade softcover : alk. paper)
  I. Title.
  PS3603.O5555L43 2012
  813'.6--dc23

                              2011034446

The Lhasa Trilogy © 2012 by Gary D. Conrad

Hardcover ISBN: 978-1-56825-127-1
Softcover ISBN: 978-1-56825-116-5
ePub ISBN: 978-1-56825-122-6

This is a work of fiction.

Illustrations by Sheridan Conrad.

The cover image, taken by the author during his October 2008 visit to Drak Yerpa, shows a Tibetan *stupa* overlooking the Yerpa Valley. A *stupa* is a domed structure that contains Buddhist relics and is used as a focal point for ceremony and meditation. The small dark spots in the foreground are yaks, which roam this sacred area.

The cover symbol, ༀ་མ་ཎི་པདྨེ་ཧཱུྃ, is a revered Tibetan mantra, *om mani padme hum*, which literally means "jewel in the lotus."

Published by:

Rainbow Books, Inc.
P. O. Box 430 Highland City, FL 33846-0430
Telephone: (863) 648-4420 • RBIbooks@aol.com • RainbowBooksInc.com

Author's Website:

GaryDConrad.com

Individuals' Orders:

Toll-free Telephone (800) 431-1579
Amazon.com • BookCH.com • AllBookStores.com

From THE TIBETAN BOOK OF THE DEAD, edited by Graham Coleman & Thupten Jinpa, translated by Gyurme Dorje, copyright © 2005 by The Orient Foundation (UK) & Gyrume Dorje. Used by permission of Viking Penguin, a division of Penguin Group (USA) Inc.

The paper used in this publication meets the minimum requirements of the American National Standard for Information Sciences—Permanence of Paper for Printed Library Materials, ANSI Z39.48-1984.

First Edition 2012
16 15 14 13 12   7 6 5 4 3 2 1
Printed in the United States of America.

To Gen Tsesum Tashi
May you be reborn in a free Tibet

The
Lhasa
Trilogy

"The tragedy of life is what dies inside a man while he lives."

—Albert Schweitzer

Prelude One

October 18, 1990 Drepung Monastery, Tibet

Lama Tenzin Tashi rubbed his eyes as he heard a loud banging on the heavy wooden door to his room. It had been a long, arduous day, and he felt irritation at this intrusion on his sleep.

Who could be disturbing me at this early hour? he wondered. He glanced at the hands of the clock sitting beside his bed — it read two a.m.

The knocking resumed, more strident than before, and this time a tremulous voice called from beyond the door, "The time has arrived."

The lama sighed and rolled from his bed.

Splashing ice-cold water from his bedside bowl onto his face, at last he understood. He dried himself with a cloth he kept at hand. "One moment," he responded and slipped into his ochre robe.

He opened the door, and Dawa Jigme came into view, a novice monk who was agitated and tearful.

Why has Dawa's training not prepared him to view death? He would have to address the subject with him . . . but not now. Dawa had been raised in a Lhasa orphanage, and Tenzin suspected he had been shielded from the pain associated with the end of life.

Tenzin looked into the young man's eyes and thought he saw a hint of anger in his handsome face. But he dismissed this early morning observation as irrelevant. When he joined Dawa in the hallway, a swarm of large,

1

ebony cockroaches scurried back into their home — inside the wall. Tenzin smiled. The insects were safe here. As a Tibetan Buddhist monk, all life was precious to him.

He motioned for Dawa to follow along, and soon they exited the monastery. Tenzin gasped as he felt the unseasonably cold early morning air strike his face. They carefully picked their way down the poorly lit ancient streets. Then, rounding a corner, they stumbled into two Chinese infantrymen, AK-47s slung over their shoulders, smoking cigarettes and hovering around a fire pot with their arms outstretched over the flickering flame. On the wall directly behind them was a large poster of the omnipresent Chairman Mao, wisely overlooking his Communist comrades.

One of the soldiers spat on the ground and addressed them, "You fucking idiots. Are you blind? Can't you watch where you are going?" They were not pleased at their misfortune of being assigned to watch on such a bitter night.

The monks said their apologies and hurried on. Now would not be a good time to be stopped and interrogated.

Wiping the cold perspiration from his wrinkled forehead, Tenzin nudged the younger monk forward, and these unwelcome invaders of their Tibetan homeland returned their attention to simply keeping warm.

The spiritual leader of the Tibetans, the Fourteenth Dalai Lama, had advised a path of nonviolence and compassion when dealing with the Chinese, but there were moments when it was difficult not to hate these foreigners who had not only brutalized their people but also had systematically and with intention destroyed their culture. Sometimes it was difficult for Tenzin to live with.

Time seemed to stand still as the two monks pressed ahead through the night. At first, the only sounds they heard were the angry howling of packs of hungry street dogs as they scrapped for food in the dark night of the new moon. Before long they became aware of the faint whisper of agonized screaming echoing from the distance. As the wails grew louder, Tenzin realized this tortured soul was at the destination he sought, and he began to comprehend the discomfort of the younger monk.

In a few more minutes they approached the front of an opulent estate with ornate gardens adorning the entrance. Brushing aside the attendant who answered the door, they entered to find an aged, balding, emaciated man in the throes of death, lying on his right side in a sunken bed.

His skin was the bright yellow of jaundice, as were the whites of his partially opened eyes. The piercing wails had diminished to low-pitched moans, and the moribund smell of approaching death penetrated the air, despite the sandalwood incense burning on a table adjacent to the bed. A small statue of the Buddha, sitting cross-legged in peaceful meditation, was perched on the windowsill and overlooked the vomit that filled the nearby basin and stained the dying man's bed-clothes. The young monks in attendance held between them *The Tibetan Book of the Dead* and were chanting softly from it with bowed heads. Tenzin paused as he heard the familiar words:

> O, Child of Buddha Nature, Matthew Walker Johnston, the time has now come for you to seek a path. As soon as your respiration ceases, the luminosity known as the 'inner radiance of the first intermediate state', which your spiritual teacher formerly introduced to you, will arise. Immediately your respiration ceases, all phenomena will become empty and utterly naked like space. At the same time, a naked awareness will arise, not extraneous to yourself, but radiant, empty and without horizon or centre. At that moment, you should personally recognise this intrinsic nature and rest in the state of that experience —

Grimacing, Tenzin stopped the chanting and dismissed everyone from the room. Only he and the dying man remained.

He gazed at the wretched skeletal form and understood why this impending death was so tortuous. Physical pain could be controlled, but this man's agony went beyond — ever so deep into the heart of his spirit.

Feeling the tension of the moment, Tenzin reverently touched a weathered picture of the Dalai Lama he had hidden in a pocket inside his robe. This was the same one his beloved hermit instructor, Geshe Choden Nyima, had given him many years ago. Somehow this gave him a modicum of peace. He then pulled out a small bronze-colored Tibetan singing bowl, also gifted to him by his teacher, and gazed at it fondly. He placed it in the palm of his left hand and pulled the wooden dowel from the center of the bowl with his right. Rotating the stick around the outside rim, a wavering melodic tone resonated loudly and penetrated every inch of the room.

The man roused and uttered a soft moan.

Tenzin replaced the bowl in his robe and leaned over him. He whispered softly, but with focused intensity, into his left ear. "Can you hear me?" he murmured. He watched closely. A slight nod of the head was perceptible. "I will do as you have asked," Tenzin said, feeling a deepening heaviness in his chest.

A slight curling of the dying man's parched lips indicated he understood. With a faint guttural moan his breath stopped, and he stared ahead, open-eyed, pupils fixed and dilated.

So be it.

Tenzin heard the monks continue to chant outside the door as he placed his right hand to the man's still-warm neck. Finding no pulse, he said without emotion, "Matthew Walker Johnston, you are now gone from this world."

Just as death has come to him, so must it come to each of us. There is no escape.

Now, he thought with a shudder, *I must do what no one has done before in the history of humankind.* A vow was sacred to him, though this one bordered on the profane.

No, this is worse than profane. This promise is blasphemous.

Will saving the lives of many thousands justify this crime? When do the ends truly justify the means?

He departed the room, leaving the body to the monk attendants. At the proper time and place, a traditional Tibetan sky burial would be performed. But, for now, this was the least of his worries.

Within the next year, he had to make preparations for a spiritual odyssey, a task he knew he never should have accepted.

Prelude Two

October 22, 1990, Drigung Til Monastery, Tibet

Dawa Jigme secured his winter hat over his head to protect him from the frigid, high altitude weather. His thick, sheep's wool robe was not thick enough.

It was approaching dawn at Drigung Til Monastery, and the early morning light faintly revealed a precarious route along the darkened barren hillside. Dawa, along with a small procession of monks, chanted as they walked the steep trail, some carrying burning torches of juniper. They were followed by two men, *rogyapas* — body breakers — who wore long white aprons. Between them they carried a bent body wrapped in white cloth.

Dawa well remembered the events of the past three days. After the abrupt exit of the lama, he and his fellow monks offered a prayer of assistance from *The Tibetan Book of the Dead*, and repeated it three times:

> O, buddhas and bodhisattvas, abiding in the ten directions, refuge of living beings, imbued with compassion, imbued with knowledge, imbued with clear vision and imbued with love, come to this place, by the power of your compassion and accept these displayed and visualised offerings! O, Compassionate Ones, as you are the fountain of all-knowing pristine cognition, of loving compassion, of effective activity, and of a power to grant refuge, beyond conception, come to this place!
>
> O, Compassionate Ones, this human being, Matthew Walker

Johnston, is leaving this world and journeying to another shore. He is being cast off from this world and approaching the great transition of death. Suffering deeply, he is without a friend, without a refuge, without a protector and without a companion. His perception of this life is fading away. He is moving on to another world, entering a dense darkness and falling into an unfathomable abyss. Entering the thick forest of doubt, he will be driven on by the potency of past actions. He will be entering a great wilderness, borne away on a great ocean, and driven on by the vital winds of past actions. He will be moving in a direction where there is no firm ground, entering a great battlefield, being seized by great malevolent forces and becoming overwhelmed by fear and terror upon meeting the executors of the unfailing laws of cause and effect. In accord with his past actions, powerless to resist, he may even, yet again, be entering the realms of rebirth. The time has come when he has no choice but to move on, alone, leaving his dear friends behind.

O, Compassionate Ones, grant refuge now to this person Matthew Walker Johnston, who has no refuge! Protect him! Be his companion! Defend him from the great darkness of the intermediate state! Turn back the great hurricane of past actions! Protect him from the great fear and terror of the unfailing laws of cause and effect! Rescue him from the long and dangerous pathways of the intermediate state! O, Compassionate Ones, be unsparing in your compassion! Grant assistance to him! Do not allow him to be expelled into the three kinds of inferior existence. Without wavering from your ancient vows, swiftly release the power of your compassion. O, buddhas and bodhisattvas, for the sake of this person Matthew Walker Johnston, be unsparing in your compassion, skilful means and ability! Seize him with your compassion! Do not allow this sentient being to fall under the power of negative past actions! O, Three Precious Jewels, protect us from the sufferings of the intermediate state!

Tenzin had given specific instructions, which they followed exactly. They maintained a vigil around the corpse for seventy-two hours, offering continuous prayers and chanting. The body was kept on its right side, mirroring the death position of the Buddha. It was not touched, except at the crown of his head, through which the *namshe* — consciousness — exited. The body was then washed and wrapped with white cloth into a fetal position, mimicking its posture when the soul entered the earth. When this ritual was completed, the corpse, along with the monks, was transported by a smoke-belching Chinese diesel truck to Drigung Til Monastery, about 120 kilometers northeast of Lhasa.

Dawa knew that this was one of the three most important *jhator* sites in all of Tibet. Tenzin had taught him much. *Jhator* meant "giving alms to the birds." When the body was presented to the vultures, they were *dakinis*, the Tibetan term for angels, which literally meant "sky dancers." It was believed that when the vultures spread their wings and flew away from this site, they distributed the body to the highest peaks of Tibet through their droppings.

Tenzin had also told him that when the Chinese overran Tibet in 1950, they viewed sky burial as barbaric and eventually banned the practice. In the 1980s they began to allow it again, realizing that much of the ground in Tibet was too rocky to dig a grave, and, given the scarcity of wood, sky burial was the most practical choice.

Dawa's thoughts were interrupted by the eerie screeching of vultures as they approached the charnel grounds. This area, about a half mile east from the monastery, consisted of a large fenced meadow with a half-circle of stones partially surrounding a flat boulder where the *jhator* was to take place. Dawa looked back at his fellow monks; most had a sallow color to their skin.

As he gazed again at the charnal grounds, his view was soon obscured by a growing flock of vultures. Some had a two-meter wing span, and, after landing, they edged just yards away from the rock on which the body was to be placed. Dawa fought back the urge to scream and run away.

The monks chanted *om mani padme hum* — "jewel in the lotus" — as they took seats on the rocks surrounding the slab. The *rogyapas* roughly threw down the body, with a cracking *thump*, on the flat rock. As they began to unwrap the corpse, one smiled and said, "Which of the monks do you think will vomit first?"

"Definitely the one called Dawa," said the other. "He is as white as our aprons." They laughed and continued their work.

Dawa choked back waves of nausea as the odor from the now unwrapped, green tinged carcass slapped him in the face and clung to every exposed inch of his skin. The chanting of the monks abruptly stopped.

The *rogyapas'* chuckles increased as they observed the reaction of the monks. The larger said, "If you baby monks would like to leave and go home to your mothers, we won't tell anyone." He winked and smiled a toothless grin.

While most shook their heads, Dawa watched as several got up and unsteadily walked back down the mountain.

One of the *rogyapas* began waving long sticks and shouting to hold back the squawking and agitated vultures, while the second lifted up an ax he had placed next to the boulder. After whetting it on an adjacent rock, he kneeled over the head of the corpse, scalped it, and broke off and removed the teeth. Then he rapidly dismembered the body, stripping the skin and muscle off the bones in long swaths. He split open the abdomen, and the stench of rotten entrails made the previous odor seem like sweet perfume.

It was too much for Dawa. He gagged and vomited as days-old yellow feces oozed slowly onto the now darkened rock. The remaining monks likewise began to retch, and before too long their morning breakfast would also be given to the birds.

The chuckles of the *rogyapas* became roars of laughter. They almost fell over as they guffawed hysterically, tears rolling down their cheeks.

One of the *rogyapas* finally regained his composure and wiped his eyes with a soiled cloth before he stepped back from the slab. His partner then lowered his arms and also moved away. Sensing that their time had come, the hungry vultures swarmed onto the rock, the larger, stronger ones in the forefront, eating the putrefied flesh and entrails, gulping ravenously. Some momentarily choked on the larger pieces.

Dawa vomited again — and again —

In a short time all that remained was a bloodied skeleton. The scavengers saw their meal had vanished and returned to an adjacent boulder. They waited impatiently while one of the *rogyapas* produced a large sledge hammer. He swung his instrument in a high arc and smashed the bones into tiny shards with repeated blows. After mixing the bony slush with *tsampa*, a Tibetan staple of roasted barley flour and yak butter tea, he again backed away.

The vultures charged back onto the slab; this time they left nothing except for old blood and the spatters of bird droppings. Sated, the heavily gorged birds clumsily flapped away into the clear morning sky, now brightened by sunrise. Song birds began to chirp, and the warmth of the rising sun gradually penetrated the cold.

With their task completed, the *rogyapas*, whose aprons were stained with blood and feces, returned to the path leading down the hillside to the monastery. They laughed and playfully walked along the mountain trail.

Dawa, still quivering and exhausted, paused a moment with what was left of his fellow monastics. They would continue their prayers for a total of forty-nine days to assist the soul in making its passage through the *Bardo*, the stages of existence that came before the next incarnation.

He stared angrily at the bloodied slab then stumbled away.

Book One

MATTHEW

WALKER

JOHNSTON

"God sometimes does try to the uttermost
those whom he wishes to bless."

—Mohandas Gandhi

Chapter 1

ohn and Edith Smith's baby died in childbirth last week.

William Johnston could not get that thought out of his mind as he paced in the living room of his small frame home in rural Oklahoma. His wife, Naomi, had been in labor for over fifteen hours, and as her contractions and discomfort increased so also did his anxiety.

Will, a simple farmer, was skilled in the delivery of four-legged creatures, but this was much too intimate for him to maintain his composure.

He stepped outside to the front porch. The sun was sinking into a cloudy haze on the horizon. He carefully searched the sky for storm clouds and saw none. He was born and raised in Oklahoma and knew tornados could strike when you least expected them.

He stared at the road and gazed into the empty distance.

How long had it been since his neighbor, Virgil Carter, had gone to find Dr. Raulston?

Damn it, where are they?

He pulled a red handkerchief from his back pocket and dabbed his sweaty forehead. He was grateful for the help of Virgil's wife, Eleanor, tending to his wife in their bedroom.

At long last Will saw a rapidly approaching carriage with a thick cloud of fine dust trailing as it rumbled over the rutted dirt road. Virgil was holding the reins and

11

whipping the horses into a frothy gallop. Sitting beside him was the dapper Doc Raulston, dressed in his usual black hat, coat and pants with a white shirt and bolo tie. The normally imperturbable physician had a look of panic as he clung to the railing of the wagon with his right hand and clutched his black bag with his left. He bounced several feet into the air with each unexpected bump.

The carriage came to a skidding halt beside the front porch, and the dust engulfed the buggy and its riders.

The doctor jumped down from his seat, black bag in hand. He shook Will's extended hand and said, "How's my patient?"

Taking Will's pained look as an answer, he dashed up the steps of the concrete porch and jerked open the flimsy screen door. It slammed shut behind him with a loud *snap*, but that didn't deter Will. He pressed on in the trusted physician's footsteps.

Doc threw his coat and hat in the direction of a frayed, green living room couch. Finally he ended up in the kitchen, washing his hands in a bowl of soapy cold water Will had set out for him hours earlier.

Eleanor cracked the door from the bedroom. "Doc, you've got to get in here right now."

He shook the excess liquid from his hands and dried them with a nearby dish towel. "Boil some water," he said to Will. Then he pulled up his sleeves and entered the bedroom, Eleanor closing the door behind him.

Just after Will had stoked the wood stove and placed a kettle of water on it, he heard the approaching footsteps of his neighbor, Virgil Carter. They shook hands and sat down together on the living room couch next to the doctor's dusty coat and hat.

"How's the wife of my best friend?" Virgil asked.

"I'm not feeling too good about this," Will replied. "If one of my cows was working this hard, I'd have my hands inside her and pulling on anything I could get my fingers on. I wouldn't care if it was only an ear. We'd have us a calf one way or another." He paused and took a deep breath. "Naomi's been having hard labor for too long. Thank God, Doc is here. Where did you find him?"

"He was at the Frederick Hospital making rounds," said Virgil. "You should have seen the look on the faces of the nurses as I jerked him away from the bedside of Mildred Culpepper. They tried to stop me from going into her room, but I went in anyway, even though four of them were hanging on me. I said, 'Doctor, you've got some pretty important business to attend to.' He looked at me and said, 'What are you talking about?' I said, 'We're about to have a baby, and you're going to be there.' He barely had time to grab his bag and throw on his coat and hat before I hustled him out to the buggy."

Will's face blushed with gratitude. "I know you've got plenty of chores to do at your farm. Wheat harvest coming up soon. Do you and Eleanor need to head home?"

"Nah," Virgil said. "Besides, I think the Doc might need some help. Eleanor is pretty good with having babies, you know. Anyway, I'd kind of like to know what's goin' to happen." He winked and smiled at Will. "Hey, what if you pass out? I'd better be around to pour some cold water on you."

"Thanks, old friend."

While Virgil was not above the occasional profanity, he was the son of a Baptist minister, and he always carried his King James' Bible with him. He pulled it out of his oversized front coat pocket and flipped opened the tattered black cover to a worn page. He read out loud.

"The Lord is my shepherd; I shall not want —"

Will heard another scream from the bedroom.

John and Edith's baby died last week.

Shaking his head, trying to rid the unwanted thought from his head, he again heard Virgil's words.

"Yea, though I walk through the valley of the shadow of death, I will fear no evil: for thou art with me; thy rod and thy staff they comfort me —"

Their baby never took a breath.

"Surely goodness and mercy shall follow me all the days of my life: and I will dwell in the house of the Lord for ever."

Please no, not my baby. Let my baby live. Please, God.

Virgil softly closed the book.

Panic and fear had invaded Will's soul.

ཨོ་མ་ཎི་པདྨེ་ཧཱུྃ ཨོ་མ་ཎི་པདྨེ་ཧཱུྃ ཨོ་མ་ཎི་པདྨེ་ཧཱུྃ

The minute Dr. Raulston entered the room, he was sure of one thing:

The baby is in serious trouble.

The length of the labor didn't particularly concern him, especially since this was her first child. However, Naomi's appearance was alarming, even to his experienced eye. She was as pale as anyone he could remember, and her blood pressure was too high, even considering the severity of her contractions. His suspicions were confirmed when he heard the baby's heart beat drop into the fifties during a contraction. This child had to be delivered soon, or it would not survive. While he was a skilled surgeon and knew he was capable of doing an emergency caesarian section, he preferred not to perform this procedure in such a remote location without an experienced nurse available.

"Naomi, put your heels together, put them close to your bottom, and let your legs fall apart." Inserting his gloved index and ring fingers of his right hand into her vagina, he felt a sense of relief when he discovered the cervix was completely dilated, with the baby's head bulging through it. He flushed as he recalled the death of the Smith's baby only eight days ago. It was also their firstborn.

This child has to live.

"It's time," Dr. Raulston said. "With the next contraction, bear down as hard as you can." He readied his birthing tools.

The next spasm came suddenly and unexpectedly early. Naomi put her hands on her knees, and Eleanor pushed her forward. With a visceral yell from Naomi, the baby's pink head delivered from the vagina under the control of Dr. Raulston's hands. He discovered that the umbilical cord was coiled twice around the baby's neck.

Ah-ha! No wonder all this difficulty.

He skillfully kept the head close to the vagina as the next contraction propelled the baby's body forward. Cradling the infant into his left arm, he then unwrapped the cord.

"It's a boy!"

No spanking was necessary, as the baby screamed vigorously in a few short seconds. Naomi and Eleanor both joined the baby in a howl of joy, and after the umbilical cord was securely clamped and cut, the child was placed on Naomi's now-blanketed abdomen for drying and a mother's love.

ཨོཾ་མ་ཎི་པདྨེ་ཧཱུྃ ཨོཾ་མ་ཎི་པདྨེ་ཧཱུྃ ཨོཾ་མ་ཎི་པདྨེ་ཧཱུྃ

A few moments later, the door opened and Eleanor motioned Will inside. He beamed as he saw his son, his hope for the future. The infant was no longer crying and was snuggled comfortably in his mother's arms. He was bright pink with a thick mop of dark hair and patchy areas of white sticky stuff over much of his face and chest. Will gently took his wife's hand.

"Husband, meet your son," Naomi said. "Son," she said as she gently rubbed his head, "meet your father."

"What shall we call him?" Will said, as he kissed her forehead.

With a knowing smile, she said, "His name is Matthew Walker Johnston."

ཨོཾ་མ་ཎི་པདྨེ་ཧཱུྃ ཨོཾ་མ་ཎི་པདྨེ་ཧཱུྃ ཨོཾ་མ་ཎི་པདྨེ་ཧཱུྃ

An exhausted Will and Naomi sat on the old green couch, legs outstretched, while Matthew sleepily nursed on his mother's breast. Just a short time ago, Dr. Raulston had re-examined both mother and child and pronounced both of them to be fit. He then repacked his bag and walked outside for a few breaths of cool air. He was exhausted.

Virgil and Eleanor put down their nearly finished cups of coffee, again extended their congratulations and followed the good doctor into the cool Oklahoma night. The sky was brightened by a full moon, and the smell of freshly turned earth lingered in the air. Will heard the carriage leave at a much slower pace than when it arrived.

He gazed lovingly at his wife and son. Even though he had been a father for only a short time, he began to feel the weight of new-found responsibilities.

Could he provide adequately for the three of them? Would his son be healthy? What challenges would Matthew face in his life, and would he be strong enough to face them? Would he, as a father, prepare him for what the world might bring?

Concerned, he glanced at his now sleeping wife and son. The only movement perceptible was the episodic twitch of Matthew's mouth as he nursed, not for sustenance, but for the comfort of his mother.

Enough worrying, he thought. *The world will present us with plenty of difficulties in the future. Right now, the love of my life is holding our son, and we are at peace. No one in the world could be happier than I am.*

He bowed his head and prayed: *Oh, God, wherever his path might lead, guide him, be with him.*

Chapter 2

Davidson, Oklahoma, 1934–1941

Christmas day, with its decorated pine tree and tinfoil light reflectors, plus a special dinner of roast chicken, dressing and pumpkin pie, had come and gone. Eight-year-old Matt was in bed, one he shared with his younger brothers Alex and Robert. They snored softly beside him.

Matt had wanted a football for Christmas; he had received a thick packet of paper and five pencils — for school — and a red scarf and mittens — for walking that mile into school — on those cold, dust filled days when the wind blew wild.

He listened to the faint voices of his parents, who continued to talk in the living room. He guessed his younger sisters Esther and Earlyne were sleeping too; their room was just down the hall, and they were as quiet as mice.

What could dad and mom be talking about?

Then his mind drifted back to the football he so wanted for Christmas. Kids on the farm had to come right home every day after school to help with the chores, while town boys got to go out and play football, just for the fun of it. Then he thought of his best friend in the whole world, Joe Hay, who lived on a nearby farm.

Maybe, just maybe, Joe got a football for Christmas.

Matt closed his eyes and tried to sleep. He couldn't. Paper and pencils. Red scarf and mittens. Around and around they traveled in his mind, and his parents' voices droned on. Finally he couldn't take it any longer.

Maybe, just maybe, they're talking about getting me that football for my birthday.

He crawled from bed and found his way to the bedroom door in the dark. Once in the hall, he could hear what his folks were saying. He settled down on the floor and listened.

"Well, I guess it went okay," his father said. "It wasn't much of a Christmas. Are you sure you've counted every dime and dollar? What with the Depression and the dust storms, it's getting harder and harder to pay the loan on the farm each month. I sure wish I could've bought you a present —"

"Will, I didn't need a present. And, yes, we've got January's loan payment saved."

"That's a relief." Silence followed, then, "Lots of folks are heading for California, claiming there're plenty of jobs out there. I'd hate to give up on the farm and do something like that."

"We're not going anywhere, Will. We can make it. I'll skimp and save, no matter what. We bought this farm in better times, and better times will come again."

Matt sighed.

This is home. I guess I'll have to live with it.

ཨོསྐརྞིངདྲེརྞ ཨོསྐརྞིངདྲེརྞ ཨོསྐརྞིངདྲེརྞ

Always at Matt's side was his dog Inky, a jet-black Lab mix. One day when Matt was nine, Inky wandered onto the Johnston property and made it home. While there were usually plenty of scraps for him, he seemed to find great pleasure in catching rabbits, and partially eaten cottontails and jackrabbits were often discovered scattered around. One fall day Matt and Joe came home from school and discovered a fresh kill.

"Hey, Joe," Matt said, pulling out and unfolding his sharpened pocket knife, "do you want a rabbit's foot? It's good luck, you know." He began sawing at one of the legs.

"You bet."

Matt removed two of the front feet and wiped the small amount of blood that oozed from them with his handkerchief. He handed one to Joe.

Joe carefully appraised his new possession, lowered his voice and spoke as if he were telling a secret. "Some of our friends are blood brothers, but we'll be something better. We'll be Brothers of the Rabbit. Nobody or nothing will ever come between us." They touched the bloody stumps together as if it were a sacred rite.

"Brothers of the Rabbit," Matt solemnly said.

"Brothers of the Rabbit," Joe repeated.

ཨོསྐརྞིངདྲེརྞ ཨོསྐརྞིངདྲེརྞ ཨོསྐརྞིངདྲེརྞ

Matt loved helping his dad pick pecans and sapodilla plums at their home. Every fall his father climbed into the pecan tree, and, before he did anything, he yelled, "Watch out below!" All five kids in the family elbowed each other, trying to get the best position under the tree.

"Okay, Dad, we're ready!" they hollered together. They then all put buckets over their heads.

Their father jumped up and down on branch after branch. Then he grabbed any available limb and shook with all his might. Matt heard *ting* after *ting* as the pecans hit his bucket, along with the giggling of his brothers and sisters. When the noise stopped, they pulled the buckets off their heads and hurriedly gathered the pecans in them, as if it were a contest.

His dad then shimmied down the tree. After harvesting a bucket of pecans for making pies and such, he said, "Who wants some nuts?"

"Me! Me! Me!"

His father had strong, callused hands. Matt marveled at the strength in them as his father grabbed a couple, pressed them together and cracked the shells. As fast as he could open them they were snatched and eaten. Matt felt a pecan hit him on his left ear. He looked over and saw Alex grinning mischievously. *I'll get even with him*, Matt thought. *But not while Dad is looking.*

Esther, the oldest sister, had a huge pile in her bucket and protected them as a brooding mother hen might. She leered back and forth as she ate the pecans her father cracked.

Matt glanced over at his youngest brother, Robert, with his cowlick and freckled face. He was sitting next to their little sister, Earlyne, sharing some of his pecans with her. Because of severe nearsightedness she wore horn-rimmed glasses and was at a distinct disadvantage when it came to gathering pecans. *Not to worry*, Matt thought, *Robert will take care of her. He always did.*

After their stomachs were bulging with pecans, his father smiled and said, "Enough for now. Keep a few more for yourself, but let's save the rest for your mother, okay?" With that, they scampered into the house, anxious to show her their treasures.

The plums were an altogether different story. Like persimmons, Matt knew you had to be careful and make sure they were ripe. No, beyond ripe, almost rotten. One bite into a not-so-ripe plum led to what Oklahoma farmers called "puckering up."

Matt saw the smile on his father's face the first time Matt did it. It happened only once.

ཨོཾ་མ་ཎི་པདྨེ་ཧཱུྃ ཨོཾ་མ་ཎི་པདྨེ་ཧཱུྃ ཨོཾ་མ་ཎི་པདྨེ་ཧཱུྃ

If there was any one thing that Matt was sure of, it was how much he hated church. He would much rather do hours of chores, and that included slopping hogs.

Every Sunday morning, unless there were pressing matters on the farm, he put on his best dress-up clothes and, along with his family, went to church, initially by carriage and in later years by a Model A Ford. For a time they attended the Davidson Baptist Church, and their first hour there was spent in Sunday school. Matt didn't mind that so much, but then came church service.

"Woe be to you, all ye sinners!" screamed Reverend Black, his greasy black hair flying in all directions. He smoothed it back to cover a large bald spot. His angry, bloodshot eyes stared at his petrified congregation.

Matt was sure he was looking at him.

"You are all destined to burn in the hottest hell unless you accept Jesus Christ as your savior." His usually pale face was beet red. "For eternity!" he shrieked.

Matt gulped. He glanced at his father and mother, who were smiling at each other. *Hmm*, Matt thought, *they don't seem too worried.* He felt his mother squeeze his hand.

"The demons of hell have sharpened their tridents and have reserved a place especially for you." Reverend Black then put his hand to his ear, as if listening. "I can hear their laughter now. They're calling your names!" Froth built at the corners of his mouth.

A scream went up from the back. A woman on the next-to-last row had passed out. Her husband leaned over her and dabbed her face with his handkerchief.

Matt made up his mind once and for all.

This is all a bunch of crap.

His dad and mom must've felt the same way. The next Sunday they went to the Davidson Methodist Church. It was a lot tamer, but that didn't matter to Matt. He still hated church.

ཨོཾ་ཨ་ཧཱུྃ་ ཨོཾ་ཨ་ཧཱུྃ་ ཨོཾ་ཨ་ཧཱུྃ་

Finally, when Matt was twelve, Alex was old enough to take up some of the chores Matt had been doing, and Matt was allowed more after-school time with his buddy Joe, who had received a football the Christmas before. Matt discovered that the pigskin just seemed to fit into his hand naturally.

"Joe, go out for a pass," Matt would say.

"How about you go out this time? I've gone out for ten straight."

"Aw, come on, Joe. Are you a man or a mouse?"

"I'm a man. Throw me the ball. Let's see you run for a while."

Matt felt lucky. Some of the farm boys he and Joe knew weren't going on in school. Their folks said, "That's 'nuf educatin'. You need to work on the farm."

ཨོཾ་མ་ཎི་པདྨེ་ཧཱུྃ ཨོཾ་མ་ཎི་པདྨེ་ཧཱུྃ ཨོཾ་མ་ཎི་པདྨེ་ཧཱུྃ

As Matt grew older, he worked alongside his family picking cotton, dragging heavy, eighteen-feet-long burlap sacks behind him. He also learned to break the fields behind a horse and a plow, and labored side by side with his family and neighbors.

One dreary day, a Monday — Matt had stayed home from school to help his dad dig a new well — he and his folks took a break and huddled around the family radio. His father tweaked the knob until he could find a clear signal. The day before, a Sunday afternoon it was, the news of Pearl Harbor had exploded across America.

They heard President Roosevelt ask Congress to declare war on Japan. Matt looked up at his mother. Tears were in her eyes. His father had his arm around her and solemnly looked at Matt. Matt wondered what he was thinking. Three days later, on December 11, 1941, Germany declared war on the United States, and now it was a global conflict.

Then and there Matt decided that, when he was old enough, Uncle Sam might need his help. He'd heard the pay wasn't bad to begin — twenty-one dollars a month. Never in his whole life had he seen that kind of money. He began to think about serving his country.

ཨོཾ་མ་ཎི་པདྨེ་ཧཱུྃ ཨོཾ་མ་ཎི་པདྨེ་ཧཱུྃ ཨོཾ་མ་ཎི་པདྨེ་ཧཱུྃ

Sometimes, when his family had all gone to bed, Matt would lie in the cool grass in the front yard at home, his coat folded beneath his neck, gazing upward at the stars. At his side was the aging and ever present Inky, snuggled up to him, needing nothing more than his master's presence.

In the dark country night, the sky appeared as a shimmering vision, so bright as to seem unreal. Matt could readily pick out the Big Dipper and followed the line of the cup to identify the North Star, the end of the tail of the Little Dipper. His favorite, though, was Orion, The Hunter, with its distinctive belt of three stars. Always close to Orion was the brightest star in the night sky, Sirius, the Dog Star.

"Hey, Inky, that star's named after you!" He smiled and rubbed the ears of his faithful friend. Inky had heard the same words many times over the years. *If dogs could roll their eyes*, Matt thought, *Inky surely would be rolling his.*

For hours he watched the celestial formations move across the sky. He pulled his coat over the two of them as the night air began to chill. He guessed he was a dreamer like his father, who was always imagining the farm was going to pay off.

Matt sighed and thought about himself in the scheme of things. While he was popular enough, he hadn't found a girl he cared to date — to spend his nickels and dimes on. Not that they didn't like him. After all, he wasn't so bad to look at — muscular, six feet tall, dark hair and eyes.

He stroked Inky and let his mind wander. To his surprise, from the darkest part of the night sky he discovered a pair of inquisitive eyes that seemed to gaze on him and him alone. He wondered: *Who are you? Where are you?*

As the night deepened, he felt a gust of cold wind stab him like a knife through his tattered overalls and the cracks in his mud-caked leather boots. No girl wanted any part of a dirt farmer. He sighed and decided:

I'm tired of being poor.

Chapter 3

November 19, 1943, Davidson, Oklahoma

Senior quarterback Matt Johnston huddled his players together for their final opportunity. Time for one last play, and it had to be a good one.

A fleeting thought crossed his mind. He smiled to himself, remembering that Christmas when he was eight and his parents were struggling to keep body and soul together. Well, he'd not received that football then, but when he finally did, he practiced and practiced until he became the best in Tillman County. What he had to do with the football now would be close to magic.

He shivered and lifted his chin against the frigid Oklahoma wind on this Friday night. He would rise above the mud and cold — all of it — he had to —

His six-man team, the Davidson Sandies, were on their own 44 yard line with five seconds left to play in the last game of the season, and the winner took home the championship trophy. Their royal blue and white uniforms revealed the sweat and grime of a hard fought battle. The defense had just forced a punt, and Matt looked up at the scoreboard, reminding him that his team trailed the much larger county seat school, the Frederick Bombers, by a score of 40 to 35. He heard the taunts from the Frederick sideline. Thought Matt:

We'll let our play speak for us.

The hometown crowd was hushed, holding their collective breath and hoping for a miracle.

The Bomber followers were whooping it up; victory was one play away.

It was hard to hear anything. Matt glanced into the stands. His dad and mom clung to each other nervously. Inky was secured to his father's left side with a leash. Between frenetic barks he whined and looked at least as concerned as Matt's parents.

Suddenly Matt felt time begin to move in slow motion. He saw, more than heard, his coach yell, "One more play!" pointing up at the scoreboard clock with a raised index finger. Next, his eyes zeroed in on the end zone — over 50 yards away. Now, in this one moment, which stood unexpectedly still, he looked at his team.

Frederick may be bigger and stronger than we are, but they sure don't have our heart.

That the score was this close proved it.

Steam came out of his mouth as he bent over in the huddle. "Joe," Matt asked, looking at his best friend, "can you beat their safety?"

"There's no one on that team that can keep up with me. They'll eat my dust."

Matt grinned.

Joe never lacked confidence.

Matt nodded his head and looked at his linemen. "Can you give me enough time for Joe to make a double move?" They nodded, though their faces were lined with fatigue.

"All right, men, let's make it happen. Standard formation. Joe to the left sideline, hook, and then post to the back of the end zone. On three!"

"Break," they said in unison, clapping their hands as they walked up to the line of scrimmage.

As they settled into their formation, Matt scanned the Frederick defense. The safeties were well over 30 yards off the ball, willing to let the Davidson receivers catch anything in front of them, knowing the game would be over if they kept them out of the end zone. He had to change the play. Matt hand-signaled the"fly" sign to Joe, who nodded recognition.

No pump fake. Let's just hope he can get free somewhere in the end zone.

Matt knelt behind the center. He barked loudly, hoping his team could hear him above the noise of the Bomber followers. "Hut! Hut! Hut!" After the third cadence, the center snapped the wet ball into his hands. As he backpedaled, Joe streaked down the left sideline.

Just give me a few more seconds.

Right at that moment he sidestepped and shook away a charging defender, who briefly grabbed him by his left shoulder pad and nearly pulled him to the ground. Pirouetting from his grasp and rolling to his right, he saw Joe get free in the back of the end zone.

Matt heaved the ball as hard as he could, just as a bulky Frederick lineman smashed into him. "Take that, pretty boy. Eat dirt!" he heard him snarl as he pressed his heavy frame against him. Matt's face was ground into the boggy mire.

Matt never saw the leaping two-handed grab that Joe made in the end zone between two maroon-and-grey-clad defenders, but he knew he had caught it by the deafening roar of the Davidson faithful. Even above that, he somehow heard a familiar male voice pierce through the din of the delirious crowd.

"Way to go, son!"

Complete chaos erupted as he was lifted from the ground by his overjoyed teammates. After they wiped the mud away from his face, Matt checked the scoreboard.

Is it really over?

The clock stood at 0:00. The impossible had happened:

Davidson 41, Frederick 40.

Immediately he and his teammates were surrounded by the ecstatic home crowd. Somehow he found Joe amidst the mob, and they briefly hugged before being swept apart by a host of country folks who were proud as punch of their boys.

ཨོཾ་མ་ཎི་པདྨེ་ཧཱུྂ ཨོཾ་མ་ཎི་པདྨེ་ཧཱུྂ ཨོཾ་མ་ཎི་པདྨེ་ཧཱུྂ

Afterward, Matt and Joe met in the parking lot, each drinking a bottle of cold Coke as they leaned against the back fender of Joe's car. Joe's girlfriend Emily waited nearby, talking with some equally excited classmates. Both players had removed their shoulder pads, but underneath their letter jackets they still wore their football jerseys — Matt proudly wearing number 8 and Joe number 81. Neither wanted the night to end.

Matt said, "You know, if number eighty-one had caught that pass I threw to him in the second quarter, we wouldn't have needed those last-second heroics. Why couldn't I have been given a decent split end?"

Joe smiled. "If number eight would have thrown the ball anywhere close, number eighty-one would have caught it. God, why did I have to play with a quarterback who couldn't hit the broad side of a barn?"

Matt laughed. "Hey, number eight-one, we'll be graduating next May. What are you planning to do with yourself? I mean, besides dropping passes that are thrown right to you?"

Said Joe, "Hey, number eight, it'll be great doing ANYTHING besides trying to catch passes from a rubber-armed quarterback!" He shrugged his shoulders, paused, and for the moment looked as serious as Matt could remember. "Buddy, I know we both have colleges looking at us, but I can't see being a bookworm and playing football when there is some serious shit taking place damn near all over the world. I think Uncle Sam needs my help. I've heard the Marines are the best and the toughest, and that's me all over. I'm going to enlist and kick some serious ass. German or Japanese, I don't care."

Matt took a swig from his Coke. "You know, you're going to need someone to baby-sit you. Who's going to change your diapers? Who's going to burp you at night? Besides that, Hitler and Tojo will never know what hit them with two Davidson Sandies fighting on the other side."

Joe extended his hand. "Matthew Johnston, you are a true asshole. Let's shake on it."

Matt firmly grasped his hand, and they shook with grins on their faces.

Looking over to his girlfriend, Joe said, "Emily, are you ready?"

She ran over to her hero, jumped into his arms and gave him a hug and kiss.

"Hey, Matt," Joe said, "Need a ride home?"

"Got room?"

"Only for my best friend. Hop in."

Nothing more needed to be said, and they loaded into Joe's car and headed to their homes to see their appreciative families and revel in their most glorious victory.

ཨོམཧཅདྲྀཧྡྲྀ ཨོམཧཅདྲྀཧྡྲྀ ཨོམཧཅདྲྀཧྡྲྀ

Life, despite the cloud of war, continued on with some modicum of normalcy. Matt continued to work long weekends in the fields, with chores before and after school. In March Matt received a letter from Henry "Hank" Iba, athletic director at Oklahoma A&M College; he offered Matt a chance to walk on for the football team.

As much as Matt loved sports, he already knew the direction he was headed. Besides that, if he didn't get a scholarship, he couldn't afford college.

Truth is, I'm just a dirt-poor farm boy.

So, after graduation, he caught a ride with Joe and traveled to Oklahoma City. There, in a stuffy, crowded room — despite the constantly running watercooler — they lifted their right hands and enlisted in the Marine Corps.

It is, Matt thought, *not only time to serve my country but also to find out what I'm made of.*

Chapter 4

Summer, 1944, Marine Corps Base, San Diego, California

June 8, 1944

Dear Mom and Dad, brothers, sisters,

Thought I was long overdue to send you a note and let you know what's up. I guess by now wheat harvest is long since done. The wheat looked pretty healthy when I left. Did we get twenty bushels? Please pet Inky for me. I think of you all often and hope you're doing well.

Joe and I knew that the Marines would be tough, but I don't really believe we had any idea what we were getting into. They say we are Hollywood Marines, but there's nothing Hollywood about it. Show me a movie star, and I'd believe it. I tell you I'd rather be that than a "hump-waiver" at Parris Island in South Carolina. That's where all the east coast sissies train.

After arriving here, we were immediately stripped of anything that reminded us of our previous lives. Our clothes were taken away and our heads were shaved. We were all given standard issue Marine boot-camp wear, none of which fits very well. Remember the black hair I used to have? Right now it's a pile underneath the barber's chair, and there is nothing but stubble on my head. I feel like a sheared sheep!

I thought I was in pretty good shape. I found out that nothing could get me ready for this. The marching is practically non-stop, and anytime someone goofs up, the whole group falls to the ground for push-ups, lots of them. I'm not sure how much weight I've lost, but it's been a lot.

The food stinks, and they give you plenty of it. We eat bushels of potatoes, and I'm getting sick of eating powdered scrambled eggs. Give me the ones from the farm any day. I keep thinking of all the wonderful vegetables from our garden. I don't think they know the meaning of "fresh" here. One thing about it, I'm sure not hungry. There's no time for that.

Enough complaining. I do know the reason I'm here, and I'm pretty proud of it. The June 6 invasion of France is talked about a lot, and our DI (that means drill instructor) is doing his best to get us ready. After around eight weeks here, we go to Camp Pendleton for infantry training. I just hope I can make it that long. The fence to the outside world looks awfully tempting.

Love to all,
Matt

ཨོམ་ཚི་པྲེཧཱུྃ ཨོམ་ཚི་པྲེཧཱུྃ ཨོམ་ཚི་པྲེཧཱུྃ

June 15, 1944

Dear Son,

It's starting to be an unseasonably hot summer. We are already into the high 90s, and there is no relief in sight. Your father has had a lot on his mind, trying to make ends meet. If the farmer doesn't get rain, it makes for hard times. Dad wanted me to tell you that we got twenty-one bushels, a pretty good crop.

I've got some bad news to share with you. I hope you're sitting down. Ever since you left, Inky sat out in front of the house and stared like he was waiting for you to come home. He would howl late into the night, and we couldn't get him to eat anything. Finally, last night, he died in the same spot where he used to lay with you and watch the stars. Your father and brothers buried him at the foot of the sapodilla plum tree. We figured that would be an okay spot with you. Inky was an old dog, and he really didn't have a lot of strength left anyway, so, all in all, we think this was for the best. I know this is a tough way for you to hear this. I've been crying nonstop since he died. How is it that you grow to love your pets so much? Surely there's a place for them in heaven.

Life doesn't seem quite the same without you. There is an empty chair at the dinner table, and it seems to us that you should be sitting in it. I set a plate there at your spot every time we eat, and I put it up once the meal is over.

The good news is that our boys seem to be doing pretty well in France. Hitler is on the retreat, but there seems to be a lot of fight left in those Germans. We are definitely winning the war in Asia as well. I sure wouldn't want to go against MacArthur. I just want you to be safe wherever you go, okay?

I'm sorry to hear that the food is so bad, but compared to your mother's cooking, what else could you expect?

Love,
Mom

ༀམཎིཔདྨེཧཱུྃ ༀམཎིཔདྨེཧཱུྃ ༀམཎིཔདྨེཧཱུྃ

June 24, 1944

Dear All,

I am here in my barracks, having just read your letter. It breaks my heart that I was not there for Inky when he went. I remember the day we first found him on the front porch of the house, just a puppy, nothing but skin and bones. Even then, when he was barely alive, he wagged his tail when he saw us. I knew right then and there that he was going to be my dog, though I think he really is the one who did the choosing. I remember how I first fed him some good leftovers. Then, I got a washtub, filled it full of soapy water and gave him a warm bath. I picked what must have been over a hundred swollen ticks off him. You never saw a happier dog after all that attention. I hope he's in a better place now.

Our schedule day-to-day is pretty much the same. We wake up every morning at 0500 to reveille played on the loudspeakers. At 0530 we are called to muster, and we then are marched as a unit to the toilets. Around 0600 we go to breakfast. There is no talking allowed, and we have to eat fast because we only have twenty minutes. The rest of the day is spent marching, doing calisthenics, obstacle courses, and learning how to shoot the M1 rifle. Just a few days ago several of our guys goofed up while marching, and we were taken to a large sand pit where we had to do sit-ups and push-ups till we couldn't do any more. Several of the guys vomited. That same evening, they wouldn't let us take a shower. Talk about a miserable night! It seems the main purpose of basic training is to take away any independence that you think you might have, so you work together as a unit. They don't want any free thinkers around here, only those who do what they're told. It makes me angry as I was not raised that way, but for right now I'm just a nose-picking grunt. Lights are out at 2200. What a life, huh?

Love,
Matt

ཨོཾ་མ་ཎི་པདྨེ་ཧཱུྃ་ ཨོཾ་མ་ཎི་པདྨེ་ཧཱུྃ་ ཨོཾ་མ་ཎི་པདྨེ་ཧཱུྃ་

July 3, 1944

Hi, Son,

Your mom is busy fixing dinner, so I thought I'd take my turn and write this letter to you. Here we are, the day before the 4th of July, and you're slap dab in the middle of boot camp. I'll bet its warmer here than it is there in sunny San Diego. We're breaking into the 100s, which makes those hot days in June look like a cold front. The ground is so dry that it's cracking, and the heat is even getting to the chickens. We lost a couple just the other day. We've also had some problems with varmints. When Inky was around, we didn't have this kind of thing happen. We might have to get another dog just to keep all the vermin away.

I'm sorry to hear that the food there isn't very good. Don't worry, we'll enjoy some of your Mother's fried chicken this evening, and I'll eat a bite for you, okay? I can just about taste that delicious crispy chicken! (Just kidding, son!)

Being the 4th of July is almost here, it's a good time to think about the many blessings that God has given us. Because of Marines like you, we enjoy our free-dom. As a country, we have been incredibly blessed.

It's time to eat! Mom just went outside and rang the dinner bell. I expect your brothers and sisters to come in soon from the fields and clean every crumb of food off this table. We pray for you every night, son, and look forward to seeing you when you finish your training.

Love,
Dad

ཨོཾ་མ་ཎི་པདྨེ་ཧཱུྃ་ ཨོཾ་མ་ཎི་པདྨེ་ཧཱུྃ་ ཨོཾ་མ་ཎི་པདྨེ་ཧཱུྃ་

July 14, 1944

Hi Dad and Mom, Alex, Esther, Robert and Earlyne,

Well, we're about six weeks into boot camp, and, believe you me, I'm counting the minutes till it's over. I've never been called so many different names by our DI. One day we're "civilians," the next we're "assholes," and another time we're "big babies."

The biggest news is that Joe got into a helluva fight this evening. You remember Joe isn't the largest guy around, and a big, husky guy named Junior from Lubbock started picking on him. At first, it was just insults, calling Joe an Okie and questioning his manhood. The final straw happened today at lunchtime when he tripped Joe and he fell, his food flying in all directions. All of Junior's Texas buddies started laughing. I stepped in and stood face to face with him. No one treats my friends that way, and I figured it was time someone taught him a lesson. Joe grabbed me by the shoulders and shoved me out of the way. He was a head smaller than Junior and about 100 pounds lighter, but that didn't stop Joe. Joe said, "Meet me tonight, back of the barracks, 1900 hours. We'll see what kind of man you really are."

Junior shoved him away and said, "After this evening, when I get through with you, there won't be enough of you left for me to shit on. I can already hear you whining, 'Please don't hurt me, Junior. I'll buy you a beer if you just leave me alone.'" With that he turned away and joined his snickering Texas friends.

Well, as you might guess, the excitement pretty much built up over the day, and the consensus was that Junior was going to pulverize Joe. I knew better. Joe is a lot tougher than they thought. Anyway, everyone gathered behind the barracks right at 1900, and before you knew it, Joe and Junior were in the middle, shirts off, circling each other.

Suddenly the DI appeared, and yelled, "What's going on?" At first I thought he was going to stop the fight. Instead when he saw what was taking place he broke out into a big grin. He pulled a cigar from his pocket, lit it up, took some puffs and moved up to the front. "It's about time we had a little action around here," he said.

Joe got in the first four or five punches, lightning quick right and left jabs. Junior kept lunging at him with wild swings that missed by a mile. Blood was pouring out of his nose as he grabbed Joe across the chest and slammed him to the ground. Junior then sat on Joe's chest, clobbering him right in the face with punch after punch. Junior's Texas buddies started cheering, and the Sarge moved forward like he was going to break it up. Somehow Joe got to his feet and busted Junior right in the gut. Junior groaned and bent over, gasping for breath. Joe then wiped the blood from the corner of his mouth and said, "Here's a special knuckle sandwich from your best Okie friend. Eat up!" and he wound up and landed a haymaker right in his chops. Junior's head jerked backward, and he buckled to the ground. A big cheer came up from the non-Texas crowd. It seems that Joe was not the only one Junior had been picking on.

Leaning over him, I heard Joe say, "You say or do anything to me or my friends again, I promise I will kick your ass twice as much again as I did today. Do you understand, you big fat Texas PUSSY!?"

Lying flat on his back and spitting out blood and bits of broken teeth, Junior nodded.

"That's what I hoped you'd say," Joe said. He smiled, patted Junior on the cheek and walked away with a swagger.

We were headed back to the barracks when the Sarge stopped us. He pulled the cigar from his mouth and said to Joe, "Damn good fight." He winked, smiled, slapped Joe on the back and walked back to his Quonset hut.

Needless to say, it was a big moment for Joe. No one, and I mean no one, picks on him anymore.

Okay, time for lights out. I hope the heat is letting up for you. After I finish this eight weeks of hell some people call boot camp, I will officially be a Marine. Then I go for infantry training at Camp Pendleton. Looks like I'll be home sometime in early September.

Love,
Matt

ཨོཾ་མ་ཎི་པ་དྨེ་ཧཱུྃ ཨོཾ་མ་ཎི་པ་དྨེ་ཧཱུྃ ཨོཾ་མ་ཎི་པ་དྨེ་ཧཱུྃ

August 1, 1944

Hey Brother,

I'm guessing by now that you are about to start infantry training. Are they finally taking it a little easier on you guys?

We are baking, and I mean really baking here in Davidson, America. It's been around 105, and nowhere is rain in sight. Virgil and Eleanor Carter were over today to borrow some water, and they asked about you. I told them you were getting ready to learn to shoot! They laughed, 'cause they remember how good you were with a rifle.

We're all still talking about the big fight that Joe had with that Texan. You should see Emily. She's so proud. Since when does a big city Texan, especially one named Junior, get the idea he can whup up on an Oklahoma country boy?

Dad and Mom tell me you'll have a month of furlough. Let's take a trip to the Wichitas for a little hike. It would be good to find the top of Sunset Peak and take in the scenery. School will be started then, and there will be plenty to do in the fields, but we'll just have to make some time to hang together, okay?

Take care,
Alex

P.S. Just because you are now a hot-shot Marine, don't think you'll have any special privileges when you return. There are about 20 dairy cattle in the barn with your name written all over their udders!

ཨོཾ་མ་ཎི་པདྨེ་ཧཱུྃ ཨོཾ་མ་ཎི་པདྨེ་ཧཱུྃ ཨོཾ་མ་ཎི་པདྨེ་ཧཱུྃ

August 14, 1944

Dear Family,

Well, here I am at Camp Pendleton, and I'm finally getting the feeling that this part of my life is about over. We still do the usual Marine Corps crap, but we're taking a lot more time on the rifle range. As to that, brother Alex, I want you to know that I have qualified as an expert for the M1 rifle. I'm pretty proud of that. All those years shooting a .22 have definitely paid off. These stationary targets are easy compared to a jackrabbit twisting back and forth through the brush.

Yes, they are finally giving us a little bit of free time. We're now getting Sundays off pretty regular. Since the beginning, we have been taking tests to see where we best qualify. I'm not scoring too badly, but it's becoming clear that no matter what you do well in, Uncle Sam needs foot soldiers. I'm pretty sure I'll be right on the front line.

There is good news from the front. Our troops have finally busted through the German lines in Normandy. On to Berlin! In the Pacific the island of Guam has been taken as well as Tinian. It looks like Hitler and Tojo are both on the run.

I'll be coming home the first week of September for furlough. I promise not to slack on the chores. Hard as it is to believe, I'm actually looking forward to working in the fields. Milking the herd again sounds just fine to me. I really don't care how hot it is there. I'm ready for Mom's cooking, a soft bed to lie in and rest before I start the real fighting. I'm looking forward to home, sweet home.

Semper Fi!
Matthew Johnston, USMC

ཨོཾ་མ་ཎི་པདྨེ་ཧཱུྃ ཨོཾ་མ་ཎི་པདྨེ་ཧཱུྃ ཨོཾ་མ་ཎི་པདྨེ་ཧཱུྃ

Matt put down his pen, lay back on his bunk and closed his eyes. As he drifted off to sleep, he saw a withered dead man lying on his right side in a smoke-filled room. He moved closer to the corpse and gazed at his face. There was something familiar about him. Suddenly the sunken eyes opened. Matt screamed and woke in a cold sweat.

It was just a bad dream, he thought, and pulled the covers back over him. He stared at the ceiling and shuddered.

That was me.

Chapter 5

September 5, 1944, Davidson, Oklahoma

M att and Joe sat side by side in the Greyhound bus as it rumbled toward home. Matt, seated next to the window, watched as the familiar terrain passed, growing drier and drier as the miles went by. Joe was fast asleep, his hat pulled over his eyes. It had been a three day trip from San Diego, and they had spent much of the time sleeping, but as they neared home, Matt had become alert and expectant.

So much had changed in the past four months. For the first time in his life, he had been away from home for longer than just a few days, and he had the opportunity to see the world on his own. As odd as it sounded, at the ripe old age of eighteen he felt like a man, one who was capable of taking on whatever the world might bring him. He had completed Marine boot camp and had risen to the challenge. Matt knew there was a fine line between confidence and arrogance, and he was not arrogant.

Nothing can beat me. Nothing.

And while he looked forward to time with his family, something inside him had changed. While he was still a son and a brother, he now was aware he was ready to stand on his own. On an even deeper level, he knew he was a leader and a damn good one. He liked not only making his own decisions, but when asked, making them for others.

When he finished this stint with the Marines, he wanted to get a college education. He knew that he was bright enough and also that it would open up a world of opportunities an Oklahoma farm boy otherwise would not have. He didn't want to even think about being a farmer. He couldn't bear the thought of a hand-to-mouth existence, and that's exactly what he would face if he chose to work the land. Furthermore, if he succeeded financially, he could help his mother and father. He wanted them to have a better home and money for more than just food on the table. He fancied himself sending all of his brothers and sisters to college and saw them becoming doctors, lawyers, veterinarians, whatever they might choose to be. And he could visualize their eventual families prospering, his nieces and nephews well fed and happily playing in fine clothes, all because of their Uncle Matt. He smiled as he thought of all he could do for his family.

I need to succeed — and not just for myself.

As the bus approached Davidson from the north, a sea of country folk waited at the bus stop, dressed in various shades of red, white and blue. He elbowed a still sleeping Joe. "Wake up, sleepy head. Your fan club awaits you."

Joe grunted, pulled his hat back off his face, sat up and peered out the front window of the bus. "No way, Matt. I think that crowd is from Frederick. They're still pissed about that football game."

Matt smiled and shook his head. "Has anyone ever told you what a complete idiot you are?"

Joe winked and said, "Only those who really know me."

Their conversation abruptly stopped as the bus approached the crowd. They heard the sounds of a brass quartet playing "God Bless America" and yells of "Welcome home, boys!" As he gazed at all of the familiar faces, he wondered if this would be the last time in his life he would see them. He had excelled at boot camp, and he was certain his assignment, wherever it might be, would not be easy.

Matt followed Joe from the bus and saw Emily leap from the crowd into Joe's arms. She kissed him repeatedly. Joe's parents were right behind. Matt searched again through the crowd and finally saw his mother and father; they were glowing with pride. Matt looked a little closer, and while he expected to see tears in his mother's eyes, he was shocked to see them in his father's.

Matt dropped his duffel bag and ran toward them, but before he could get there he was bear-hugged by his brothers, Alexander and Robert, who burst from the crowd, knocking his Marine hat from his head.

Alexander pulled him close and said, "Brother, you need to be brought down a few notches, and I'm the one to do it." He slugged him in the shoulder. "By the way, welcome home."

Robert's face was red and puffy from crying. He wrapped his arms around Matt's chest. He stammered, "We . . . missed . . . you."

Matt hugged Robert. "I've missed you, too." Looking at Alex, he smiled and said, "I'm going to tie you up in knots before this evening is over."

Before Alex could reply, Esther and Earlyne rushed up. Matt was shocked to see the emotion in Esther's usually distant manner. "Welcome home, brother," she said as she warmly slipped her arms around him.

Earlyne tucked her head in the nape of his neck and said, "Matt, home hasn't been the same without you." Perhaps it was his imagination, but she already seemed a head taller.

A few seconds later his parents arrived. His father shook his hand and said, "Son, looks like to me the Marines have made a man out of you."

His mother hugged him, saying, "Matthew Walker Johnston, I think you were a man *before* you left home."

Matt grinned. "Well, could be I'm more man than I was."

"A lot more," his father said. "That much I'm sure of."

"Are you hungry?" his mother put in.

"Does the sun rise in the morning?" Matt paused and asked, "Do you have any fried chicken?"

"Of course, son," his mother said. "Let's go home."

Matt reached down and picked up his hat. He dusted it off and placed it on his head. He then retrieved his duffel bag, and they bustled off to the car. Matt jammed himself into the back seat of the family car along with his brothers and sisters.

The band ceased playing, and the small crowd scattered. Each of them had a father, son, nephew, uncle — someone at war. Matt reckoned that they all hoped someday, somehow, their loved ones would come back on that same bus.

As their car roared away, Matt thought:

There's no place like home.

Chapter 6

September 6 through October 3, 1944, Davidson, Oklahoma

The month back home was the quickest of Matt's life, though certainly not a leisurely one. There was farm work to be done, and he was glad to pitch in. It felt good to wear his civvies again. He now had a whole new appreciation for Round House overalls and the simple freedoms civilian life offered.

The family had a new dog, a mutt named Chippy, but she could never replace Inky. At the end of the day, Matt often found himself sitting under the branches of the sapodilla plum tree next to where Inky was buried.

I would give anything to scratch you in your favorite spot behind the ears again. I miss you, Inky.

When the sky darkened, he headed inside for bed; he had to get up at six each morning to milk the cows with his brothers and sisters, and repeat the chore in the evening. He helped his mother churn butter and spent hours in the fields learning to drive their newly acquired John Deere tractor.

All went well for the first week. Then one day his father walked up to Matt and his brothers while they were hoeing in the garden.

He said, "Boys, stop what you're doing and come with me."

"What's up?" Robert asked.

"It's your favorite chore," he said. "It's time to cut the calves."

Matt felt himself break into a cold sweat. As he had grown older, there was nothing he disliked more than castrating calves. He knew the reasons they had to do it: if there were more than one bull, there would be fights and injuries. Also, bull meat was tough as a boot, and it just didn't taste good. On top of all that, his father was notorious for letting the calves get too big.

His brothers felt the same way. Matt tried to think of an excuse to get out of it. Before he could speak, Alex said, "Dad, Mom wants us to work in the garden this afternoon."

"It can wait. C'mon now."

With that he led them back to the corral where four very nervous calves circled. As they got closer, Matt's worst fears were confirmed.

Good God, they're not calves; they're practically bulls.

Esther and Earlyne hung around the outside of the enclosure. Esther had a big smile on her face; Earlyne looked worried.

Matt said, "Hey, Dad, don't you think they're a little too . . . well . . . *big* to cut?"

His father smiled. "Son, if they look too old it's because we've been waiting for you to get back home. I know how much you love this." He winked at Matt.

"Okay, enough stalling. Let's get the hardest one done first," his father said as he looked at a calf that was the biggest of the lot. He then opened the gate to the corral, and they entered. Matt gulped as their dad closed it behind them.

Alex and Robert had looks of resignation on their faces as they slowly closed in on the fidgety calf from the front. Once they had its attention, Matt crept up from the rear, then leaped and clutched him around the neck. Matt grabbed his ear and twisted while Alex and Robert joined in the fray. The frantic bucking calf dragged all three twice around the pen, finally falling to the ground in a cloud of dust. As the calf flailed, Matt was kicked in the head twice, and Alex and Robert were thrown off against the fence a time or two. Quickly they all rejoined the battle. In the background were peals of laughter.

Esther laughed and yelled out, "Ride 'em, cowboys!"

Even Earlyne started to smile.

Finally, after the three cowpunchers had restrained the overgrown calf, their father approached with his sharpened pocket knife, slit the scrotal sac and removed the testicles. Then he dabbed the area with kerosene. The calf bawled to high-heaven right in Matt's ear, blowing slobber all over his face. As they released the animal, their father said, "Good job, boys! Only three more to go . . ."

Matt grimly stared at his brothers; they looked like they had been run over by a truck. He was sure he wasn't looking any better. He thought:

Three more?

ཨོཾ་མ་ཎི་པདྨེ་ཧཱུྃ ཨོཾ་མ་ཎི་པདྨེ་ཧཱུྃ ཨོཾ་མ་ཎི་པདྨེ་ཧཱུྃ

The later part of September was one of the busiest times of the year — cotton harvest. As King Cotton was the biggest cash crop, it was the most important gathering of the farming season. Along with his family, he picked the fibrous hulls, and with each round trip, they dumped the fluffy cotton into a trailer waiting at the end of the row. Once full it was taken to the Davidson cotton gin, where 2,200–2,400 pounds of cotton would make one bale. It had been a hot, dry year, so Matt's father felt fortunate to get a third of a bale an acre.

Matt appreciated his family more than he ever had.

Toward the end of his furlough, Matt and his brothers took a trek in the Wichita Mountains. One of Matt's teachers had told him that in the ancient past the mountains had been among the tallest in the Americas, with peaks ranging up to 20,000 feet in elevation. The ravages of time had made them only a bit more than hills.

In the early afternoon Matt, Alex and Robert arrived at the trailhead and began their hike to the western part of the reserve. Dodging the generally docile but unpredictable buffalo, they picked their way along the poorly defined trail.

Within two hours they had ascended Sunset Peak. They fell silent as they sat down and sipped water from their canteens, realizing it might be their last time together. For Matt, the moment was precious beyond words.

Matt gazed at the eastern horizon. Mount Scott was in the distance. And in that point in time he suspected his destiny lay far beyond.

Japan?

In a few days he would wave goodbye and board the bus bound for San Diego. He sat down and lifted his face to a warm breeze. A mourning dove cooed its sad refrain.

A shiver moved up and down Matt's spine. He wondered:

Is it mourning for me?

Chapter 7

January 27, 1945, Guadalcanal

Matt lay on his assigned bunk in a Quonset hut close to Henderson Field on Guadalcanal, having received his orders earlier that day. Soon he and his fellow Marines would take to sea and sail to an unknown location for their first combat action.

Perspiration beaded on his forehead. Music from Radio Tokyo blared from the loudspeakers around the camp, playing the all-too-familiar tune, Glenn Miller's "In the Mood". Matt remembered that Miller's plane had disappeared in bad weather over the English Channel during the December just passed; he'd been en route to perform for American troops in France. The world didn't seem quite right without Glenn Miller in it.

When the music stopped, the sultry voice of the woman the American troops called Tokyo Rose followed. Matt was aware that the purpose of these programs was to demoralize the U.S. military. On the contrary, at the least they made him smile, and often he would laugh out loud.

It had been a whirlwind experience since he and Joe had departed Davidson. After returning to San Diego, they had a brief period of reorientation, then they were flown to Guadalcanal, a training base in the Solomon Islands. The intensity of their preparation had been ratcheted up, and it was certain they were getting ready for an amphibious assault.

Matt knew that Guadalcanal was the site of the lengthiest and one of the most challenging campaigns the Marines had faced in the Pacific conflict, lasting for over six months. The island was infested with mosquitoes, and malaria was endemic, making the battle all that much more difficult.

Hearing a familiar buzz, Matt looked over his head and swatted one of the pesky mosquitoes, which had somehow found its way through his netting. He opened his hands and grimaced at the remains of the bloody, mangled insect.

Realizing that soon he was about to enter his first battle, Matt had begun to experience fear at a more intense level than he ever had before. A few days earlier during a break he had overheard a conversation between two of the sergeants, veterans of the island assault on Peleliu, sharing with each other their renditions of bloody, hand-to-hand combat. Finally one of them said in a whispered voice, "There's no way we can get them ready for what they're about to face."

Matt began to wonder what it would be like to die. He was no stranger to death, having participated in the slaughter of numerous farm animals. He also recalled the agonizing, prolonged death of his Uncle Peter from cancer. Over a six month period, he saw a vital, vigorous man wither away into a shell of a human being. When Matt's family visited at his uncle's home in Lawton a few nights before his death, Matt was shocked at what he saw: A confused, combative, skeletal man who was restrained with leather straps, thrashing side to side in the bed.

Matt remembered the pained look on his Aunt Wilma's face as she tried to comfort him. Uncle Peter gave no indication that he knew her or anyone else. Matt felt certain that if any of their family pets had experienced such suffering, his father would have quickly and painlessly ended their lives.

Why is it so different for human beings?

He hoped that, if he were mortally wounded, he would die quickly. He didn't want to lie on a battlefield with his intestines protruding from his abdomen, his arms and legs bent into unnatural positions. He could see his shredded arteries spurting out bright red blood, far from his body at first and later only slightly oozing as he bled to death. Maybe there would be a corpsman nearby who would administer morphine.

Perhaps Joe would be close at hand to comfort him as his consciousness faded.

He thought about his family.

How would they take the news?

In his mind's eye he could see the Western Union man knocking on the front door of his home back in Oklahoma. Then he watched his mother scream and buckle to her knees as she read of his death and saw his father as he gripped her tightly in despair. He saw his brothers and sisters crying — grouped around his parents. He shook his head and pulled his consciousness back to the present. He looked at his hands. They were trembling.

Will I be brave? Will I fight off the urge to run?

He dried his eyes — and not a moment too soon.

Joe, Junior, and several other members of their unit walked through the door, making preparations for their departure. Matt smiled at Junior, and he smiled back, still missing his two upper teeth knocked out in the fight with Joe last summer. Since then, Joe and Junior not only tolerated each other but had actually become friends. Matt smiled sardonically as he realized that the impending threat of combat had a way of drawing people together.

Hell, even I am starting to like Junior.

Matt's mind drifted back to his previous thoughts.

I must survive this.

Somehow, he knew he would.

But at what cost?

He rose from his bunk and began to pack his duffel bag in preparation for the next step of his journey, whatever that might be.

Chapter 8

February 19, 1945, Iwo Jima, Japan

A sulfurous odor greeted the Marines as they approached the island of Iwo Jima. In the seafaring amtrac were fifteen terrified young men, many engaging in their first battle.

"This must be what hell smells like," someone said behind Matt.

Matt stood next to Joe. He had never known Joe to be frightened, but there it was, written all over his ashen face.

He's scared to death.

And so am I.

Matt reached into his pocket with his right hand and found his precious rabbit's foot. He felt the familiar soft fur and hoped there was still some luck in it. He wondered if Joe still had his.

The Marine on the other side of him pulled a rosary from his pocket and nervously moved the beads between his fingers. He silently mouthed, *Hail Mary, full of grace, the Lord is with thee . . .*

Matt looked up at the rapidly approaching island of Iwo Jima. He couldn't take his eyes off Mount Suribachi; it loomed menacingly from the southern end.

Except for the waves splashing up against their boat, dead silence prevailed. Matt prayed the previous seventy-four-day bombardment of the island from the air and sea had decimated the Japanese defenders and hoped beyond hope that only a mop-up operation would be required.

As the lurching amtrac struck land at 0859 hours, one minute ahead of schedule, Joe moved close to Matt and shook his hand.

Joe whispered, "Semper Fi, old buddy, Semper Fi."

Matt's heart was pounding wildly in his throat. He looked at Joe and whispered back, "Semper Fi." He braced himself for what he must now do.

The landing crew clutched their weapons, some crossed their chests and a few bowed their heads for a final prayer.

The moment the door slammed open and hit the ground, the small contingent advanced onto a beach of fine volcanic ash. They quickly followed their sergeant in concealing themselves behind a fifteen-foot terrace of the grimy stuff that lay just beyond the shoreline. Rather than the withering fire they had expected, a surreal silence prevailed.

Matt surveyed his surroundings. There was nothing to indicate the presence of an enemy. Wave after wave of landing vehicles arrived without resistance.

Maybe they're all dead.

Sarge urged them forward. Then five hundred yards inland, the Japanese opened fire from well concealed positions, and chaos erupted. Matt and Joe dove face-first to the ground. Nowhere was safe.

Matt wished he had a hole to crawl in. Wave after wave of his fellow Marines were mowed down as they tried to bear down on the Japanese positions.

Shit! Shit! Shit!

Marines were scattered all around — dead Marines. Some looked as though they were asleep, others were mutilated beyond recognition. The fear he had experienced at Guadalcanal was nothing compared to this waking nightmare.

There's no way I'll live through this.

The noise was deafening, though any brief pause in the barrage was filled with the screams of the wounded. Mayhem rained down upon the troops. Any glimmer of hope disappeared as Matt watched their armored support vehicles foundering in the ash.

Matt felt a bullet whistle past his head and yelled, "Hey, Joe, we're sitting ducks here. The Japanese gunners have made this a No Man's Land. I don't think we have any choice."

"What?" screamed Joe.

Matt crawled up beside Joe and yelled again at the top of his lungs, "I don't think we have any choice."

Joe stared at Matt, as if he might be crazy. "What in the hell are you talking about?"

"We charge and see how many of those bunkers we can take out."

As if the sergeant had overheard them, he waved the contingent forward. They gradually advanced against the hidden Japanese positions, inch by inch, foot by foot, yard by yard. The Marines quickly discovered rifle fire was ineffective against the enemy. Grenades and flame-throwers, though, at least gave them a fighting chance. As he saw flaming Japanese soldiers run screaming from their caves, the smell of burning human flesh became indelibly etched in Matt's mind.

ཨོཾ་མ་ཎི་པདྨེ་ཧཱུྃ   ཨོཾ་མ་ཎི་པདྨེ་ཧཱུྃ   ཨོཾ་མ་ཎི་པདྨེ་ཧཱུྃ

Matt and Joe collapsed in a shallow rocky pit as the sun dropped low in the sky. Matt had thought this day would never end. He choked back tears. Night was falling, and many of his friends were dead. If he hadn't hated the Japs before today, he did now. They were his enemy. It was clear they wanted to kill him just as badly as he wanted to kill them.

Tracer flares began to light the darkening sky. Sarge had warned them about a possible banzai attack during the night, and he assigned Junior and one of his Texas buddies to take the first watch. Matt and Joe sipped on the water from their canteens and tried to sleep.

They couldn't. They had seen too much.

Matt remembered the words of William Tecumseh Sherman, "I tell you, war is hell!"

No, Matt thought, *it's a lot worse than that.*

Chapter 9

February 23, 1945, Iwo Jima, D+4

Survival was the name of the game.

Every second had become precious. To touch, to breath, to see, to eat; all were priceless gifts.

As on D-day, the next three days the Marines fought from one cave to another. This was the first assault on the Japs' god-Emperor's homeland, and they fought the Marines ferociously, not only with determination, but also religious fanaticism.

On the evening of D+4 Matt's group had found a rocky crater near the base of Mount Suribachi. The cloudless night sky seemed almost peaceful under a nearly full moon. Matt, Joe, Junior and six others settled in for what they hoped would be a quiet night. Two sentries worked opposite sides of their little nest.

Junior whispered, "Hey, guys, wanna hear a joke?"

"Come on, Junior, we're sick of your stupid-ass Texas jokes," a voice quietly said.

Someone else whispered back, "Shut up, you idiots! We're not the only ones on this godforsaken island. Do you want the Japs to hear us? I got my hand on my knife. One more yap from any of you, and I'm gonna do the Japs a favor."

Matt jumped as he heard the sharp crack of gunfire, and a gaping red hole appeared in the middle of Junior's forehead. He fell forward, lifeless. Almost simultaneously, a second shot rang out — a guard spun and tumbled face-first into the dugout. Now a Jap appeared from nowhere, grabbed the second sentry from behind and slit his throat with a sharpened bayonet before he flung him to the ground.

Suddenly Japs were everywhere, screaming and shooting at close range.

Matt stood and reached for his gun — he was struck in the head by a rifle butt. He dropped to the ground, dazed, then managed to stagger to his feet. He fumbled at his belt strap and pulled his .45 from its holster, and by the light of the moon he saw his sergeant die like a puppet on a string, killed by a burst of submachine gun fire.

Oh, my God . . .

He gasped. A Jap was pointing a pistol directly at the head of his best friend in the whole wide world — Joe Hay.

Matt pulled his shaking right hand up and aimed his .45 directly at the Jap. Joe yelled at Matt, a feverish last attempt to live. Matt started to squeeze the trigger, but paused as he felt his pants dampen with shit and piss. That was all the time the enemy needed. The Jap fired, and Joe was dead.

Matt felt pieces of Joe's brain splatter across his face. He screamed and too late pulled the trigger. The Jap buckled, convulsing briefly as he collapsed.

Feeling nothing but rage, Matt surveyed the scene. The only ones standing were Japs, and, before they could react, he bent his knees and shot repeatedly and accurately. One bullet for each man. The pungent odor of fresh blood filled the air. The movement stopped.

Matt was the last one standing.

As he wiped his face, stark reality struck him. At his feet lay Joe, dead, staring straight ahead. Every part of his body was limp except for his right hand, tightly clenched around something. Matt reached down and slowly unwrapped his fingers. Out fell a worn rabbit's foot.

Matt jumped back in horror and fell to his knees. He screamed until he had no breath. He had failed his best friend, and he had failed himself. The pain was too great to bear.

He recalled his thoughts from five months ago:

Nothing can beat me. Nothing.

He grimaced, took a deep breath and steeled himself. Now he had to prove it.

He scrambled to find more power — grenades, Japanese and American, were scattered on the ground; he stuffed them into his field pack. He picked up a smoking Tommy gun and slung it over his shoulder. It was time to do as much damage as he could.

As other Marines arrived on the scene, he headed out — in a rage and on the prowl, looking for Japs.

Those worthless bastards will pay for this.

Chapter 10

February 24, 1945, Iwo Jima, D+5

No longer did the Iwo Jima night frighten Matt. He was a man on a mission, a well-trained fighting machine — and this, coupled with his innate country good sense and seething anger, made for a deadly combination.

It was early morning after that devastating attack on his entrenchment, and Matt sat exhausted in a makeshift foxhole. It was only a bit more than an indention in the rocky terrain, but it was the best he could find. He was so tired he had begun to hallucinate, seeing and hearing Japanese soldiers who weren't there. He had begun to fire at shadows — mere figments of his imagination.

What is real? What isn't?

Matt felt trapped in a macabre blend of dream and reality, and there wasn't a damn thing he could do about it.

At last, dawn creased the eastern horizon. He wondered:

How many have I killed?

It didn't take long for him to answer his own question.

Not enough.

He had located and charged hidden position after hidden position, sparing no one. He emptied magazines of bullets until the gun was too hot to touch. It made no difference to him at all if they tried to surrender. They had given no quarter to Joe, so why should he offer any? When he ran out of ammo, he either broke their

It's springtime here. The garden is planted, and everything is bright and healthy looking. No doubt soon we'll have a battle with the insects who think the same. The winter wheat is starting to grow tall and green. I'm afraid that the war, along with the deaths of Joe and the president, has pretty much taken the wind out of our sails.

All we can think about now is getting you back home safe and sound. Write soon! We love you son.

Mom and Dad (Alex, Esther, Robert, and Earlyne)

ཨོཉཐིངདྲེརཱྀ ཨོཉཐིངདྲེརཱྀ ཨོཉཐིངདྲེརཱྀ

June 10, 1945

Dear Mom, Dad and family,

I'm sorry I've been so long in writing. All the things that have happened since my last letter have left my head spinning. Before I get into that, though, there is some good news. I have been promoted to corporal! This means a little more pay, and I plan to start sending more money back home. There's no point in refusing. I know you can use it.

Now for the hard part. Yes, I was with Joe when he was killed. It was the most horrible thing I have ever experienced, and please forgive me if I don't give you any more details. There are things about his death that have really stuck in my craw, and I can't talk about them just yet.

Now I know that you all believe that there is a God that watches over and cares for us. I have to ask this question: If there is a God, how could he let things like what I've seen happen? I'm afraid that I am pretty much becoming a disbeliever.

For the time being, I'm not sure where I'm headed from here, and if I knew, I couldn't tell you. According to the censors, my travels are top secret.

I think of all of you often and find myself ready to come back home. I just want to get on the seat of our John Deere tractor, plow the fields and let my head clear. I think being at home will help me get rid of some of the demons inside my head — believe me, there are plenty of them. The first thing I would do, though, after I hug all of you, would be to lie out in front of the house at night and watch the stars float by. With all that's happened, I've lost what I thought were my dreams. Home will go a long way to help me find them again, that is, if they still exist.

Love,
Matt

Matt folded the letter and stuffed it into an envelope. He placed it on the table and stared at it. Never in his life had he thought he was going crazy, but he knew that he was on the edge of insanity. He had always believed that those with mental problems were weak, spineless creatures who couldn't handle what life had to offer. Now he knew better.

Too many thoughts . . . Too many thoughts . . .

He wiped away the tears that fell on the envelope.

Chapter 13

August 15, 1945, Iwo Jima

M att was alone in his tent when he heard a chorus of excited whoops along with the chatter of celebratory M1 fire. It didn't take a scholar to figure out what the news was. Matt shook his head; it was hard to believe it was finally over.

The Japanese had surrendered.

Matt chose not to go outside and join his fellow Marines. There was no way he could bring himself to play the fool and act happy with all that had happened.

Since the deaths of many of his close friends, Matt had become more and more of an isolate. He took a slow drag from his cigarette. He had discovered there was one tried and true way to dull the images swirling in his head.

Booze.

When he first started drinking, a beer or two might do the trick. The depression and nightmares continued, though, and it required more and more. He took it any way he could get it — beer, wine, whiskey . . . whatever.

How else can I sleep?

He couldn't remember the last time he had a shower, and patchy black stubble dotted his face. When he'd get too far out of hand, Sergeant McKensie would direct him to a shave and shower. *At least someone cares*, Matt thought, *even if it is a damned sergeant in the Marines.*

Matt no longer responded to the letters from his family. It was just too painful and brought up too many memories. He had so wanted his parents to be proud of him. He could easily imagine the look of disappointment on their faces when they heard the truth of what happened to Joe. What was worse, he couldn't bear the thought of going home and having them see him this way.

Matt was glad there was still a need for him in the Marines. He had heard rumors that his company would be among the initial forces to occupy Japan. He found himself wondering if he would have a chance to kill more of those filthy Japs.

Matt reflected on how the proud Japanese were brought to their knees. From the articles he had read in *Stars and Stripes*, he learned the atomic bomb had been developed by the Manhattan Project and had been successfully tested on July 16 of that same year at the Alamogordo Test Range in New Mexico. It was the opinion of Secretary of War Henry Stimson that up to a million American servicemen would be killed if they directly invaded the Japanese mainland, and the use of nuclear weapons was the best option. After Iwo, and seeing the fierceness of the Japanese defense, he had no trouble believing that estimate.

He remembered how the Enola Gay had flown from the island of Tinian with two other B-29s and dropped the uranium weapon, "Little Boy", over the city of Hiroshima on August 6. The destruction was beyond belief, and he was shocked that the Japanese government still refused to capitulate. The plutonium bomb, "Fat Man," was then dropped over the city of Nagasaki on August 9. At long last, they conceded defeat.

It is time for a celebration.

The war is over.

He leaned over his bunk and took a swig from the Jim Beam bottle he kept hidden under his bed. He smiled to himself.

Now he had found another reason to drink.

Chapter 14

November 6, 1945, Hiroshima, Japan

W hat do you mean you didn't fire? And you could've saved Joe's life if . . . if . . . Why didn't you fire? You, his best friend . . . you didn't fire?

Matt sat up in bed and clasped his hands over his ears. He screamed out loud, "SHUT UP! SHUT UP! SHUT UP!" He heard the lights click on; the other five occupants of his Quonset hut were sitting up in their bunks, staring at him.

"Come on, Johnston — get a grip!" said the Marine next to him as he lay back down and clicked off his light.

"Every so often is one thing," grumbled another, "but every night?

Matt reached for his trusty bottle of whiskey. It was empty.

He wrapped his head in his pillow.

It would be another long night.

Matt was now stationed at the Allied headquarters in Kaidaichi, just south and east of Hiroshima, and Sergeant McKensie had told him it was time to spiff it up. They had left the hostilities of Iwo, and an unkempt appearance would no longer be tolerated. Matt was ordered to clean up and do so regularly. But that didn't wash away the guilt of Joe's death — it still hung heavy, and he took up his new duty as a means of not going home to face the consequences.

Matt's main responsibility was to patrol the outskirts of Hiroshima daily and distribute food to the surviving Japanese. During his first few weeks Matt thought with a smile, *The bomb is just what these Jap assholes deserve.*

As time passed, though, an unexpected change of heart occurred; when Matt was able to come to grips with his own pain and the voices faded, he was able to see more clearly the anguish of the Japanese.

Thousands of them wandered the streets in ragged clothes — burned, scarred and starving. Keloid tumors marred what should have been attractive faces. Matt saw that even though they were in a state of near starvation, they stood patiently in line for their portions of rice, politely holding out their bowls.

What affected Matt most were the numerous children, many of whom seemed to be without family. Nearly all were bald, and Matt couldn't help but wonder if this was an aftereffect of the bomb. He noticed, over a period of weeks, one particular child in Saeki-ku, a ward on the periphery of Hiroshima where the damage from the bomb was not so severe. Sadness was etched into the boy's features; he looked no more than seven years old, and Matt's heart was touched by him. One day Matt said, "Hey, Charlie, would you like some chocolate?" Matt held out a Hershey's bar.

The kid grabbed it and bit off a large chunk. As he hungrily chewed, he said in broken English, "My name not Charlie. My name Shigeshi. What your name?"

Matt smiled in spite of himself. "Just call me — Matt."

"Are you Private Matt, Corporal Matt, or maybe you General Matt?" the boy asked seriously.

"I'm Corporal Matt." Matt smiled again. "But you can just call me Matt."

"Okay, Corporal Matt. That's what will call you. I got to go. Can you give more chocolate?"

Holding out a second bar, Matt asked, "Can I call you — Charlie?"

He snatched it from his hand. "You give chocolate, you can call anything!" With a faint crack of a smile, the boy vanished into a crowd of gathering children.

Matt rummaged around in his knapsack for more chocolate.

Looks like this group will have to share.

He laughed out loud for the first time in a long while and glanced up to see that Sergeant McKensie had driven up in his jeep. The Sarge was looking directly at him, nodding approval.

ཨོམཧྲིཧྲཱིཧྲཱུ ཨོམཧྲིཧྲཱིཧྲཱུ ཨོམཧྲིཧྲཱིཧྲཱུ

After that day, every time Matt and his platoon arrived in Saeki-ku, Charlie would be there. He was now sporting a Cincinnati Reds hat, one that Matt had purchased for him at the PX. Matt also discovered that he and many other children loved Wrigley's Spearmint Gum, and he found himself purchasing large quantities of it to share with them. Matt began to feel a real affection for the boy, and in time his curiosity got the best of him. He asked, "Hey, Charlie, where's your mother and father?"

He answered, "Father dead. Killed by Americans. Mother live here."

Killed by Americans? Matt winced. "Do you have any brothers or sisters?"

"One sister. Her name Aika. She here visiting from college when bomb went off. Was only few kilometers from ground zero. She protected by concrete wall, or she be burned bad. She teach me English she learned in school. Aika very smart. She busy at home taking care of mother. I bring her here in day or two. Aika need to get out of house."

"Okay, Charlie," Matt said, "I'll see you tomorrow. Don't take any wooden nickels, okay?" Matt smiled as he saw the puzzled expression on the boy's face.

"Tomorrow, Corporal Matt," he said, giggling, "I make sure I take no wooden nickels."

ཨོམ་ཛི་ལྲེ་རྱ་ ཨོམ་ཛི་ལྲེ་རྱ་ ཨོམ་ཛི་ལྲེ་རྱ་

The following day as Matt was scooping out rice, he felt a tug on his sleeve. And there was Charlie, beaming a smile at him.

Pointing to a figure standing far back from the crowd, the boy said, "There my sister — Aika. Come with me. I tell her who you are."

"Okay, Charlie. Just a second." Matt whistled to a Marine standing guard nearby. "Take my place," Matt said. "I'll be back in a few minutes." He took a final drag off his cigarette and mashed the butt into the ground.

Matt walked hand in hand with Charlie to the waiting woman. She was slender and seemed to be about twenty years of age. Like her brother, she was completely bald. Her arms were folded across her chest; she wore sunglasses, and there was an air of defiance about her.

Charlie said, "Corporal Matt, this my sister, Aika. Sister Aika, this Corporal Matt."

Matt put on a smile and extended his hand. "Nice to meet you, Aika."

She kept her arms folded, glaring straight ahead through her dark glasses, and Matt awkwardly withdrew his hand.

Not noticing the icy chill, Charlie said, "I go now and get in line for rice. You get to know each other. I be back." He scurried off to join the lengthy queue.

Aika spoke in surprisingly fluent English, saying, "You've been very kind to my brother, and I appreciate that. And I also am thankful for the rice your government has given us. Many have been saved from starvation. But we don't need or want your chocolate, your gum or any other gifts.

"Shigeshi says you call him . . . Charlie. He already has a strong Japanese name, and it is Shigeshi. He constantly wears his baseball hat, and it reminds and sickens me that he has adopted an American Marine as one of his friends. Have you not seen what your bomb has done to my city?" Her voice rose in anger. "And look at what it has done to the people who live here." She was now trembling with rage.

Matt replied, "Well, you did the same thing to us at Pearl Harbor."

She furiously erupted. "Pearl Harbor was a military base! How many do you think were killed there?"

Matt shrugged his shoulders.

"You don't know? Well, I'll tell you, Marine. Somewhere around twenty-four hundred. We had tens of thousands die in the first second, and there will be many more to come. You obviously have no idea what happened here. Would you like to know more?"

Matt felt the color drain from his face. He hadn't expected this.

"I thought you would," she angrily said. "After the blast, I was stunned and wandered to the river along with many others who were so severely burned you could not tell who was male and who was female. Their skin hung from their bodies like draperies. They struggled into the rivers of Hiroshima, seeking relief from their pain, and there they died. The river was full of bodies mixed with dead fish. I saw a baby nursing the breast of its dead mother, who only moments before had been killed. I heard the moans of the wounded crying for water. Most died before receiving any. Then came the black rain — rainwater mixed with dust. All were poisoned who drank it."

Her anger increased in intensity. "In the first few days afterward, the wounds of the injured were infested by maggots, and starving children ate these detestable insects, thinking they were rice. I can't begin to describe the horrors our people have experienced because of you. How dare you compare this to Pearl Harbor!" Tears were now streaming down the sides of her face.

Matt would have liked to have held and comforted her, but thought the better of it. While he knew what she said about the bombing was true, he found himself starting to bristle with rage. *The Japanese weren't exactly lily white; just ask the Chinese about Nanking. What about the Bataan Death March? Or Japanese*

POW camps? They sure as hell weren't health resorts.

Matt felt he had to change the subject; she was starting to get under his skin in a big way. "I'm actually from Davidson, Oklahoma. My first combat assignment was on Iwo Jima, and —"

She interrupted him abruptly, slowly pulling the glasses from her face. Her beautiful dark eyes blazed hot. "Did I hear you say that you were in Iwo?"

"Yes," he said.

Before he could react, he felt the shock of a hard slap across his face. She was quivering and sobbing uncontrollably. "My father . . . was killed on Iwo . . ." As she raised her shaking right hand to slap him again, he reached out quickly and grabbed her wrist.

She was surprisingly strong. "Aika, I didn't know."

She jerked away from him and hissed, "You Americans, I hate you, I hate all of you! Stay away from my brother!"

She ran away crying as Shigeshi returned from the line. He looked puzzled. "Corporal Matt, I follow her. She look unhappy. I see you tomorrow." He ran after her.

Matt watched them both until they disappeared from the dusty, crowded street. Slowly he walked back to his spot in the line. He was so mad he wanted to scream.

"I'll take over now," he said to his replacement and began filling bowls with rice.

A cool breeze touched his face, but it didn't calm his anger. She was pretty, no doubt. But pretty only goes so far.

I hope I never see her again.

Chapter 15

November 21, 1945, Hiroshima, Japan

Matt began to worry.

Where is Shigeshi?

It had been three days since an angry Aika had left him with Shigeshi following closely behind her. Each time when the food convoy approached Saeki-ku, Matt scanned the crowd from his jeep and saw no trace of him. Not that he expected or wanted to see Aika. Truthfully, he couldn't think of anyone he would rather see less.

It was just as well, he decided. Just being American was enough to trip her trigger. And the fact that she was Japanese, well, didn't exactly bring up good feelings. All he could do was think of Joe and all the friends he had left behind on Iwo Jima.

Today seemed no different than usual, and as the truck screeched to a halt at the drop off spot, he hopped from his jeep. Along with the other men, he began unloading supplies. He heard a loud whistle. One of his men was waving at him.

"Hey, Matt," he yelled. "There's someone out there trying to get your attention."

Matt looked in the direction he was pointing. A woman dressed in black Japanese pantaloons was waving at him. It was Aika.

What is she doing here?

Matt smiled to himself.

She's probably come to finish me off. I hope she doesn't have a knife.

He took his time walking up to her.

She was not wearing sunglasses, and puffiness around her eyes told him she had been crying. Despite that, he had to admit she was easily the most beautiful woman he had laid his eyes on. He had a strong feeling that he had somehow seen or known her before. As he came to her, he shook himself from his reverie; he was determined to not let her get the best of him again. Matt was just getting cranked up and ready to argue when she bowed to him in greeting. Matt was caught off guard. He did not return the bow.

She said, "Corporal, I need your help. Shigeshi is sick."

Matt was still exasperated with her and kept it short. "He seemed just fine a few days ago."

Aika continued, "Shortly after we left you he started having pain in his stomach. I became even angrier at you because I thought it was all the sweets you had been giving him. Later that night he started vomiting, and his fever went up. I took him to the hospital — such as it is — the next day, and they prescribed him some medicine. It didn't help, and he hasn't kept anything down since. I went back this morning and talked again with the doctor. He was too busy to see him and told me to bring him in tomorrow. When I returned home his pain was worse, and he hurts to move. My mother and I are both worried. Please — is there any way you can help us?"

Her pleading dark eyes slowly convinced him. "If you'll take me to where you live, I'll peek at him and see what I think."

"Good —"

"I know a doctor back on base. If it's necessary, I think I can get him to look at Shigeshi. Will you trust me?"

She warily looked at him then finally nodded.

It would have been nice if she had apologized to me for her behavior the other day. Oh, well, he thought, *the kid needs help, and I will help him if I can.* He motioned for her to follow him to the jeep. "Private," he called out to the driver, "go ahead and help the guys distribute food and water. I'm borrowing the jeep."

The private looked first at Matt and then at Aika. He winked, softly whistled and said, "Oh, yeah," then hopped from the jeep.

Matt chose to ignore him. "I'm going to be gone for a bit. When you're finished here, head back to HQ on the truck. I'll see you there."

ཨོཾ་མ་ཎི་པདྨེ་ཧཱུྃ་ ཨོཾ་མ་ཎི་པདྨེ་ཧཱུྃ་ ཨོཾ་མ་ཎི་པདྨེ་ཧཱུྃ་

A short drive later the jeep stopped in front of a modest Japanese home, wood-framed with a thatched roof. Matt saw the planks and thatch were darkened on the side that faced ground zero.

Even this far away.

Aika said, "Corporal, wait here." She stepped down from the jeep and up to the front door, cracked it open, and called out to someone within. Shortly an attractive middle-aged woman appeared at the doorway. Aika gestured for him to approach. The woman was slender, her graying hair was piled up on her head, and she wore a dark brown kimono with a black obi sash.

When he reached the door, the woman bowed to Matt, and he clumsily reciprocated.

"This is my mother, Miyo Tanaka. Mother," Aika said, "this is Corporal Matt."

With a motion of her hands she invited him into the home. He politely held his hat in his hands and stepped inside. The first thing he saw was a decorated shrine sitting in front of a room partition. There were several pictures of older Japanese couples sitting on it. In the foreground, though, was a picture of a man wearing the uniform of a Japanese soldier. There was no smile to be seen, and he was standing ramrod straight with a sword hanging from his belt. Matt swallowed hard realizing he must be Aika's father.

The older woman bowed again and spoke in clear English. "Corporal, we thank you for your help. Please come see Shigeshi. He is very sick." Walking into an adjacent room, they found him wrapped tightly with blankets and barely awake.

"Corporal Matt," he said softly, "you come to help Charlie?" A faint smile crossed his lips.

Matt looked closely at him. He appeared far worse than he had imagined. Shigeshi winced as Matt gently probed in the right lower part of his stomach.

This could be appendicitis.

"Everything will be okay, Shigeshi. We're going to see the doctor." Pulling the blankets over the boy, he lifted him up and started toward the front door.

Miyo said, "I will stay here. Aika, go with your brother. I know you and Corporal Matt will take good care of him."

Matt studied her closely as the three loaded in the jeep. He saw more than concern; she was beside herself with worry.

ཨོཾ་ཨཱཿཧཱུྃ་ ཨོཾ་ཨཱཿཧཱུྃ་ ཨོཾ་ཨཱཿཧཱུྃ་

Matt, Aika and Shigeshi sat in the waiting area at the military hospital in Kaidaichi. A white-coated doctor wearing a surgical hat approached. Matt stood and saluted.

"Why, Corporal Matthew Johnston," he smiled and said as he walked up to them, saluting in return. After they shook hands, the doc continued, "It's been a long time since Iwo." He glanced down with concern at Shigeshi, who shivered uncontrollably in spite of the blanket and his sister's embrace. He looked back at Matt. "Marine, what can I do for you?"

Matt whispered in his ear. "Dr. Lewis, I'm real close to this boy, and I'm afraid he might have appendicitis. Do you mind looking at him?"

"For you, Matt, anything." He pointed to a nearby bed. "Put him on this stretcher."

Matt carefully picked Shigeshi up and placed him there.

Dr. Lewis then examined Shigeshi's abdomen. The young boy moaned as the surgeon probed in the right lower area. Finishing his evaluation, he said to them, "I think the little guy has appendicitis. I don't believe that it has perforated yet, but he'll need surgery as soon as possible."

Looking at Aika, he said, "Do I have your permission?"

Matt saw the tension written all over her face, and at the same time sensed her inner strength. "Of course," she said softly.

"Okay then. Anesthesia is already here, and we'll be only a few minutes. I'll be back shortly, and we'll take him to the operating room."

As the surgeon exited, to his great surprise, Aika took his hand and squeezed it warmly for a brief second. He felt his anger at her begin to melt away.

She said to Shigeshi, "Little brother, you are going to have surgery. You will go to sleep and when you wake up your pain will be better."

"So," Shigeshi said, "chocolate not make me sick?"

"No," Aika said, "it wasn't the chocolate."

"Corporal Matt?" Shigeshi asked. "That mean you still can give Charlie chocolate?"

Matt felt his eyes well with tears. "Little buddy, I promise you will get a basket of chocolate when you get home, okay? I might even throw in some Juicy Fruit gum."

The attendants came and wheeled the boy away.

Following close behind was Dr. Lewis. "He'll be fine," he said. "I'll see both of you in about an hour. And, by the way, I can tell this is one special kid. I promise I'll take good care of him."

Matt again felt Aika take his hand. With a sudden jolt he finally realized where he had seen her before. Matt had dreamed of her while lying in front of his home in Davidson, Oklahoma, Inky curled to his side.

The eyes I saw on those starry nights were the same ones I am staring at now.

Chapter 16

December 1, 1945, Hiroshima

Matt arrived promptly at 10:00 a.m. at the Tanaka home and was greeted warmly at the door by Aika. He was led inside to the receiving room and seated on a tatami mat. Aika sat gracefully to his right.

"Where is Shigeshi?" asked Matt

"He is at a friend's home. What we are doing tonight is for adults only."

"Really?" Matt said as he raised his eyebrows.

Aika playfully shoved him. "Not that, foolish one. My mother is most grateful for what you have done for Shigeshi, and she could think of no greater gift than a tea ceremony."

"Oh," Matt said as he tried to appear disappointed. But, as he thought about it, he had to admit he was curious. In Oklahoma, country folks went for the coffee. Tea was something for little old ladies who had too much time on their hands. "Tell me more," he said.

"Well, Matt, my mother is a tea master, as was my grandmother, and many generations before her. The Japanese tea ceremony, if done properly, takes years to learn. And something you don't know about me," she proudly said, "is that I am a student of my mother."

Matt nodded. He was starting to get the picture.

"Even my father, Toshiro, before being ordered into the Japanese Army, was a tea marketer. My countrymen are great lovers of tea, and this has continued despite the travails of war. Since his death . . ." she paused and cleared her throat, "we have survived by the modest fees my mother earns from the shop and her students."

"I see. Is there anything that I should know about this ceremony?"

"No," she said. "Just relax, and it will flow as it should."

Matt took a few deep breaths, and as he appreciated the light scent of jasmine incense, his mind wandered to the day after Shigeshi's surgery.

ཨོམཚིཔྱེཧཱུྃ ཨོམཚིཔྱེཧཱུྃ ཨོམཚིཔྱེཧཱུྃ

When Matt walked into the room, Shigeshi was lying in bed as Dr. Lewis examined his abdomen. Miyo and Aika sat at the bedside.

"Corporal Matt!" Shigeshi yelled. Matt smiled at him as the doctor lifted his stethoscope from the boy's stomach. Matt and the surgeon exchanged salutes.

"Hey, Shigeshi," Matt said. He then looked at the doc. "How's the patient doing?"

Dr. Lewis said, "He's doing great. We'll let him go home in four to five days — if he is able to take solid foods. I tell you, Matt, you got him here just in the nick of time; his appendix was on the verge of rupturing. Good work, Marine."

Dr. Lewis then walked out of the room, but stuck his head back in and said, "Matt, could I have a moment with you? When he joined him in the hall, Dr. Lewis said, "Matt, you and I both know that Iwo was a crazy place. In spite of that, I thought that not only did you have a good head on your shoulders, but also a heck of a lot of good old common sense. Have you considered going into medicine when you finish with the Marines?"

"Doc, funny you should ask. Since I've left my home in Oklahoma, I've discovered how much I miss working with animals, that is, except cutting calves." Matt and Dr. Lewis shared a smile. "If anything, I'd like to use the GI Bill to get training to be a veterinarian."

"Well, I think you'd do a damn good job at it. Good luck."

As Matt walked back in the room, Miyo looked at the basket Matt had left at the bedside. "What's that?" she asked.

"Oh, it's nothing. Just a whole lot of chocolate and gum for my good buddy." He handed it to an open-mouthed Shigeshi.

Shigeshi squealed out loud at the sight of the overflowing basket. Miyo was not happy. Matt could tell she wasn't completely convinced that the chocolate wasn't the culprit in the first place.

ཨོ་མ་ཎི་པདྨེ་ཧཱུྃ ཨོ་མ་ཎི་པདྨེ་ཧཱུྃ ཨོ་མ་ཎི་པདྨེ་ཧཱུྃ

As he and Aika continued to wait in silence for the tea ceremony, Matt thought about his busy routine since the surgery. Between distributing food and taking his turn on patrol, his mind had been occupied with thoughts of Aika. He had fantasized about how life with her might be. Where would they live? How many children would they have? What would it be like to lie in bed with her? It was far too early for such ideas, but he entertained them just the same. As he pictured Aika's beautiful face, an old desire returned:

Money — I need money.

He wanted Aika to have the best of everything.

He also recalled the pained look on her face when he had lit up a Camel on the night of Shigeshi's surgery. No words were spoken, but he knew he had to quit. Further, he was still drinking far too much. In the days to come, he would completely stop. He was living in a whole new world, and he liked it.

The day after Shigeshi's operation, Matt was stunned to learn that not only had he been recommended for the Silver Star, but it had been approved. General Corbett had flown in just for the occasion, and, only yesterday, Matt and others received medals for their actions on Iwo Jima. As it was pinned on his chest, it took all the strength he had not to rip if from his uniform and throw it in an adjacent trash can. It was as if the medal spoke to him and said:

You are a lowly coward.

Today, as he was in formal Marine wear, he wore it just above his left front pocket. He could barely stand to have it there, but he owed it to the Marines and his country to display it, and display it he did.

ཨོ་མ་ཎི་པདྨེ་ཧཱུྃ ཨོ་མ་ཎི་པདྨེ་ཧཱུྃ ཨོ་མ་ཎི་པདྨེ་ཧཱུྃ

"It is time," Aika gently said and jarred him back into the present. She motioned for him to follow her.

The chill of winter had held its breath for the day, and he felt comfortable as they exited out the back door. They entered a brightly colored garden with flat stepping-stones surrounded by an almost fluorescent green moss.

Matt watched Aika sidestep ants and other crawling insects that appeared. As far as he was concerned, bugs were for mashing when they got in your way.

I have much to learn about her.

In a few moments they approached a stone basin through which bubbling water was flowing. Several small shrubs and statues of Buddha were placed around it.

"Do as I do," Aika explained. Then she crouched next to the basin and picked up a small wooden dipper. After she scooped some of the sparkling water, she poured it onto her hands and into her mouth. She then dried her hands on an adjacent towel and spat into the grass. Matt repeated the act, and she said, "This is the place of cleansing. This is where we prepare to receive the tea ceremony."

From there, they walked farther and came to a bench against a wall with a covering roof.

"This is the waiting area," she said. "Here we will sit and enjoy the peace of the garden."

Matt resisted the strong urge to put his arm around her shoulders.

Mrs. Tanaka then appeared, dressed in an elegant dark blue patterned kimono with a red obi.

Aika and Matt both stood as she approached, and they all bowed to each other. They remained while she returned to the tearoom, and, shortly afterward, a soft gong was heard.

"We have been called," Aika whispered. They proceeded to the teahouse and found a large, flat stone sitting at the foot of a narrow entryway that was elevated off the ground. They stepped on the rock and stooped as they entered the tea house.

Following after Aika, Matt saw Mrs. Tanaka sitting on her knees, beaming a sweet smile. In front of her was a steaming pot of water being heated by a charcoal fire. As they entered, she sprinkled incense onto it, and a pleasant aroma filled the air. To her left were several tea bowls and the instruments for tea-making sitting in a tray. They sat on mats directly in front of her.

"Would you like a dessert?" Mrs. Tanaka asked Matt. With his nod, she placed a sugared candy in the shape of a leaf on a plain paper napkin and handed it to him. She repeated this with her daughter.

As they ate, Matt said, "Mrs. Tanaka, why is the entryway to the teahouse so small?"

She said, "It is this way for a reason, as all who enter this place must stoop, and everyone, whether important or not, are humbled and without distinction." She smiled at Matt. "Now I will prepare the tea."

Mrs. Tanaka then went through an elaborate ritual of cleaning the tea instruments with a cloth. Then a tea scoop was used to remove a green powder from its container, and hot water was dipped from the pot and added to the bowl. Using a bamboo whisk, the mixture was whipped into a froth. Mrs. Tanaka presented a bowl to first Matt and then Aika.

"Corporal Matt," she explained, "this is matcha."

Matt took a small sip. He enjoyed its somewhat bitter taste.

Mrs. Tanaka continued. "Tea's beginnings were in the Yunnan Province of China. At first, its main purpose was medicinal, though later it was used by monks and priests who found that its stimulating properties would help keep them alert during long meditations. As Buddhism, Taoism and Confucianism spread, so did the use of tea."

After they finished their tea, Miyo performed the cleaning ritual. With slow and precise movements, each bowl and instrument was cleaned and placed in its proper position.

Then Mrs. Tanaka rose along with her guests. They exchanged bows with their host and exited the tea room. Aika walked Matt to the front door.

"I want to see you again," she abruptly said and kissed him lightly on the lips. "Will you be able to get a pass for next weekend?"

As Matt looked at her beautiful face, he suddenly saw transposed upon it the face of a screaming Japanese soldier who was pointing a gun at the head of Joe. His own voice echoed in his head.

I hate the damn Japs . . .

He suddenly soaked his uniform with a cold sweat.

"Aika," he stuttered, "I'll . . . I'll . . . need to check on that. Can I tell you later when I see you at the food distribution site?"

"Of course," she said. They then bowed to each other.

Her dark eyes sparkled as she gently closed the door.

As Matt walked away, he realized that he had never felt such inner conflict. While he was no psychologist, he guessed that it would take more than just a little time to get over months of an all-encompassing hate. He smiled to himself. He was an Oklahoma farm boy; he was not only tough, he was a quick healer.

He did not doubt his vision; he did not doubt how he felt.

I am in love.

Chapter 17

Davidson, Oklahoma

January 3, 1946

Dear Son,

We can't begin to tell you how happy we are to receive the letter from you and hear the BIG NEWS! We are so thrilled for you. Aika sounds delightful, and we can't wait to meet her. But, like you say, it is early and some time will tell you (and her) a lot more. You say she is Buddhist? Of course, we had to know more, so your father and I went to the Frederick Library a few days ago and picked out a book on Buddhism. It may take a bit, but we'll try to get up to snuff.

Most around here think if you don't accept Jesus as your savior, you are going to hell. That doesn't make any sense to me. The way I see it, there's no difference between a good Christian and a good Buddhist. What's important to us is that she loves and cares for you.

We are so proud to hear that you have been awarded the Silver Star! After we heard from you, there was an article about it in the Frederick newspaper, and we are about to bust our buttons with pride. We are very proud of you. Congratulations, son!

Merry Christmas and a Happy New Year! Now we have had two strange holiday seasons in a row, as both have been without you. We've taken your presents from under the tree and couldn't decide whether to send them to you, or just wait till you get home. Sounds like you'll be there for a while getting to know Aika, so I'll go ahead and put them in the mail.

It was a bad cotton harvest this year, and your father has been trying to figure out how we're going to make it. The extra money you have been sending has helped, that's for sure. You know we sometimes have droughts, and this has been one of those years. At least the cattle have been giving a lot of milk, so I've got lots of homemade butter to sell. We'll get by, one way or another.

A little about your brothers and sisters: First of all, they are all on Christmas break from school, and it's pretty windy and snowy outside. Because of that, aside from milking the cattle, I think they are all getting pretty lazy. Alexander, being as tall and lanky as he is, has been playing center for the Sandies basketball team. They played in a tournament over the holidays, and placed 2nd out of 16 teams! Your brother averaged 25 points, and the coach thinks he'll get a scholarship offer. Esther decided last summer to try out for cheerleader, and she made it. So, she's had to go to all of the sporting events, and I think one of the football players has his eye on her. Robert and Earlyne are still like two peas in a pod. You never see one without the other.

Son, I must admit that I feel like part of me is missing, and, of course, that is because you are so far away. Some of the other young men who went into the armed forces are coming home now that the war's over, which makes things even worse. It sounds like you'll be staying on for a while, and I don't want to rush you back. After all, you do have your own life to live.

Much love,
Mom

ༀ་མཎི་པདྨེ་ཧཱུྃ་ ༀ་མཎི་པདྨེ་ཧཱུྃ་ ༀ་མཎི་པདྨེ་ཧཱུྃ་

March 3, 1946

Hi Family!

Busy! Busy! Busy! They have been working us day and night getting ready for the Aussies, who will officially take our places on March 6. About 100 of us, including me, have volunteered to stay and help with the transition. For now, I don't know how much longer we will be here.

I have to tell you I have seen a lot of suffering here because of the bomb. You would think the immediate death and destruction would be bad enough, but even worse seems to be the lingering illnesses. I must admit that I'm more than a little worried about how Aika might be affected. She's doesn't seem concerned, so I guess I shouldn't be.

Our relationship is going great guns. Once the Aussies take over, I should finally have some evenings off to spend with Aika. But, till then, we have to limit our time together to weekends. One of our favorite places to spend the day is Miyajima. This is a wooded island just south and west of Hiroshima. You have to take a ferry to get there, and one of the first things you see is a beautiful Shinto shrine standing in the water called the O-Torii. Also, lots of wild deer inhabit the island. I think the word "wild" is an exaggeration, as the deer practically mug you to get food!

I have learned a little more about Buddhism. First of all, Aika and her family are Zen Buddhists. They believe in living mindfully and finding inspiration through a type of meditation called Zazen. If I understand it correctly, they sit still and listen to their breath as it goes in and out. This hopefully eventually leads them to satori or an awakening. Another part of their practice is koans, which is like a puzzle to which there is no answer, and they hope it sort of shocks you into satori. They also believe in reincarnation. Truthfully, this is all Greek (Japanese) to me. I am grateful that Aika and her mother don't seem to mind that I don't believe the things they do. Honestly, I'm not sure what I swear by anymore.

Thanks for filling me in on all the happenings with my brothers and sisters. I can't believe that Alexander is such a basketball stud. When I come home I'll show him who the boss really is. I'm sorry to hear about the bad cotton crop. It's amazing to me that anything can survive long in Davidson. Not enough rain, way too hot in summer, well, you know what I mean.

Don't worry at all about me. In my patrols I occasionally run across Japanese soldiers who finally figured out that they lost, and they surrender without any resistance. All in all, life is pretty easy and sweet.

This Saturday Aika and I have plans, and I'm thinking it's about time to pop the question. I know it's only been a little over three months, but I know I'm ready. The big question is: Is she?

Love,
Matt

Chapter 18

March 9, 1946, Hiroshima

Matt felt like he was about to jump out of his skin. It was approaching 4:00 p.m., and a jeep headed his way had dropped him off down the road. Every step he took drew him closer and closer to the Tanaka household.

In his right front pant pocket rested a small jewelry box with a diamond ring. He had spent all morning shopping, and when he saw the diamonds arranged on a simple gold band formed in the shape of a lotus, he knew it was the one. He spent every last penny he had; he wanted something special for the most special woman in the world.

"Aika Johnston." He liked the way it sounded. He repeated it again. "Aika Johnston."

He hadn't quite yet figured how he was going to ask her. He hoped he wouldn't stutter.

After knocking on the door, a few moments passed before Aika answered, now with a full head of shining black hair, artfully arranged. "Matthew, how good to see you." She drew him close and kissed him. "Mother has been cooking all day, and I think she has something special prepared." The minute he entered he appreciated a delicious aroma in the air. The availability and variety of food had definitely improved since those first few months after the bombing, and he couldn't wait to sample home cooked Japanese food.

Shigeshi leapt into his arms. "How you doing, Corporal Matt?"

"Shigeshi, I am as happy as a pig in poop," Matt replied.

"What that mean?"

"I'll tell you later," Matt said, a bit embarrassed.

"Hey, how come you no call Charlie anymore?" Shigeshi asked.

"Well, let's just say you already have a very good name, and we'll stick with Shigeshi." Pulling him closer, Matt whispered in his ear, "If you want, when it's just you and me, I'll call you Charlie. But let's keep it our secret."

"I got it, Corporal Matt," a grinning Shigeshi said.

With that, a gong sounded from the dining area.

"Dinner is ready," Aika explained.

They followed the fragrance into the dining area where Mrs. Tanaka stood by a low-set table in another dazzling kimono, this one styled in green with a beige obi sash. In contrast, Aika wore a black silk blouse and a matching skirt.

"Welcome to our home, Corporal Matt," Miyo said as she gracefully bowed.

After bowing in return, they sat on floor mats. There was no silverware, only chopsticks. During these months here in Japan, Matt had gotten quite good at using them. Aika squeezed his hand under the table.

How I love this woman.

While the meal of green tea, miso soup, edamame and salmon teriyaki on rice was being enjoyed, Matt noticed a distinct difference in the way the food was eaten as compared to Oklahoma. Back home each meal was a race to gobble down the food as quickly as possible.

"Mrs. Tanaka?" Matt asked.

"Corporal Matt, it's time you started calling me Miyo."

"Yes, Miyo, but only if you start calling me Matt."

"Yes, Matt?" she replied with a smile.

"Why is everyone eating so slowly?"

"Matt, as you know, our family embraces Zen Buddhism. Aika tells me you have been studying about how we believe, and that pleases me very much. Part of our practice is being mindful in as many ways as is possible, and this includes eating. When you see food, how do you view it?"

"Well, I think of it as nutrition for our bodies."

"Of course, it is, but we think of food in other ways. Take for example the rice in the bowl. In the rice is earth, where it was nurtured. Part of it is water and sunshine, which helped the plant grow. Another portion is the labor and love of the farmer, who not only helped the plant grow healthy and strong, but later harvested it and took it to market. So, when we chew and chew slowly we think of earth, water, sunshine, labor and love. All of these are in each bite, and we are very thankful. There is much more here than just food." She added, "Do you understand?"

Matt could only nod. He had never thought of food in that way before.

So, what would have been a five minute eat-and-gulp-down meal in Davidson, Oklahoma, was a one hour affair in Hiroshima. After the meal was completed, Matt thanked Mrs. Tanaka, and he and Aika excused themselves. Shigeshi stayed to help clean up with his mother. Miyo winked at Matt as they left.

Does she know what's about to happen?

Matt found himself sweating as he sat next to Aika. The ring in his pocket began to feel as hot as a flaming coal. He noticed that Aika was looking at him intently. But he needed to talk to her before he asked her to marry him.

"Aika, there's something you should know about me. It's something no other person in the world knows. Remember me telling you that I was a Marine on Iwo?" He saw the slightest wince on her face. "One late evening when I was with my best friend, we were attacked, and there came a moment when I had the chance to save his life. I was so frightened that I froze, and in that second he was killed. In spite of all this brave Marine talk you've heard, you need to know that I am a coward, and I betrayed one that I loved." His eyes welled with tears. "Are you sure you still want to continue to see me, knowing what I am and what I have done?"

Tears formed in her eyes as well. "Matthew Johnston, you are not a coward, and you did not betray your best friend. You were in one of the most brutal battles of the Pacific war. You, like everyone else, including your Japanese opponents . . ." she held her right hand to her heart ". . . were scared out of their minds. I know my father was. The letters he wrote gave us a small window into the horrors of war.

"To have fear is expected. To be slow in reacting is normal. I know who you are, Matthew Johnston, and you are not a coward. You saved the life of my brother. You are brave and courageous, and you are the man I love."

Whoa, now. Did I hear what I thought I heard?

"Aika, I love you, too," he found himself saying without even thinking.

Okay, here we go. I'm a battle-tested Marine. Why am I so nervous?

Finally he spoke in a voice that, to his embarrassment, quivered a bit. "Aika, over the past three or so months we've gotten to know each other really well. And there is still much more to learn. I know that I don't have much to offer you. I'm a poor country boy from Oklahoma. But this much I do know: I love you, and I want to be with you the rest of my life." He gulped. "Aika, will you marry me?"

To his dismay, she paused and looked down at the floor. He could see that she was gathering her thoughts.

Finally she looked up at him. "Matt, I love you too, but I can't answer your question just now. Tomorrow I want you to come back for a Japanese tea ceremony. I have been practicing for months, and I believe I am ready. My mother has watched my preparations and has given her approval. Come here tomorrow evening at six o'clock, and I will answer your question."

"But, Aika, I . . ."

"No arguments. Tomorrow," she repeated as she directed him toward the door. She kissed him lightly on the cheek. "I am touched by your honesty, Matt, and the man that you are. You have opened your heart to me, but before I answer your question, I must be sure. I will sit in meditation tonight and contemplate what has happened here. Good night." She closed the door behind him before he could answer.

A confused Matt stumbled out to the road in hopes of hitching a ride back to the base, thinking:

Six tomorrow? How can I possibly wait that long?

ཨོ་མཱ་ཎི་པདྨེ་ཧཱུྃ་ ཨོ་མཱ་ཎི་པདྨེ་ཧཱུྃ་ ཨོ་མཱ་ཎི་པདྨེ་ཧཱུྃ་

March 10, 1946, Hiroshima

The following day, at 5:59 p.m., Matt walked up to the Tanaka home. He was more anxious than ever and was still puzzled by her ambivalence.

He knocked on the front door and waited, and waited.

Did I get the right time?

He was about to knock again when he heard measured footsteps approach. The door cracked open, and he was stunned by what he saw: Aika was dressed in a formal kimono, a gossamer white with a crane stitched on each sleeve. Her obi was also white. Her hair was pulled back on top of her head, and she looked radiant.

"Come in, Matthew Johnston."

As he stepped inside and removed his hat, he was aware of something different about the home: silence. As if reading his mind, Aika said, "Matt, my mother and brother are visiting my aunt. We are by ourselves. Come in and sit with me." Matt felt her arm lightly touch his back as she led him inside.

After they sat, she said, "I would like to recite haiku, a Japanese poem, I have written for you."

A poem . . . for me . . .?

She spoke slowly:

> Frigid winter winds
> Have become warm spring breezes
> The smile on your face

Matt felt his heart in his throat.

Aika said, "I go now to prepare the tea ceremony. I will leave the back door slightly ajar. When you hear the gong, repeat the steps we performed together the first time. After you hear a second gong, you may enter the teahouse. I will be waiting for you inside." Aika then stood and walked out through the back door.

Matt waited as calmly as he could.

Why is she making me wait? Will she marry me?

In about ten minutes he heard the first ringing of the gong. He rose and went outside. Though still not understanding why or what for, he avoided the insects on the stepping-stones, and before too long came to the place of symbolic cleansing, where he knelt and repeated the ritual as Aika had taught him. Arising from there, he walked to the bench and edgily sat. Soon he heard again the gong sound. Rising, he followed the pathway and stooped as he entered the teahouse. Inside was Aika standing behind the water pot and looking quite serious. They bowed to each other before they sat. The pleasant smell of charcoal and incense filled the air.

"Would you like a confection?" Aika politely asked.

Matt nodded, and carefully she placed a conch shell shaped dessert on a piece of paper. Putting it in front of him, Matt felt her hand brush against his. In most situations he would have thought the touch was inadvertent, but tonight he felt intent, and he began to feel the gradual building of passion. As he ate, she began the ritual preparation of the tea utensils. She seemed completely focused on her work, but to him each motion felt sensual.

She then carefully measured the *matcha* into the bowl, poured the hot water and whipped the green mixture. When it was prepared she set it before him. As he reached for it, he felt her place both of her hands around his, and together they clasped the tea bowl. Aika closed her eyes, and Matt did as well. Time stretched while their hands intertwined. She brushed her fingers against his as she pulled her hands away. He then put the bowl to his lips, silently sipping the green mixture.

Somehow the flavor was deeper and richer than it was the first time. They sat in silence. After a second, third, and finally a fourth drink, the bowl was emptied, and he set it at his feet.

"Would you like more?" she asked.

"No, that was wonderful."

She then began the step-by-step cleansing of the bowl and the tea utensils. He watched her every move, her every motion. Somehow the music from the slow movement of Haydn's Opus 76, number 5 string quartet came into his head. He closed his eyes and listened. His music teacher in high school had played it many times on a wind up phonograph, and while it moved him then, there was no comparison to what he was feeling now. He swayed with the rhythm and the intensity that built with each motion she made. Every second was sensual, and his arousal increased.

When he opened his eyes she was gazing at him. This time she leaned forward, placed her head on his right shoulder and whispered, "The tea ceremony is over. I will be out shortly."

As he rose, she also stood. She placed her arms around him, and as he reciprocated, she pressed her chest against his. She raised her face, and they kissed, at first gently, feeling the texture of each other's lips. As their passion increased, he began to nuzzle and kiss her soft, warm neck.

"Yes."

"What?" he questioned.

"Yes, I will marry you. Please wait outside at the bench. I will be out when I finish my work here."

He reluctantly pulled himself from her, exited and waited impatiently. She joined him shortly and, intertwining their arms, they walked back into the house. As he headed for the front door, she stopped him and pulled out the wooden sticks holding her hair in place. She shook her head; her hair radiantly tumbled to her shoulders. "Matthew, my bedroom is this way," she said, pointing to her right. "Mother and Shigeshi won't be back until tomorrow afternoon. I know you have to be at work in the morning. I promise I will let you go before then. Please come with me."

As she turned and began to walk, he lifted her up and carried her into the bedroom. They held each other and kissed again, open-mouthed, allowing their tongues to dance with each other. The ring was still in his pocket. He would show it to her in the morning. Now there were other things on his mind.

ཨོཾ་མཉི་པདྨེ་ཧཱུྃ་ ཨོཾ་མཉི་པདྨེ་ཧཱུྃ་ ཨོཾ་མཉི་པདྨེ་ཧཱུྃ་

Telegram from Hiroshima to Davidson, Oklahoma, March 11, 1946

WESTERN UNION
SHE SAID YES! LETTER COMING!
MATT

ཨོཾ་མཉི་པདྨེ་ཧཱུྃ་ ཨོཾ་མཉི་པདྨེ་ཧཱུྃ་ ཨོཾ་མཉི་པདྨེ་ཧཱུྃ་

March 11, 1946

Dear Family,

Like you heard in my telegram, she said YES! We see no reason to wait, and we'll be getting married in two weeks. The date is already set for March 24, on a Sunday at 2:00 p.m. Her mother, Miyo, is in a bit of a tizzy thinking about all the things she needs to do. We have decided to get married on Miyajima. There is a special place there called the Itsukushima Shrine, which is right in front of the O-Torii, and we will be married by a Shinto priest. My best man will be none other than Sergeant McKensie. I just hope we can fight off those wild deer I was telling you about.

I am a little worried about something, and I thought I might mention it. Aika has been having these spells where she almost passes out. If it keeps up, I'll take her to the doctor and have it checked out.

Okay, I know you want to know about the ring. The more I've been around Aika, the more I realized how important her religion is to her, so I wanted to get her a ring that contained a symbol of her faith. For Buddhism, an important one is the lotus. I don't really understand much about this, so let me put down what it says in this book I bought:

The lotus symbolizes the growth of the soul as it moves from the mud of this existence, through the waters of life, and finally arrives into the luminescent sunshine of enlightenment.

Anyway, when I showed it to her she began crying and said it was the best gift anyone had ever given her. By the time this letter gets to you, we will be married.

We have been given permission to live off base, and after looking a bit, we found a place. It's a small home close to her mother and brother. Aika didn't feel comfortable moving too far from them for the time being, and that's okay with me.

By this time, I guess that the state basketball playoffs are over. I'm hoping that brother Alex had some good games and that they won state. I think of all of you a lot.

It seems that life is sweeping me along for the ride. The idea that one has any sort of control in life is really pretty silly.

Love,
Matt

ཨོསམ་ཆི་ལྡི་ཧུ་ ཨོསམ་ཆི་ལྡི་ཧུ་ ཨོསམ་ཆི་ལྡི་ཧུ་

April 11, 1946

Dear Son,

My eyes are flowing with tears as I write this letter. I can't believe that Aika is now my daughter-in-law! She has such a lovely name; I'd love to know what it means. Please send pictures of her as soon as possible.

The ring you selected looks to be perfect for her. Sounds like you put a lot of thought into it. I do hope that her weak episodes are nothing serious. Please keep us posted.

You have grown up way too fast, Matthew Walker Johnston. But, you know, I've always felt you were very mature for your age.

About basketball: You won't believe it, but the Davidson Sandies won state! In the finals with us were the Frederick Bombers, but they didn't stand a prayer. Alex scored 38 points, and they could do nothing to stop him.

The wheat crop is looking pretty good, and we're hoping for a lot of bushels. After the disaster we had with the cotton, we have to do well to at least break even. Your father keeps working hard and thinking up ways to raise money. It's not an easy time, but has it ever been?

I'll make this letter short so I can catch the mail pick up. We love you, son. Send our love to Aika as well. We can't wait to meet her.

Love,
Mom
P.S. We'll be expecting a grandbaby within the year!

Chapter 19

Married life for Aika and Matt was as sweet as either could have imagined. The routine at the base had definitely loosened up over the past months, and Matt, while still just a Marine grunt, was only required to work nine to five, Monday through Friday. During the day Aika spent time with her mother, helping her with simple household chores and keeping an eye on the rambunctious Shigeshi.

Each day when Matt returned from work, Aika had dinner prepared, and if time allowed, they would take a long walk, hand in hand, enjoying the cool of the evening. One day when on a stroll Matt looked at his bride and noticed paleness and a sense of fatigue in her beautiful face.

"Aika," he said, "are you feeling well?"

"Just a little tired, dear."

"It seems to me that you've been more and more tired lately."

"Did you ever think there might be a reason for that?" she said and looked away.

Matt knew she was hiding something from him. "What might that be, dear?" he said with more than a little curiosity.

"Well, Matthew Johnston, in another five months you will be a father," she said, giving him a playful punch in the side. "I saw Dr. Yamamoto at the hospital just last week while you were at work. Today he called, and the pregnancy test came back positive. Well, Dad, what do you say? Think you are ready to have a son?"

"Holy shit! I mean . . ." He hugged her tightly and gave a loud whoop. "When is your due date?"

"February the first, dear husband."

"How do you know it's a boy?"

"Matthew Johnston, you should know better than to ask. Sometimes women just know. And I know as surely as you're standing in front of me. By the way, would you like to know his name?" she asked.

"Don't I get any say in it?" he said, feeling a little hurt.

"Husband, many times in our relationship, you have had the final word. But this has to be my decision. I know what our baby's name should be. Please join with me in this." She paused for a second. "Please," she repeated softly.

Feeling his male ego bruised, he looked at her skeptically. "Okay. But what if I don't like the name?"

"You'll like it."

"What is it?"

"Take a guess."

Matt was puzzled. "Let's see . . ." He placed his hand on his chin and stared up at the azure sky. "George? Methuselah? Donald Duck? Okay, I give up. I have no earthly idea. Tell me!"

"Rinji," she said. "Rinji William Johnston."

He liked the way it rolled off her tongue.

"So far I like how it sounds. What does the name mean?"

"Rinji means 'peaceful forest'. It reminds me of how I felt when we walked in the forests on Miyajima after our wedding. Of course, the middle name is from your father, who you have told me so much about."

Matt screwed up his face, as if to argue, then broke out into a smile, hugged her and said, "I love it. Rinji William it will be. That is, if the baby is a boy."

"Of course it's a boy."

"Whatever you say. Come to think of it, I did wonder if you were getting a bit poochy down there." He pointed to her lower abdomen. "I was starting to believe you were overeating." He hugged her teasingly.

She smiled and then just as quickly became serious. "Dear husband, one more thing," she said with some hesitation. "The doctor said he was concerned about my blood work and wanted me to come back tomorrow for some more tests. I don't think it's anything to worry about, but hopefully I will know something by the following week."

"Does this have something to do with your episodes of weakness?" Matt said.

"It's probably just the pregnancy, but I really don't know. We'll just have to wait and see," she said and shrugged her shoulders.

Matt decided to say no more, but he was sure he had noticed these times of fatigue well before the pregnancy. The demons of fear stirred within him. He shook them away. He had great anticipation of not only being a father but also of spending his life with Aika.

Nothing is going to get in the way of that.

Chapter 20

September 13, 1946, Hiroshima

Matt never believed there was any bad luck associated with Friday the thirteenth, but he was starting to wonder if there might not be something to it.

A week ago Aika went to Dr. Yamamoto's office, had more blood tests drawn and later that day went to the hospital, where she met with another physician, Dr. Satou. Aika had told Matt that he had performed a bone marrow aspiration. Whatever the reasons for the tests, Matt hoped they didn't amount to anything. Apparently, though, the results were serious enough for them to schedule a meeting today with the doctors. To Matt's relief, Aika had assured him they were both fluent in English.

Shortly after he and Aika were seated in the consultation room, Dr. Yamamoto and Dr. Satou entered. Both were wearing long white coats with starched shirts and dark ties. Matt and Aika stood as they came in, and, after they greeted each other with a bow, the group sat down. Dr. Yamamoto spoke first.

"Aika, I know for some time you have been feeling fatigued, which you felt was simply due to the pregnancy. The tests I did last week, however, not only showed you were pregnant, but also that your white blood cell count was abnormally high. Usually this is around five to ten thousand in the normal person, but in your case the number was seventy-five thousand. I was quite concerned and asked Dr. Satou to consult.

"Aika, he has confirmed you have acute myeloid leukemia. Unfortunately, we seem to be seeing this more and more, and we're not sure why. I'm so sorry . . . I wish I had better news."

Matt said, "What exactly is leukemia?"

Dr. Yamamoto said, "It is a cancer of the blood."

Matt and Aika sat in stunned silence. They grasped each other's hands.

"Dr. Satou, would you take it from here?" Dr. Yamamoto asked.

"Of course," Dr. Satou responded. "Up till very recently, there was nothing we could do to treat leukemia. But now there are some medical centers offering chemotherapy, which is a harsh medicine that helps to control or kill cancer. This is quite new and still largely unproven, but it is likely in the next few months this option will be available. The problem we have is that you are pregnant, and the chemotherapy agents are extremely toxic to the fetus. They would in all probability severely damage your baby or could even end the baby's life. Therefore, we are going to ask you to have an abortion, so, if chemotherapy does become available, we can safely treat you. Once the course of treatment is finished, you can try again to get pregnant, though it is possible, with the damage that might occur to your reproductive system from the chemotherapy, that you would not be able to do so."

Dr. Yamamoto nodded in concurrence.

Both doctors waited for a response.

Matt was dumbfounded. He glanced over at Aika, and while he saw rage on her face, the words that came out of her mouth were measured.

"Doctors Yamamoto and Satou," she said. "I would like to talk about another option. Is it not possible that we could delay treatment until after the baby is born?"

Dr. Yamamoto responded. "We don't recommend that. It appears your leukemia is progressing rapidly, and as the tumorous growth begins to displace the cells that make blood in your bone marrow, you will become more and more anemic. Also, as a result of the leukemia, you will have thrombocytopenia, or low platelet count —"

Matt interrupted. "What do platelets do?"

Dr. Yamamoto said, "They help the blood clot. If they are decreased, this would dramatically increase Aika's risk for hemorrhage during labor. It would be too dangerous, not only for her but also for your baby."

Aika then spoke with a controlled anger: "Doctors, my husband and I will talk about this, but I want to be clear about a few things. First of all, there will be no abortion. My baby will not be killed. He is already four months old, and I plan to have him. Secondly, I will not consent to chemotherapy until he is born. You can treat me in ways that are supportive. I will take anything that will not harm my baby. You are doctors. You know the things you can do." Her voice quivered with rage.

"Aika," Dr. Yamamoto said, "we don't believe it is wise for you to have this baby. But I have delivered babies for over thirty years. As you know, I delivered you. I have the highest regard for you and your family. Your father was a friend of mine, and I bought many a tin of wonderful tea from him. I have also attended a number of tea ceremonies with your mother. She is a true master at her work. But enough!

"What I want to say is this: I strongly recommend that you have an abortion. It is the safest and the best way. But if you refuse, I will do all I can for you. For your delivery, I will call on the top pediatrician in all of Hiroshima, Dr. Suzuki. And since the end of the war, here at Hiroshima Teishin Hospital we have acquired the most up-to-date equipment and have learned the latest resuscitation techniques from our Western colleagues. We will be prepared as anyone could be. That said, if you change your mind about terminating the pregnancy, please let me know."

He then took her hand, patted it, rose and left the room with Dr. Satou.

"Aika . . ." Matt had tears in his eyes. "Aika, I can't take the risk of losing you. I've waited too long to find you. Are you sure about this?"

"Husband," she carefully replied. "I have waited a long time to find you as well. Sometimes I began to wonder if you even existed. But here you are. We will go through this together, the three of us, you, me and Rinji. Whatever happens, good or bad, we are a team. I want just as much as you to live a long life together. I cannot kill our baby to do that. I cannot . . ." With that, the veneer dropped, and she wept.

Matt handed her his handkerchief and held her as tightly as he could.

Yes, we are a team.

ཨོཾ་ཅི་དྲེ་སྐྲེ་ ཨོཾ་ཅི་དྲེ་སྐྲེ་ ཨོཾ་ཅི་དྲེ་སྐྲེ་

September 15, 1946

Dear Mom and Dad and Family,

I have some good and some bad news to share with you. First, the good news: Aika is pregnant. Right now, she's four months along, and her due date is in early February. She is sure it's a boy, though how I don't know. She's even picked out a name, and it's Rinji William. How about that, Dad?

The bad news is that Aika has a deadly kind of leukemia, a type of blood cancer. They want her to have an abortion so she can receive chemotherapy, but she has absolutely refused, thinking she can get by until after the delivery. I'm really confused, as I want the best for both her and my son (if that's what it is).

I'm feeling pretty blue right now, but I just do the best I can to be helpful. Her mother and brother are taking it hard, but one thing I have discovered is how stoic the Japanese are. It takes a lot to get them down, and Aika and her family are no exception.

After hearing all this news, Sergeant McKensie has given me as much time off as I want. I still like to do patrol, though, as it gives me a chance to think. Sort of reminds me of the days in the country when I would go rabbit hunting with Inky.

Sometimes I think I'd like to get a dog again. I like wagging tails and big doggy smiles. Here it might be easier to have a cat, but I never really cared for the aloofness of those critters. They're just too independent. I'd take a dog any day.

You are already aware that I don't believe in God. How could I, after what I have seen? I know, though, that you do. And, since I try to cover all the bases, I would appreciate it if you'd offer up a prayer or two. Aika and I need all the help we can get.

Love,
Matt

P.S. Aika means "love song." Isn't that perfect for her?

ཨོཾ་མ་ཎི་པདྨེ་ཧཱུྃ ཨོཾ་མ་ཎི་པདྨེ་ཧཱུྃ ཨོཾ་མ་ཎི་པདྨེ་ཧཱུྃ

October 15, 1946

Dear Son,

I wrote as soon as I received your letter, and I pray that Aika is doing well, and that her son, Rinji William, is growing as a baby should. Son, I pray for you as well. I imagine the burden you are carrying is awfully heavy. It seems to me that not only are Aika and the baby depending on you, but also her mother and brother.

Son, trust me, if Aika says it's a boy, then it's a boy. I remember all too well a little more than twenty years ago when I had you. My intuition was very strong that you would be a boy. Also remember this, no matter how hard the things are that you are given, or how much you succeed or fail, God is always watching over you. That much I'm sure of. I hear what you are saying about your disbelief, and given what you have had to go through, it's completely understandable. Someday, dearest Matthew, your father and I will no longer be here to remind you of this very important fact: God loves you and is very aware of you and your life. Son, I respect you and how you believe, but please remember these words.

As you have given your permission, I will add not only your name, but also Aika's and Rinji William's to the prayer list at the Davidson Methodist Church. Our prayers will surround you. There are many here in Oklahoma who care deeply about you.

Love always,
Mom

Chapter 21

January 27, 1947, Hiroshima

"Husband, wake up. It is time!" Aika shrieked.

Matt woke quickly, as he had been expecting her to go into labor at any moment. They had been making numerous visits to Dr. Yamamoto's office with irregular contractions, and the doctor was becoming more and more concerned. It was now far too late to consider an abortion; the only option left was to have the baby.

Some time ago Dr. Yamamoto had approached them with the idea of doing a planned caesarian section. Only a few days ago she had agreed, and it had been scheduled for the morning of the 28th.

It's too late now.

"How far apart are your contractions?" he said and glanced at the clock. It read 3:10 a.m.

"Two minutes!" she yelled.

Matt threw back the covers as he hopped out of bed. He saw a flood of blood-tinged fluid streaming from between Aika's legs, and all his doubts vanished.

As she dressed, Matt phoned the hospital. Then, hanging up, he assured her, "They have notified the doctor, and he will meet us there." He pulled on some clothes and then placed another call. "Miyo, Aika's in labor . . . Yes, it's the real thing this time . . . Trust me, it is. We'll meet you at the Hiroshima Teishin Hospital."

Matt helped Aika out of the house and into the jeep he had borrowed for just such an emergency. He hopped in, and they sped to the hospital. Aika clenched her teeth as the spasms increased.

They pulled in front of the emergency entrance of the hospital, and they were greeted by a team of medical personnel. A cold rain began to fall as she was loaded onto a stretcher. They raced to the labor suite, where Dr. Yamamoto and Dr. Suzuki waited, garbed in medical scrubs.

The carrier was pushed into the room, shoved to a position adjacent to the delivery bed, and Aika slid onto it. With a sense of urgency, Matt muscled to her side in between the nursing staff. He tenderly ran his fingers through her hair. "Aika, dearest, I love you. Take care of yourself and our son. He is a boy, isn't he?" he said, trying somehow to lighten the situation.

She smiled in spite of herself. "Matthew, I love you too. More than you could ever know. And, yes, he is a boy, and he wants to meet you."

A nurse had a no-nonsense look on her face. "Sir, you must go to the waiting area. We will call you when your baby is delivered."

Reluctantly Matt slipped away and entered a small waiting room. There he found Miyo and Shigeshi.

"How is my daughter doing?" Miyo demanded anxiously.

He didn't want to worry her. "Hopefully, soon, we'll have a baby. I know they'll do their best."

He sat down next to her and motioned to Shigeshi. He pulled him up and sat him on his lap. "How are you?"

"I worried, Corporal Matt. Aika look sicker and sicker. You think she be okay?"

He nodded, and the conversation died. Words seemed to fail them. As time passed, each moment became more and more agonizing.

Suddenly a series of high-pitched tones from overhead pierced the silence, followed by a number of agitated Japanese words. Matt checked his watch. It showed 4:30 a.m., and the quiet hospital area had sprung into frantic activity with dozens of personnel running rapidly in the direction of the labor room.

"What was that?" Matt demanded of Miyo.

Miyo put her hands to her face. "That was a call — please no — not my Aika . . . not her . . . for an emergency in labor and delivery."

Shigeshi leapt from Matt's lap and clung to his mother.

Matt's head swam. He couldn't think, he couldn't talk, he didn't want to hear any more.

Maybe it's someone else. Please let it be anyone else.

In a few moments, one of the nurses appeared. She spoke in broken English. "Dr. Yamamoto want me to tell you Aika Johnston and her baby have quit breathing and hearts have stopped. He and Dr. Suzuki trying to help them. Soon know more. I go back to help."

"May we see them?" Matt asked.

"No, sir," she replied. "You be in our way. We let you know soon as possible."

Matt, Miyo and Shigeshi huddled together and tried to find strength. There was no consolation to be found.

Time passed, and Matt tensed as he began to see nurses slowly emerging from the labor area. Matt recognized some of the faces as the ones that had earlier rushed by. He saw them glance in his direction as they walked by, carefully avoiding his gaze. Soon a somber Dr. Yamamoto and Dr. Suzuki entered the waiting area. They bowed and sat down across from them.

Dr. Yamamoto spoke first, taking the hand of Miyo. "Miyo, your daughter is no longer with us. She delivered a son just before she died. There was much bleeding."

Matt felt like someone had hit him in the throat. He gasped for breath as his eyes filled with tears.

Miyo sobbed and said. "My baby . . . I've lost my baby girl."

Shigeshi huddled close to his mother.

Dr. Suzuki then said, "The boy —"

My son . . .

"— responded for only a few seconds before he died. We both tried many different medicines in our attempt to resuscitate them, and . . ." he paused, "we were unsuccessful. We are both sorry beyond words. Do you have any questions?"

Matt could barely find his voice. He finally stammered out, "Doctors, is there anything else . . . we could have . . . done?"

Dr. Yamamoto considered his words carefully. "Sir, you and Aika's family did as much for her as anyone could. I've know her ever since she was a little girl. She was an exceptional student and very driven. And, as you know, Miyo, only the very brightest are accepted to Tokyo Imperial University, especially," he nodded proudly, "given the fact she was a woman." Then he turned to Matt. "You loved and cared for her, and I've never seen her happier in all the years I've known her. No, given the circumstances, we . . ." his voice broke ever so slightly, "all did the best we could. Again, we are very sorry." Dr. Yamamoto and Dr. Suzuki then stood, pushed their chairs back, bowed and slowly walked away.

A nurse then came for them. The three followed her to the delivery room where the bodies of their loved ones waited. The nurse exited as they gathered 'round.

Miyo sat in the chair on the right side of the bed with Shigeshi in her lap. She pulled Aika's hand from her side and rubbed it as a mother would to comfort a child. She softly sang a song in Japanese. It sounded to Matt like a lullaby. She rocked forward and backward as she sang, holding Shigeshi to her chest.

Matt stood on the opposite side and studied the faces of his wife and baby.

Are they sure that they're not just asleep?

Of course, he knew the answer.

Rinji William was no doubt the most beautiful child he had ever seen — bushy black hair and a face that somehow seemed wise. Matt stroked Aika's still beautiful black hair with his hand. He carefully pulled her left hand from beneath the sheet. The diamonds grouped together as a lotus on a gold band — still there. He twisted the band, removed it and placed it on his own left little finger.

Aika Johnston, this ring will never leave my hand. I will always love you. Always . . .

Time passed. Soon Matt, Miyo and Shigeshi would have to go away without them.

All too soon . . .

They said their final farewells and disappeared into the now bitterly cold Hiroshima night. Matt was numb with pain.

There is no God. There never was.

ༀ་མ་ཎི་པདྨེ་ཧཱུྃ་ ༀ་མ་ཎི་པདྨེ་ཧཱུྃ་ ༀ་མ་ཎི་པདྨེ་ཧཱུྃ་

January 27, 8 a.m., Telegram from Hiroshima to Davidson

WESTERN UNION

AIKA AND BABY DIED DURING CHILDBIRTH. I'M DEVASTATED. LETTER COMING.
MATT

January 27, 4 p.m., Telegram from Davidson to Hiroshima

WESTERN UNION

WE ARE DEVASTATED TOO. YOU ARE IN OUR PRAYERS.
LOVE,
DAD, MOM AND FAMILY

ༀམཎིཔདྨེཧཱུྃ ༀམཎིཔདྨེཧཱུྃ ༀམཎིཔདྨེཧཱུྃ

February 3, 1947

Dear Family,

Thanks for the telegram. I'll tell you more details later. It's too painful to talk about just now.

The past three days have been a nightmare. Two days after their deaths, there was a wake given by a Buddhist priest. Aika was dressed in the white kimono that she wore the night she performed the Japanese tea ceremony for me, and Rinji was in black. The funeral was the following day, and they were given new names. The reason they say they do that is because it keeps the deceased from returning when their name is said. I have no idea what those names were, and I don't care. They were cremated the next day, and their ashes are in urns at the family shrine. In the next week or so, they will be deposited in the family grave.

I've talked with Sergeant McKensie, and he thinks that I should be able to be discharged from the Marines in the next month or so. I want to come home and be with my family.

The past two years have been unbelievably bad. Joe is dead, and now both Aika and Rinji are dead. Many others of my friends died in this damned war. I'm ready to smell fresh-turned, red Oklahoma dirt.

Love,
Matt

After he had finished writing the letter, he reached in his back pocket for his wallet, and flipped through the pictures till he found the one of his Oklahoma family. He looked at each and every face.

You're all I have left.

ༀམཎིཔདྨེཧཱུྃ ༀམཎིཔདྨེཧཱུྃ ༀམཎིཔདྨེཧཱུྃ

February 5, 1947

Matt felt drained when he reported back to duty. The Sarge had said he could take off for a few weeks, but he had to come back to work, if not for any other reason than just to keep his mind occupied. He filed the paperwork for his discharge, and while part of him regretted leaving Miyo and Shigeshi, he yearned to go back home.

Just as he walked back onto the base after being on patrol duty, he heard a familiar voice.

"Hey, Matt," one of the privates yelled. "The Sarge is looking for you. I think it might be pretty important."

"Thanks, I'll head that way," Matt said and went in the direction of Sergeant McKensie's Quonset hut.

He knocked on the door and cracked it open. "Hey, Sarge, are you there?"

"Matt? Come on in. I've got some something for you."

Matt entered and saw his friend rise from his desk, signaling for him to sit down.

"Sarge, what's up?"

"Matt," he said as he sat back down, "you know I've been asking you to call me by my first name when we're in private. Just call me Sean."

"Sorry, Sar . . . Sean."

"A telegram came for you this morning, and I thought you'd better see it as soon as possible."

Matt grimaced. It was rare that telegrams brought good news.

He accepted the sealed envelope. He pulled out his pocket knife and slit it open. Removing the folded paper, he read with disbelief:

WESTERN UNION
RARE WINTER TORNADO HIT DAVIDSON YESTERDAY. YOUR
FAMILY ALL DEAD. TWELVE OTHER NEIGHBORS KILLED. COME
HOME SOON.
WE LOVE YOU,
VIRGIL AND ELEANOR CARTER

Matt flipped the telegram over to his friend, and put his hands to his face. Matt thought:

How much can a man take?

Sergeant McKensie shook his head as he grimly read it. He placed his right hand on Matt's shoulder, "The shit always hits the fan at the same time, doesn't it? Goddamm it." He sighed. "I'm going to grant you leave to get back home, but I want you to come back here for another month before we discharge you. You are like a son to me, Matt, and I want to keep an eye on you for a while longer. Understand?"

"Yes, sir."

"Anything else I can do for you?" he said.

"Yes, sir, there is," Matt said. "I want to go out on patrol again today."

"What are you talking about? You're in no shape to be out in the field."

"With all due respect, I can't be by myself, and I can't burden Aika's mother and brother with this news just now."

"Okay, you got it. But tomorrow you are relieved from duty till you get back from Oklahoma. I should be able to find a military transport back to the States in a few days."

"Yes, sir," said Matt. He then put his head down on the desk and wept.

Sergeant Sean McKensie kept a hand on his shoulder.

ཨོམ་ཙ་ིང་ཧྲཱི་ྂ ཨོམ་ཙ་ིང་ཧྲཱི་ྂ ཨོམ་ཙ་ིང་ཧྲཱི་ྂ

Later that evening a chain-smoking Matt walked the wooded hills with six other Marines around the outskirts of Hiroshima. He reeked of cheap whiskey. For the time he was glad to be with his fellow Marines. They knew what had happened and understood why he was as drunk as a skunk.

Matt felt the effect of too much liquor, and he yelled over to the group, "I'm going to take a piss. Be back in a few."

He saw their nods and walked around to a secluded, woody area. Unzipping his pants, he began to pee and suddenly became aware of an odd combination of shadows on the side of the hill. He pulled up his zipper and walked closer to it, moved aside a brushy overhang and found an entrance to a cave. Matt took his flashlight from his pack and entered, feeling the scratches of thorny shrubs against his side. He was shocked to find a large underground storehouse in the cave. He moved his light from side to side and saw a huge stockpile of Japanese weapons and ammunition.

Why was this left behind?

In an instant he understood: When the bomb exploded, the soldiers who knew about this were likely all killed. Just then he heard a faint voice from the distance, "Johnston — you okay?"

Stepping outside the cave, he said, "Yeah, there was more to do than just pee. Give me five more minutes." He lit a Camel and took a deep drag.

"If you need to take a crap, take your time. Join back with us at the jeep. We're all done here."

"Won't take long." With that, he disappeared back inside the musty cave. He pulled a pencil and paper from his backpack, took a quick inventory and began to wrestle with what to do.

The right thing would be to turn this in.

But then another thought entered his head. He remembered how miserably poor he and his family had been. Now with all his recent losses, he was destitute in more ways than one.

He thought quickly. He had heard of a Chinese weapons dealer named Li Wei who frequented a bar in one of the seedy areas of town. He had been described as having a black eye patch with a large scar underneath. He was always asking soldiers for weapons.

Matt grimaced as he walked outside the cave and hurried to the jeep.

ཨོམ་ཧཿ་རྐྱེ་ཧཱུྃ ཨོམ་ཧཿ་རྐྱེ་ཧཱུྃ ཨོམ་ཧཿ་རྐྱེ་ཧཱུྃ

The next night Matt sat at the bar in The Lonely Rooster. He had far too much to drink, but he really didn't care. The air was thick with smoke, and the tavern was crowded with GIs. Sometime after midnight, a large slovenly Chinese, with a black patch covering his right eye, entered the bar. His stained, long sleeved black shirt barely overhung a grossly paunchy belly.

He was disgusting. He looked like he hadn't had a bath in weeks, and the scar was far worse than Matt could have imagined. It was as if someone had purposely carved his face with a dull knife.

After a few minutes, Matt rose from his spot, walked over and pulled out a chair at the man's table. The stench was overpowering. "You Li Wei?" he tried in English.

He was smarter than he looked. He came right back at Matt in English. "Yeah, that's me," he said with a growl. "What do you want?"

"I hear you are looking for weapons, and I know where there are plenty."

"Bullshit. This area has been cleaned out. And I need more than you can supply."

"Okay," Matt said. "I know others who will want them." He stood up and turned to walk away. He felt a huge fist wrap itself around his right arm and pull him back to his chair.

"What have you got?" Li Wei demanded.

Matt reached in his front pocket, pulled out a wrinkled piece of paper and handed it to him.

His eyes grew wide and dark. "I could be interested. Where have you got them?"

Matt snapped back, "Do you think I'm stupid? You pay me first, and then I tell you the location. How much are they worth to you?" He yanked the paper from Li Wei's hands and slipped it back into his pocket.

Li Wei stood up, grabbed Matt's collar and pulled his face close. "If you are lying to me, I will find you and kill you. And I won't kill you fast. I will break every bone in your body first and strip every inch of skin off. You will live for days as a bag of broken bones and raw flesh. I will piss on you as I walk by. You will beg me to kill you."

Matt deftly pulled Li Wei's right arm behind his back. "Would you like me to break it right now? Or just dislocate it? I can do whatever you like." He had trained too long in hand-to-hand combat to be intimidated by a Chinese goon.

Li Wei groaned. "Let go!"

Matt released him.

Li Wei painfully rotated his shoulder a few times. "Let me look again at your list." He sat down and studied the inventory. Taking a shot of whiskey and slamming it to the table, he muttered quietly, "Fifty thousand U.S. dollars. That's more than they're worth."

Matt, now sitting across the table from him, glared at him. "You know damn well they would bring more than that. Hundred and fifty thousand. That's as low as I go."

Li Wei countered, "You drive a hard bargain, Marine. Here's my final offer. One hundred thousand U.S. dollars. Take it or leave it."

"You drive a harder bargain," Matt said. "I'll take it. When can you have the money?"

"Two hours. When I get back you tell me where they are, and we'll stay while my men check it out. If it is what you say, you leave with the money."

"I'll be here."

Li Wei snarled, "You'd better be." He rose from the table and sauntered out into the cold Hiroshima night.

ཨོམ་ཚི་དྷེ་ཧཱུྃ་ ཨོམ་ཚི་དྷེ་ཧཱུྃ་ ཨོམ་ཚི་དྷེ་ཧཱུྃ་

Two hours and a few minutes later Li Wei walked back through the door of The Lonely Rooster to find six burly Marines armed to the teeth and sitting at the table with Matt. Matt stood up, slowly walked up to him, and the two of them moved to an unoccupied table in a dark corner. "Show me the cash," Matt said.

Li Wei looked carefully around, and seeing no one was watching, pulled open the duffel bag he carried, revealing stacks of one hundred dollar U.S. bills.

Matt flipped through the Benjamins — the amount was close to accurate. Matt nodded and handed him a map. "The map is marked. Send your men there."

Li Wei nodded to a diminutive Chinese hovering near the doorway. He dashed up to Li Wei, grabbed the map and rushed out the door. Matt set the duffel bag in his lap and leaned back in his chair. He smiled at a scowling Li Wei.

A short time later Li Wei's accomplice came through the door and nodded. Li Wei's questioning look morphed into an evil grin. He said, "It's a done deal, as you Americans say," and threw back another shot of whiskey. He added, "My buyer will be most pleased."

"Who is your buyer?"

"Wouldn't you like to know, Mr. Asshole Marine?" Li Wei grunted as he stood and waddled out the door.

He can sell them to the Devil for all I care.

Matt then picked up the duffel bag and rejoined his friends. They finished the last of their drinks and prepared to leave. No one at the table aside from Matt knew what had happened. Matt had asked them for a little protection and that was reason enough. Tomorrow morning, Matt decided, he would find somewhere to stash his new-found fortune.

Money — I've finally got money —

He looked down at his left little finger.

Tears filled his eyes as he walked out of the bar into the cold dark lonely night. One of the guys with him had managed a jeep for the evening and said he'd drop Matt off at home — the home he'd shared with Aika — the home he hoped to share with his son.

Once he had a family waiting for him in Oklahoma.

But now . . .

No one waited for him . . .

Anywhere.

Chapter 22

February 11, 1947, Davidson, Oklahoma

wo days later Matt was able to catch a military transport and cross the Pacific to San Diego. There he boarded a flight to the army base, Fort Sill, in Lawton, Oklahoma. He borrowed a car from an old army pal of Sergeant McKensie's and drove to the Carter home where he spent a restless night. Virgil and Eleanor were warm as they always were, but it felt uncomfortable to be with his old neighbors without his family. He could tell it was awkward for them as well.

The next morning he visited the Hay family and Emily. They, of course, wanted to know more about the circumstances of Joe's death. Matt told them as much as he was able, but he couldn't bring himself to tell them of his cowardice. In spite of Aika's reassuring words those months ago, he still wasn't convinced he was not to blame. The guilt clung to him — dark, heavy and foul smelling. Matt wondered if he would ever be able to shake it.

His second stop that day was the Johnston homestead. It was cold and frosty as Februaries in Oklahoma invariably were. He gulped as he pulled up the gravel drive. The house and outbuildings — what was left of them — were in shambles.

He got out of his car and slowly walked around the destroyed structures. He took a deep breath as he gazed upon the family pecan tree, their supplier of nuts for so many years, lying uprooted on its side. He imagined that when the tornado violently ripped it from the ground, its exposed dark roots screamed for the comfort of the earth. Now, though, there was only silence.

He paused for a few moments at Inky's burial place by the sapodilla plum tree, which, miraculously enough, was still standing.

I miss you, Inky.

He stood in one place and slowly turned a full circle. Memories flooded in upon him — good times, warm recollections. He continued to walk the area, taking his time. Then, with a stinging jolt, the deaths of his family flooded into his consciousness. He clutched his pounding head with his hands.

I can never set foot in this place again.

There was too much of the past here to have a present or a future.

What to do?

Matt took refuge in the car, started the motor and turned the heater on high. He was freezing, shaking, almost unable to control himself. He wanted to scream, to cry . . .

No wife, no child, not even a family.

Matt made his decision. He would have old Mr. Grimes, the in-town real estate agent, sell the farm for what little value it had and let someone else start a new life there. It wouldn't take long to swing by his office in the bank building on Main Street and sign the necessary papers.

ཨོཾམཎིཔདྨེཧཱུྃ ཨོཾམཎིཔདྨེཧཱུྃ ཨོཾམཎིཔདྨེཧཱུྃ

That done, his last stop was the Davidson cemetery two miles north of town. He pulled his car into the parking area. Virgil Carter had told him where to look, but he really didn't need to. Six freshly dug graves in a row were not hard to spot in the small cemetery. He read the markers — made at the quarry from the appropriately named town of Granite, Oklahoma. As he walked past them, he saw that they had been placed in order: William Jefferson Johnston; Naomi Anna Johnston; Alexander Roy Johnston; Esther Mae Johnston; Robert Edward Johnston; Earlyne Amelia Johnston.

How could it be?

He heard the sounds of twittering mockingbirds in a nearby tree. He picked up a rock and threw it at them. The birds scattered and flew away.

He looked back at the grave sites and thought: *There's no point in trying to find the living among the dead.*

Head down, grim and washed out, he returned to his car, started it and headed toward Lawton.

Soon he would find a military plane that could make connections back to San Diego and ultimately a transport to Hiroshima and the Marines. He felt like an orphan in many ways. Not only that, there were no more dreams for the young man from Davidson, Oklahoma.

As he lit up a cigarette, he began to have a craving for whiskey. He needed something to dull his senses. There were too many thoughts in his head. As far as he was concerned, the Zen Buddhist idea of mindfulness was complete bullshit. He had too much pain to fully grasp the present moment.

Far too much.

His features hardened. No longer would he allow himself to love. To him, love meant agonizing pain. All he had cared for were now gone. He would never again open his heart to anyone.

What next?

Go to college? Later to vet school? No. His brain was scrambled, and he thought it would be that way for a long time. He couldn't imagine picking up a book and studying.

Stay in the Marines? No. Too many bad memories. But one of the men in his unit had talked about mercenary work. That might just be the ticket. He felt encouraged.

I hear they make good money.

He thought about the funds he had deposited at the brokerage firm back in Hiroshima. Money didn't matter now. Still, mercenary work might give him a future.

It was all he had left.

Chapter 23

March 22, 1947, Hiroshima

Matt puffed on a cigarette as he hurriedly packed his belongings. He had already changed into his civvies and had everything he owned stuffed in an oversized duffel bag. He had earlier said his goodbyes to all of his buddies with the notable exception of Sergeant McKensie, who had said he would stop by.

So much had happened in the past month. Matt had signed a contract to join a group of mercenaries. He had no idea where he would be or what he would be doing. All he knew was his new employers had the need for tough men to do their dirty work. Since he was a Marine who had proved himself on Iwo, he was the perfect choice for the job. At this point he really didn't care what he did or who he hurt.

As far as the money from the sale of the Japanese armaments was concerned, he decided to leave it with a brokerage firm in Hiroshima. They had recommended a little-known business called Tokyo Tsushin Kogyo K.K. He put every penny of the $100,000 into it.

What in the hell do I have to lose?

Matt heard a knock on the door of his Quonset hut. "Matt, are you there?" said a familiar voice.

"Sure, Sergeant, come on in."

"Call me Sean, dammit!" he said as he stepped inside. "If this is the last thing I get you to do, then my job will have been a success."

105

"Okay, Sean — you've got it." Matt looked beyond the door for his ride. "I've only got a few minutes, but go ahead and take a seat." Matt pulled up a chair and sat down in front of him. "What's on your mind?" he asked.

Sergeant McKensie minced no words. "Matt, I know I've talked about this to you before, but I've got to ask you again. Are you sure you want to join this group of mercenaries? My sources tell me that they're a band of cutthroats who will do anything their employer tells them to do. There's no such thing as morals as far as they're concerned. In war, you kill because you have to; it's completely different when lethal force is used to intimidate and control."

"Sean, we've already been through all this."

"Hear me out," he said. "Matt, we share a bond that few men have, and it is that of being warriors together. We have fought side by side in the greatest war this world has ever known.

"Remember, I've got lots of connections in New York City, and I'm sure I could get you a damn good job. You could stay with my wife and children till you get your feet on the ground. I'll be out of the service in a few months, and I'll join all of you there. I'm a big Yankees fan, and we could take in a game every now and then. What do you say?"

Matt repressed the emotions that arose. "Sean, I've made up my mind. Leave me your contact number, though, just in case."

The Sarge's shoulders sagged, and he sighed in disappointment. He then pulled a scratch pad from his shirt pocket, hurriedly scribbled out a number and handed the paper to Matt.

Matt folded it and placed it in his wallet. Just then, a horn sounded outside the door. "Gotta run, Sar — I mean, Sean. Goodbye." He grabbed his hand, shook it, and threw his duffel bag over his shoulder as he ran out the door.

Glancing back, he saw one of the few friends he had left in the world was staring at the wall in front of him.

ཨོཾ་ཨཱཿཧཱུྃ༔ ཨོཾ་ཨཱཿཧཱུྃ༔ ཨོཾ་ཨཱཿཧཱུྃ༔

The jeep pulled in front of the Tanaka home. While some time ago Matt had told them he was leaving, he steeled himself for one last goodbye. He jumped from the jeep and told the driver he'd be out in a few minutes. He hurried up to the door and knocked.

Slowly it cracked open, and Matt saw part of the face of a tearful boy wearing a Cincinnati Reds hat. "Hey, Charlie," Matt said.

The door suddenly popped open, and before he knew it, the boy had jumped into his arms. "Corporal Matt," he said, "You can't go. Charlie want you to stay."

Holding him in his arms, Matt stepped into the house that held so many memories.

Miyo then appeared from around the corner, wiping her eyes with a wadded handkerchief. Matt bowed with Shigeshi in his arms, and Miyo bowed back. "Matt, please sit down." She motioned him to a chair.

He sat, still holding a clinging Shigeshi.

It wasn't that long ago that I was sitting here in this same room with Aika.

Miyo said, "My dearest son-in-law, husband of my only daughter, father of my only grandchild, you know we don't want you to go. You have become an important part of our lives. But I know the time has come for you to leave; the world calls you." She stared at the floor for a moment before she looked up at him. "Will you promise me one thing?"

Matt could only nod.

"Let us hear from you again."

"I will, Miyo," he promised. Just then, a series of loud beeps sounded from the jeep. "I'll be in touch." Extracting a still clinging Shigeshi from his arms, he rose and quickly escaped the house, a place of many memories.

Will they ever cease to haunt me?

Chapter 24

July 4, 1969, Laos, Ho Chi Minh Trail

Commander Matt Johnston and his 200-man company had set up camp on both sides of a muddy rutted road on the Ho Chi Minh Trail. Matt was being paid big money to be there, and all he cared about was staying alive in this hell hole and maintaining control of his men — each, it seemed, with a claim to fame in another life, or so they said. Still, he had to keep an eye on them. Most of them were hardly old enough to shave, and he was their leader.

Every so often some felt the need to test him, and as much as he hated to admit it, it was getting harder and harder to kick ass.

But he still could — even at the age of 43. He was sure they all feared him, and some even hated him. That was okay; he desired no friends. All he required was their respect, and he got it. And slowly but surely they were learning from him, the old man.

Where had the years gone?

How Matt had arrived there was a tale unto itself. Over the years Devcon Corporation, his employer, had turned out to be in bed with the CIA on more occasions than not, and the decision had been made by the U.S. government to do all they could to stem the flow of men and supplies from North Vietnam into the South.

The covert mission also saw other groups of mercenaries from Devcon scattered along the trail, each waiting for convoys. Survive it, and he'd soon be moving on to an administrative role at Devcon.

"Just a few more 'boots on the turf,'" his boss had said before he departed corporate headquarters in Baltimore, Maryland.

Matt had responded, "Is that a promise?"

"Hit the road, and you'll get more than a big pay raise."

Matt had hit the road, knowing he was special with Devcon. He had earned that pay raise and an upcoming cushy job, as he had accomplished tough mission after tough mission.

It might've been the Fourth of July, but he didn't plan to celebrate. Not in this rain. He'd pitched a small tarp over a vine and at least was glad for his tiny shelter. He had hoped this might encourage his troops to do the same. But most of the fools just sat there, soaked in the rain, too stupid to remember a very useful small sheet of tarp in their back pack.

As the rain continued to fall, he thought of the investment he had made all those years ago from the sale of that weapons cache. For a brief moment, he wondered if it had ever amounted to anything. Someday he would check on it.

Now, though, while not wealthy, he was pretty well set. He had maintained a small apartment in Hiroshima, and, while in the area, he would on rare occasions stop by and see Miyo and Shigeshi.

These visits had slowly but surely decreased in frequency. He saw the looks on their faces when they asked questions of his life that could not be answered. Distance had grown between them as the years passed. *Perhaps*, he thought, *it was just as well.*

He was last there a few months back. Shigeshi was now married, and he and his new wife Asami had just discovered that she was pregnant with their first child. Matt cringed with the memories that brought up. He glanced uncomfortably at the lotus ring on his left little finger.

Meanwhile, Shigeshi had decided to follow in the footsteps of his father and mother, and took over the family tea shop. Sometimes an aging Miyo would still perform tea ceremonies there. Shigeshi was also heavily involved as a volunteer at the Hiroshima Peace Memorial Museum. After witnessing the effects of the nuclear blasts of 1945, he had become a peace activist.

Peace, bullshit!

Much had happened since Matt had left the Marines. He had been transported all over the world to various areas of conflict. He grimaced as he thought of the countless numbers he had killed — but that was the name of the game, and he had, he felt, mostly been in the right. Since he was spending day after day in the field, it didn't take an Einstein to realize he had to moderate his alcohol consumption. A split second could make a difference whether he lived or died, and he couldn't be a drunk and survive as a crack mercenary.

As he fingered his Uzi in his little shelter in the pouring rain, he knew that, unlike the Pacific conflict, there was no way the United States was going to win this war. The supply lines were too many and too long for anyone to control them, and he sensed a determination in the soldiers from the North that was missing in the South. Besides that, he hated Richard Nixon and Spiro Agnew.

How did these two assholes get to be the leaders of our country?

Jebonski, his second in command, came slogging through the rain. "Commander Johnston," he whispered urgently, "enemy approaching from the north."

"Then let's prepare to greet our guests," Matt whispered back. "Get the men ready and in position. Send Rimmington over to the other side of the road — just in case those guys are asleep at the wheel."

"Yes, sir."

Matt pulled on his floppy go-to-hell canvas hat, checked his weapon and stepped outside his shelter. He believed in a hands-on approach and always joined his men at the front of the fight.

Moving to a concealed position near the side of the road, he spied a small convoy of trucks approaching in the rain. They lurched as they slowly ground their way through the axle-deep mud. He looked through his binoculars and counted to himself:

Six trucks, with around 30 men on foot. Could be personnel in the trucks, but probably only supplies. This is going to be easy.

As they drew nearer, Matt was able to see the faces of the North Vietnamese regulars through the pouring rain. He could see fear in their eyes as they nervously looked from side to side.

Shit! They're just a bunch of kids.

When the convoy came abreast of him, his shot signaled his men, and they lay down a murderous barrage. The trucks exploded, and it was quickly over. The only survivors were four young men trying to hide between two of the burning trucks. They stood and dropped their weapons. They threw their hands high above their heads.

"We surrender! We surrender!" they chorused in garbled English. They could barely be heard as the rain suddenly became a deluge.

Matt and his men approached them with weapons raised. He looked up and down at these boys who claimed to be soldiers. He turned his back on them and walked away. He shouted to his men:

"Kill 'em!"

The North Vietnamese screamed, fell to their knees and begged for mercy. His men opened fire, and it was over.

Four less gooks to deal with.

He then ordered his men to dig a trench, and they threw the dead into it. They covered them with mud, and the rain kept pouring down. The burned-out vehicles were left where they were.

Let that be a warning.

Matt's radio man sent the news to other mercenaries waiting along the trail. Matt surveyed his men and discovered only one minor flesh wound.

Pretty good day's work.

Matt smiled to himself.

Devcon would be proud of me.

Chapter 25

January 8, 1990, Hiroshima

Matt had not been feeling well.

Four months ago it had started with a mild, but persistent cough, which gradually worsened. With that, he began to have some discomfort in the right upper area of his abdomen. Perhaps he was imagining things, but it seemed that his eyes had begun to develop a faint yellow tint. Something was wrong, but, whatever it was, he hoped it would pass.

He had been unable to see a doctor, because he had been busily involved in Angola. The National Union for the Total Independence of Angola (UNITA) was selling so-called "blood diamonds" to finance their operations in a bloody civil war. Matt had been organizing mercenary troops and covertly supporting UNITA. Despite Devcon's promise those twenty-some-odd years ago, the work in Africa more than occasionally required him to take up his weapons again. Devcon was happy with him; they were charging exorbitant fees for their services. The work, though, was the toughest with which he'd been involved. The brutal mistreatment of the African people to finance this war was beyond even his comprehension.

Since he had taken on more of an administrative role, he had packed on the pounds and was never without a cigarette in hand. Not only that, his thick black hair had been replaced by thinning gray. When he was at long last no longer in the field, he reverted to drinking excessively. Never mind. He had a ruthless and sharp military eye. Devcon could care less about his personal habits.

While he now had a safe house in Maryland, in addition to his place in Hiroshima, he kept an apartment in Paris for stopovers. Finally last week, when there was a pause between missions, he flew to Hiroshima and made an appointment to see a doctor. Initially, extensive laboratory studies, EKG, and chest X-rays were performed. Two days later, after evaluating these tests, his physician ordered CAT scans of his chest and abdomen, which eventually led to a biopsy of his right lung. The worst was confirmed. He had squamous cell carcinoma of the lung with widespread metastases not only to his liver but also to his bones. His doctor had consulted with three different oncologists, looking for a gleam of hope, but the answer from all was the same. Any treatment was at best palliative. There was no cure. He had less than a year to live.

He had just returned home from the hospital and had glumly sat on the couch when his phone rang. He groaned. Probably the office calling. But he answered to hear an unfamiliar Japanese voice say, "Is this Matthew Johnston?"

No one, I mean, no one, has this phone number — except Devcon.

"Yes, who is this?"

"This is Jomei Nakamura, the president of Hiroshima Investments. Our firm has been trying to find you for over twenty years. We have tried everything." He paused for a deep breath of what seemed like relief.

"Everything!" he repeated. "We finally employed a private investigator to track you down. It seems that your name and identity had vanished into thin air."

That was how it was meant to be, he thought. *Working as a mercenary was not a life in the limelight.* "Why do you need to speak with me?" he asked cautiously.

"Do you remember the purchase you made in nineteen forty-seven, the investment of one hundred thousand American dollars in a firm then called Tokyo Tsushin Kogyo K.K.?"

Matt scratched his head. He figured it, just like his life, had hit rock bottom. "Yes, I remember . . ."

"The company is now called Sony. We have spent over one million American dollars looking for you, which you will have to reimburse. Minus that, your position is still worth well over three hundred million dollars. Mr. Johnston, you are now a wealthy man."

What?

Hearing no response, the man said, "Mr. Johnston, are you still there?" He clicked the receiver repeatedly. "Mr. Johnston?"

Matt Johnston, rugged Oklahoma farm boy and hardened mercenary, was stunned beyond words. He had dropped the phone on the floor. Some minutes later, when he picked it up, the line was dead.

Is this a sick joke?

His mind was racing, but he collected his wits about him and called Nakamura back. No, it was no joke. He hung up the receiver.

Matt had not spent a lot of time thinking about dying since the deaths of all of his loved ones. For him, death seemed like something that would never happen, something so distant in the future it was not at all worth being concerned about. Now, all of a sudden, the specter of death was looking him right in the eye and seemed to be amused by the whole series of events.

All things considered, he had never really given up on being rich. Matt had changed a lot since the disasters of 1947, but one thing that had not changed was his desire to be wealthy. And now that he finally was, he was going to die within the year

I feel so screwed.

Looking at the diamond lotus design on his little left finger, he began to re-member what Aika had told him. It was her belief that after death one would be reincarnated into another form. Karma, in other words, reaping what you have sown, determined what your next incarnation would be.

Then, he began to remember what she had once said about the reincarnations of the Dalai Lamas, the spiritual leaders of Tibet. When the Dalai Lama dies, a selected group of monks begin a search for his next birth. Once discovered, he was taken to the Potala, the palace of the Dalai Lamas in Lhasa. There he would assume not only his position of power, but would also control the enormous wealth which the Dalai Lamas had accrued through the centuries. Gradually, a completely insane idea began to form in his mind.

It can't be done. But why couldn't it be?

Surely he had gone mad. But he had less than a year to live. What did he have to lose?

He again reached for the phone and called Jomei Nakamura. There was much to be done.

It was time to arrange a flight to Tibet.

Chapter 26

Matt fidgeted uncomfortably in his narrow airline seat next to the window. He hated commercial flying. Invariably there would be a baby somewhere close to him screaming bloody murder, or the person seated next to him would be airsick. In this case both were true. He held his nose and breathed through his mouth, hoping to avoid the distinctive odor of vomit, while at the same time trying to cover his ears. He was trapped; there was no escape.

Much had happened in the past month. Jomei Nakamura had sold the Sony stock at his request and had delivered by courier a cashier's check for the full amount in American funds. Using his connections, Matt converted most of it into rare gemstones, which he bought on the black market. That made it easier for him to covertly transport vast amounts of wealth.

He thought back to the day when he had first gathered his fortune before him. As he looked at the stones, he initially was mesmerized by their sheer beauty. Then he realized they contained another quality, one much more pervasive.

Power — power beyond imagining —

He had studied them closely. There were, of course, many clear and colored diamonds. He was especially proud of the large red ones, extremely rare and incomprehensibly valuable. He examined the alexandrites, mined in Brazil. He moved the stones from daylight to incandescent light and watched them turn from a lovely green to a purplish red. He gazed at the beautiful mix of blue sapphires, some a dazzling cornflower blue, the finest he had ever seen. Of course, there were several huge rubies and emeralds. He supposed that many were pilfered from statues of Buddha in Southeast Asia.

Given his extensive connections across the world, this gathering of rarities was not a difficult task. He had trained well over the past forty-plus years and had no difficulty hiding these precious assets in not only his clothes, but also his carry-on luggage. No one would find them.

He nearly jumped out of his seat as the baby let out a piercing scream.

Change it, feed it, burp it, do something!

No, he couldn't think of anything he had missed. He had liquidated all of his assets, and everything in the world he owned was in his possession. He had rented a nicely fitted home within walking distance of Drepung Monastery. The lease was set for one year, probably longer than he needed given his rapidly declining health, but he wasn't one to take chances. He had also retained the services of a Tibetan guide to help him with the inevitable red tape one has in a foreign country, and three days after his arrival he would have a meeting with the abbot of Drepung.

Yes, I'm ready.

Finally, after some time, the baby went to sleep, and the sickening smell began to wane. It was time to write a letter.

February 12, 1990

Dear Shigeshi,

Please humor an old friend for a few moments. Take this letter and go back to your bedroom. Are you there yet? Good. Now look under your bed. What do you see? I'm hoping you have discovered a black leather briefcase. Go ahead and put it on the bed. Now open it. Shocked? I thought that you might be. There's no need to count; it totals 500,000 American dollars. I know trying to care for a mother, wife and three daughters on your income cannot be easy, so it is my hope this will lighten your financial load. Please forgive my intrusion into your home. In the big scheme of things, I didn't think you'd mind.

Use it in whatever way you would like, but I would be especially pleased if you would apply some part of it to your children's college educations. In the distant past I had hoped to help my Oklahoma family live a better life through higher education. In this way, though not quite how I imagined, my dream can still be fulfilled.

Please accept my apologies for all of these years of being out of touch. While I loved you and Miyo, every time I would see you it would remind me of Aika. It was just too much to bear. Please relay my best wishes to your mother. While she must be in her mid-80s, I can't imagine Miyo not aging gracefully.

About me: In the past month I have discovered two things. One, I have a terminal disease and will likely be dead in less than a year. And second, I am wealthy. The circumstances are unbelievably bizarre, but they are what they are.

The sad truth is I have become something I'm not proud of: an unhappy, cynical man who has done enough horrible things to be damned to hell a thousand times over. Today I am flying to a place far away to die. This will be the last you hear from me.

I am envious of you, Shigeshi, as you have a wife and children. Never forget how much you have. This possibility was taken away from me many years ago.

Matt
P.S. You'll always be Charlie to me.

Matt pulled an envelope from his briefcase, addressed it and sealed the letter within. He would use his sources to make sure that it was delivered without a postmark.

He did not want to be found.

Chapter 27

February 15, 1990, Lhasa, Tibet

Matt stood in an incense filled room with his guide, Tsering Kalden, and awaited an audience with the abbot of Drepung Monastery. Despite all his worldly travels, the atmosphere was foreign to him, and he found himself longing for one of his comfortable apartments.

It was hard to believe that only three days ago he had landed at Lhasa Gonggar Airport, twenty-eight miles southwest of Lhasa. He had thought that he could handle just about any temperature until he got off the plane at over 12,000 feet. The frigid wind had easily penetrated his layered clothing, and the lack of oxygen at that altitude was enervating.

He was standing in a large chamber filled with chanting monks. Multicolored draperies hung high on the walls mixed with scattered paintings of garish figures.

Matt whispered over his shoulder, "Tsering Kalden? . . . Tsering Kalden?"

"Yes?" the aged guide responded.

"What is that?" Matt said, pointing to a painted figure with dark skin and adorned with skulls.

"Sir, this is what we call a 'wrathful deity.' It is not as bad as it appears," he said with a thick accent. "This is a representation of an entity that takes this form to guide sentient beings to enlightenment. It is not to be feared."

"Looks pretty scary to me."

His guide smiled a toothless smile.

Matt was not encouraged. He looked around: large golden Buddhas of different shapes and sizes seemed to be everywhere, all staring forward without expression. He had carefully planned what he was going to say, but that still didn't keep him from being nervous. He was about to make a request that had likely never been made before. How would he be received? Soon he would know.

All of a sudden the door in front of them cracked a bit, then opened halfway.

"The abbot will see us now," said Tsering Kalden. "Follow me."

They entered a small room, and directly in front of them were two monks seated on the floor. They both smiled warmly.

"Please be seated," the elder of the two said. "My name is Lobsang Gyatso, and I am the abbot of this Monastery. This is what you might call my second-in-command, Lama Tenzin Tashi. We are both fluent in English, so there is no need to go through your translator." He motioned toward two nearby blankets, which Matt and his guide sat upon. "What can we help you with?" he asked politely.

"Sir, my name is Matthew Johnston, and I am an American who, not long ago, lived in Hiroshima. Just recently I have discovered that I have a terminal disease and have less than a year to live."

The two monks nodded sympathetically.

"Only a short time ago I was awarded a large sum of money. I would like to donate a substantial portion of that to your Monastery. You may use these funds to help others in whatever way you wish. I believe this would create what you might call 'good karma.'" He paused a few moments for his words to sink in. "Are you interested?"

Lobsang Gyatso looked kindly at him. "Of course, we are. To help others in such a way is very appealing to us," he softly said. Then, with a knowing look, he added, "What, may I ask, do you want in return?"

Matt knew this was the moment of truth. "Sir, I ask one small boon. It is my understanding you have the ability to find the next incarnation of a being. Is that correct?"

The monks exchanged glances. The abbot nodded and said, "Yes, that is true. But we only perform such actions in auspicious circumstances; for example, when we look for the reincarnations of the Dalai Lama or Panchen Lama. It is not done routinely."

"To clarify," said Matt, "my request is this. I feel the money I received should continue to be mine. I want to use it to help others during my next life. So, I would like you to find my next incarnation and give it back to me."

The monks' eyebrows rose.

"When you have completed this work, you will take a portion of these funds. Your part would total around fifty million American dollars. You could feed many with that money."

The younger monk's eyes widened.

"Think of all the good you can do. Think of all the suffering you can ease."

Lobsang Gyatso remained quiet.

Matt waited.

Finally the abbot responded, "Mr. Johnston, you have been direct with me as to your request, and I will be direct as well. It would seem to my simple mind the primary motivation for you is not the betterment of others. It appears that you want to be wealthy again in your next lifetime, and you will go to any extreme to keep your money. Truthfully you are one of the most selfish men I have ever met." He said this without the least bit of hostility.

"So, my answer to you is no. Our ability to track incarnations is sacred and never done casually. Especially not to satisfy someone's greed. You would be well to donate all of your money at your death. You can then reap the karmic reward of such a gift."

Matt felt his face flush with anger. "You don't understand. With that money you could even build a new monastery!"

Lobsang Gyatso spoke evenly and with firmness. "Sir, our conversation here is done. I wish you the best as your life approaches its end. I'm afraid we cannot grant your request. I can offer you this, and that is if you choose to die here in Lhasa, I can have monks assist you as you approach death, and afterward during your Bardo experience. Think about that. For now, though, we are finished. Tenzin, would you see our guest to the door?"

Matt erupted, saying, "Damn you. Damn all of you to hell! You'll regret this decision every time you see the starving faces of children, every time you see disease which could have been treated. When you do, you'll know that YOU are responsible."

Lama Tenzin Tashi firmly grabbed his arm and, along with his guide, led Matt to the front door. Shaking his fist at the retreating abbot, Matt roared, "You'll regret this. You'll see!"

Off he angrily stomped into the night, his guide close behind him, headed toward his house. As a mercenary, he always had a Plan B. This time, though, he had reached a dead end.

He would die in this godforsaken country by himself, extremely wealthy — and not a damn thing left he could do about it.

Chapter 28

February 20, 1990, Lhasa, Tibet

The cold snap Matt had experienced when he entered Tibet returned with a vengeance, and he huddled under a pile of blankets in his drafty home. Snow and dust blew in flurries, and he heard the popping sound of particles of ice and dirt hitting the front windows and door.

He found himself wishing for the warmer, humid climate of Japan. Not only was the weather strikingly different, but also the political system. As opposed to the free world, civil liberties were severely curbed in Tibet. Of course, he had heard their claim that Tibet was actually part of China.

Only a moron would believe such propaganda.

He had done some research on Drepung Monastery and had discovered that, at one time, it was the largest in the world, housing over ten thousand monks. Now due to Chinese restrictions, the number was limited to a few hundred. The day he visited the abbot, he saw the Chinese military prowling the monastery grounds like a pack of wolves, watching every movement, every step. Matt sensed the silent resentment of the monks.

His cook came and brought him a tray with a steaming cup of yak butter tea, a Tibetan concoction of tea, salt and yak butter. Matt managed to sit up in bed, and the cook placed it on his lap. He'd learned to like the stuff, as it seemed to beat back the cold and pain he felt gnawing away at the inside of his being.

As he sipped his drink he was baffled as to what his next step should be. He was stunned that the abbot had turned down fifty million dollars on principle alone. He had thought every man had a price. His guide had gone back on several occasions to press his cause with Lobsang Gyatso. Despite his efforts, the answer was always the same.

No.

At the same time Matt was aware that his health was rapidly declining. He was losing weight faster than he would have expected, and his weakness and jaundice were also worsening.

He heard an unexpected knock at the front door. He yelled for the cook to answer it. The knock came again. Unhappy about his hired help, he moved the tray to the side, threw back the blankets and unsteadily made his way to the front door. Without opening it, he cautiously asked, "Who is it?"

A voice muffled by the weather answered, "It is Lama Tenzin Tashi. I wish to have words with you."

Matt opened the door and admitted the heavily clad monk. "Come in. I'll have the cook bring some hot tea for you." Matt struggled to the couch, shaking with the effort. He pulled his blankets closer and huddled there, calling out, "Cook! We have a guest. More hot tea here."

The cook came shortly, carrying a second cup of tea. The monk gratefully accepted it and sat on a chair across from Matt.

"Is it always so cold this time of year?" Matt asked.

"Not usually," Tenzin responded. He sipped on the tea then loosened his coat. "The highs in February in my country average almost fifty degrees Fahrenheit, and the lows around twenty. This is much colder. But we, as a people, can tolerate these conditions. In Tibet the weather is predictably unpredictable."

"They talk about the same thing in Oklahoma," Matt said. "The saying is, 'If you don't like the weather today, wait till tomorrow.'" Their eyes met, and they both chuckled.

"You are from Oklahoma?"

"Why, yes. Why do you ask?"

"I have studied much about the United States," the monk said. "I find, in particular, the history of your state to be most interesting. The plight of the American Indian is well known to me. Especially after the persecution of my people by the Chinese, I have made it a point to learn about cultures which have been subjected to genocidal policies. I believe it is true that Oklahoma is derived from the Choctaw language and means 'Land of the Red Man', does it not?"

Matt said, "Yes, indeed, it does. You know more about Oklahoma than I would have guessed."

The monk smiled. "But I am here on another matter. My abbot is a very wise man, and he said much that was true those five days ago. I believe he has read your motivations correctly. I think you are a greedy and egotistical man. You somehow believe the world revolves around you and you alone.

"On the other hand," Tenzin said, "in my time as a monk, I have seen much poverty and disease among my people. As a poor monastic, there has been little I could do to help. After I heard your appeal I realized such a large sum of money would do much good. I was born in nineteen-forty, and now at fifty years of age I have made little progress in helping my fellow Tibetans."

I like the direction he is heading.

"About the task of finding your next incarnation: I have spent decades of my life working on my meditation practice, and feel I would have as good a chance as any of finding your next birth. It would be one of the most difficult challenges I have ever faced, but I believe I can accomplish it. So, I accept your charge. I will seek out your next incarnation, but only if you agree to the following conditions."

"Go on."

"First of all, I will need travel expenses, not only for myself, but also to transport your reincarnation back to Tibet. There will also be funds needed to purchase a high quality passport forgery. When I am out of the country, it will be necessary for international travel. Secondly, you must agree to my abbot's offer to take the assistance of our monks as you move toward death. I must know you are making some attempt to better yourself. Thirdly, our agreement here must be totally secret; no one can know of it. If word of such an action was known by my abbot, I would likely be expelled. Finally, I have the last say in all major decisions." His dark eyes studied Matt. "Is this acceptable to you?"

Matt couldn't believe what he was hearing. "Yes," he agreed.

Tenzin continued: "Now, since you previously grew up in Oklahoma, I might guess you will choose to be reborn there. Wherever, once my meditations give me a good sense of where you are in your next life, it will be necessary for me to travel to confirm your location. I will do this while you are very young, but I will not attempt to contact you until you are of age. In your country, I believe that occurs sometime around eighteen years old?"

Matt nodded.

"Around that time I will attempt to convince your incarnation to come to Tibet and let him or her claim your fortune."

"Him or her?"

"Yes," Tenzin said. "In the chain of reincarnation, one does not stay either a male or a female. One needs experiences as both sexes for the greatest spiritual growth."

Matt's jaw dropped. "You've got to be kidding."

Tenzin broke into a little smile and said, "No, I'm not." He then continued, "There are secret ways through the mountains to get in and out of Tibet through Nepal. These are difficult, but they can be accomplished. Now I must ask you: How is your fortune stored?"

Matt admitted, "Precious gemstones. I have them in a safety deposit box at the Bank of China branch here in Lhasa."

"They are easily transportable then." He gathered his thoughts. "Sometime in the months to come, after I have obtained my new passport, I will shed my robes for the clothes of a Tibetan civilian. We will then enter this bank, and I will become a signatory on the account. At the proper time I will remove them and hide them in a location known only to me. It would not be wise to leave them there for too many years. The Chinese need no excuse to invade someone's privacy. We must do all we can not to arouse suspicion.

"So, Matthew Johnston, I believe that, for the time being, we are finished. I have a question to ask you."

"Yes?"

"What do you do in your country to formalize an agreement between two people? Do you sign papers?"

"No," said Matt. "In Oklahoma we shake on it." He extended his right hand.

"Shake on it," Tenzin repeated, and he clasped Matt's hand firmly.

Tenzin finished his tea, pulled his coat about him, then took his leave into the frigid Tibetan winter. As the door closed behind him, a miserable Matt took a long sip of his tea — then smiled.

Most have their price. Most — but not all —

ཨོཾ་མ་ཎི་པདྨེ་ཧཱུྃ་ ཨོཾ་མ་ཎི་པདྨེ་ཧཱུྃ་ ཨོཾ་མ་ཎི་པདྨེ་ཧཱུྃ་

February 21–October 16, 1990

As expected, Matt's health continued to decline. His weight plummeted, his jaundice worsened, and he became plagued with vomiting. In spite of his increasing emaciation, his abdomen swelled with fluid, and he knew this was from his the cancer that had spread to his liver.

Probably the worst thing, though, was the mental and emotional pain he went through as he began to look back on his life. He shuddered as he recalled the death of Joe and the responsibility he felt for his demise. He recalled Aika and Rinji's deaths and found himself still wishing that he could have done something to prevent them. He was saddened he was never able to say goodbye to his Oklahoma family. Worst of all were the many crimes against humanity he had committed as a mercenary. No, he didn't imagine a peaceful death, only one wracked with misgiving and guilt.

The most uplifting moments of the recent past were his association with the monks from Drepung. They were young and inexperienced, but he appreciated their freshness and innocence, qualities he had lost long ago. He became especially fond of Dawa, and they would have long conversations late into the night when Matt fell well enough.

One evening, in mid-October, as death rapidly approached, a knock came at the door of his bedroom. "Come in," he called out, being too weak to raise himself from his bed. He was pleased to see Dawa enter.

Dawa closed the door behind him and sat on the chair facing his bed. He too could speak English. This friendship provided no small measure of comfort.

"Are you still alive?" he teased.

"As alive as you are," said Matt. "You know, Dawa, I think I'm going to outlive the lot of you monks. I'm too ornery to die."

"I hardly think so. You have the look of approaching death on your face. I think you will die before the end of the month," he bluntly said. "Soon we will stay with you twenty-four hours a day. You are approaching the time when you will be unable to walk, and you will need to be spoon fed. The adventure of the Bardo rapidly approaches. Before you know it, you will be leaving the world."

"Dawa," Matt asked, "will you be with me when I die?"

"If at all possible. Have no worry, at least one of us will be in your presence."

"Dawa . . . I'm scared . . ."

Dawa said, "All have fear as they approach the great transition. If anyone says they are not frightened, it is likely they are not being truthful. If one looks deeply, one realizes that all that you have known will be taken away. This includes not only your body, but also your surroundings — everything familiar. It is no wonder it is unsettling. Remember this: It is a journey you have made many times before, even though you don't recall it.

"During your after-death experience, listen for our voices. We will guide you through the Bardo, the state between death and rebirth, with The Tibetan Book of the Dead. It won't be as bad as you might think. We will do the best we can to guide you to a good rebirth."

Matt remained silent.

If he only knew . . .

Chapter 29

October 17, 1990, Lhasa, Tibet

For Matt the day began as any other; roosters crowed in the morning when he woke, and he slowly drank the yak butter tea his cook had brought to him. He took a few sips for its warmth, then set it aside, closed his eyes and gradually slipped into a semi-comatose state. He did not feel the diaper that was placed on him. Later that evening he opened his eyes and remembered where he was.

He fondly recalled how much he used to enjoy the taste of a good old chicken-fried steak and gravy dinner back home. Now nothing sounded good, and everything he swallowed ended up in or around his vomit basin. He remembered how strong he used to be; now every movement was difficult. As the monks had taught him, he concentrated on his breathing.

He again thought of Aika. They had so many hopes, so many expectations for their life together, only to find their dreams shattered. He also reflected on their child, Rinji William.

Where are they now, if they still exist?

Were they snuffed out like the flame of a candle?

He welcomed death, the very same death he sought out all those years ago on Iwo Jima. He heard the sound of his voice screaming, not from physical pain, but from the misery of a wasted existence.

He realized, though, that over the past few months he had the beginnings of a shift in his consciousness, which had intensified as he approached death. The greed that had permeated his being for so long was starting to change into a desire to be of service. He smiled, if only for a brief second. Maybe the old Matt still lurked in the depths of his being, the one from solid Oklahoma stock, who was much more of a giver than a taker. One who cared about others more than himself.

He hoped that if somehow he could dodge hell, and there was a lifetime to come, he could find a way to make amends. Perhaps he would have the wisdom to use his enormous wealth for the good of humankind.

Also, in the recent past, Matt had begun to reflect back to the words that had been written by his mother. As hard as it was to believe, he had started to wonder: *Could there be a God?*

The murmur of monks chanting softly permeated his space, and he caught a hint of sandalwood incense. Little else filtered through the haze that fogged his mind.

It shouldn't be long now.

His heartbeat began to slow, and he barely heard the door to his room open and close. But he did feel the presence of Lama Tenzin Tashi and the resonant ringing of a Tibetan singing bowl. The vibration of the bowl entered his forehead, and he became slightly more aware.

Whereupon the monk repeated his promise.

Could the lama really keep his word? Could he reach into the chasm of death and discover its secrets?

. . . Out of nowhere Matt became aware of an intense, blinding white light that filled the center of the room. It was without circumference or center, moving as a panoramic mirage. It was bright to the point of being uncomfortable. But the discomfort did not come from the brilliance itself. Rather, it arose because it made the darkness inside him all that much more apparent.

He found himself eager to escape it. The monks now stood outside his room, their chants murmuring through the closed door:

> O, Child of Buddha Nature, Matthew Walker Johnston listen! Pure inner radiance, reality itself, is now arising before you. Recognise it! O, Child of Buddha Nature, this radiant essence that is now your conscious awareness is a brilliant emptiness. It is beyond substance, beyond characteristics and beyond colour, completely empty of inherent existence in any respect whatsoever. This is the female Buddha Samantabhadri, the essential nature of reality. The essence of your own conscious awareness

is emptiness. Yet, this is not a vacuous or nihilistic emptiness; this, your very own conscious awareness, is unimpededly radiant, brilliant and vibrant. This conscious awareness is the male Buddha Samantabhadra. The utterly indivisible presence of these two: the essence of your own awareness, which is empty, without inherent existence with respect to any substance whatsoever, and your own conscious awareness, which is vibrant and radiantly present, is the Buddha-body of Reality. This intrinsic aware ness, manifest in a great mass of light, in which radiance and emptiness are indivisible, is the buddha nature of unchanging light, beyond birth or death. Just to recognise this is enough! If you recognise this brilliant essence of your own conscious awareness to be the buddha nature, then to gaze into intrinsic awareness is to abide in the enlightened intention of all the buddhas.

Despite the entreaties of the monks, Matt hesitated only momentarily and turned away from the dazzling, unbearable light. He was relieved when the radiance began to fade. There was the inner sense, though, of a missed opportunity.

His thoughts were interrupted by a loud, uncomfortable buzzing sound. It was as though he had entered a large beehive, and the annoying reverberation was all around him. He suddenly felt himself moving through what seemed to be a narrow dark passageway, and when he reached the end he looked back and discovered he was floating above the body of an emaciated corpse.

Matt shuddered as he came to the realization that he was seeing his own physical body, motionless and devoid of life.

He glanced up, saw the lama leave the room, and the monks returned to his bedside.

At first he felt panic and a desire to re-enter his body. He spoke to the softly chanting monks, but they did not hear him. When he willed himself over to touch Dawa on the shoulder, he saw his hand pass through to the other side of his body.

Matt took a closer look at himself, and as far as he could tell, his current form seemed to be similar to the dead man lying on the bed, though weightless and more pliant. A column of light with the appearance of a silver cord extended from the head of the body to an area between his shoulder blades. As he gazed at it, this translucent cord thinned in the middle and snapped apart, separating him from the immobile corpse.

No more going back now.

There was an odd feeling of timelessness. Rainbow colors surrounded the scene, iridescent in quality, and hues he had never known sparkled around him. He felt an alertness and expansion of his consciousness that was somehow familiar.

He also discovered his vision was markedly accentuated, and he could see beyond the walls of his home — even to the interior of Drepung Monastery, where a caretaker angrily chased rats and slapped at them with a broom. He found the thoughts of some of the monks in the room were transparent to him and that Lobsang, the youngest of the group, was thinking about the attractive nun he had chatted with earlier. If only his colleagues could know, he chuckled to himself. He looked at Dawa and was surprised to see an unmistakable rage written all over his face.

Even he is angry at death.

As his mind power increased from second to second, he again saw another intensely bright illumination, which first approached and then completely surrounded him. He gazed deeply into it, and while not as brilliant as the first light, it was still far too scintillating for him to face. It also made him all too aware of his imperfections, and deep within he knew that merging with this light meant giving up all earthly attachments. He heard the monks again chanting:

O, Child of Buddha Nature! Meditate on this, your meditational deity. Do not be distracted! Concentrate intently on your meditation deity! Meditate that the deity appears, and yet is without inherent existence, like the reflection of the moon in water. Do not meditate on the deity as a solid corporeal form!

I have no Jesus, no Buddha, no Mary, no saint, no bodhisattva, to call to my side, he angrily thought.

Again he turned away from the brilliance, though the light maintained its place around him as if extending a prolonged invitation, a beckoning. He continued, though, to pull away. Eventually the light, as the first, began to fade, and Matt felt a sense of relief.

Hey, this isn't so bad.

It was at this moment he became aware of something behind him. As he turned, almost upon him was a large black amorphous form with glowing yellow bloodshot eyes. The odor was unbearable. To his horror, the creature began to speak:

Matthew Walker Johnston, I have come for you. Come —

Matt screamed and felt terror beyond his wildest imaginings. As the creature reached its clawed forelegs for him, his expanded consciousness contracted, and he fell into a swoon.

Chapter 30

Matt woke from his unconscious state and found himself floating above a small group of chanting monks, two holding smoking plumes of juniper, walking up a steep hillside. He recognized Dawa, who, in the lead, carried an open copy of *The Tibetan Book of the Dead* in his hands. Behind them were two men with white aprons shouldering a bent body wrapped in white. Remembering his prior experience with the dark creature, he swiftly floated closer to the monastics and listened carefully as Dawa read:

> O, Child of Buddha Nature, that which is called death has now arrived. You are leaving this world. But in this you are not alone. This happens to everyone. Do not be attached to this life! Do not cling to this life! Even if you remain attached and clinging, you do not have the power to stay — you will only continue to roam within the cycles of existence. Therefore, do not be attached and do not cling! Think of the Three Precious Jewels!
>
> O, Child of Buddha Nature, however terrifying the appearances of the intermediate state of reality might be, do not forget the following words. Go forward remembering their meaning. The crucial point is that through them recognition may be attained.

Alas, now, as the intermediate state of reality arises before me,

Renouncing the merest thought of awe, terror or fear,
I will recognise all that arises to be awareness, manifesting naturally of itself.
Knowing such sounds, lights and rays to be visionary phenomena of the in-
termediate state,
At this moment, having reached this critical point,
I must not fear this assembly of Peaceful and Wrathful Deities, which manifest
naturally!

Go forward, reciting these words distinctly and be mindful of their
meaning. Do not forget them! For it is essential to recognise, with certainty, that whatever terrifying experiences may arise, they are natural
manifestations of actual reality. O, Child of Buddha Nature, when
your mind and body separate, the pure luminous apparitions of reality
itself, will arise: subtle and clear, radiant and dazzling, naturally bright
and awesome, shimmering like a mirage on a plain in summer. Do not
fear them! Do not be terrified! Do not be awed! They are the natural
luminosities of your own actual reality. Therefore recognise them as
they are!

From within these lights, the natural sound of reality will resound,
clear and thunderous, reverberating like a thousand simultaneous peals
of thunder. This is the natural sound of your own actual reality. So, do
not be afraid! Do not be terrified! Do not be awed! The body you have
now is called a 'mental body', it is the product of subtle propensities
and not a solid corporeal body of flesh and blood. Therefore, whatever
sounds, lights or rays may arise, they cannot harm you. For you are
beyond death now! . . .

Matt shrank back as he now witnessed the unwrapping of his putrid body.
One of the men in white aprons dismembered his corpse, and later used a sledge
to crush his skull. Matt watched as large ravenous vultures devoured his flesh and
eventually his bones.

Soon he heard muffled, guttural sounds all around him. He sensed more than
saw innumerable dark forms gathering, not unlike the one he had seen earlier. He
heard their demonic laughter as they stealthily moved nearer and nearer like hunters closing in on their prey. To his dismay, he heard his name called out time and
time again.

Matthew Walker Johnston . . . Matthew Walker Johnston . . .

He could see them more clearly now. While they varied in size, some were the most enormous creatures he had ever seen. They had coarse, black-matted coats and sharply pointed teeth, and the odor of a thousand bloated animal carcasses preceded them.

Despair struck him, and he felt as if he might be suffocating. The bright colors that had entranced him had been replaced with shades of grey and brown.

The expanded state of consciousness that he had enjoyed now shrank to a point somewhere inside his new body. He began to hear deafening thunder-clap-like sounds. He covered his ears but could not escape the pealing noise. He appreciated a wet, musty smell as he seemed to fall deeper and deeper into himself with a accelerating spinning motion. He grunted as he felt himself hit a firm loamy surface.

When his mind cleared he was flat on his back in the middle of a golden brown wheat field. A pleasant warm breeze caused the shafts to sway side to side with a distinctive rustling sound only a farmer would know. The scent of freshly turned earth brought back warm memories. He saw the sun as it gently peeked through the waving wheat. He heard the distinctive call of the scissor-tailed flycatcher, and he smiled, remembering this sweet melody from his youth.

With a start he searched the horizon for any trace of the dark creatures and sighed as he detected no sign of them. He brushed the dirt, grass and wheat stems off as he stood up in the soft indention where he had fallen. He was wearing blue denim Round House overalls over a plain white tee shirt and his shoes were brogans, as a farmer might wear.

In the distance stood a familiar house with nearby sapodilla plum and pecan trees. Turning in the opposite direction, his suspicions were confirmed as he viewed the quiet country town of Davidson, Oklahoma. He rotated back around and approached the small country home through the field of waving wheat. He saw what he thought was movement in the front window.

Patiently he walked on toward the modest house, raptly taking in the entire scene. There, to the left, was the barn where he, along with his brothers and sisters, had milked their small herd of cattle. He could see the storm shelter which doubled as a root cellar peeking out just behind the home to the left, and the wrap-around porch where the family would sit in the evening and watch the twilight deepen.

As he stepped onto the porch, he saw a figure through the open curtain to the left of the front door. He peered inside and saw a young version of his mother holding a newborn infant in her lap; it was wrapped in a quilted patchwork blanket. He gulped as he realized the child was him, and he was seeing a scene from the first few days following his birth.

The infant was a bright shade of pink with a thick shock of dark hair and was sleeping comfortably in his mother's arms. There was the soft clicking of an old wooden rocking chair as Naomi Johnston gently rocked her son back and forth. He looked closely at his mother.

How beautiful she was! How had I never noticed?

He was stunned as he saw her bright blue eyes gazing steadily at him, her precious baby. Suddenly he found himself transposed into her arms, and he once again was an infant. He noted the gentle scent of talcum powder with which his mother had dusted him after changing his cotton diaper. His now-baby eyes opened and sensed the divine caring only a mother could give. Naomi beamed at him and kissed him on the forehead. Abruptly the scene changed.

A small child, maybe four years old, stood there, wearing the all-too-familiar Round House overalls. His head was covered by a cotton-lined hat with ear flaps, straps coming from both sides, snapped securely across his chin. This child carried a BB gun in his arms. To his left walked a lanky dark-haired man who held a .22 rifle. Matt watched the man glance down at his son with a look of pride.

He was seeing himself and his father on a hunting trip. It was a cold, blustery day and both wore thick coats.

"Keep your eyes peeled, Matthew Walker," Will whispered. "We'll likely have only one shot."

As they walked through a brushy field with scattered mesquite trees, a rabbit bolted from the underbrush and ran away in a zigzag pattern. A cotton-white tail clearly marked its trail. Both hunters quickly pulled their rifles to their chests, took aim and fired. The rabbit dropped quickly to the ground, a .22 bullet through its head. They sprinted over to the dead animal and kneeled over it for a moment. And Matt found himself looking at his father through the eyes of the boy.

"Great shot, son," Will said as he picked up the animal and placed it in his satchel. "Thanks to you, our family will have meat tonight, and we will not be hungry."

Matt found himself smiling at his father's praise.

"Remember this," he continued. "We kill because we have to survive. We slaughter the hogs, butcher the cattle and wring our chickens' necks because our lives depend on it. We never take life for pleasure. We never kill to have the biggest trophy on the wall. All life is sacred and deserves our respect. Some day you may find that you have to kill, maybe even take the life of another person. Never find joy in that, and only do it when absolutely necessary. Son, do you understand me?"

"I do, Dad," he heard himself saying.

He shuddered.

How could I have forgotten?

He gazed up at his father. How strong he looked! His arms and chest were toned from years of hard labor, and his hands were dark with the grime of near-constant work with farm equipment. His face was weathered, though there was a contented glow written into his premature wrinkles. His father smiled at him. In those dark brown eyes he saw unconditional love.

Will put his arms around his son and hugged him tightly. Matt felt his tiny body warm as he embraced his father, his little arms only reaching to his father's sides.

He ached to hold this priceless moment, but in a flash he found himself sitting outside on a cool autumn day beside his brothers. Alex had a particularly mischievous grin on his face. He was situated to the right of Matt, and on Alex's other side was their younger brother, Robert, who looked more than a little nervous. They were squatted behind two hay bales stacked upon each other, with a large pile of corn cobs scattered between them. Directly in front of Alex were their secret weapons, a heap of heavily saturated corn cobs which they had soaked overnight in their mother's washbasin.

"They feel like they weigh a ton!" Robert whispered.

Alex winked at him. "They do, brother. They do."

About twenty feet away from them were two other stacked bales with four of their Davidson classmates lurking behind with their own large pile of cobs — they were ready for a fight.

"You Johnstons are a bunch of wieners!" one yelled.

"Get ready to get your butts kicked!" Alex screamed back.

"Okay, here we go. On your mark, get set — go!" yelled Alex.

With that, the boys from both sides rose up from their crouched positions and began flinging corn cobs. The contest seemed even for a short while. Matt caught a corn cob in the throat, which knocked him to the ground and left him breathless for a second. Alex beaned one of the boys on his left ear, but he took a shot to his nose, leaving it trickling with blood.

Robert was neither hit nor did he hit anyone, but kept the other side ducking from his rapid erratic throws.

Immediately after Matt rose to his feet, both he and Alex were simultaneously smacked in the face, stunning them both. The other side sensed victory, gave a series of war whoops and charged the Johnstons' position, flinging cobs as they ran.

Alex quickly jumped from his prone position and flipped some of the soaked corn cobs to his brothers. Within moments two of the other boys were hit on their foreheads and knocked down. Another was popped in the mouth, loosening several of his front teeth. The fourth lad, seeing what had happened, threw down his cobs and ran screaming from the field of battle along with his moaning friends.

Matt, Alex and Robert gave chase with their loaded cobs, hitting their foes several times in their backs before they finally escaped.

"Come back and fight like men, you chickens!" Robert yelled.

Exhausted by the effort, the three brothers rolled on the cold evening ground and laughed. They then sat in a small circle and stacked their right hands together in the center.

"Good job!" Alex proclaimed to his brothers as he held pressure on his still bleeding nose.

"Way to go!" Matt said to Robert. Matt saw the beam of pride in his little brother's eyes as he knew he was now initiated into his family's fraternity.

Alex said, "Hey, guys, we are like The Three Musketeers. One for all and all for one!"

The scene faded and Matt found himself floating below the ceiling in the Davidson High School gymnasium. His little brother, Robert stood with Lillian Jenkins, one of his first grade classmates, on the floor of the basketball court. They were in front of a packed house of students and parents, preparing to perform for the school assembly. Robert's hands trembled as he held the music for the two of them.

From his high vantage point, Matt saw himself and Alex sitting in the front row with a group of friends. They were cheering loudly, stamping their feet on the wooden floor to make even more noise. Alex put his two little fingers in his mouth and whistled.

"Let her rip, brother," Matt yelled, to the chagrin of his mother, who was sitting with Will, Esther and Earlyne in the middle of the bleachers. She was growing redder by the minute, and if looks could kill, Matt and Alex would have both died instantly. Will tried unsuccessfully to hide his smile, which only added to her anger.

Robert and Lillian then meekly sang a song they had practiced for months, "Home on the Range," much to the delight of the audience.

When the final stanza was sung, initially there was polite applause. Then Matt and Alex stood and yelled at the top of their lungs, "Encore! Encore!"

The singers both turned a shade that looked to be a mix of sickly green and purple, and they hurriedly took their places in the bleachers. That, however, did not stop the cheering.

"Encore! Encore!" his brothers repeated over and over. They finally stopped when Alex, looking back and seeing the reaction of their mother, elbowed Matt to quit. They laughed so hard they cried. From his vantage point above, Matt found himself smiling.

How I loved my family.

Again, he wanted to stay at that place. Instead he floated up into a dense fog. There he pondered what he had experienced in this part of the *Bardo*. He realized that he, as a child, had known the joy of unconditional love, not only from his parents, but also from his siblings, something not every youngster had.

What went wrong?

Matt began to wonder about the monks. He could no longer hear them chanting. Dawa had told him that their ritual would continue for forty-nine days after his death.

He recalled again the demons that pursued him. While the reading from *The Tibetan Book of the Dead* assured him that these creatures were not real, he felt little comfort from this and wondered when — not if — they would confront him again.

Before he was ready, the fog parted.

Chapter 31

Matt descended from the parting fog and found himself over an island. It took a few moments for the scene to register, and then, with horror, he saw the distinctive outline of Mount Suribachi.

Oh, shit! It's Iwo Jima.

He desperately flailed his arms as if to swim away. But the island drew him like a magnet, and he was helpless to resist.

The U.S. fleet floated offshore, firing nonstop with a deafening roar. Planes from an aircraft carrier strafed Japanese positions, and smoke and flame rose from the explosions of too-many-to-count artillery shells. Numerous glowing spirits rose above lifeless bodies.

His speed accelerated toward the island. In moments he was in a bunker with his Marine buddies. Joe stood beside him, taking a swig from his canteen. Matt wanted to scream out, "Get ready! We're not safe!" Instead he found himself as an actor, filling a role he was unable to change, no matter how much he wanted to alter the script.

Without warning they were overrun. Matt heard the screams of his fellow Marines as they died one by one. He felt a blow to his head and was knocked to the ground. He staggered to his feet and pulled out his .45. He then saw a Japanese pointing a revolver at the head of his best friend. He heard Joe yell, "Shoot him, Matt. Oh, God, shoot him!"

Matt pointed his gun at the Japanese and shrieked to himself, "Shoot, you asshole! Shoot! Shoot! Shooooooooooooot!" He paused as piss flowed down his legs and diarrhea filled his pants.

The weapon of the Japanese discharged.

Matt screamed as Joe fell lifeless to the ground. And then he did it — too late — putting a bullet through the head of Joe's killer. He shot all the others invading his bunker. Then the Matt that he had been gathered his weapons and charged out of the bunker, shouting as a madman, firing as he went. But the spirit Matt stayed behind, weeping as he sat on the rim of the bunker, his face covered by his hands.

Matt then heard an eerie shuffling sound and looked up to see Joe standing unsteadily in front of him, staring at him with the unfeeling eyes of a dead man. He edged back as Joe stumbled toward him, Joe whispering quietly, "Coward . . . you are a coward. Not a Marine. A lowly coward. I thought you were my best friend, but you betrayed me. You peed and crapped in your pants like a little boy. You're not a man, you are a scum-sucking worthless piece of shit!"

Matt stood and backed away. He turned to run and found his exit blocked by other mangled zombie-like creatures, some Japanese, some American, all gaping vacuously at him, stumbling as they approached. Soon they all were in a circle around him, moving closer and closer, chanting relentlessly and gradually louder, "You are a coward . . ."

The group parted and a large man with a bullet hole in the middle of his forehead roughly pushed his way to the front. Matt gasped: It was Junior.

He reached up to Matt's chest and ripped off the Silver Star that had appeared there. He threw it to the ground, unzipped his torn pants and then, in a circular pattern, methodically urinated on the medal. Zipping up his trousers, he glared at Matt, poked his right index finger into his chest and said, "You are a fucking coward."

Matt screamed and slumped to the ground. Suddenly he felt both of his arms tightly gripped and discovered that two of the demonic creatures had reappeared, one on each side, their sharp nails pinching deep into his skin. They lifted him high into the air. He first struggled against them, but soon relented, as they were far stronger than he was and seemed to relish his futile attempts at escape. The threesome then ascended into a dense cloud. From seemingly nowhere, he heard the monks again repeat the phrase:

". . . it is essential to recognize, with certainty, that whatever terrifying experiences may arise, they are natural manifestations . . ."

Matt shook his head.

They seem pretty damned real to me.

Suddenly the creatures released him, and he again floated downward, this time through the roof of an unfamiliar building. The minute he entered, though, he knew his location; it was the Hiroshima Teishin Hospital. Admittedly, he yearned to see again the two people he loved more than anyone in the world, Aika and Rinji William. In a moment he found himself floating above a delivery room where Aika was in labor.

How pale and tired she looks.

He saw the blood that was being given through her IV. The leukemia she contracted had certainly done its worst. He floated down to hold and comfort her, but found that he was unable to touch her, and she could not hear him speak. He looked through the wall and recognized a much younger version of himself pacing in the waiting area. Seated nearby were Miyo and Shigeshi.

He heard Aika call his name in the Japanese accent he had come to love. "Matthew . . . Matthew, where are you?" Her head rolled side to side in delirium.

He whispered tearfully, his face inches from hers, "I'm right here, sweetheart," but again he could not be heard. He had never known she had asked for him during her labor.

Why in the hell didn't the doctor send for him?

One glance at the look on Dr. Yamamoto's face, and he understood. He had his hands full.

Aika's body lurched as she had a contraction, a hard one. A large dark blood clot expelled from her vagina. Doctor Yamamoto listened to Aika's and the baby's heart beats. Matt could read and understand his every thought.

Aika's heart rate is far too fast — and the baby's is much too slow.

Matt saw him do a vaginal exam.

Dr. Yamamoto nodded at the nurse, who went to the head of the bed.

He heard her speak in Japanese as she whispered in Aika's ear, but he somehow heard the words in English. "It is time. Push down hard with your next contraction."

Matt watched in stunned silence.

Aika, who was beautiful even in her wan and sickly state, felt a contraction and leaned into it with a fervent scream. Soon a thick-haired baby's head appeared. The doctor felt Aika's pulse. Matt continued to see into his mind.

We've got to deliver this baby with the next contraction.

Dr. Yamamoto listened again to the baby's heart beat. His cool demeanor hid his panic.

Oh, my God! It's still beating too slowly! We have to do a C-section!
He yelled frantically at the nurse.

Iodine was rapidly splashed on her abdomen, and the anesthesiologist prepared to induce general anesthesia. Before he could put the mask on her face, Aika grunted and pushed mightily. A male baby was propelled from the vagina with a large gush of bright red blood and dark clots. He fell into the arms of Dr. Yamamoto and took a single gasping breath. Aika slowly lifted her head, saw her critically ill infant and smiled. Suddenly her head fell back and she became unresponsive.

"Call an emergency!" Dr. Yamamoto said as he clamped and cut the umbilical cord. Like before, Matt could hear his words in English. Dr. Suzuki grabbed the infant and started the resuscitation at an adjacent table. Dr. Yamamoto focused his attention on Aika. In moments the room became crowded with hospital personnel.

Matt looked through the walls and saw himself and Aika's family in the waiting area as the nurses rushed past them. How well he remembered the helpless feeling he had.

Matt's eyes filled with tears as the medical team worked frantically. He stared dumbfounded as he began to see the looks of resignation on the doctor's faces. "Don't stop," he yelled. "Keep trying!"

Doctor Yamamoto soon recognized the futility of their efforts. He looked over at Dr. Suzuki, who shook his head. "It is time to stop," Dr. Yamamoto said. "They are both dead. We can no longer help them."

He removed his gloves with a rubbery *pop*, and the physicians, along with their assistants, began to leave the room. The nurse attendant then cleaned and wrapped the infant corpse in a blanket and placed him on the right side of his mother's chest.

Matt's spirit rose from the corner of the room where he had been sitting and silently weeping. He never even minutely comprehended that the deaths of his wife and son had happened in such a violent fashion. He floated over and gazed at the dead twosome. He placed his arms around the both of them, and while unable to feel their skin, could appreciate the ebbing warmth. He knew he only had a few moments. His eyes welled with tears as he spoke.

"Aika, my dear wife, I miss you more than you could ever know. We were supposed to grow old together. Why were you taken away from me?" He turned to his son. "Rinji William, I never had the chance to watch you grow up. I was supposed to see you become a young man, go to college and raise a family of your own. Son, I . . ."

Before he could say more, the door softly opened, and the young Marine that Matt had been, along with Miyo and Shigeshi, walked to the bedside.

He couldn't bear to see any more.

Thankfully he found himself floating up through the ceiling and into the rainy Hiroshima night.

Chapter 32

Matt's consciousness once again faded, and when he came to he found he was walking in a most familiar wheat field, bright green with the young shoots of winter wheat. Again, he was wearing his Round House overalls. There was no sign of the Tibetan monks, and the dark creatures that had pursued him were nowhere in sight.

Directly ahead of him sat the Johnston homestead warmed by a bright sun. It seemed to be the early afternoon, and there were several cars parked around the house. He walked onto the porch and peeked through the front window.

Around a large dining table sat his entire family preparing to enjoy a big meal. The aroma was enticing. There were pork chops, a large bowl of mashed potatoes with gobs of butter melting on top, and all sorts of wonderful country food. Best of all, though, were his mom's renowned homemade noodles.

Matt smiled as he looked around the table. His father proudly sat at the head next to his mother, who scurried back and forth from the kitchen to the dining room preparing the table. There was Alexander, who was obviously pleased to be seated next to the noodles. To his left was his sister, Esther, who was sitting next to a young man wearing a royal blue and white football jersey.

"Wendell, would you please pass me the green beans? Esther said.

Matt saw her nuzzle her head into his neck.

She has never been that sweet to anyone — she must be in love.

Next to Wendell was Robert, looking older than he remembered, and seated by him was Earlyne. By her was an empty chair with a plate in front of it with silverware stacked on a cloth napkin. On the plate was a framed picture of Matt taken when he was home on leave.

His father gazed at all those around the table and leered at Alex who was preparing to take a big bite of one of the pork chops. "I know we're all hungry, but let's pause a moment for the blessing." As he bowed his head, so did the rest of those at the table.

"Heavenly Father, it is by your mercy that we have this food before us. Thank you for your love and grace. But, most of all, surround Matthew Walker with your protection while he fights for our freedom. Father, return him to us safe and sound. Amen."

Upon hearing the magic word, they charged pell-mell into the food, and Alex practically lunged at his pork chop.

Matt smiled once again, but suddenly felt a sense of trepidation as the bright sky began to fill with boiling dark clouds approaching from the northwest. From the green tinged cloud, the long arm of a large black funnel searched the ground for something to devastate. Debris flew in all directions each time it chose to touch the earth.

Matt ran through the wall of the family home. "To the root cellar!" he heard himself screaming. "Go! Go! Go!" He felt a wave of nausea; as before, he could not be heard.

The front door abruptly banged open, and all within heard an all too familiar roar. His father jumped from the table, ran to the open door and looked outside. "Quick, let's move!" he yelled over the deafening noise.

As the family rose from their seats, Matt kept an eye on his father, the solid rock of the family. He had never before seen panic on the face of the man he knew could handle anything. Yet, there it was.

Lightning struck rapidly and closely. The roof of their home was torn free and lifted away, and Matt cringed as Robert and Earlyne were ripped by the force of the wind from the clutches of their terrified mother. Screaming, they clung to each other as they were twisted up and away. They were killed instantly as they slammed into a heavy fence post, well over a hundred yards away.

As the rest rushed for shelter, the tornado struck the dairy barn, and the large wooden planks from the barn flew into them, mowing them down as a crop cut by a sharpened scythe. Matt was beside himself; he buckled to the ground in the downpour.

Just as rapidly as it came, the storm dissipated. Matt rose and stumbled around the wreckage. He found his anger growing, boiling.

He pointed his fist to the sky, shook it and shouted, "Damn you . . . damn you, God!" He pointed to the bodies littering the ground. "I see what you do to those who believe in you. Stay away from me!"

He sadly looked again at his loved ones.

The scene shifted, and a still furious Matt now floated above a city he had never seen before. The scent of salt in the air led him to believe he was near the ocean, and as he looked to the north, he saw a large expanse of water. Closer now, he finally recognized some of the landmarks. He was good at geography. His work had demanded it.

There, bordering the city to the south was the Xindian River, and to the northwest was the Tamshui River. Yes, he was above the city of Taipei and he rapidly accelerated toward the heart of the metropolis. He floated next to a woman who was vending cigarettes when she was accosted by a policeman. He attempted to take her tray and money from her, and when she resisted he cracked her head with the butt of his pistol. Blood poured from the wound, and she died instantly. An angry mob gathered and was dispersed only when the police wildly shot into the crowd.

Matt remembered this historical incident. The Japanese had ruled Taiwan from 1895 until their surrender in 1945. When the Chinese Nationalist forces first arrived, they were greeted as liberators and initially were welcomed by the Taiwanese. They discovered, however, that the forces of Chiang Kai-shek were repressive and brutal, and after more than a year of corruption, tensions boiled over.

Suddenly time began to fast-forward, and Matt saw images and events pass to that day when there was a full scale invasion by the hardened troops of Chiang Kai-shek from mainland China. A massacre of epic proportions took place right in front of his disbelieving eyes.

Police indiscriminately roamed the streets, shooting into unarmed crowds. There was widespread looting and rape, and the wails of the injured echoed in Matt's head. It had been reported that up to 30,000 Taiwanese were brutally murdered by the Chinese, and Matt believed he had seen almost all of them.

Finally he silently mouthed to an empty sky, "Why am I seeing this?" As if in answer to his question, the scenes began to slow, and the picture coned down to the weapons being held by the assailants. Matt looked closely; a number of firearms he recognized. The revolvers were of Japanese issue, as were the rifles. The scenes began to move more rapidly, and he saw more Japanese weapons, all in mint condition.

Suddenly Matt knew. He hung his head in shame.

Li Wei was working for Chiang Kai-shek.

Matt recalled his previous words, and thought:

I did sell them to the devil.

Suddenly he was surrounded by countless hordes of the demonic creatures. Their satanic laughter preceded their appearance, and the bloody drool from their open maws dripped from the corners of their mouths as they guffawed. They seized him roughly by his arms and legs, though Matt did not care. He had already known he was damned for eternity, but now his fate seemed certain. He slumped as the cackling creatures carried him through the crust of the earth, deeper and deeper. Matt began to perspire from the heat of molten rock. The fears of fire and brimstone from his childhood rose to meet him.

His worst fears were confirmed.

I am headed for eternal hell.

He gladly slipped into a stupor.

Chapter 33

Matt woke to find his arms and legs chained to a hot iron chair, blackened with soot. He tested the restraints; they were tightly secured. A host of demons and other dark creatures danced happily around him in a large cavern, many carrying tridents with razor sharp points. Others were cracking whips and popping them uncomfortably close to his head. Volcanic lava was spurting from nearby geysers, producing cloudy fumes that reeked of sulfur. The heat was unbearable, and his throat was parched.

So this is hell.

Matt again heard one of the creatures call his name. This jogged an old memory.

Reverend Black, how did you know?

Salty perspiration dripped into his eyes, but he was unable to wipe them. Glancing to his right, a long line of unfortunate souls were bound in a similar fashion, and a chorus of moans was heard echoing throughout the chamber.

Hearing some movement to his left, he turned to see another line forming. It stretched far into the distance.

The first person in the queue walked in front of Matt and glared at him. It was a diminutive Asian female. She said, "The troops of Chiang Kai-shek knocked on our door and forced their way in when my husband opened it. They held one of the revolvers you provided to his head. First, he was bound to a chair, and then his tongue was cut out before he was bayoneted through the heart. My daughter and two sons were then bludgeoned to death with clubs, right before my eyes. I was unfortunately allowed to live so that I could remember their screams. I died in an asylum."

He shrunk as low as he was able in the chair and said, "I am so sorry. If you can find it in your heart, please forgive me."

She said nothing but pursed her lips and walked away, looking back with angry glances. Then the next person in line took her place before him. It was a tiny black child, perhaps five years old. She appeared familiar.

"Sir," she politely said, "you came into my village one day looking for a bandit. My mother and father did not know you were there, and when they went outside our hut, you murdered them with your weapon. I had no family to care for me, and so I was raised in an orphanage. I later died of starvation."

Matt recalled those years as a mercenary in Africa. He often shot first and asked questions later. After his experience in Iwo Jima, he had promised himself never to delay when faced with danger. He now recalled the little girl coming out of the hut and embracing the bloody bodies of her parents, which were riddled with bullets. He remembered the shame he felt, but he had made no apologies; rather, he resumed roaming the village with his automatic weapon, finger on the trigger, ready to fire and fire quickly. He killed many more before he shot the diamond thief as he ran from hiding. He looked down at the child, who had tears in her eyes.

"Oh, little girl," he said, his eyes moist, "I am so sorry for what I did. I thought that your parents might be the bad person I was looking for. How awful it must have been for you to spend your life without them." He gulped and felt a large lump in his throat.

How could I have been so heartless?

The small girl then walked away, slowly, sadly, head down.

ཨོཾ་མ་ཎི་པདྨེ་ཧཱུྃ་ ཨོཾ་མ་ཎི་པདྨེ་ཧཱུྃ་ ཨོཾ་མ་ཎི་པདྨེ་ཧཱུྃ་

The never ending flow of those whom he had hurt in one way or another continued. Matt shook his head. How long had this gone on? Was it days? Weeks? Months? He had no way of knowing. All he knew was that he had apologized and begged forgiveness from all. The dark minions continued to gleefully dance, and when they felt like it they jabbed him with their tridents, bloodlessly piercing his skin.

The crack of their whips also began to find their mark, but he felt no physical pain from either; instead, his mental anguish seemed to block out all other sensations. The line to his left never diminished, and Matt felt depleted and absolutely hopeless. Finally, in a moment of complete desperation, he said something he had not said for many, many years and had seemed utterly impossible only a short time ago.

Weeping and pulling a deep painful breath into his chest, he whimpered almost imperceptibly, "Oh, God . . . oh, God . . . please help me . . . please."

No sooner than he had spoken these words, a portion of the rock-studded wall in front of him dissolved into nothingness, and a glowing male figure with flowing robes emerged.

Smiling, he came to Matt and placed his cool hands on his shoulders. "Matthew Walker Johnston, your time here is over. Take my hand." With that, the iron shackles fell away, and he gripped Matt's right hand and pulled him from the chair. He beamed at him. "It's great to see you again, my child. It's time to go back home."

He effortlessly lifted a semi-comatose Matt onto his shoulders, and they both floated back into and through the luminous portal.

Chapter 34

Matt awoke beside a pool of crystal clear water. He found himself lying on his back, resting on a comfortable bed of grass. He sat up and studied his reflection in the water. He appeared and felt as a man of twenty-five, brimming with a new-found strength. He was now wearing a soft white tee shirt and faded denim jeans. The old man he was had vanished.

He gazed at his new environs. A glowing sky illuminated a series of interconnected pools between verdant rolling hills. Trees were scattered throughout the landscape, many hanging with brightly colored fruit. Birds happily chirped as they hopped from branch to branch, and a gentle breeze wafted through his now thick black hair. This place somehow seemed familiar. He smiled his first happy smile in a very long time. Then the memories of the recent past flooded his brain. He couldn't help but wonder if they simply were a bad dream.

No, they were all too real, all too painful.

As Matt looked around he became aware of a robed figure sitting in meditation next to him. His eyes were closed, and he held his hands on his knees, palms facing upward. Matt recognized him as the one who had rescued him.

Matt studied the man more carefully. The man's tightly curled black hair was pulled back behind his neck and gathered with a dark beaded tassel. He had a closely trimmed black beard and mustache, and his facial characteristics seemed Arabic. A feeling of strength and masculinity emanated from him. The effeminate depictions of Jesus and the heavenly saints he remembered from his youth were nothing like this man.

Suddenly he opened his eyes and turned to look at Matt. "Welcome to heaven," he said.

The warmth from the man's face was palpable. "Who are you?" Matt asked.

"My name is not important, though, if you wish, you may call me Abraham. I have assumed this appearance because I know it is one with which you would be comfortable, though long ago I abandoned my human form. These surroundings should seem familiar to you, as I have greeted you in this place between each incarnation. I see you have questions. I will try to answer them." He stared into the distance, as if he had entered into another time and space.

How does he know I have questions?

Abraham began to speak again:

"Many eons ago, from a time too ancient to remember, the spark of God that you are entered into the human race. At that moment, I, Abraham, took a sacred vow to guide you through your gradual evolution until you stepped fully aware into the pure consciousness of God. For you to get to this point has required many lifetimes, and it is likely you will require many more. Though," his eyes twinkled, "sometimes enlightenment can happen sooner than one might guess.

"I also see that you are wondering about your youthful form. While this image no longer exists, it is the one you most identify with and wish to project. This might change, depending on who you are with. This is true for other souls as well —"

"Abraham," Matt interrupted, "I feel . . . I feel so terribly guilty for the things I've done."

"My son," Abraham said, "guilt is a useful feeling; it makes you aware of a wrongful doing. There its purpose ends. When one feels guilt, one should try to correct the misdeed, and if unable to do so, ask forgiveness of the one you have wronged. If for some reason even that is not possible, direct your plea to God, and there your responsibility ends."

Matt experienced a sense of relief.

Abraham continued. "Karma, though, is created with each and every act, and at some point in time you have to face the effects of what you have created. But karma is not about punishment, it's about learning. Its purpose is to help you understand the results of your actions and how they impact others. To carry guilt puts an unnecessary weight on your soul. Remember — when you injure another you inadvertently become a catalyst for their growth and learning. If you reflect back on your life, you will realize that your greatest teachers are those who have harmed you the most. There is a silver lining in every cloud and an opportunity for advancement with each experience.

"Take, for example, a baby girl learning to walk. She rises and falls over and over again. But through her experience of learning, she is able to walk, first one step, later two and finally a whole string of them.

"Do you know of any mother or father who would spank her when she stumbles? Or would berate her when she didn't succeed the first, the second, a third or even a tenth time? Such it is with God. God understands that one must begin with baby steps."

Matt frowned. "I wouldn't call my life's actions baby steps. They were the lowest of the low."

"Hush. In the scope of our eons of existence, we have all been guilty of the most horrific crimes. Thus, there is no place for criticism, no place for vilification — ever! As we judge the misdeeds of others, so also we judge ourselves."

Matt nodded, encouraged and hopeful. *Maybe*, he thought, *it's not too late for me — even now.*

Abraham stretched his legs and propped his arms behind his back. "The Earth, while a beautiful creation of God, was not created to simply be a place of comfort. It was meant to be a rigorous institute of learning. If the Earth were always blissful and perfect, one would never learn the lessons required for growth."

Perplexed, Matt asked, "When I died, what were the lights that I saw? Was I really taken to hell?" He quivered with the memory.

"The after death experiences you had are what is called the Bardo. You were first presented with the Clear Light of the Void, the essence of your own true nature. If you had been able to blend with it, then you would have immediately escaped the wheel of reincarnation. Later as you hovered above your body, you saw the Secondary Light, not nearly so radiant, but still your own essential nature. Had you been able to hold this light, you would have escaped the rest of the Bardo experience and still attained liberation."

"So?" said Matt, urging Abraham on.

"Unfortunately, because of your karma, you then entered the next phase of the Bardo; some call it the Lonesome Valley. While many of the portrayals of your previous existence were a reality, the demons, zombies, fire and brimstone — the picture of hell itself — were all illusions created by your own consciousness for your learning and understanding. Remember those in the long line you had wronged? While the events were accurate, the people were all an illusion, concocted so you might know the devastating effects of your acts."

Confusion now overwhelmed Matt. "I was told as a youth that, after my life, I would go to heaven or hell forever."

Abraham chuckled and shook his head. "Matthew, for the sake of argument let's suppose you have one and only one life to live. You could die as a baby and experience only a few hours or few days of life. Perhaps you might live fifty, sixty or maybe even one hundred years of Earth's time. Knowing the infinite nature of God's love, does it make any sense at all to you that He would banish you to an eternal existence of suffering for the sins of one life? On the other hand, do you think that one good life deserves an eternity of joy and happiness? Think about it. The love of God is so boundless that you will always be given another chance; thus, we have been given the gift of rebirth.

"No, Matthew, there is no eternal hell, only eternal, limitless forgiveness." Abraham smiled, stood up and went to rummage through a pile of nearby rocks. Finally he picked up a flat one and skipped it across the top of the still water of the lake. "One — two — three— four — five — six skips. Want to give it a try?"

Matt rose and picked through the stones until he found one he thought might be a winner. Aiming it parallel to the surface of the water, he let it fly.

Abraham counted out, "One — two — three — four — five — six — seven. That's pretty good," he conceded. "I'll have to practice for our next meeting. Get ready for a whipping!" He broke into a big smile and started to chuckle.

Abraham's laughter was contagious, and Matt found himself grinning back, feeling as contented as he had felt in a long while.

They both then sat on the grass, and Matt asked, "Abraham, I really like it here. How do I keep from being born again?"

Abraham grew serious and answered, "Matthew Johnston, there are many pathways to eventually escape the wheel of incarnation. Do you know what the word yoga means?"

"No."

"Yoga describes any number of disciplines that help one attain liberation from the material world and eventually find union with the Supreme Being. The paths of yoga apply to all; it doesn't matter what your faith is.

"To name a few, Jnana Yoga is the pathway of discovering God through knowledge and understanding. This might be accomplished by reading the teachings of the world's great sages. For the Christian, this could mean study of the Bible. Hatha Yoga is concerned with physical and mental purification; this allows the soul as pure a vehicle as possible to work through. Karma Yoga achieves oneness with God through service to mankind. Mantra Yoga allows one to find God consciousness though the repetitious chanting of a word or phrase. The Tibetan mantra, om mani padme hum, is one such example. For the Catholic this might mean repeating the rosary. There are many other different types of yoga, and many on the spiritual path choose a combination of these.

"Matthew, you will discover your own sacred way to God. While Jesus, Buddha, Mohammed and others have shown us their paths to enlightenment, yours will be totally distinctive for you and you alone. Look to these avatars for guidance, but seek your own way."

Matt then asked, "How do I stay in the presence of God?"

Abraham said, "Matthew, you have never been and never will be separate from God. While it may seem that way when you are going through your learning experiences, the idea that you are ever apart from God is an illusion."

"I think I understand —"

"Of course, you do," Abraham said. "But the time for questions is over. There are some things I need to tell you, and I want you to listen carefully. Very soon you should consider re-entering the human form."

"But . . ."

Abraham held his hand up to silence him.

"In a normal situation, one has ample time to digest the experiences of one's previous life and take the knowledge gained into the next. However, due to your astonishing selfishness in wanting to carry your wealth with you, you have, at the same time, created a most unique opportunity. I cannot force you to do anything against your will. If you wish to stay here longer, you have every right to do so, and after a time of assimilation, you will re-enter the Earth at the moment you are ready, carefully selecting your parents and your birth environment. That said, I strongly advise your prompt rebirth." Abraham paused and added softly, "What is your decision?"

Matt sighed and took a deep breath. He gazed again at the lush surroundings. He also remembered the intense suffering he had experienced. He looked at Abraham's face with its gleaming dark eyes of promise. "May I ask another question?"

Abraham nodded. "One last question."

"If I do go back now, is there a chance that I could make amends for the wrongs I have committed?"

Abraham might have been looking into his soul. He whispered intently, "If you so wish — if you so wish."

Matt acutely understood the anguish he had created. He hadn't forgotten those scenes from the *Bardo*. Matt sighed and said, "Yes, I'm ready to take another crack at life. Surely this time I will do better."

Abraham smiled his approval. "Your future mother is now in labor, and your delivery is approaching. What happens now happens because you have loved and loved deeply." He stepped back and melted into nothingness.

Matt was alone now. Silently alone.

Am I truly about to be born again — a baby?

The twitter of the birds abruptly stopped, as if in anticipation.

Matt waited.

Chapter 35

"Ruff!"

"Maaaatheeeeeeeew!"

"Ruff! Ruff!"

"Maaaatheeeeeeeew!"

Matt was only able to get a quick glimpse of something large and black running at lightning speed straight at him, followed close behind by — who?

Before he could react, they all barreled into him, knocking him to the ground. He felt a tongue on his face just before he was smashed down face first into the grass.

"Grab his arms!"

"I've got them! You sit on his back!"

The licking had stopped. Now loud barking made the voices hard to distinguish.

"Okay, we've got him! Start the tickling!"

Probing fingers worked their way into his armpits, and soon he was screaming with laughter, rocking side to side, trying to unseat those on his back. The harder he fought, the deeper the fingers jammed into his ribs. Mercifully the tickling finally stopped, and he discovered he had been placed in a headlock — while a rapidly wagging tail thrashed him repeatedly in the face.

"Scob his knob!" he heard another voice say.

A closed fist rubbed deeply into his scalp. "Yeow!" Matt screamed.

"Say uncle!" the voices demanded.

"Uncle!" And he was freed.

He rolled over on his back, spat the grass from his mouth and sat up. The first thing he saw was the smiling face of a large black Lab mix too excited to sit still.

"Inky!

"Inky! Is it really you?" As Matt rubbed Inky's favorite spot behind the ears, four beaming faces surrounded him.

"Hey, brother!" they all yelled.

Matt couldn't believe his eyes. There were Alex, Esther, Robert and Earlyne. Like him, they seemed to be in their early twenties, and they all individually hugged him before sitting together on the ground.

"We've been waiting for you," Alex said. "And about that tickling and scobbing, remember, you were our older brother, and we owed that to you."

Said Esther, "Welcome home, Matthew Johnston. We've all missed you more than you can imagine." She leaned over and kissed him lightly on the cheek.

Of course, Robert and Earlyne greeted him together. "Hey, brother," said Robert, "as you can see, heaven is a pretty terrific place. But without you, well —"

"— things just didn't seem quite right," Earlyne finished.

"Welcome home!" they both finally managed together.

As the Johnston's continued to chat with one another, Matt stroked Inky's head. Inky turned his head to the side and jerked his right leg, his face twisted in ecstasy. Matt grinned and broke into the pure laughter of joy.

Then Matt became aware of another pair that approached. The man wore Round House overalls over a flannel shirt, and the woman was dressed in a loose cotton dress.

Matt breathlessly stood and stared. "Mom . . . Dad . . . !" He ran into their arms, unable to control his tears.

"There, there, Matthew Walker Johnston," his mother murmured. "It's all okay now. Everything is as it should be."

"We love you, son," his father said as he wrapped his arm around his shoulders.

Matt wrenched himself away and said, "But how could you love me? I wasted my life. I don't deserve your love."

His mother pulled him close. "Son, listen to me and listen well. Many years ago, even before you were born, I knew you were a bright, pure soul. As the years went by, we were so proud of the strong young man you became. But I knew you would be tested and tested harshly. God gives his greatest challenges to the most spiritual, and I felt that even with your strong constitution, your mettle would be tried. Remember this: the love I have for you is greater than any of your actions." She then placed her hands on the sides of his face. "I love you, Matthew Walker Johnston, and always will." She kissed him on the forehead and held him until his sobbing ceased.

"I love you too, Mom," he managed.

His dad then placed one arm around his wife's shoulder and one around his son's. "Matthew, I don't understand why you had to face so much. But no one is perfect, and no one always does the right thing. That goes for all of us. You did your best, and no one could ask for more.

"Oh, son — one more thing. That touchdown pass back in 1943, the one you threw to Joe? The one that beat Frederick?"

"Yes?"

"There's never been a better pass thrown in the history of mankind. Don't ever let anyone tell you different, okay?"

Matt blushed and smiled.

"Well, speak of the devil. Look what the cat drug in," his father said, looking over Matt's shoulder.

Matt turned and found himself bear-hugged by a wiry young man wearing a royal blue and white jersey, with the number 81 on his back. He clasped a football with his right hand.

Matt choked back tears as he blurted out, "Joe . . . Joe Hay . . . is it really you?

"The one and the same, old buddy," Joe said. "Hey, I've got a football. Wanna play catch? No one here in heaven comes close to throwing the ball as good as you." Matt looked over at his parents, who nodded and turned back to his brothers and sisters.

"Sure. Toss me the ball." Matt found himself now wearing a matching jersey with the number 8.

Joe flipped him the pigskin.

"Okay, Joe, deep post pattern. But don't run into the trees on the other side of the meadow."

"Just throw it, and I'll catch it."

"On one — ready — hut!"

Joe took off to the left side of the clearing. Matt backpedaled, faked a handoff and threw a perfect spiral, which stuck to the fingers of Joe's outstretched hands.

"Hey," Joe said, "you've still got it. Throw me another one."

And so, they took their time and just played catch. After all the years, it was clear they had not missed a beat. Finally, when they sat down in the grass to catch their breath, Matt said, "Joe, remember that day on Iwo Jima . . . when you were killed?"

Joe looked straight ahead, as if bringing up the memory, and slowly nodded.

"After all those months of Marine training, I can't believe that you died because . . . well . . . I froze. Joe," Matt's voice cracked. ". . . You were my best friend. How could I have not pulled the trigger? I was such a coward. Can you find it in your heart to forgive me?"

"Matt, there's nothing to forgive. We were both kids, fresh out of high school. Sure, we thought we were tough Marines, but we were as frightened as anyone would be. And I know something you don't —"

"What's that?"

"— it was my time, my time to die. If you had shot and killed that Japanese, it would have made no difference. My life would have been taken in some other way." Joe smiled and hit Matt in the shoulder. "Fellow Sandie, we both played our roles and did our best. You'll forever be my best friend. And, by the way, you are the farthest thing from a coward I know. As I left my body, I saw how you charged the enemy lines. It scared me to see how brave you were. If I were a Japanese soldier, I would have been scared shitless of you. By the way, that Silver Star looks damn good on you. Wear it well, old buddy. You deserve it."

A shining medal had appeared on Matt's chest. "Thanks, Joe," he said. "Hey, do you think we'll see each other again in another lifetime?"

"You can count on it," Joe said. "Next time I plan to be the quarterback, and I'll let you chase around trying to catch my passes. I'm going to run your ass off. Besides that, Brothers of the Rabbit never part for too long."

"Yes," Matt said. "Brothers of the Rabbit always stick together. Always —"

Joe then looked upward and to the left; he appeared to be listening to someone. "Well, Matt, your friend Abraham just whispered in my ear. Something about a tight schedule and others who want to see you. Give me back my football, I going to hang with your folks for a few minutes. And, Matt, one more thing," he leaned forward and whispered so that no one else could hear, "Semper Fi, old friend. Semper Fi." He reached over and shook his hand.

Matt smiled and handed him the football. "Semper Fi, Joe, Semper Fi."

No sooner had Joe turned to greet Matt's family, a loud voice pierced the air. "Daddieeee! Daddieeee! Daddieeee!"

A small pair of arms wrapped tightly around the front of his legs. He looked down to discover a beautiful bright-eyed Eurasian child jumping up and down with excitement. "Daddy! I've been waiting so long for you! Where have you been?"

Matt was stunned for a brief moment, and suddenly he knew. "Rinji! Oh, God! Rinji William!" He lifted the boy up and smothered his face with kisses. He then felt a warm hand touch his forearm.

It was Aika.

"Welcome home, husband," she murmured.

They jumped into each other's arms while Rinji clung to his father's neck. Matt whispered in her ear, "I love you. I've missed you more than you could imagine."

"My husband, I love you too," she said as she kissed him on the neck and wrapped her arms around him. Matt saw tears form in her eyes. "I knew that some day this moment would come, but after so, so long, it began to feel like it never would." She blushed ever so slightly. "Would you like a cup of tea?"

Before he could answer, Abraham appeared. "Hey, Rinji," he said. "Would you like to learn how to skip stones?"

Rinji eagerly nodded his head then looked at his father and said, "Daddy, promise me you won't leave till I get back, okay?"

"I'll be right here, son," said Matt.

Rinji gave his father a parting hug and skipped away with Abraham, holding hands as they laughed and danced toward the lake.

A blanket materialized on the grass beside Matt and Aika with a pot of steaming tea and two cups sitting in the middle. Matt stretched out on his side, and Aika sat on her knees pouring the tea. As they sipped the hot *sencha*, he was flooded with wonderful memories. He also remembered how their arguments, while passionate, were usually short-lived and forgotten after a few days. He somehow knew she was also thinking about old times, and they both smiled together.

"My husband," she said, "our time here is short, and there are some words that are important for me to express. After Rinji and I died so many years ago, we continued our lives in this beautiful place. The sadness and the pain of not being with you were almost too much to bear. It has been said there is only joy and happiness in heaven, but that is simply not true.

"And you do know, Matthew, that I love you as much as anyone could love another person. We have shared many lifetimes together, and, because of that, we both somehow recognized each other in Hiroshima. Not at the start, of course." She smiled and laughed softly.

Matt smiled back. How much he missed her laughter — how much —

"Dear one," Aika continued, "I have written a haiku for this moment. Would you like to hear it?"

Matt was speechless, but cleared his throat and somehow squeaked out a
"Yes."

The words lilted from her:

Clear days and sunshine
Coolness and soft autumn rains
Like us — intertwined

Matt could not keep his eyes off her face. He immersed himself in each and
every word.

Aika then said, "My husband, the moment of your departure is close at hand.
Would you please stand?" With a puzzled look on his face, he rose with her and
they faced each other.

"Hold me, dearest, hold me tightly," she whispered.

They wrapped their arms around each other, their hearts and souls open. As
their bodies pressed together, the boundaries that separated their forms thinned
and grew indistinct. They gradually blended into a single glowing ovoid form,
floating several feet above the ground. Matt was overwhelmed with intimacy and
pure ecstasy.

The oneness of this spiritual joining made their previous sexual connections,
while memorable, seem pale in comparison. He realized that human sexuality was
a vain attempt to mimic this sublime experience.

It doesn't even come close.

While he was completely at one with Aika, at the same time he had his own
thoughts and feelings. They were paradoxically separate and, at the same time,
indistinguishable from each other.

Is this what it is like to merge with the consciousness of God?

Time seemed to stretch to a place that time, in and of itself, did not exist. His
consciousness danced with Aika's. They frolicked across the Universe, touching
far distant stars and discovering planets deep in remote galaxies. They bathed in
foaming water at the base of towering waterfalls. They discovered creatures of
every shape and configuration. They found themselves at one with a love and
intelligence that felt nurturing and accepting.

Without warning their consciousness suddenly separated from their ecstatic
state, and they were once again in each other's arms. Matt memorized the feel of
her body and the scent of her hair.

Some day I will experience this with you again.

Aika smiled, knowing his thoughts, and nodded.

Abraham suddenly reappeared with Rinji. "It is time," Abraham said. He grouped father, mother and child together for a final embrace.

Matt kissed each tenderly then reluctantly released them. "Stay close to me, my darling," he said to Aika.

Tears rolled down both of their faces.

Abraham then stepped behind Matt and waved his right arm in a wide clockwise swath. As he repeated this motion, a shimmering cloudy whirlpool of light materialized, lengthening and stretching across the heavenly meadow. The conical area gradually widened, and at its depth the abdomen of a pregnant woman appeared. The moans of labor reverberated from the depths of the whirlpool.

As Inky, Matt's brothers and sisters, mother and father, Joe, Aika and Rinji gathered close to him, Matt realized this was the last time he would see them, in this form at least, and he felt his heart sink.

The love we share will never die.

This thought, though, was of little comfort.

"I will see all of you again," Matt said as he looked at his loved ones.

They all tearfully nodded in response. The only one who didn't seem to understand was Inky; he was whining forlornly.

"I am ready," Matt finally said.

Matt backed up to the swirling vortex with Abraham standing on his right side and waved goodbye. Aika and Rinji blew kisses. He blew a kiss back to them. He felt himself being gradually being pulled into the whirlpool as his consciousness began to fade. He looked at his arms and legs, and saw them dissolving. "Abraham?" he said.

"Yes, my son."

"Will you always be there for me?"

"I have never left you." As he spoke, he touched Matt between the eyes, and he simultaneously saw not only innumerable past lifetimes, but also the lifetimes of the future. In each he saw Abraham standing by his side.

Matt heard him say, "I have never left you and never will."

He had one more question. "Abraham, do you love me?"

Abraham smiled and slowly said, "Matthew Walker Johnston, just as God loves you with all His Being, so do I. There are those who love you as much, but none more than I." A solitary tear rolled down Abraham's right cheek.

It was the last thing Matt saw.

Book Two

LAMA

TENZIN

TASHI

Elevate your experience and remain wide open like the sky.

Expand your mindfulness and remain pervasive like the earth.

Steady your attention and remain unshakable like a mountain.

Brighten your awareness and remain shining like a flame.

Clear your thoughtfree wakefulness and remain lucid like a crystal.

—Dakpo Tashi Namgyal
from *Clarifying the Natural State*

Chapter 1

June 25, 1991, Drepung Monastery, Tibet

Lama Tenzin Tashi sat in deep meditation in Drepung Monastery. It had been over eight months since the death of Matthew Johnston, and he had made final preparations to begin his quest. He had obtained a backpack and had been able to procure some good walking shoes. It was a long trek to Drak Yerpa, the place he had chosen to begin the most formidable task he had ever attempted: the tracking of an incarnation.

The last remaining detail was for him to obtain permission from the abbot, Lobsang Gyaltso. He expected little resistance from his friend but knew a formal request had to be given. With the close observation of the Chinese, his abbot had to do everything to the letter of the law.

He relaxed and allowed his mind to wander. After all, he had been sitting in contemplation for over six hours, and it was time for a break. He remembered back to his childhood, when he was first taught meditation by Geshe Choden Nyima, a hermit who lived on the mountain overlooking his home village of Batang. Geshe preferred to be called *Gyen la*, Tibetan for teacher.

As a boy, Tenzin's name was Sampa Dhondup. When he took his vows as a monk, his name was changed to Lama Tenzin Tashi. He remembered well one of his first lessons so many years ago.

ༀ་མཿཎི་པདྨེ་ཧཱུྃ ༀ་མཿཎི་པདྨེ་ཧཱུྃ ༀ་མཿཎི་པདྨེ་ཧཱུྃ

"Sampa, you say you want to learn to meditate like me?"

"Yes, Gyen la," said Sampa.

"Very well, then. First, I want you to put a blanket on this rock and sit on it with your back straight. Now put your hands on your knees and watch carefully."

Sampa's teacher sat in the lotus position. Geshe put his hands on top of his interlocked legs and closed his eyes. "Some day I will teach you this pose. For now the sitting position will be fine for you. Go ahead and close your eyes."

Sampa found himself transfixed by the image of his teacher but closed his eyes as instructed.

"Now, young learner, I want you to concentrate on your breath. Feel it as it enters your nose, then into your sinuses and into your lungs. Now when you exhale, feel it leave your lungs the same way it came in. Repeat this cycle over and over again. We will first do this for only a short time. Keep your eyes closed and concentrate."

Sampa couldn't help himself. He opened his eyes to look again at his teacher.

With his eyes still closed, Geshe said, "You must shut your eyes."

Sampa obeyed and began concentrating on feeling his breath go in and out. After a few minutes his mind wandered, and he began thinking about a fight he had with another boy the previous day.

"Sampa," he heard his teacher whisper softly, "your thoughts are not on your breath."

Sampa returned to his breathing, and after only a few seconds, he felt an insect crawl across his leg. He brushed at it.

"Sampa, go back, go back."

Again he refocused on his breathing, only to find his mind drift away again.

"That's enough for now," Geshe said. "Honorable student, what you are experiencing is called monkey mind. This is when your thoughts are playing and chattering as a monkey, wandering in all sorts of directions. This animal inside your head," Geshe chuckled, "needs a little training. So, the next time this happens, and it will, over and over again, smile at the thoughts, do not judge them and return to your breath. This will take some time, but you will find that your monkey mind will gradually be less and less of a problem. Do you understand, little one?" Geshe smiled at his student.

Sampa loved the warmth of his smile. "Yes, Gyen la."

ཨོཾ་མ་ཎི་པདྨེ་ཧཱུྃ་   ཨོཾ་མ་ཎི་པདྨེ་ཧཱུྃ་   ཨོཾ་མ་ཎི་པདྨེ་ཧཱུྃ་

His consciousness returned to Drepung Monastery, and he thought of the novice monks when they first joined the monastic order. When many started meditating they had the idea that one's mind should simply float from thought to thought.

First one must learn to sharply focus the mind.

With the directions that Gyen la had given him over the years, his meditations had gradually become deeper and deeper. As he moved his legs out of the lotus posture he heard a friendly voice call to him.

"Do you have a few moments to speak?"

Looking up, he saw Abbot Lobsang Gyaltso standing over him. "Of course," Tenzin replied. After rising, he bowed deeply to his old friend and followed him to a private sitting area. They sat on rugs facing one another.

Lobsang began, "Tenzin, I have seen that you have requested to go to Drak Yerpa for three months of meditation in the caves, and, of course, I give you my approval."

He continued, "My friend, both you and I know this is one of the holiest areas we have in Tibetan Buddhism. Some of these caves were in use before the time of our Lord Buddha. Even Guru Rinpoche and Atisha have meditated there. As you are aware, the monastery that was in this sacred location was destroyed during the Cultural Revolution. So, I have had a conversation with the abbot at nearby Ganden Monastery, Gen Palden Chung, and he will be happy to not only prepare a cave for you but to assist you while you are there. When do you plan to leave?"

"In the next few days. As you know, it is about thirty-one kilometers, and I plan to walk. It will be a good preparation for my meditations." Tenzin then noticed a subtle look of discomfort on his friend's face. "Venerable abbot, is something troubling you?"

Lobsang said, "Tenzin, I should have known better than to try to hide anything from you. Your years of meditation have been good for your intuition. Very well, then, I want to tell you a story."

Tenzin smiled. He loved stories. Even now.

Lobsang began, "Once there was a monk who had great sympathy for those less fortunate than he. He spent his whole life wondering how he could help. He had great knowledge of the properties of medicinal herbs, and often he was asked to recommend remedies for those who became ill. One day, while he was begging for food in front of his monastery, an aged woman approached him. She said, 'My husband is dying. I want you to help me.'

" 'Ah, so you want me to recommend a treatment for him?'

" 'No,' she said.'

" 'Then what is it that you want?'

" 'Beloved monk, it is past that. He is soon to leave the world, but his suffering is so great. We have tried everything to take away his pain, but nothing works. He is ready to die. You have knowledge of plants and their properties. We want you to give him a potion that will end his life. Please help him.'

"The monk was stunned by her request. 'Surely you know that I, as a Buddhist monk, believe that life is sacred. To end his existence prematurely would be the greatest of crimes.'

"She said, 'Wise monk, you know that my husband has much money. If you do as we ask, then this is yours.' With that, she opened a satchel, revealing an ancient golden statue of Buddha, a family relic that the monk knew was priceless.

"The monk was taken aback. He thought of all those he could help and pondered what he should do. He was caught in an unsolvable conundrum.

"My friend, Tenzin, what course do you think the monk should take? On one hand, he has the opportunity to relieve the pain not only of the suffering man, but also of many others. On the other hand, to do so would break a most sacred vow."

Tenzin looked into the depths of his friend's eyes.

He knows. How is this possible?

"How long have you been aware?" Tenzin asked.

"I knew that very moment of our conversation with the dying man. I believe his name was Matthew Johnston."

"Why have you said nothing?"

"Valued friend," Lobsang said, "I have always respected and had high regard for your opinions, though I might not always agree with them. Now that the die is cast, you must abide with this choice. I will do all I can to support you in your quest. There is no better place to start than Drak Yerpa."

Slowly he stood and walked from the room.

Chapter 2

June 27, 1991, Drepung Monastery

I t was early morning when Tenzin departed Drepung Monastery. The sun had yet to rise, but he could see the light starting to appear over the mountainous horizon. As he gazed at the beams of light in a partially cloudy sky with shades of purple and orange, he was certain that nowhere else had more beautiful sunrises than Tibet. The colored sky drew him forward, and he felt sure he could reach his destination with two days of brisk walking.

Tenzin pulled out a container from his backpack and tasted the salty yak butter tea. It was delicious, as usual. Dorje Dondrub, the cook at Drepung, made the best tea he had ever tasted, and he savored it even more knowing that, for the next three months, there would be another preparer. As he replaced the container in his backpack, he smiled upon his sacred Tibetan singing bowl resting safely there.

The roosters announced the coming of the morning. It was the perfect time of year for a trek, for in July came the monsoon season, making hiking nearly impossible. He felt good about his progress; in an hour or two he should be in the heart of the sacred city of Lhasa — and then on to Drak Yerpa. He had never been there before and was eager to sense the energy that accompanied such a holy place.

He began his journey by doing a walking meditation. First, he began to time his breathing with his steps. With each in-breath, he took four steps, and with each out-breath, he took the same number. Repeating this pattern over and over again, he began to feel a sense of peace along with an increased awareness. Soon

169

he began to put a mantra in time with his breathing and his steps. *Om* was chanted silently with the first in-breath, *mani* with the first out-breath, *padme* with the second in-breath, and *hum* with the second out-breath. This chant had first been taught to him by Geshe Choden Nyima, and its familiarity was comforting to him.

Tenzin picked up his pace. Soon he was in Lhasa and in view of the storied Potala Palace. The sight of the magnificent structure, no matter how many times he had seen it, always took his breath away. The massive thirteen-story white and ochre building was built on the top of Marpo Ri, the Red Hill, and looked more like a fortress than the previous home of the spiritual leaders of Tibet. It was the residence of the 14th Dalai Lama until March 17, 1959, when under immense pressure from the Chinese he fled Lhasa under the cloak of night, disguised as a Tibetan soldier. He then met his family near the Kyichu River, and from there they traveled across the Himalayas to exile in India.

Tenzin sighed deeply. He had some extra time and decided to join those who were circumambulating the Potala in a clockwise manner. They were chanting their mantras, doing prostrations, and a number of older men and women were spinning prayer wheels. Many wore traditional Tibetan garb. Armed Chinese soldiers patrolled the area in riot gear. Tenzin walked on, determined.

The Chinese will never defeat our spirit.

After he finished his circumambulation, Tenzin pulled some *tsampa*, a mixture of roasted barley flour and yak butter tea, from his backpack and ate as he approached the Jokhang Temple. While he was in Lhasa, he again had to see the most sacred Buddhist temple in all of Tibet. He smiled as he approached the Jokhang with its roof of gilded bronze tiles. The two golden deer statues sitting on the roof facing an eight-spoked dharma wheel seemed pleased to see him. Before entering, he bowed three times. As he walked inside, he appreciated the thick smell of yak butter lamps and incense, and gazed at the rows and rows of candles burning in the smoky atmosphere.

Young and old spooned globs of yak butter into the basins holding the candles. The chanting of mantras created a low continuous murmur. It was hard to imagine that during the Cultural Revolution the Chinese had converted part of this cherished temple into a pig sty. He grimaced at the thought, then slowly walked over to prostrate himself before the gilded gold statue of Jowo Shakyamuni, sitting peacefully with his left hand face-up in his lap. He was snapped out of his reverie as he felt a strong hand grab his right arm and swing him around. "Lama Tenzin Tashi!"

Much to his surprise, he was face-to-face with Dawa. He blurted out, "What are you doing here?"

"Wise one, our abbot has instructed me to go with you to Drak Yerpa. He said I needed to spend more time in meditation. He has arranged a cave for me as well."

Tenzin fought back his anger.

One thing I do not need is a young pup of a monk following me around.

As he thought deeply, he understood. The abbot was concerned for his safety.

Very well.

"Dawa, you are young and have much to learn, but I will be glad to have a companion. Are you prepared for the long walk to Drak Yerpa?"

Swinging an Eddie Bauer backpack over his shoulder, Dawa said, "Esteemed lama, you are old and feeble. I am young and strong. You will have a hard time keeping up with me. I will help you, though, if you stumble and fall."

Tenzin smiled at the pun. "Very well, then, young and vigorous one, let us be on our way. By the way, be careful of your attachment to the backpack." With that, the two men left the Jokhang with the lingering odor of yak butter lamps and incense clinging to their ochre robes.

ཨོམ་ཙི་དྲེཧཱུྃ ཨོམ་ཙི་དྲེཧཱུྃ ཨོམ་ཙི་དྲེཧཱུྃ

To Tenzin's delight, much of the time his companion struggled to keep up with him. As the altitude increased, Dawa fell farther and farther behind, gasping for breath as he walked bent over at the waist. Tenzin yelled back over his shoulder, "We are supposed to be at Drak Yerpa tomorrow, not in three days. The abbot of Ganden will wonder what has happened to us. Perhaps he will think a wild animal has attacked and sent us both to the Bardo. Come along, oh young and vigorous monk!"

Dawa could only grunt in response.

It was approaching evening when they reached an acceptable stopping place — high in the mountains. To their right, off the edge of a steep cliff, wound the Kyichu River with its many serpentine branches; above them, numerous Tibetan prayer flags flapped in response to the mountain wind. Tenzin felt great joy at being in the Tibetan countryside. It gave him no small amount of pleasure to be away from the direct oppression of the Chinese.

This is an illusion. The Chinese are everywhere, and they watch everything.

Tenzin located a place to camp, and Dawa set out to find some dried yak dung for a fire. In a short time both were comfortably sitting around a glowing fire, eating *tsampa* and sipping the remnants of their yak butter tea. Even though it was in the middle of summer, at this high altitude the beginnings of a chill could be felt. Both pulled yak wool blankets around themselves. As he stared into the mesmerizing embers, Tenzin reflected back to his childhood.

ཨོཾ་མ་ཎི་པདྨེ་ཧཱུྃ ཨོཾ་མ་ཎི་པདྨེ་ཧཱུྃ ཨོཾ་མ་ཎི་པདྨེ་ཧཱུྃ

"Gyen la, the flames grow larger," said Sampa.

"Yes, little one, the heat feels good, doesn't it? Add some more wood."

"Yes, Gyen la." As he stoked the fire, the sparks flew up and around them.

"Sampa, take a few moments and gaze at the flame." After a short span of time, he asked, "What do you see?"

Sampa looked at the fire closely. He wanted to say something that would impress his teacher. "Gyen la, I see the flame in the middle is a blue color. From there, it turns from orange to yellow."

"Very good, my observant student. Let us look for a while longer." With that, both teacher and student sat quietly, staring at the fire, which was sometimes still, sometimes dancing to and fro in the wind.

Geshe finally spoke. "Just as you have learned about focusing your mind on your breath, the flame can also be a place of concentration. As you look at the fire, you will discover that your thoughts — your monkey mind — move in and out of your awareness. Let them flow past as a river. Now close your eyes and picture the flame in the middle of your head.

"Student, you are doing well. Hold the brightness inside your head for a few more minutes." Soon he spoke again. "Now, open your eyes, little one, and look again at the fire. The flame represents your life and its expression. The wood symbolizes the length of your life. One day," he said as he pulled a small flaming twig from the fire and extinguished it with the tips of his fingers, "your life will end, just as the flame is put out. Part of the twig has disappeared. What do you think has happened to it? Did it die? Is it gone forever?"

"I don't know," Sampa admitted.

Geshe studied his student and softly spoke. "Sampa, what has happened is that part of the twig has merely transformed into light, heat and ash. Nothing dies; it only changes into different expressions. And that is true for everything," he paused, "even for you. Do you understand, little one?"

"Yes, teacher, I do."

"Very well, then," said Geshe. He warmly smiled at his student.

ཨོྃ་མ་ཎི་པདྨེ་ཧཱུྃ   ཨོྃ་མ་ཎི་པདྨེ་ཧཱུྃ   ཨོྃ་མ་ཎི་པདྨེ་ཧཱུྃ

Tenzin stirred from his thoughts and saw Dawa shivering in the cold night air. Tenzin pulled an extra blanket from his pack and wrapped it around his dozing companion. The odor of burning yak dung emanated from the fire. The hypnotic sound of a meandering stream murmured nearby.

ཨོྃ་མ་ཎི་པདྨེ་ཧཱུྃ   ཨོྃ་མ་ཎི་པདྨེ་ཧཱུྃ   ཨོྃ་མ་ཎི་པདྨེ་ཧཱུྃ

Tenzin awoke with a crushing feeling on the right side of his face and thought he must be having a nightmare. Instead when he roused he discovered a steel-toed boot was planted squarely on his right cheek. He felt the bone crack under the pressure, but when he tried to rise and move away, he found his arms were pinned to his sides.

"Monk boys out for a campout?" he heard a harsh voice say in Chinese.

As he finally was able to twist his face free, he saw that Dawa was being savagely pummeled by a group of Chinese soldiers. He only caught a glimpse before he felt a crushing pain in his ribs from a kick to his side.

He screamed and doubled over in agony.

His arms were released, though the beating continued. There was no way to resist. Finally the soldiers tired of their game and abruptly stopped. The monks heard the soldiers clear their throats and felt spittle hit their faces.

Their assailants then turned toward their jeeps, laughing. "Go ahead and pray to Buddha, monk boys. See if he will help you." One flipped a card in their direction. "Here's someone you can pray to. I'm sure he will assist you."

After they drove away, Tenzin did a quick survey on himself, and could not identify one place on his body that was not swollen and tender. He pulled a cloth from his robe and wiped the blood and saliva from his face. He crawled over to Dawa, who was lying on his back. The swelling was such that Tenzin could barely recognize him.

I'm sure I don't look a lot better.

"Dawa? Dawa? Talk to me." Tenzin sat beside his companion. He poured water on his cloth and dabbed the wounds on Dawa's face.

Dawa opened his eyes. "Tenzin, I feel like I've been run over by a truck." Slowly sitting up, he added, "How are you?"

"Other than being beaten to a pulp, I'm fine." Tenzin reflected for a moment. "Dawa?"

"Yes?"

"I saw the beating that you took, and it was one of the worst I have ever seen. But I never heard you express any measure of pain." Tenzin then discovered a loose upper tooth. He cleared his throat and spat out a mouthful of blood. "How did you control your discomfort?"

Dawa said, "When I was a young boy in the orphanage, an old holy man would come to visit. He would tell us stories of ancient saints with miraculous powers. He took a liking to me, and one day after his teaching session, he sent all the others back to their rooms. He said, 'I see that you have experienced much pain in your life. Would you like me to teach you a way to withdraw yourself from your discomfort so you don't feel it so intensely?' Of course, I told him, 'Yes,' and then, over a period of almost a year, he taught me a method to separate my awareness away from any pain I might have, whether physical or emotional.

"So, when I felt the blows of the Chinese I pulled my consciousness deep inside myself. It was like they were hitting someone else. Trust me, I feel everything now."

Tenzin laughed in spite of himself and felt his right cheekbone crack. He looked around in an arc, and finding no restriction of his eye movement, hoped it would eventually heal. He thought about what Dawa had said; it was a technique he would like to learn.

Tenzin then saw the card that the soldiers had thrown. He started to leave it where it was, but curiosity got the better of him, and he reached for it. In the light of the ebbing fire, he could see a picture of Chairman Mao. He crumpled it into a ball and flung it into the embers. As it unfolded in the fire, he watched as Mao's countenance burned into ashes. He glanced over at Dawa, who nodded his approval.

Now the older monk studied the sky. It looked to be around six in the morning. They took a few moments, drank some water from their canteens and threw their backpacks on. It was time to leave this wretched place and move on to sacred ground.

They were ready to go to Drak Yerpa.

Chapter 3

June 28, 1991, en route to Drak Yerpa

he two monks started with a slow pace and accelerated as they felt their stiff joints loosen. Minutes stretched into hours, and they made gradual progress. Neither of them felt like talking, and Tenzin's mind began to drift back into his youth, the unspoiled time before the Chinese invasion of Tibet in October of 1950.

ཨོ་མ་ཎི་པདྨེ་ཧཱུྃ ཨོ་མ་ཎི་པདྨེ་ཧཱུྃ ཨོ་མ་ཎི་པདྨེ་ཧཱུྃ

Sampa Dhondrup had been born in 1940 in Batang, which up until 1934 was on the eastern frontier of Tibet. At that time an armistice with China ceded the area to the Chinese, yet the populace and culture remained Tibetan, and they were essentially left alone by their new rulers. A high, snow capped mountain towered above the many apple and apricot trees that flourished there.

His father, Jampa, and his mother, Dolma Yangzom, were simple peasants; they survived by growing crops of barley and turnips. He had three older brothers, Tenpa, Choephel Tsering and Kalsang Tenpa, and three younger sisters, Tsering Wangmo, Bhumo Dolma and Dolkar Lhamo. Like most Tibetan children their names were given by a high lama. They lived in a two story mud-brick home with a stone foundation.

Of the seven children, it could easily be said that Sampa was the most difficult.

Though he was the youngest boy, he would often prevail in the frequent fights he had with his brothers. But Sampa had an advantage as one of his friend's father had given him boxing lessons, and he had mastered the art of fisticuffs. Besides that, he was lightning quick and could usually land three or four punches before they could get their fists raised. It was only when they grabbed hold of him that they had any chance at all.

As a boy, he was curious about anything and everything. His mother often said, "Sampa, why do you ask so many questions to which there are no answers?" Finally in exasperation, she said, "Sampa, many years ago the abbot of Chöde Gaden Pendeling Monastery left to become a simple hermit. He was a lama at the Monastery, but now he just goes by Geshe Choden Nyima." She pointed to a spot high on the mountain. "They say he is in that place, living in a humble cave. Go to him and ask your questions."

His mother packed him a lunch, and he headed up the mountain to meet this answerer-of-questions. He couldn't wait to meet the one who could satisfy his endless curiosity.

Sampa had heard his friends talk about this hermit before, and many of the stories were not only strange but exceedingly hard to believe. There were rumors he was able to converse with animals and lived on nothing but wild roots and berries. Some had even reported he had been seen in two places at the same time.

Is he a man or a god?

As Sampa ascended the mountain, the tree lined pathway soon became barren and rocky. The aroma of flowers filled the air. After over an hour of hard walking he encountered the entrance to a small cave partially hidden by brush. As he approached, he saw an aged man, wearing only a loincloth, sitting quietly in the lotus position. His eyes were closed, and he seemed to be deep in meditation.

Sampa moved in for a closer look, and the hair on his neck began to stand on end. The ancient one had long white hair pulled back from his face and a matching white beard that hung untrimmed upon his chest.

"Hello, Sampa, I have been expecting you. Why has it taken so long for you to come see me?" the old hermit said as he opened his eyes, startling the young boy who had dared to move so close to him.

"Wise one, how did you know my name, and how did you know I was going to visit you?" said Sampa, regaining his composure.

"Let's just say that when I gave you your name — how long has it been, five years? — I knew then I was going to be your teacher. I told your mother at that time, and I might guess she had something to do with your visit here today. I had expected you to come to see me sooner than this, so we have much to talk about."

Said Sampa, "I'm not sure I need a teacher. I am learning all I need from my mother and father." He folded his arms in defiance.

"Little one, you require a teacher. Your family does not have the means to provide you with a proper education, and you need someone to instruct you on not only the Tibetan alphabet but also other means of broadening your education. Well, what do you think?" the old hermit asked. He seemed to bless the small child with twinkling eyes and a warming smile.

"But you haven't answered any of my questions, and I have many," Sampa protested. "How do I know you are wise enough to be my teacher?"

"Why don't you start by asking me a few, and then you can make your decision?"

Sampa put his forefinger to his mouth and thought a few seconds. "What are all the lights in the night sky?"

"Little one, those are stars, which are actually suns, many like the one above this earth." He pointed at the blazing orb above them. "When they are so far away they look like tiny sparkles. At night when you see many grouped together, that is what is called the Milky Way. Some have planets orbiting around them just like our sun." He waited for Sampa's approval.

"That was a really good answer, " Sampa admitted. "But that wasn't hard. Now are you ready for a tough question?"

The ancient one nodded and smiled.

"Why was I born?" Sampa asked.

"Oh, that's a very difficult question," the old man replied with a chuckle. "Do you really want to know the answer?"

"Yes," said Sampa. He again folded his arms across his chest, trying to look stern.

"You were born because you had desires for things of this world. Tell me, what do you like most?"

"Let's see. I like gathering eggs in the chicken coop. I like the vegetable dumplings my mother fixes. I like playing war with my brothers, and, most of all, I like really scary stories about demons and ghosts."

Geshe shook his head in amusement and then became more serious. "You see, little one, when you have desires for things of the world, you come back to this earth to experience them. Let's suppose that you fell off the cliff going back home and were killed. Because of your wants, you would come back in another body to partake of them. If you have no need for anything, then you have achieved nirvana, which means 'without desire.' Do you understand?"

"Well, I think so," said Sampa. "Does that mean I can't do anything I like?"

"Not at all, young Sampa. Do many things that you like, but don't be attached to them."

"I don't understand."

"Someday, perhaps, you will. But that's enough for now. It is getting late in the day, and I expect that your mother is concerned about you." Then he asked again, "Would you like me to be your teacher?"

"I'll think about it," Sampa said, and he ran down the mountain along the rocky pathway, arms extended from his sides and gliding from side to side, pretending he could fly.

ཨོཾ་མ་ཎི་པདྨེ་ཧཱུྃ་ ཨོཾ་མ་ཎི་པདྨེ་ཧཱུྃ་ ཨོཾ་མ་ཎི་པདྨེ་ཧཱུྃ་

Tenzin pulled his consciousness back to the present and discovered he was on an especially steep incline — gasping for breath. This intensified the pain from his aching wounds. But then —

Where is Dawa?

Tenzin had gone so deep inside his mind he had lost track of the world around him. He stopped and looked back. A small dot far below him was moving at a snail's pace.

Young, indeed!

He removed his backpack from his shoulders and pulled out his canteen and enjoyed a long drink. The sun was a dark red color and drifting low in the sky. He took a closer look at the ascending road and saw a large white *stupa* — a Buddhist monument — with more up the hillside. The prayer flags were so thick they almost obliterated his view of the mountainside. Lines of caves dotted the grounds.

He had arrived at last.

Drak Yerpa.

Chapter 4

July 5, 1991, Drak Yerpa

enzin sat in his meditation cave. It was approaching the end of the day, and he had been in near-constant meditation since he arrived. His routine was simple and predictable. Every morning after he rose he listened with deep awareness to his Tibetan singing bowl. Once a day, usually late in the evening, he was brought a simple meal of *tsampa* along with a container of yak butter tea. He would exchange smiles with his monk provider from Ganden, but conversation was nil — it was a retreat of strict silence.

Once a day he would empty his excrement bucket a discrete distance away from the cave. At the same time he would walk down a steep trail to fill his canteen with cold water, which was bubbling from the rocky mountainside. At night he would sleep for no more than five hours. Other than these occasional distractions, he was in contemplation.

Tenzin had participated in lengthy meditations before, but never one as ambitious as the three months he had just begun. Dawa was situated in a cave not far away, but they would not see or speak with each other for the entire period.

It was hard to believe that already a week had passed. Gen Palden Chung had greeted them on their arrival and was dismayed at their battered appearance. He was not surprised, though; the Chinese military had a habit of harassing the monk populace.

Tenzin was pleased with his cave. Even during the heat of the day, the interior was cool and comfortable. As he looked outside and saw the Yerpa Valley, with its lightly green-tinged hills, he understood why Buddhists for centuries had come to these sacred grounds to seek enlightenment. This was not an area to lightly touch and leave; rather, it was a location in which to obtain the deepest realization. One had to go inside oneself and discover the dark places, the places not only of this lifetime but also of the previous ones. Some imagined the path to enlightenment was a soft, easy experience.

No, it is the hardest of work.

Not only that, he had a daunting task before him, the finding of an incarnation. He had no doubt Matthew Johnston had already experienced rebirth. The trick was finding out where he was — beyond a reasonable doubt.

Tenzin began to ponder the previous quest for the 14th Dalai Lama and the extreme difficulty the monks had in searching him out. When the 13th Dalai Lama had died in 1933 at the age of fifty-seven, while the embalmed body was out for public view, his head had somehow turned from facing south to facing northeast. It was felt that indicated the direction from Lhasa that the reincarnation had taken place.

The Tibetan Regent later had a vision looking into the sacred waters of Lhamo La-tso, the oracle lake. This body of water, south and east of Lhasa, had long been the object of pilgrimages to seek the revelations that appeared in its waters. The Regent saw three different Tibetan letters, *Ah, Ka* and *Ma,* followed by the vision of a three-storied monastery with a gold and turquoise roof. Also, he saw a little home with oddly shaped guttering.

The search committee was thus sent in a northeast direction toward the province Amdo, which they believed the letter *Ah* symbolized. When they arrived at Kumbum they found the monastery there was indeed turquoise-roofed and three-storied, and it was felt that the symbol *Ka* represented the monastery. Once they discovered a house in the village with a roof of gnarled juniper wood, they felt they had found the home of the next Dalai Lama.

The group decided to remain incognito and asked at the home for lodging. Their leader, Kewtsang Rinpoche, represented himself as a servant and closely observed the youngest child in the household. The youngster, Lhamo Thondup, seemed to somehow know the old lama and called him, "Sera lama, Sera lama." Sera happened to be the monastery in Lhasa where the old lama was from.

Several days later they brought forth objects owned by the 13th Dalai Lama and mixed them with others. The young lad picked out each correctly, saying, "It's mine. It's mine." That convinced the committee, and soon he was acknowledged to be the 14th Dalai Lama.

Tenzin worried as he recalled this story. In the search for the Dalai Lama, there were a number of advanced monks involved. For Tenzin's task there was only him. So far he had been in the process of adapting to his environment, and he had not expected to have any major revelations at this early time. He hoped in the near future, though, to begin opening some doors into the mystery of Matthew Johnston's rebirth.

For the moment, he allowed himself to return to the memories of his time with Geshe Choden Nyima. Of course, after their first meeting the obstinate young boy that Tenzin was chose him as his teacher. One thing he recalled was how much he treasured hearing tales from the ancient one.

ཨོམ་ཅི་དྲེཧྱུ ཨོམ་ཅི་དྲེཧྱུ ཨོམ་ཅི་དྲེཧྱུ

"Gyen la, I want to hear a story today!" said Sampa impatiently.

"Again?" the old mentor said. I have told you stories each of the past three days, and we need to spend more time on the Tibetan alphabet. And soon you must also come to know The Forbidden Library, where you will learn English and read many important and interesting books."

"Please," the young boy begged. "I promise I'll study hard if you tell me a story first." While Sampa was intrigued by anything that was forbidden, it was still just a library. "Tell me a story. Please, oh, please."

Geshe smiled his biggest smile. "Very well, but only if you promise." Seeing the boy's excited nod, he proceeded.

"Once there was a very famous lama who lived high in the Tibetan mountains. He carefully remembered his sacred vows about the sacredness of life and vowed to never hurt any sentient —"

"Sentient? What does that mean?"

The old hermit patiently said, "Anything that can sense or perceive. For example, we are able to smell the mountain flowers, so we are sentient beings. Also, even the worm is able to understand the type of soil it is burrowing in, so it is also sentient. The ant is able to tell what kind of food she needs to bring back to the colony, so she is also sentient. Do you understand?"

"Yes, Gyen la, I do."

"Anyway, he promised to never hurt any sentient beings, even the tiny insects that sometimes would find their way into his cave. One day he heard something very small scratching in his waste bucket. After many years of silence, his hearing had become very sharp. He rose from his blanket and peeked inside. Much to his surprise, he saw a beetle floating in the excrement, churning his legs as fast as he could. He was trying to get out, and was scraping his legs against the sides of the bucket. The lama could tell the poor insect was in a panic and also knew he would drown if he did not act soon.

"He quickly looked around, and found a long, thick string. The lama then carefully dipped it into the bucket, putting the end right next to the legs of the frightened insect. In the movement of the bucket, some of the contents splashed on the arms and face of the compassionate lama. Even then, he kept his focus and continued to keep the string close to the beetle.

"Much to his delight, the beetle was able to grab hold of it, and the lama gently lifted him out of the bucket and onto the ground. The insect happily crawled around the dirt floor of the cave. Imagine his delight at not drowning in that awful bucket!"

Sampa silently nodded understanding.

"But the lama was now distracted; he wished in the worst way to wipe the foul-smelling fluid from his face and hands. He rushed around the cave, finally finding a wet rag to wash himself. He felt very satisfied and maybe a little smug — he had saved the life of the beetle.

"Next he began to look around the cave for the bug and much to his dismay, discovered he had squashed the helpless insect when he was looking for a cloth to clean himself!

"So, my young charge, what do you think the lesson of this story is?"

Sampa shrugged his shoulders. "You are the teacher, Gyen la. You tell me."

"Ah, young Sampa, indeed I am the teacher. But the best teacher encourages his students to think. What is your guess?"

"That you should pay attention if you rescue a beetle and not step on him?" said Sampa seriously.

Geshe laughed. "That's certainly true. But if we focus our attention on this situation, we see that deep in the heart of the lama, he wished to help the little beetle. But, he unfortunately killed it. For me, the lesson I learned is what is most important is the intent behind the effort. The outcome is not as significant."

"So, what you're saying is that you should try your hardest in everything you do, and if it doesn't turn out the way you wanted it to, then it's not for you to worry. Right?"

"Young one, I think you've got it. Very good!" he said as he patted Sampa on the head. "Now let's get back to the Tibetan alphabet."

Sampa whined, "Do we have to?"

"Yes, little one."

ཨོ་མ་ཎི་པདྨེ་ཧཱུྃ ཨོ་མ་ཎི་པདྨེ་ཧཱུྃ ཨོ་མ་ཎི་པདྨེ་ཧཱུྃ

Tenzin smiled as he remembered his teacher's praise. Now it was time to get back to work. Reassuming the lotus position, he straightened his back and concentrated on his breath.

Focus — Focus — Focus —

Chapter 5

July 25, 1991, Drak Yerpa

A sweating and miserably uncomfortable Lama Tenzin Tashi roused himself from his meditation. It was almost midnight, and normally it would be time to prepare to sleep.

That day's meditation had been unusually deep. The silence had enveloped him as if he were covered with many layers of yak skin blankets. In the past few hours, though, he had perceived an area of uncomfortable darkness. He must enter there; for him to discern the current incarnation of Matthew Johnston, he had to be the cleanest vessel possible.

Was now the time? This murky area had to be penetrated before he could go any farther.

Of course, it was.

He re-entered the still of his mind, and he was surprised to see himself as a little boy playing with his oldest brother.

ཨོཾ་ཆི་པ་རྗེ་རྒུ ཨོཾ་ཆི་པ་རྗེ་རྒུ ཨོཾ་ཆི་པ་རྗེ་རྒུ

"Hey, Sampa, look over here!" yelled Tenpa.

He ran through the rocky field and found his brother with his hands cupped around something. "Do you really have something, or are you just playing with me?" he said.

184

"You won't believe how big this is," Tenpa replied.

Sampa looked through the cracks in his brother's fingers and saw a monstrously large grasshopper trapped against the ground. "That's the biggest one I have ever seen!" he yelled. "What are you going to do with it?"

Tenpa said, "I've got an idea, but we have to make sure he doesn't get away. Help me pull his legs off."

Somehow Sampa didn't think that Gyen la would approve.

But, after all, it's only an insect.

"Pinch him with your fingers and turn him over," Sampa said.

Tenpa did as his brother asked, and Sampa grabbed each of the front legs and pulled them off with a jerk. The insect flailed wildly, but all to no avail. Despite the sharp stab of his conscience, he proceeded to yank each of the four back legs from the body.

Tenpa said, "Now the fun begins. Watch this." Holding the grasshopper pinched between his fingers, he walked over to an ant bed, Sampa close behind. He then placed the insect over the ant hole, and the ants swarmed over their prey. In a few moments the insect was motionless, and the ants began to move it down the hole.

Tenpa laughed and said, "Let's find another one." He ran away into the fields, jumping at the profuse array of grasshoppers that deftly sprang away from his grasp.

ཨོམ་ཚི་འརྗེ་ཧཱུྃ ཨོམ་ཚི་འརྗེ་ཧཱུྃ ཨོམ་ཚི་འརྗེ་ཧཱུྃ

Tenzin recoiled from this childhood scene. Suddenly, in his mind's eye, he became a carefree grasshopper, enjoying the most beautiful sunny day. He had just found a luscious leaf to chew on when a pair of rough hands surrounded him. He was enveloped by fear. As he was rolled to his back, he thought:

What is happening to me?

Soon he felt the agonizing pain of first his front legs being pulled from his body followed by the back ones. Green ooze appeared at each of the stubs. He then found himself surrounded by ants, angry that he had blocked the entryway to their hill. Tenzin felt sting after sting over his body. As the ants ushered him down the hole, he gasped for air under their crush. Finally his consciousness faded, and he found himself as Sampa, face-to-face with Geshe.

ཨོམ་ཚི་འརྗེ་ཧཱུྃ ཨོམ་ཚི་འརྗེ་ཧཱུྃ ཨོམ་ཚི་འརྗེ་ཧཱུྃ

"Gyen la, I must tell you what I have done today," he said. "I am feeling sad." As he looked at his teacher, he saw Geshe's eyes were filled with tears.

"There is no need, young one. I am aware of what has happened. Have you learned anything from your experience?" he asked.

"Yes," he admitted.

"And what is that?"

"You must not harm anything . . . not even insects," he said.

Geshe wiped the tears from his face. "Yes, Sampa, that is correct. One of the main lessons our Buddha taught us is that all beings inevitably endure suffering. Anything we can do to decrease suffering is good. Let me ask you this: Will you ever again knowingly injure another living thing?"

"Never, Gyen la, never."

"Well, then," the old hermit said, "I suspect the grasshopper is glad to give up his life to teach you this most valuable lesson. His karma is indeed good." He smiled and hugged his student.

ཨོཾ་མ་ཎི་པདྨེ་ཧཱུྃ ཨོཾ་མ་ཎི་པདྨེ་ཧཱུྃ ཨོཾ་མ་ཎི་པདྨེ་ཧཱུྃ

Tenzin wiped the sweat from his forehead and consciously slowed his breathing. He was glad to access the memory and release it.

Even though he was well trained in controlling his emotions, he found himself starting to worry more and more. Despite a month of deep probing, he had made little progress in reaching his goal. Certainly he had a small breakthrough tonight, but the tracking of the incarnation seemed farther away than ever.

He kept a small picture of Matthew Johnston with him as a meditation aid. He looked at the photograph at least once a day, hoping it would steer him in the right direction. Every time he felt he was making progress, though, he would run straight into a thick, lavender curtain. He attempted to pierce it, find an opening or simply shove it aside. He tried to go over, under and around this obstruction with no success.

He had sat at the curtain time and time again, chanting sacred words and phrases, such as *om mani padme hum, shanti* — Sanskrit for "peace" — and finally in frustration, remembering his reading of *The Arabian Nights* from The Forbidden Library, he said crisply, "Open Sesame!"

He had tried everything. Nothing, nothing seemed to penetrate this veil. He had two months to go, and there was still plenty of time. But he began to have doubts.

September 26, 1991, Drak Yerpa

Panic was the only way to describe how Lama Tenzin Tashi felt. He had done his best over the past three months to gain information concerning the incarnation of Matthew Johnston. He had attempted every technique he had learned over his many years as a monastic and tried them repeatedly. Still the lavender curtain refused to budge. There was nowhere left to turn.

He looked at the sun; it was around three o'clock in the afternoon, and normally he would not take a break until his sparse dinner was served later. He was beginning to realize that perhaps he had been too intense and maybe it was time to simply relax. He unfolded his legs and decided to sit and mindfully watch the gathering clouds. He heard the gentle patter of raindrops. In Tibet, most of the precipitation occurs during the monsoon season, which lasts through September. This would be one of the last rains of the ongoing cycle.

As he watched, copious dark clouds gathered in the sky, and rolling thunder echoed across the valley. At his high vantage point he watched lightning split the sky, silver streaks that beckoned sheets of driving rain. Water poured across the mouth of his cave, and he felt at peace.

After about an hour of a torrential downpour, the rain slowed to a drizzle, and the sun began to peek through the thinning clouds. He spotted a sparkling pool of water outside the cave entrance, and light began to reflect from it. Rainbows of colors danced from the pool, and as Tenzin looked up into the sky he saw that a beautiful double rainbow decorated the high mountain landscape. He gazed in rapt attention. Rainbows in Tibetan Buddhism were an auspicious symbol.

Suddenly he was startled by the flapping of large wings. A dark shadow crossed his face, and before him, drinking from the pool of water, stood a mammoth white eagle. This majestic bird gradually stood fully erect, spread its wings to their full ten foot span and screeched loudly. Its steely eyes met with Tenzin's, and the two held each other's gaze. He felt a powerful, visceral energy emanating from the bird, and all at once, through the eyes of the eagle, he saw Green Tara, a female bodhisattva, smiling benevolently at him.

Abruptly the bird leapt from its place in front of the cave and flew into the starkly blue Tibetan sky. Tenzin followed its flight as it disappeared into the rainbow. He closed his eyes and floated deep into his mind, soaring just as the eagle did. He went around the clutter of sensory phenomenon and the past, present and future images of his mind. Before long he was again face-to-face with the lavender curtain. This time he tried no magical words, no magical phrases. He simply sat and dispassionately observed.

The curtain slowly began to rise.

At first, an amorphous, blurry blue figure began to appear; it gradually sharpened into the image of a stunningly beautiful lake. A snow-capped mountain rose above it. He looked closely. He had never been to this location before, but he had seen pictures of it. It was one of the four sacred lakes of Tibet: Yamdrok-tso. The key to finding the next incarnation of Matthew Johnston had been given to him. It was there he would find his answers.

He held the image as long as he could, and it finally faded. He smiled as he realized that he had been trying far too hard. His own desire for success had obstructed the vision. He would stay here for the next few days and enjoy his meditations. Next summer, when the days began to lengthen and the Tibetan air began to warm again, he would venture to the holy lake.

Chapter 6

June 16, 1992, en route to Yamdrok-tso

Lama Tenzin Tashi, along with Dawa Jigme, bounced up and down in the back of a Chinese built pick-up truck headed for Nangartse, a small village located on the west side of Yamdrok-tso. It was early in the afternoon, and the warm wind whistled past their heads. They hunkered down, realizing that it was more than a four hour drive to their destination.

While Tenzin would have been glad to have walked, his abbot remembered his last encounter with the Chinese troops and insisted upon the transportation. He again dispatched Dawa to be his companion. Granted, two monks against a cadre of Chinese military was not an even match, but it was certainly safer than traveling alone.

Earlier that same day, Tenzin had changed out of his robes into the garb of a Tibetan commoner and entered the Bank of China in Lhasa. As he opened the safety deposit box, he peered inside and saw a large, tightly sealed plastic bag. It appeared to be waterproof.

Perfect.

He removed it, placed it in a burlap sack and cinched the drawstring tight. He carefully placed it in his backpack and headed out the door toward Drepung. When he was certain he was not being followed he ducked into a dark, secluded alleyway and changed back into his monastic robes. He arrived in plenty of time to catch the truck that had been arranged for their travel. He remembered his conversation with Lobsang Gyaltso the previous evening.

ཨོཾ་མ་ཎི་པདྨེ་ཧཱུྃ ཨོཾ་མ་ཎི་པདྨེ་ཧཱུྃ ཨོཾ་མ་ཎི་པདྨེ་ཧཱུྃ

"Tenzin," Lobsang said, "everything is as you wish it to be. Your transportation has been arranged and all the preparations are complete. I have one final question for you."

"Yes?"

"I know you have said you wish to go to Yamdrok-tso. I do not want to question your decision, but is there any other place that would satisfy your needs? As you know, here in Tibet we have four sacred lakes, the others being Lhamo La-tso, Nam-tso and Manasarovar. All have the quality of inspiration, and I can easily make arrangements for you to go to any of the other holy lakes for as long as you would like."

Tenzin studied his friend carefully. Lobsang was not one to say something like that unless there was a reason. He whispered in his ear, "What is on your mind, my abbot? Is there something else I should know?"

Lobsang hesitated, looked around, then whispered back, "The walls have ears. Let us go outside."

When they reached an open courtyard, they sat down on the hardened earth. Lobsang quietly spoke. "Tenzin, I'm sure you are aware the Chinese watch us closer and closer as each day passes, so we must be careful. What I tell you now must be kept in the strictest confidence."

Seeing Tenzin's nod, he continued, "The abbot of the small monastery at Nangartse has recently been replaced. This new abbot, Penba Wangyal, is Tibetan and has completed his monastic vows, but there are those who believe he has been subverted to the will of the Chinese. It is not at all unusual for other monks to wish to travel and spend time at this holy lake, so I don't believe he is suspicious of you. But beware, my friend, watch what you do. Any misstep will be recorded, and I don't believe he would hesitate at all to turn you in for questioning. And you know what happens in Chinese interrogations."

Tenzin felt a lump in his throat as he recalled the stories of the torture teams who came to Lhasa in 1987 after the unrest that September. Monks were bound with metal cuffs, stripped of their clothes and beaten with bludgeons that had nails driven through the ends. Their testicles were crushed by policemen who stood on them. Cattle prods were used not only on the monks but also used to instrumentally rape the nuns. Attack dogs were unleashed, ripping into prisoner's legs and genitals, male and female alike. After the demonstrations outside the Jokhang Temple in October of 1988, it was reported that many who were arrested were not only severely beaten but also forced to rebuke the Dalai Lama and Tibetan independence.

Tenzin felt venom toward the Chinese begin to rise into his consciousness. He breathed into it and thought to himself:

It is not the Chinese people — it is their government.

Tenzin said, "What do you recommend?"

"Do not do anything suspicious, and do as the other monks do. I suspect if you don't make yourself obvious, there will be no trouble."

Tenzin grasped the shoulder of his friend in appreciation.

ཨོཾ་མ་ཎི་པདྨེ་ཧཱུྃ་ ཨོཾ་མ་ཎི་པདྨེ་ཧཱུྃ་ ཨོཾ་མ་ཎི་པདྨེ་ཧཱུྃ་

As they drove out of Lhasa, Tenzin saw rock walls along the roadway with white ladders painted on them, indicating the pathway upward to enlightenment. Cattle, yaks and goats lined the fences adjacent to the highway. He sadly saw the construction of typical Chinese buildings and many young Tibetan students, dressed in turquoise and white uniforms of Chinese design, walking on their way to school.

They want to remake us in their image. Can they not forget that we are not Chinese and never will be? How can the sun become the moon? How can fire become water?

Old men and women were sweeping the road with long brooms. He lost track of all the trucks, which were loaded with freshly cut trees, coming from the opposite direction.

They will stop stripping our natural resources only when they are completely depleted.

As they left town, the brown Kyichu River wound to their left, and Tenzin smiled as he watched a yak skin boat being paddled along the river bank.

Soon the truck left the paved road and started up a river valley. The terraces of vegetable crops wound upward along the road as it rose in elevation. He looked over at Dawa, who was idly whittling on a stick of wood. Tenzin tucked his backpack in the corner of the truck bed and leaned against it. Within moments he nodded off, and his dreams took him back to Batang.

ཨོཾ་མ་ཎི་པདྨེ་ཧཱུྃ་ ཨོཾ་མ་ཎི་པདྨེ་ཧཱུྃ་ ཨོཾ་མ་ཎི་པདྨེ་ཧཱུྃ་

Sampa Dhondrup was most excited; he at last had a full day with his teacher. It was early in March, the chill of winter was finally beginning to lessen. Days with Gyen la were precious to him, and as soon as he could complete his household chores he would say goodbye to his family and head up the mountain to the old hermit's cave. His mother always knowingly smiled when he left.

It was hard to conceive that he had been seeing the aged one for around five years, and already he was ten years old. During that period, never had Geshe repeated a lesson. That is, except for the Tibetan alphabet.

Of course, as promised, in due time he had been introduced to The Forbidden Library, which was safely hidden away at the Chöde Gaden Pendeling Monastery. It seemed his teacher had gathered a collection of books for him and for him alone — and all in English. Geshe had also arranged for one of the younger monks, Gen Tsesum, to give him English lessons. Sampa loved reading, and as his English improved, he ravenously plowed through them. Just when he thought he was about to read them all, more would mysteriously appear.

One day he asked the aged one, "Why do I have to learn English?"

"You don't have to learn anything, but I highly recommend it."

"Why?"

"Let's just say that it will be of great benefit to you in the future."

"How do you know?"

"I just do." Geshe smiled. "Some things, little one, you just have to accept. I promise, someday you will understand."

As much as he loved the library, his favorite moments were with Gyen la. Over time, though, Sampa became concerned about his teacher, as his aging seemed to be accelerating. His mind, though, stayed as sharp as ever. While his physical body deteriorated, the joy in his eyes practically jumped out and kissed you on the face.

Sampa brought his mind back to the present — he was almost to the cave. As he arrived at the entrance, he found his teacher sitting solemnly in meditation. He had learned not to disturb Geshe under such circumstances and sat down quietly at his feet. Before long the old man roused and spoke.

"Little one, I see a dark storm gathering in the east, and it approaches soon. When it arrives the fabric of our society will be wrenched away from us. The ancient teachings will be destroyed, and there will be much pain." He opened his wizened eyes and looked across at his student. "The time is coming soon when I will not be here. We must hurry — you still have much to learn."

Sampa felt his eyes fill with tears. He never thought there would be a moment when he and his teacher would not be together. "Gyen la, I want you to stay here with me. We are strong, and we can fight the evil storm."

Geshe was touched by his sincerity. "Yes, together we are very strong, but not enough to resist what is about to happen. Listen well: Even though we may not be face-to-face on this earth, we will always be together. Do you understand?"

Sampa wasn't sure, but he nodded yes anyway.

"Now," the old hermit said, "enough of this talk. We have a full day of lessons. First, I am going to tell you a story."

"Yeah!" Sampa clapped.

"Once upon a time," the old man said, "there was a boy named Sampa, and he lived happily in the village of Batang with his parents, three older brothers and three younger sisters."

Sampa smiled. He enjoyed hearing stories in which he was the main character.

"One day when he was walking in the woods by his home, a beautiful white stallion magically appeared. Sampa snuck up on the horse and was able to put a rope around his neck. When he arrived at home with the horse in tow, his family was very excited, and his father exclaimed, 'How good this is! We will put him in the barn along with our two yaks.' His mother proudly kissed him, and his brothers and sisters all asked if they could have rides on Sampa's new horse.

"After the stallion had been there for about a week, Sampa decided to take him out and show him off to the neighbors. The animal was prancing over the hill with Sampa on his back, when without warning a snow leopard pounced from the bushes and jumped onto the horse. The beautiful animal was killed, and Sampa broke his leg in the fall. Not only that, he was badly mauled before the leopard ran away.

"His mother, who was a gifted seamstress, sewed up his many wounds, while his father cut thick strips of yak leather and splinted his leg.

"His brothers and sisters said, 'How bad this is! If only Sampa had not found the horse, he would not be in this condition.'"

Sampa grimaced at the idea of being so horribly injured.

Geshe saw the look on his face and playfully tousled his hair. "The next day men from the army came to their home, looking for young boys to carry water for them. Sampa's brothers happened to be far away, working in their neighbor's fields. When they saw how badly injured Sampa was, they left him to find others.

"His mother said, 'How good it is that you found the horse and were injured. Otherwise, you would have had to go away from home to be in the army!'"

Sampa smiled at the obvious irony.

"Now, young one, the tale could go on and on, but we will stop here. What do you think that this story is trying to say?"

Sampa pondered for a few moments. "I think that sometimes it's hard to tell the difference between what is good and what is bad."

The old hermit smiled. "Very good, student of mine. That is an excellent answer. One might even say that sometimes the lines between good and bad are blurry, and perhaps there is a place where there is no real difference between the two. It all depends upon one's interpretation."

With a look of satisfaction, the old man added, "Sampa, let us go over again your Tibetan alphabet."

A look of disgust appeared on the boy's face.

"Then we will take some quiet time to build a fire and gaze at the glowing embers. I have some hearty vegetable stew and bread to share with you. And if you have done well on your lessons, I just MIGHT tell you a story about the monstrous ghost of the Potala. Are we agreed?"

Sampa clapped his hands in joy, somehow forgetting the ominous warning he had been given earlier. "Oh, yes, Gyen la!"

ཨོཾ་མ་ཎི་པདྨེ་ཧཱུྃ ཨོཾ་མ་ཎི་པདྨེ་ཧཱུྃ ཨོཾ་མ་ཎི་པདྨེ་ཧཱུྃ

Tenzin was woken by the many jarring bumps their four-wheel drive vehicle was making. Looking at the surrounding terrain, he guessed that they should arrive in a few more hours.

He hoped he would have unobstructed times for lengthy periods of meditation and that the sacred waters would reveal the hidden secrets he needed to discover. He couldn't help but wonder if Penba Wangyal would create any difficulties. Thanks to the warnings of his abbot and friend, though, he would proceed carefully.

The clues to the reincarnation of Matthew Johnston would not let themselves be known easily. They would resist and fight, just as a bear defends it den. But there was no doubt that, if they were to be uncovered, Yamdrok-tso was the right location to do so. Once he had secured the necessary information, he had a plan for the gemstones. But he had to be certain first. There could be no guessing.

Too much is at stake.

Chapter 7

June 17, 1992, Yamdrok-tso

The remainder of their journey was even more jolting. The condition of the road was atrocious, and the terrified monks clung to their seats as the truck, time after time, nearly caromed over the precipice of the narrow road. As they rounded the top, though, they were stunned by the majestic panorama.

Yamdrok-tso.

The varying shades of turquoise water took their breath away. As they headed to Nangartse, they were unable to take their eyes off the hypnotic lake that stretched to their left. Looming above the lake stood the magnificent white-capped mountain, Nojin Kangtsang.

Just as I saw in my vision.

Upon arrival, they were greeted warmly by the monks of the monastery, and even by the abbot, Penba Wangyal. However, his appearance was strangely unnerving. He looked to be around fifty years old, was tall and unusually muscular, and there was something intimidating about him. Not only that, his face was pinched as though he might be chronically in pain. Shortly after their arrival, the abbot asked them into his office.

"Welcome to Nangartse and our humble monastery, " he said. "I understand you are here for three months of meditation by our sacred lake?"

Both nodded, and Tenzin began to wonder where this conversation was leading to.

"Many come here to experience the serenity that only this place can bring, and I welcome you. I would like to think you are here for strictly spiritual reasons. Other sorts of adventures will not be tolerated. Do you understand?"

Tenzin felt sweat beading on his forehead.

Does he know?

Tenzin said, "I'm not sure what you mean."

The abbot looked sternly at the both of them. "As I'm sure you are both aware, our Chinese brothers are planning to drain water from the lake to produce electricity. This will be Tibet's largest hydroelectric plant. The 10th Panchen Lama voiced opposition to its construction, and you know what happened to him."

Of course I know. He mysteriously died after giving a speech critical of the Chinese.

"Let me make myself perfectly clear: If you are here to assist the resistance movement, you will be crushed." With that, he slammed his fist on the table with a loud crack. "Such behavior will not be tolerated. Do you understand me?"

Tenzin was taken aback. He had never known any Tibetan monastic to behave in such a way.

He has betrayed his own people.

"Yes," Tenzin heard Dawa meekly say.

The abbot nodded his head in recognition.

"What about you?" he grumbled, looking questioningly at Tenzin.

"I understand completely," Tenzin said deliberately, his tone thick with hidden meaning.

"Well, now," the abbot said with an evil smile that looked like it could split his face apart, "we are in complete agreement. Enjoy your meditations." With that, he dismissed them from the room.

The next morning Tenzin and Dawa joined the small group of monks for their morning meditation. Afterward, they went their separate ways. Since meeting with the abbot, Tenzin decided it was time to hide the gemstones.

Carrying his pack with him, he walked several kilometers away from the monastery on the west side of the lake. When he was sure he wasn't being followed, he found a pile of rocks which he was certain he could identify again. He pulled a small spade from his pack and dug a hole in the stony soil. He reached inside and pulled out the bag of gemstones. He started to place it into the hole — then paused.

Now is a good time to see this treasure.

He looked around one more time — surveying the landscape. Seeing no activity, he carefully unknotted the drawstring of the burlap bag and pulled it open. In a second he had the inner protective plastic bag undone. He looked inside and saw the gemstones were all individually wrapped in folded white paper. Tenzin saw a smaller sealed plastic sack at the bottom, also filled with wrapped stones. This would be his portion once the incarnation was found.

He felt his breath quicken as he unwrapped a handful. He gasped as the clouds overhead passed by and the bright Tibetan sun shone down. Just the few that he had opened burst into color and sparkled intensely. A feeling of lust and desire swept over him. He fell to his knees.

Tenzin carefully moved his fingers through the glimmering stones. He heard them clicking against each other. It was as if the stones were talking to him.

Keep us — Keep us — Keep us —

Why couldn't I? Think of how many more people I could help.

Maybe one or two, just for me?

He broke out into a cold sweat. He shook his head.

No. No. No!

Tenzin quickly rewrapped the stones, replaced them in the sack, sealed it and pulled the drawstring tight. He put the bag into the hole, covered it with dirt and pulled a heavy stone on top of it, mentally and emotionally exhausted. He was reminded of when he read *The Lord of the Rings* some years ago, when the miserable creature Gollum became mesmerized by the all powerful ring, which had been forged by the evil Sauron at Mount Doom.

My precious . . . My precious . . .

He quickly rose and vacated the area. The sooner he got away from there, the better.

ཨོམ་ཚི་དྲེ་ཧཱུྃ་ ཨོམ་ཚི་དྲེ་ཧཱུྃ་ ཨོམ་ཚི་དྲེ་ཧཱུྃ་

Tenzin returned from evening meditation late the same day and discovered his small room had been searched. His backpack was in complete disarray, and he was relieved he had emptied it of the gemstones. Also, he couldn't escape the feeling that he was now being watched.

I've got to get away from here.

After some thought he decided the best way to accomplish that would be to perform a ritual circumambulation of Yamdrok-tso. This devotion, called a *kora*, would allow him to focus on the task at hand.

It would take about seven days and would not be refused by the abbot. He knew he had to do it alone. Dawa would be disappointed, but there was no other choice. As he drifted off to sleep, his mind again wandered to Gyen la.

ཨོམ་ཚི་པྲེཏྠུ ཨོམ་ཚི་པྲེཏྠུ ཨོམ་ཚི་པྲེཏྠུ

Sampa practically ran up the mountain to see his teacher. Several days before, he had been promised "something special" for the next lesson, and he couldn't wait to find out what that was. He was also worried about the previous warning he had received from Gyen la. He so hoped the time of their parting would be far, far away. When he arrived he was gasping for breath and found Gyen la sitting peaceably on his meditation blanket. He had a sad smile on his face, and there was a metal bowl sitting on his lap.

"Welcome, honored student," said the old man.

Sampa bowed deeply to his teacher.

"Sit in front of me," Geshe said as he gestured to a blanket. As Sampa sat, he added, "I know you must be most curious about what this is on my lap. It is a Tibetan singing bowl and was given to me by my monk teacher when I was your age. Now I will play it for you. Close your eyes."

Sampa shut his eyes for a moment, then peeked through his partially closed eyelids. He saw Geshe pick it up, place it on the palm of his right hand and rotate a wooden dowel on the outside edge of the bowl; it produced a high pitched tone, which became louder with each circling of the dowel.

"Sampa," Geshe said, "you must close your eyes." Realizing he had once again been caught, he squeezed his eyes shut. "Now, Sampa, pay attention to the sound. Listen closely."

Sampa initially felt the vibration of the bowl all around him, but as it started to fade, it seemed to enter his forehead. Gradually it became inaudible.

"Go ahead and open your eyes," the old hermit said. "Where did you feel the sound?"

"Gyen la," said Sampa, "I felt it enter my forehead just above my eyes."

Geshe beamed. "Well done, student. Now close your eyes again."

As Sampa did, he felt his teacher touch his forehead. Suddenly he felt his consciousness explode to the ends of the universe, though, just as quickly his vision contracted back into a little boy sitting in front of an old man on blankets in front of a cave. But instead of seeing just physical forms, he saw a radiant, pulsating light individually surrounding each of them with a column of brightly colored spinning areas, up and down the length of their spines. He was able to somehow see the sitting pair, though his eyes were closed. It was then he heard their voices, but neither of them moved their lips.

"My student, what you are seeing is your spiritual body, and the different chakras up and down your spine. The glowing light around you is what is called your aura. Look at it carefully."

"Teacher?" Sampa asked.

"Yes."

"The light around you is bright and clear, and the light around me has a whole bunch of black spots. Why is that?" said Sampa.

"Little one, the dark parts of your aura are there to simply show you the work you have to do while you live in your body. Your job is to make them bright and shiny."

"Why don't you have any black spots?" said Sampa, starting to get worried.

Geshe said, "Sampa, there is no cause for concern. I have simply had more lifetimes and more opportunities. Some day your aura will be at least as clear as mine."

"Oh," said Sampa, feeling a little better.

"Look at the spinning areas up and down your spine. Tell me the colors from the bottom to the top."

"Let me see, red at the bottom, then orange, yellow, green, blue, and, let's see . . . the top two are like two different kinds of purple."

"Exactly right," said Geshe. "The one at the forehead is actually indigo, and the other at the top of the head is violet. These seven so-called chakras are the energy centers of the body. Now watch what happens when I play the singing bowl."

As Sampa observed, the tone appeared as a golden luminous light, which emanated from the bowl to his forehead. From there, it entered his spine and traveled to the green chakra which was overlying his heart. The slightly dull green light in that area became brighter, more radiant, and the spinning also increased.

His teacher again spoke. "Tibetan singing bowls originated in our country thousands of years ago. They were originally constructed for healing purposes, but with time the deepest use of these instruments was forgotten, and they were used simply to enhance meditation. If the bowl is constructed properly, when it is intoned it will sense where your weakness is and provide healing to that area. Today your heart chakra, the green one, needed some care.

"Do you have questions, little one?"

An entranced Sampa merely shook his head.

The old hermit again touched him on the head, and Sampa once again found himself back in his body, sitting cross-legged in front of his teacher.

"Would you like some yak butter tea?" Geshe asked after a few moments had passed.

"Yes, please," Sampa replied, but he could say no more; he was still in awe of what he had experienced. They sipped their tea and sat in front of the cave in silence.

Finally Geshe spoke. "My student, it is time to talk about what is about to be. Remember long ago when I talked to you about dying, and how we, as the twig does when it burns, do not die, but simply change forms?"

"Yes, Gyen la."

"Tomorrow, little one, it is time for me to change forms. The cycle of my life is complete, and I move into the next chapter of my existence. The storm I spoke to you about is almost upon us, and I am not to be here when it arrives."

Sampa felt tears drip down his face.

"Now we have some business to finish." Geshe smiled at his student. "Sampa, I believe that for some time you have known that you are to be a monk this lifetime. Is that correct?"

Sampa nodded.

"I have talked with your mother, and she has agreed — if it is your wish — to take you to the Chöde Gaden Pendeling Monastery in the coming week. There you will continue your life's work."

Sampa heard a slight choking of the hermit's voice and saw his eyes mist over.

Geshe cleared his throat and continued, "The abbot there, Sangye Phuntsog, is an old friend of mine. He says he will be glad to continue your training, as he has heard good reports from not only your English teacher, Gen Tsesum, but also from me.

"Sampa, you are an excellent student." He winked at his pupil. "That is, of course, except when you decide to peek when you are supposed to close your eyes."

They both forced a laugh.

Then the old hermit became serious again. "Sampa, there is something else that you need to know.

"I'm afraid there is something I have not told you. My student, you are the reincarnation of a wise and venerated lama who died shortly before your birth."

Sampa raised his eyebrows in disbelief.

"So, little one, you will be taken into the monastery as a lama. I have talked with your mother and father about this, and they are most proud. They have arranged to make a feast offering, and the day after you enter, a banquet will be held on your behalf."

"But Gyen la . . ."

Geshe sternly interrupted, saying, "Sampa, you must know that with such an honored background you will have greater tests and responsibilities than many of your fellow monks. You have prepared well over these years, though, and I have no doubt that you are ready."

He smiled again deeply and lovingly. "Now, Sampa, it is time for you to go, as I have many preparations to make. When you leave here, go to the monastery and ask for the abbot. If the monks refuse to grant your request, mention my name, and you will be brought to him. Simply tell him that I will be making my transition and ask him to come with you tomorrow morning to my cave."

Sampa openly sobbed, "Gyen la, I can't bear the thought of being without you. Please say that you won't leave."

Geshe extended his arms and hugged the weeping boy. "Remember what I have told you. We will always be together, even though you may not be able to see me. I am tired and am ready for a much needed rest.

"Farewell, Sampa, may your life be blessed."

Sampa slowly pulled away, "Goodbye, Gyen la." After he walked a few steps down the mountain path, he turned back for a final glimpse and saw his beloved teacher with eyes closed, tears streaming down his face.

Sampa turned away for the final time. There were no more looks back. He sprinted down the mountain and headed for the monastery.

ཨོཾ་མ་ཎི་པདྨེ་ཧཱུྃ་ ཨོཾ་མ་ཎི་པདྨེ་ཧཱུྃ་ ཨོཾ་མ་ཎི་པདྨེ་ཧཱུྃ་

The following day Sampa led Sangye Phuntsog and several monks up the hill to the Geshe's cave. As they slowly approached, Sampa discovered his teacher was exactly as he had left him. His head was slumped forward, and on his face was a beatific smile. There was a faint glow at the top of his head.

"Gyen la?" Sampa said, hoping for a response, but not expecting one. In his lap still sat the bronze colored Tibetan singing bowl.

The abbot slowly walked over to Geshe and stood for a few moments in front of him. Then he lifted the singing bowl from his lap, turned and walked over to Sampa.

"He wanted you to have this," he said as he handed it to him. Sampa clutched it to his chest, as if the bowl were Gyen la himself.

No, we will never be apart.

The monk attendants looked in the cave and gathered Geshe's few meager belongings. They then wrapped the body into a fetal position in white cloth and hoisted it up. It would be a long carry down the mountain. In three days, there would be a sky burial.

Sampa already knew he would not be in attendance.

Chapter 8

June 18, 1992, Yamdrok-tso

Tenzin began his clockwise walk around the holy lake in the early morning. As he had expected, the abbot had offered no resistance to his plan, but there was a definite look of distrust on his face as he agreed.

Or was it unease?

Tenzin began to wonder what it would be like to be under the thumb of such a powerful country that had no compunctions. One slip-up and the horrible things you've seen them do to others they now do to you.

Of course he is uneasy.

As far as Dawa was concerned, he seemed saddened that he was not invited but accepted Tenzin's somewhat flimsy excuse of needing to be alone.

It was a beautiful, sunny summer day. Tenzin walked by the place where he had buried the gemstones, and was pleased to see that it seemed undisturbed. He left it alone, though, as he had a feeling he was being followed. There was nothing to confirm his suspicions, but long ago he had learned not to ignore his intuition. He went into his walking meditation and focused on his breathing. But every so often he felt a pair of eyes boring into his back. No, there was no doubt about it; he *was* being followed.

He reflected upon who it might be. While it was possible it could be Penba Wangyal himself, more likely than not it was one of his lackeys doing the dirty work. While his friend and abbot Lobsang Gyaltso had made no mention of any others who were sympathetic to the Chinese, it made sense that Penba Wangyal might bring with him monks he could order around. Nuba and Somba seemed two likely candidates, as they were both young and constantly at his side. They reminded Tenzin of two puppy dogs who badly wanted to do their master's bidding.

He had given much thought to his circumambulation ritual. He would perform a walking meditation for a good portion of the day. When the sun was out he also wished to do sitting meditation and spend no small amount of time gazing at the surreal, kaleidoscope-like colors of Yamdrok-tso. It was there he would find his answers — of that he was certain. In the evenings he would let his mind be peaceful and spontaneous. He had learned there was such a thing as too much intensity.

It was late in the afternoon when he stopped his walk. He pulled out a blanket and sat on the rocky shoreline. He reached in his inner pocket, and pulled out the picture of Matthew Johnston, the one he had taken with him to Drak Yerpa. As before, he studied it carefully before he replaced it. Then he pushed his consciousness deep into the waters of the lake. To his surprise, the lavender curtain again appeared. Remembering Drak Yerpa, he did not try to force it open. Instead, he sat patiently and waited. Before long the curtain rose, and an indistinct picture appeared that gradually came into focus. This time there was not just a solitary fixed image but rather a series of them. The scenes unfolded before him.

He saw what appeared to be a number of American Indians running from homes that had been set afire. He observed while blue clad troops plundered their property and shot and killed any who resisted. He saw them being forced into camps with barbed wire surrounding them, and afterward they were herded together for a forced march. Slower and slower they walked in the driving snow, a number falling down to die.

The final image was that of an Indian boy, leaning over what appeared to be his mother; she lay dead upon the frozen ground. The boy seemed to stare directly at him, and Tenzin shuddered.

His consciousness gradually returned to the shores of the Tibetan lake. It was already night, and he pulled a blanket from his pack and covered himself. He removed some yak dung from his pack and created a small fire.

As he chewed on a piece of *tsampa*, he thought about what he had seen. It was clear he was viewing scenes from early American history. He stared into the now dark waters of the sacred lake, and like a flash of lightening the answer came to him. He had read about this from one of the books in The Forbidden Library.

In the early part of the 19th century, it was decided by the United States government that the five civilized tribes were to be removed from their homelands in the southeast. Thousands eventually died on the trek to what was now called the state of Oklahoma.

From his readings, Tenzin remembered that the Cherokees had an apt term for this brutal march, calling it The Trail of Tears.

Oklahoma. Matthew Johnston has chosen Oklahoma.

Tenzin smiled. His time at Drak Yerpa had prepared him well.

He was brimming with confidence.

Chapter 9

June 19, 1992, Yamdrok-tso

The peace of the previous evening had left Lama Tenzin Tashi. While he felt certain he was on the right track, the feeling that he was being followed returned with a vengeance. He decided to hide behind a hill and see if his spy would walk past. Sure enough, after a few minutes, he heard the sound of footsteps approaching.

The moment a figure appeared from around the corner, he pounced. "I've got you!" Tenzin said. He pushed the stranger's face into the sand while roughly twisting his shoulder behind his back. "What are you doing following me? I want answers, and I want them now."

Much to his embarrassment, he immediately heard the wailing of an infant and realized a baby was strapped onto his culprit's backpack. Not only that — and even worse — he discovered he had captured a young woman. After he released her, she rose from her face-down position and twisted to face him — a Tibetan, taller and more slender than most, and she was easily the most attractive woman he had ever seen. He guessed her age to be in the early twenties. As their eyes met, he saw a distinct look of terror.

"Who are you? And what are you doing?" she yelled in anger at the mortified monk. She brushed the fine sand from her face and cried, "Oh, my baby, are you well?" She removed the infant from her back, undid her blouse and allowed it to nurse. The child suckled eagerly and seemed as good as new.

"My name is Lama Tenzin Tashi," Tenzin said apologetically as he dusted the remaining sand from her face. "I am a monk from Drepung Monastery, and I am doing a circumambulation. I am so sorry. I thought that you were following me."

"Is that your only excuse for attacking a woman and her baby?"

"I'm afraid so."

"There is a police station back in Nangartse. I'm going to go there and report you. I think you are dangerous."

"I am not a criminal. Please accept my apology." Seeing the skepticism on her face and understanding he was making no progress, he begged, "What can I do to make it up to you?"

Finally seeming somewhat mollified, she said, "My name is Pema Dhargye, and my daughter's name is Lhamu Adhe. We are also doing a walk around the lake. While this is a sacred place, I have seen some young men drinking barley beer. They whistle at me and make obscene suggestions. I do not feel safe. I want to walk with you."

Tenzin was dumbfounded. The last thing he needed was the distraction of a beautiful woman and her infant. "You say your name is Pema?" He saw her nod. "Pema, I cannot allow you to walk with me. You and your baby will interfere with my meditations."

"Well, then, don't be surprised when you see the police. I'm sure that assaulting a woman and her baby will put you in jail for many months."

He sighed. There was no other choice. "Very well, you may come with me," he conceded, "but with one condition. I must have time to meditate. Is that acceptable?"

"Of course it is," she said.

What have I gotten myself into?

Tenzin said, "Then let us proceed." Her baby was now sleeping, and they set off. He found his mind too cluttered to do a walking meditation, so he let his thoughts slip into the past.

ཨོཾ་མ་ཎི་པདྨེ་ཧཱུྂ ཨོཾ་མ་ཎི་པདྨེ་ཧཱུྂ ཨོཾ་མ་ཎི་པདྨེ་ཧཱུྂ

After the death of his teacher, Sampa and his family made preparations for his life in the monastery. What he did not know was that his mother had anticipated this moment and had secretly sewn three monk's robes for him; one for winter, one for summer and another for special rituals.

The day he was to leave he took a solitary hike up to Gyen la's cave. He wanted to visit one last time.

So many memories.

He walked up to the front and saw the place where Geshe usually sat. He sighed and entered the cool depths of the cave. Much to his surprise, in a small niche, he discovered an envelope with *Sampa* written on it. Excitement filled him, and he opened it to discover a picture of the Dalai Lama. He was just a young boy, not that many years older than Sampa. He turned the picture over and read the writing on the back.

To my best student, Sampa,

I want you to have this picture. I knew that you would return to this cave, and I know how you love surprises.

Soon you will begin your life as a new monk, and many adventures await you. The difficulties you face and how you handle them will determine whether or not you will be born again on this earth. Whatever happens, always remember that the greatest pain and even the greatest joy is never permanent. Everything of this life is transitory.

Gyen la

Sampa tucked the picture into his pocket. Along with the singing bowl, he now had two priceless memories of his teacher. He walked outside, faced the cave and bowed one final time.

Back home he discovered his mother had prepared a special meal of *drel-sil*, a mixture of sweet potatoes, sugar and rice. He was greatly pleased.

When he finished his meal and had packed his belongings, he found that all of his brothers and sisters, in order from oldest to youngest, were waiting just outside the door. After a prolonged and tearful hug from his mother, he walked outside, and as he passed, each of his brothers and sisters placed a white Tibetan scarf, a *khata*, around his neck. Then he climbed on a pony and was led away by his father.

On his arrival at the monastery he was warmly greeted by the abbot, Sangye Phuntsog, and taken to his small room that overlooked the valley. That same day an elder monk entered his meager accommodations and shaved his head, leaving a small lock of hair on the crown.

After that, he was taken to the main prayer hall and found the abbot sitting on a pedestal in front of the room. There were many monks present. After an elaborate ceremony, Sampa was led to stand in front of the abbot. Sangye Phuntsog took a pair of scissors and cut off the remaining bit of hair.

The abbot smiled at him and said, "Will you be content to live a life devoted to religion?"

"Yes."

"Very well, then. Your name is no longer Sampa Dhondup. You will now be known as Lama Tenzin Tashi. From this point on, your connections are severed to your previous existence. Geshe Choden Nyima has spoken well of you, and I can see that all he has said is correct. Welcome."

Tenzin smiled at his abbot. Even though Tenzin was a reincarnated lama, he was now simply a *getsul* or novice. He was ready to begin his new life.

ཨོཾ་མ་ཎི་པདྨེ་ཧཱུྃ་ ཨོཾ་མ་ཎི་པདྨེ་ཧཱུྃ་ ཨོཾ་མ་ཎི་པདྨེ་ཧཱུྃ་

Tenzin happily pondered these memories. How young and immature he was! But, then again, with the advantage of time, everything always seemed much more defined and clearer. Sometimes he wished he could transfer the wisdom he now had into his decisions of the past. But such was not the way of learning. The past was sacred, no matter how it appeared in the days to come.

Late in the evening the trio came to a good stopping place, and the lama sat for another meditation. While mother and baby rested, Tenzin again focused on the sparkling, mystical waters.

It took more time than usual to put aside the distractions of the day. As he went deeper into his mind, he heard a faint cry from Lhamu. Soon his senses would be completely withdrawn, and there would be nothing that could disturb him.

The lavender curtain again appeared before him. Within an hour or so, it again gradually opened. This time the image was immediately sharp, and Tenzin saw a man dressed in what he knew to be cowboy clothes — hat, bandana and boots. What was most striking was how well he could handle the rope he was carrying.

Tenzin had never seen anyone with such skill. He could spin the rope up and over his head, and jump through and around the loop. The man lassoed a goose, a dog, a cat and even a mouse. In the next scene, he threw three ropes nearly simultaneously, one going around the legs of a horse, the second encircling the horse's neck and the final one the rider. Tenzin was astonished. Such a performance! And he found himself wanting to cheer, even knowing that the scene he observed was not real.

Who was this man?

Certainly Oklahoma was known for its cowboys, and this looked like one of the best. Tenzin waited patiently, hoping for another clue. He then saw the same man flying as a passenger in an airplane with a pilot who wore a black patch over his left eye. He saw their airplane have engine trouble and crash, killing both.

Soon the scene blurred, and Tenzin feared that the curtain would close.

Just one more sign. Please . . .

As if the images had consciousness, an English phrase gradually formed in front of him: "I . . . never . . . yet . . . met . . . a . . . man . . . that . . . I . . . didn't . . . like."

The image gradually faded, and soon Tenzin found himself looking at the dark waters of Yamdrok-tso. He glanced at his surroundings; it was far later than he had imagined. Pema and Lhamu were fast asleep under their blankets.

He began to put the clues together. Given what he learned from the previous night, he guessed the man was from Oklahoma. He was obviously a talented cowboy, good enough to perform before audiences.

Tenzin had studied a book from The Forbidden Library on Oklahoma history, and he had gained much knowledge from it. Somewhere within that text he had read about that man. He was sure he was an important person in the early part of the 20th century.

Suddenly he knew.

The man was Will Rogers, cowboy-turned-stage-performer, comedian and political commentator. He was known as Oklahoma's favorite son. He was killed in a plane crash, and Wiley Post, the man who died with him, was his friend and the pilot. *Now let's see — where was Will Rogers from?*

He pulled up his memories. Will Rogers lived near Claremore, Oklahoma. Even when the Rogers family lived in New York, they spent summers in Claremore. The Will Rogers Memorial was there.

Claremore.

Tenzin breathed a sigh of relief.

Another piece to the puzzle.

There was still much to discover. He had five more days of circumambulation and hoped the answers he needed would come to him during that time. Maybe he wouldn't need to stay in the presence of that oppressive abbot for the full three months.

He wrapped his blanket around himself. His goal was within reach.

He glanced over at the mother and baby, who were sleeping soundly. They weren't as much of a distraction as he thought they might have been. As a monk, he was used to being a loner, but this was a pleasant change.

He told himself, "Enjoy the moment."

As he slipped off to sleep, a sweet smile clung to his face.

Chapter 10

T enzin awoke to the sound of a crying baby. He looked up at the sky. It was around six in the morning; the sun had just started to lighten the darkness of the night, and the chill was paralyzing. He wanted to roll over and go back to sleep, but he saw that Pema was not feeling well. She was squatting and the sound and odor of profuse diarrhea filled the air. Tenzin could see the stain of vomit on her clothes.

"Venerable lama," he heard her groan, "Lhamu needs to be changed and fed. Could you, please? I feel like I'm about to pass out." She barely was able to pull her Tibetan skirt back up before she flopped to the ground on her back.

Tenzin had never changed a diaper in his entire life, and he didn't want to start now. And how was he going to feed a baby who was being breast fed? He quickly rose and went to her pack. The baby was now screaming constantly at a high pitch. He found himself becoming increasingly annoyed.

I am a lama. I am not a nursemaid!

Shaking off his frustrations, he picked up the infant and tried to comfort her. Her wails only increased. With his free hand he rummaged through Pema's pack and much to his relief discovered some prefilled bottles. He quickly shoved one into the baby's mouth, and the shrieking stopped. He placed the baby on her back, propping the bottle up on a folded blanket.

Now — about that diaper.

He glanced over at Pema, hoping she had recovered enough to complete this chore. She was still on her back moaning. He grumbled to himself.

Oh, no . . .

Seeing no choice, he again picked around in Pema's pack and found a moistened rag with a handful of cotton diapers. He pulled off the baby's baggy pants and nearly vomited when he removed the diaper. The smell reminded him of the latrine when the entire monastery had dysentery. He had never smelled anything more horrible than this diaper, and he had been to many a sky burial.

Tenzin tried to hold his breath while he speedily washed Lhamu's bottom, all to no avail. He choked when he finally had to inhale. He dried her with the sleeve of his robe and replaced the diaper. He then bundled the baby up in her blanket, held her in his arms and continued to feed her.

Much to his surprise, the oddest feeling came over him: the joy of nurturing — of fatherhood. One thing he had never previously understood was why parents fussed so much over their children. For the first time in his life he began to comprehend. A surprising warmth filled him, and he found himself feeling love for the infant he had met only the previous day. "I think you are a little bodhisattva," he whispered in an uncharacteristic high-pitched voice.

She suckled on her bottle and stared at him with her bright dark eyes. Perhaps it was his imagination, or did she turn the corners of her mouth up into a little smile? He sat down on the ground and gently rocked.

Tenzin could have continued in this way for hours, but a short time later Pema roused from her stupor. "I feel better. How is my baby?" she asked as she sat up and reached for her child.

He reluctantly handed the infant back to her. "She is fine. Take a few moments to get some fluids. We should begin our walk soon — when you feel you are able."

She pulled out her water bottle, took a swallow, and said, "Yes, I am ready." With that, she rose with the child in her arms, put on her pack and started off. As Tenzin trailed behind her, he thought:

She is strong.

They began at a brisk pace, and Tenzin found himself looking at the rhythmic motion of her hips as she walked. Granted, traditional Tibetan wear did not readily display female anatomy, but he found himself thinking about women and what it would be like to be with one — such as this beautiful woman.

When he was a young boy, his mind often wandered to thoughts of girls. He had been friends with many in his home town and had been especially fond of

Gu-Lang Yudan. Often they would take long walks in the flowering fields, holding hands as they laughed and skipped in the mountainous foothills.

One day he pulled her next to him and lightly kissed her on the lips. She gasped, put her hand over her mouth and ran away. He chased and called after her, but she was faster than he was, and before long she had disappeared, leaving him completely alone.

The kiss . . . the kiss . . . it had ruined everything.

After that, when he came to her home to see her, her mother shooed him away like a pesky gnat.

Tenzin smiled as he remembered the impetuousness of his youth.

Before he entered the monastery, he was told by his religious parents that one could progress faster on the spiritual path with a monastic life. As he thought about it, he wasn't completely sure that was true.

What if he had been the oldest male in the family and inherited his father's meager estate? He might have been able to convince his parents to arrange a marriage with Gu-Lang Yudan, and he could have felt the warmth of her body next to his when they slept at night. They might have had many children together. He could have had the joy of seeing his little boys and girls grow up and could experience not only their lives but also the lives of grandchildren.

So, which is better, the isolation of the monastery or the life of the householder? Is there greater growth from separating from life or engaging it?

There was no clear answer.

One thing was certain — as he saw the swaying body of Pema before him, he understood why male and female monastics were kept in separate institutions. The daily temptations would simply be too much. He smiled again. At fifty years old, he was far too old and too ensconced in the monastic tradition to think about such things. But the thoughts were there — the thoughts were there — just the same.

After a few hours of brisk walking, they decided to rest. They sat on the rocky beach, and Pema proceeded to nurse Lhamu after she changed her diaper. Tenzin took out his canteen and slowly drank.

She turned to him. "I suppose you are wondering how it is that I am out walking around this lake with such a small baby?"

"I hadn't given it much thought."

She went on, assuming he wanted to know more. "I live in the village of Nangartse with my mother and two younger sisters. We run a small grocery business there. My father died some years ago at the Drapchi Prison. He was arrested during the 1988 demonstrations outside the Jokhang Temple. What caused his death is uncertain, but we were told through the underground that he died while being tortured. You know how brutal the Chinese are."

Tenzin nodded his head in sympathy. He understood far more than she could ever know.

"A little more than a year ago," she went on, "I started seeing Senge Lhentsog. He was so kind and gentle, and said he wanted to marry me. My mother was insistent that I have an arranged marriage to someone else. I don't believe she approved of him; he was a simple farm laborer.

"Before too long, I discovered I was pregnant. I was so excited and couldn't wait to tell Senge the news. When I told him, he looked shocked and said he would have to think about things. I said, 'What's there to think about? We are going to have a baby. You said that you wanted to marry me.' He said, 'Of course, I do.'

"I haven't seen him since that night. Some say he has gone to live in Lhasa, others that he has decided to escape to Nepal through the mountain passes. No one, not even his parents, know for sure." Tears were in her eyes.

"But now that my baby is two months old, I began wondering whether or not I should begin a new life at another place. I thought that the circumambulation would help to clear my head. What do you think, oh, wise lama?"

Tenzin thought for a moment and said, "I believe it is always wise to consider major decisions carefully. Is there any pressure from your mother for you to leave?"

"No. She loves little Lhamu."

"Are you comfortable in your family home?"

"Yes."

"What do you want to do with your life? What are your aspirations?"

"When I was younger I dreamed of being married and having a large family. But now, of course, with the two-child limit placed by the Chinese, I will be allowed to have only one more child." She sadly looked down at the ground. "I still want to be with a good man, one I can spend my life with, and I want to raise my children as Tibetans and not as Chinese. Is it wrong to have such simple goals?"

Tenzin paused before he answered. He was reminded of the mobile birth control teams the Chinese initiated in 1982. There were horrifying reports of Tibetan women being rounded up by force and taken for compulsory sterilization or abortion. Some saw their full-term babies killed by injections in the soft spot of their heads.

Tenzin shook his head and returned to her question. "No, it is not wrong. Goals are goals, whether they are lofty or simple. Do you truly want my opinion?"

He saw her tearfully nod.

"I think you are doing exactly what you are supposed to be doing. I know you are badly hurt by the loss of your love, but he has given you a great gift, your baby. No, I would not leave your home. Your family needs you.

"You are strong, Pema. Perhaps someday you might meet someone who appreciates your strength. Then you can have another child. Sometimes life gives us turns we least expect, and we have to do the best with them that we can. Hold your dreams tightly. Never give up on them, never." When he finished, he wiped a tear from her face and kindly patted her on the shoulder.

Suddenly Tenzin felt embarrassed by the lustful thoughts he had earlier and took a few deep breaths.

They were just thoughts, nothing more. I release them.

They then continued on their pilgrimage around the lake. Tenzin discovered that he enjoyed carrying little Lhamu and gladly did so. As the afternoon drifted into evening, he decided it was time to meditate. This was only the third day, but the sooner he got the answers he needed, the better. As mother and child rested, Tenzin sat and stared at the magical waters of Yamdrok-tso.

The colors again danced before him.

He mentally dived into the waters and felt a sense of peace as the lavender curtain again appeared before him. He chuckled to himself. At Drak Yerpa the curtain was an adversary; now, it was a comfortable and consistent friend.

With the passage of time, the curtain gradually lifted. As if to mock his previous conceptions, everything suddenly changed, and rather than viewing the picture, he *was* the picture. He was walking in a place he had never been before. He could see and hear everyone, but they seemed to be unable to see him.

He heard cars honk and saw students walking on the street. He saw signs pointing to the Will Rogers Memorial. Any doubts about Matthew Johnston's city of rebirth vanished into the ethers.

His feet guided him across some railroad tracks and into a residential area. He crossed onto a street called Cherokee and found himself transfixed by a small home with an interesting pattern of brown and tan bricks. A large American elm tree shaded a screened-in front porch.

Sitting on the porch was a young couple, the man with a small child on his lap and the mother holding a baby. They all had big smiles written across their faces. He looked at the home and read the address. 507. . . 507 Cherokee Street.

Tenzin took a close look at the older child.

Matthew Johnston.

In a moment he was back in his body, sitting in front of Yamdrok-tso. He breathed a sigh of relief. It had only been three days, and he had all the information he needed. He had only to complete his circumambulation and find a permanent hiding place for the gemstones.

In this moment of peace, he reflected back to Gyen la, how the aged one had introduced him to The Forbidden Library and his insistence that Tenzin learn English. Without this nudging, Tenzin was well aware that he would now be in a blind alley.

Thank you my teacher — thank you —

While it seemed he had been in meditation for just a few minutes, it had obviously been hours. Pema and Lhamu were fast asleep, and the dark of night was upon them. He felt great joy and knew he could finally let his mind rest.

He had earned it.

Chapter 11

June 24, 1992, Yamdrok-tso

oday was the seventh and final day of his circumambulation, and Tenzin was light at heart. He looked at the brilliant turquoise blue lake to his right and felt grateful for the answers she had given him. He was starting to feel a bit sad — like someone spending a final day with an old friend. The feeling of loss somehow preceded the actual separation.

Over the past days he had given much thought to his final plans. After parting company with Pema and Lhamu at Nangartse, he would walk to and unearth the gemstones he had so carefully hidden. It would be dark at that time, and he hoped to borrow one of the yak-skin boats he had seen tied up at the shoreline. He planned to navigate across the water and bury them at a more remote location on the other side of the lake that would be easy to identify when he returned years later with the incarnation.

Yes, everything seemed to be happening just as he desired. He glanced over at Pema and Lhamu. He was enjoying very much their companionship and hoped to stay in touch. He felt as a father to little Lhamu, a new but most enjoyable feeling. There were many more hours to go, though, and he let his mind wander.

ཨོཾ་མ་ཎི་པདྨེ་ཧཱུྃ་ ཨོཾ་མ་ཎི་པདྨེ་ཧཱུྃ་ ཨོཾ་མ་ཎི་པདྨེ་ཧཱུྃ་

In the summer of 1950, a jarring earthquake was felt in Batang, and many at Chöde Gaden Pendeling Monastery felt this was an omen. Two days later a surprise attack of a Tibetan border post by the Chinese military was subsequently followed by a full-scale invasion in October. The country was quickly overrun.

In the beginning the Chinese were very kind to the Tibetans. At their initial meetings, the people in attendance were given silver coins. They gave interest-free loans to impoverished farmers and allowed the Buddhist monastic traditions to continue as before. It was a time of relative peace, so, one year after he had entered the monastery, Tenzin took his novice vows. He promised not to steal, to abstain from untruth, never to take life and to practice celibacy. Several years later he took his final vows.

Shortly after he became a fully ordained monk, the Chinese intrusions increased in frequency and severity. Soon they were all required to attend struggle sessions or *thamzing*. The purpose behind these meetings was to break down the unity of the populace. People were expected to spy on and report not only their neighbors, but also their families. One day Sangye Phuntsog called him into his office.

"Good morning, Tenzin," the abbot said perhaps a little too casually. "I suppose you might be wondering why I have asked for you?"

"Well . . . yes."

"First of all, I must share with you that I have been getting good reports from your monk teachers. While you are very young, it is clear you are ready for higher learning. There are several of the older monks who are traveling to Drepung Monastery in a few days. Of course, they will first pass through Lhasa. I would like you to go with them."

Tenzin was astonished. "Abbot, to study at Drepung would be a dream come true. Besides, I have never set foot on the soil of our sacred city."

Sangye smiled at his response. "I know you will miss your family, but it is time for you to begin more intensive learning. Would you like to go?"

"Yes! Yes!"

"Very well, then." Abruptly he took a much more serious air. "Tenzin, I have some most important words for you, so listen well."

"Yes?"

"As I'm sure you know, the Chinese have become more and more difficult, and I expect at any time they will directly begin to persecute us. They have already started to seize land owned by our monastery. I read a declaration just a few days ago that stated religious life is useless to society. Do you remember the play they presented? The one where they hired some local beggars, dressed them as monks and nuns, and had them declare that they were going to marry?"

"I'm afraid I do —"

"Well, it is clear they now expect us to break our vows of celibacy and become householders. Just this morning two of our elder monks, Pemba Trulku and Chogyal Gyaltsen, committed suicide rather than conform. Unfortunately, I expect more in the near future."

Tenzin gulped and tears came into his young eyes. He knew well the wizened monks, and he was greatly saddened.

"There is something else you need to know. The Chinese have requested that the monks of our monastery attend a town meeting in Batang this evening. It is likely to be a thamzing session. I suspect they will want to display a show of force and make an example of one of us. I expect that person to be me."

Tenzin stared, open-eyed, at his mentor.

"Tonight, no matter what happens, no matter what you see, I want you to remain silent. It is the only way you will remain safe. I would like for you to go to Drepung as planned. These difficulties are widespread in our country, and when you arrive there, you are eventually going to face similar problems. No matter how angry you become, now or in the future, you must hold your tongue. Do I have your promise?"

Tenzin could not respond.

Sangye looked kindly at him. "Fellow monk and seeker on the path, these are most difficult times. Geshe knew of all this, and I promised him I would look after you. Before you walk out of this room, I must know you will be free from harm. Can I have your assurance?"

Tenzin forced himself to mouth the word, "Yes."

"Very good. Now, let us share some tea together. The time quickly approaches, and we must enjoy these moments. Perhaps it will not be as bad as I expect."

ཨོཾ་མ་ཎི་པདྨེ་ཧཱུྃ་ ཨོཾ་མ་ཎི་པདྨེ་ཧཱུྃ་ ཨོཾ་མ་ཎི་པདྨེ་ཧཱུྃ་

In the evening the monks from Chöde Gaden Pendeling Monastery and the townspeople gathered for the prescribed meeting. Tenzin looked around nervously. There were many Chinese soldiers, and the crowd grouped around a central clearing.

Soon a female soldier appeared in the middle. She angrily pointed a finger at Sangye Phuntsog and said, "In the name of religion you have been using the common man for your own evil purposes. Come!" She waved for him to approach her.

He slowly walked forward. To the disbelief of the group, she shoved the old lama to the ground and forced him to his knees.

Several in the crowd yelled out, "What are you doing to our lama? He does not deserve this!"

Those who protested were roughly grabbed by the soldiers and shoved into the back of a waiting truck.

Tenzin wanted to rush into the circle but remembered the oath he had made. He saw the abbot glance at him and give a knowing nod.

The female soldier then took a rope, threw it around the abbot's head and put it into his open mouth. She then jumped on his aged back and jerked his head with the rope. Blood trickled from the corners of his mouth, but he remained silent.

One of the soldiers handed her a large glass filled with urine. "Drink this, vile one!" she ordered.

When he refused she poured the steaming liquid onto his face. He sputtered and choked, and then she yanked him to his feet. The rope was then slipped onto his neck, and he, along with several other of the elder monks, were also forced into the truck. The door was slammed shut just before the truck was driven away.

As the soldiers vacated the premises, the people of Batang stood and stared at each other. At last they understood.

The Chinese are not our friends. They are our enemies.

Two days later, still in a daze over the previous events, Lama Tenzin Tashi, along with two of his fellow monks, walked away from their sacred home. They could take only what they could carry, and he sadly had to leave his precious library behind. With all that had happened, it was the least of his concerns. His beloved abbot Sangye Phuntsog was either dead or in prison. The scourge of the Chinese was everywhere.

A little over two months later, as they approached their final destination, they saw what appeared to be sparkling mounds of white against the hillside. They then understood how the monastery received its name. Drepung literally meant "a heap of rice," which it had all the appearance of being. A relative peace greeted them.

But it was only a matter of time.

ཨོཾམཎིཔདྨེཧཱུྃ ཨོཾམཎིཔདྨེཧཱུྃ ཨོཾམཎིཔདྨེཧཱུྃ

Tenzin, as he walked around Yamdrok-tso, realized that he now had tears in his eyes. He had so loved his first abbot.

He gathered himself and looked to the sky. He saw that the night was coming early this evening; there was a dense cover of clouds, and any moon that might have been seen was obscured.

Pema, with Lhamu, walked quietly by his side, and soon they saw the dim lights of the village of Nangartse. As they came into the bustling center, he glanced at Pema and saw an unexpected look of fear upon her face. He kissed the head of Lhamu and turned to Pema. "It is time for us to part. Have you made any decisions about your life?"

She nervously looked around and said, "I will do as I must. I will stay with my mother and sisters, and raise little Lhamu as best as I am able. Someday, somehow, I hope to meet a good man like you."

Tenzin was surprised to feel himself blush.

"Well," she said, "perhaps someone a little younger." Then she added abruptly, "Brother Monk, there is one other thing I must share with you." Suddenly, her eyes welled with tears, and she struggled to speak. "I . . . I . . . think it might be important." She paused, looked over his shoulder, and panic appeared on her face. "But . . . I . . . can't." With that, she dashed away into a crowded street, quickly disappearing.

Tenzin turned and looked for what might have frightened her but saw just a milling crowd. He shrugged his shoulders, turned back and thought about pursuing her, yet knew it was hopeless. It was too dark, and the hour was growing late. Besides, he had important business to attend to.

What was it that disturbed her so much?

It was a pitch-black walk out to where the jewels were buried, and Tenzin felt some apprehension about whether or not they had been discovered.

Finally he spied the familiar stack of rocks with his flashlight. He held his breath as he moved the obstructing stones to the side and began to dig. Soon he felt resistance and let go a sigh of relief as he pulled the burlap bag from the ground.

He opened the drawstring and saw that the thick plastic bag was still sealed. He opened it and again saw the pile of wrapped stones. For a second he felt their magnetic pull but pushed it aside and pulled the bag shut.

Enough of that.

He studied the darkened shoreline and finally found what he was looking for, a yak-skin boat tied to a mooring. He untied it and began to row. The sky remained lightless, and he had to occasionally point his flashlight across to the opposite shore to keep his way.

The boat glided smoothly across the top of the water, and before long he felt it strike land. He tied the mooring rope to a large rock and walked slowly up the steep slope of the rocky hillside. Soon he came to a small plateau. He carefully looked around. The area was isolated.

This place is ideal.

He sat down for a few moments, took out his canteen and drank deeply.

Finally, feeling rested, he stood and pulled out a small pick ax he had packed. With his first swing he felt like he was striking concrete. But with further tries, the rocky soil began to break up. He put the flashlight on the ground and tilted it toward the hole, which slowly but surely grew larger as he worked.

Suddenly he felt a strong arm wrap around his chest, and a sharp blade press against the skin of his neck.

A gruff voice spoke. "Move, and you will die. Drop your ax."

Tenzin let go of the tool and heard it *thump* on the ground. He twisted to see who was behind him and felt the blade cut into his skin. Warm blood dripped down his neck.

"Move once more and it will be your last. Do you really want to die now? If you do, I will be happy to oblige you. Now put your hands behind your back."

Tenzin reluctantly did as he was told — and felt the knife drop from his neck. A rope was secured around his wrists. "I know who you are," Tenzin said as he felt the rope tighten.

"Who am I?" the voice mocked.

"You are Abbot Penba Wangyal. You have been watching me ever since I arrived here."

Tenzin heard a loud guffaw.

Something about that voice sounds familiar.

"So, you think I'm the abbot?"

"Well, if you're not him, then you're working for him."

"Sit down," the voice said.

Tenzin roughly landed on the hard ground, hands tied behind him. The figure moved around in front of him, his face obscured by the dark night. He sat down across from Tenzin. The flashlight, still on the ground, revealed only a dark profile. "You must be either Nuba or Somba," Tenzin ventured.

The voice that was now in front of him laughed again.

It can't be!

Just at that moment, his attacker picked up the flashlight and shone the light on himself.

"Dawa?"

"Surprised?" Dawa said. "I thought that you might be."

"But . . . Dawa . . ." Tenzin stammered, "I thought we were friends."

"We were never friends, you useless old fool. I used you, and I'm proud of it. Now let me take a look at my treasure."

Tenzin grimaced at his words but remained silent.

Dawa reached inside Tenzin's pack and removed the bag. He untied the drawstring and carefully opened the inner plastic sack. He unwrapped one of the gemstones, and when he flashed the light upon it, he gasped as the large red diamond he held reflected into his bulging eyes. To Tenzin's surprise, Dawa began to laugh, at first a mere snicker, then gradually increasing until he guffawed the sadistic laugh of a madman. When the laughter finally died down, Dawa rewrapped and replaced the gemstone. He sat the bag to the side and wickedly smiled. "Old monk, in a few minutes, I will cut your throat. I will laugh as I watch you bleed to death, but I thought you might like to know the truth before you die." He brandished the razor-sharp knife in his hands. "Well?"

Tenzin somehow managed to nod his head.

"As you know, I was raised in an orphanage in Lhasa. No one knew why my parents were not around or why no relatives claimed me. Not a single soul was interested in taking me into their home, so I was stuck with a bunch of lice-infested brats. I realized that the only way out was to profess the desire to be a monk. I never cared about religion. Personally I believe Chairman Mao was right. Religion is poison. Not only that, I think the Buddha was full of shit."

Tenzin couldn't believe what he was hearing.

"Anyway, when that dying old man, I believe his name was Matthew Johnston, came to our monastery those months before he died, I fed him all the crap I had heard from elder monks like you. He actually seemed to believe some of it, and he started to open up more and more to me. The day he died, when he was in and out of consciousness, he told me the real reason he had come. I couldn't believe that old fart convinced you to find his next incarnation. What a laugh! But when he told me about the gemstones, I sat up and paid attention. I knew this could be the break I'd been waiting for. But there was one big problem. No matter how much I tried to get it out of him, he wouldn't tell me where they were. I became very angry and felt like choking it out of him the night of his death."

Tenzin then remembered the look of anger he saw on Dawa's face those many years ago.

Why did I not pay attention?

"But I knew if I were patient, I would find out soon enough. When I heard you were going to Drak Yerpa, I begged our abbot to let me go with you, thinking I would get some clue. But you didn't say a word. When we were beaten up by the Chinese, I began to wonder if this was all worth it or not. And sitting in that cave in Drak Yerpa for three months was completely miserable. One can only sleep so much.

"Then I had to wait until your trip here. After what happened on the way to Drak Yerpa, I knew the abbot would ask me to accompany you again. Once we got here, I waited for my chance, and when you left your pack at the monastery, I thought, *This is it*. But when I searched it, I found nothing. I guessed then you had hidden the gems, probably earlier that day, but I didn't know where.

"When you decided to take the walk around the lake, I was pretty sure that you would soon have the jewels in your possession, but it was too risky to follow you myself. When I saw that woman and her baby walking in your direction I knew I had the answer. I told her I needed her to catch up with you and keep an eye out. She at first refused, but when I flashed the five one-hundred yuan notes in front of her, she grabbed them and ran off to catch up."

Tenzin interrupted. "Five hundred yuan?"

Dawa scowled. "You are so damn naive. Don't you see? No one expects a monk to rob them. Getting that money was easy."

Tenzin shook his head.

"Anyway, I was waiting for the both of you when you finished your little stroll, but she took off before I could get the information I needed." A look of maniacal anger crossed his face. "After I leave here, I'm going to find her and teach her a lesson. After I'm finished with her, I'll grab that little shit baby of hers. I think she will be a nice addition to the slave market. I should be able to get a good piece of change for her."

Not Pema and Lhamu . . . no . . .

"Anyway, tonight, when you took off out of town, I followed you. I saw you dig up the jewels and take the boat across the lake. I found one of my own and followed behind. And look what I found!" Dawa lustfully gazed at the sack of gemstones.

"Dawa . . . why?"

"Old man, are you blind? With this money, I could have anything I want. You've seen those wealthy Chinese when they come into town. They are driven around in new Mercedes and BMWs. They eat the best food and have the most beautiful women. Have you ever been with a woman before, I mean, REALLY been with one?"

Tenzin blinked his eyes in disbelief.

"Well, I haven't either, and I want to be. Look at me. I have nothing. I am nothing. This will make me wealthy, important and anything else I want to be in this forsaken life. You ask me why. I ask you, why not? This fortune gives me everything. If you don't know that, you are a complete idiot, old monk. You deserve to die."

"What will you do with my body?" Tenzin said. "Surely you know I will be reported as missing, and they will look for me."

"They will never find you. I brought some wire with me, and I saw some heavy rocks on the shoreline. I will sink your body under the water. I will tell our abbot that you just disappeared. He might be suspicious, but what can he do? He would not be able to prove anything. You are as good as dead." Dawa smiled, pleased with himself, and he began to throw the knife from one hand to another.

Tenzin saw his chance.

He quickly raised his knees and forcefully kicked Dawa in the middle of his chest. The unexpected blow dislodged Dawa from his knife and sent him spinning down the hill.

Not if I can help it.

Tenzin saw the tumbling figure rapidly disappear into the night. He awkwardly sat down, and with his roped hands searched the ground behind him for the knife.

Where is it? Hurry!

After fumbling around for far longer than he would have liked, he finally grasped the cold steel. He twisted it around in his right hand, and sawed on the rope. It held him tight. He sawed harder.

Finally, with a snap, the rope popped off his wrists.

Triumphantly he stood up, and the moment he rose, Dawa was on him, striking him in the chest with his shoulder. They both fell to the ground, the knife jarred from his hand. As they stood up, Tenzin and Dawa both saw the knife sitting between them. They feinted for position to grab it, circling around the weapon.

When Dawa finally lunged for the knife, Tenzin hit him with a flurry of stinging punches, driving him away from the knife. A crushing uppercut knocked Dawa to the ground.

Just like the old days.

Tenzin reached for the knife, but he unexpectedly felt a kick to his groin, and he doubled over in agony. As he glanced up, he saw Dawa was already on his feet.

"You forget, oh, high lama," Dawa said as he wiped the blood from the corner of his mouth, "that pain does not affect me."

They both then leaped for the knife, grabbing it simultaneously. They rolled side to side in the dark night, episodically silhouetted by the dimming flashlight as they struggled back and forth.

"Old man," Dawa said. "Have you forgotten that I am younger and stronger?"

Tenzin was breathless. Soon Dawa was on top of him, and the knife blade was pointed at his chest. He felt the point scratch against him and the strength of Dawa's arms. The younger monk's crazed face was inches away from his.

"Prepare to die, you old fool," Dawa said as he grimly smiled and leaned into the knife.

All at once, time stretched, and Tenzin saw his life flash before him. He had a vision of himself playing in the fields with Gu-Lang Yuden, holding hands, smiling and laughing. He saw himself meditating with Gyen la inside his cave. He felt his last lock of hair being removed by Sangye Phuntsog. He observed the withered body of Matthew Johnston, taking his last breaths. Then, he saw the face of Lhamu Adhe, smiling, with her alert, dark eyes. A voice from somewhere inside screamed.

I won't let him hurt you! Never!

"NOOOOOOOO!" he yelled. From where, he could not tell, he felt a surge of strength and pushed the knife away with all his might.

Suddenly, with a jerk, Dawa went limp, his eyes rolled back into his head, and bloody saliva streamed from his open mouth. Tenzin gasped and pushed him to the side; the knife was lodged to the hilt in the middle of Dawa's chest. He grimly searched for a pulse in his neck. There was none. Tenzin put his face into his hands and wept.

Dawa is dead.

ཨོ་མ་ཎི་པད་མེ་ཧཱུྃ་ ཨོ་མ་ཎི་པད་མེ་ཧཱུྃ་ ཨོ་མ་ཎི་པད་མེ་ཧཱུྃ་

Tenzin felt numb as he methodically dug again. Making the hole a few inches deeper, he placed the bag of gemstones inside it and pressed the rocky soil on top, tamping it down with the handle of his pick ax.

Now — it would take some work getting Dawa's body back down the hill. Once at the edge of the water, he would weigh it down with stones and pull it out to water deep enough so it would not be seen. In a matter of time the flesh would be absorbed in the waters of the sacred lake. Tenzin knew his intent was not to harm his fellow monk, but that didn't stop the intense feelings of shame.

I have murdered another man.

ༀ་མ་ཎི་པདྨེ་ཧཱུྃ ༀ་མ་ཎི་པདྨེ་ཧཱུྃ ༀ་མ་ཎི་པདྨེ་ཧཱུྃ

Once he had disposed of the body, Tenzin bathed in the frigid lake, though he could barely feel it. He needed to wash away not only the stains of blood but also those of guilt. He put on his spare robe, tied Dawa's boat to the back of his and quietly rowed across the lake, returning them to their places on the opposite bank.

Tonight he would have a restless sleep on the shore. In the morning he would carefully conceal the cut on his neck, make his excuses and find a way to return to Drepung.

Now the sacred lake held another mystery.

The body of a dead monk.

Chapter 12

June 25, 1992, Yamdrok-tso to Drepung Monastery

A s he bounced around in the back seat of a four-wheel drive jeep on his return to Drepung, Lama Tenzin Tashi was in his own personal hell. He had inappropriately used his honed meditative skills to find the next incarnation of Matthew Johnston. That was bad enough. Now the blood of one of his fellow monks was on his hands. While he knew that he did not directly try to injure Dawa, by his action of agreeing to hold the lucrative wealth of the jewels, he had placed an enormous temptation in front of one who was simply not capable of resisting it. Even he, a senior lama, was barely able to control the urge to take some of the gems for himself. He had been a fool, and because of his bad judgment, a man had died. He looked at the empty seat beside him.

Dawa should be there.

He also felt betrayed by Pema. Tenzin had always been a trusting man, though, in this case he had allowed himself to be badly fooled.

He wondered if he should turn himself in to the police. But he had committed no crime, and all a trial would do is land him in jail or worse. Undoubtedly the motive for Dawa's attack would be explored, and the gemstones might be discovered — and certainly they did not belong in the hands of the Chinese. He shuddered at the thought and began to think again of the young monk he used to be.

ཨོཾ་མ་ཎི་པདྨེ་ཧཱུྃ། ཨོཾ་མ་ཎི་པདྨེ་ཧཱུྃ། ཨོཾ་མ་ཎི་པདྨེ་ཧཱུྃ།

Tenzin fell happily into the daily routine at Drepung. Well before sunrise he would awaken for his private studies, and at dawn a beginning monk would chant a sacred Buddhist text. After this was the sounding of the conch, and the monks gathered for morning yak butter tea. At noontime he would assemble with other monks for discussion groups, and the novices were taught the art of debate.

As expected, the pressure from the Chinese authorities began to increase, and when the Dalai Lama left the country in March of 1959, conditions became even worse. The military camp less than a mile away from Drepung was continually being reinforced, and Tenzin knew that eventually the Chinese would invade their sanctuary. The monks began to leave in droves, hoping to find other safe havens.

Before long, the monastery itself was shelled and then invaded by the Chinese military. The remaining monks were arrested. Many were taken to various prisons for interrogation and so-called re-education.

Tenzin, remembering his promise to Sangye Phuntsog, offered no resistance and was allowed to stay. He and the rest of the remaining monks were placed in menial positions and subjected to numerous *thamzing* sessions. The next twenty years were no doubt the worst of his life. He saw sacred Buddhist scriptures either used as toilet paper or burned outright. Precious rare *thangkas* — Tibetan silk paintings — were used by the Chinese as saddle pads. Many of his monastic friends were tortured in the most horrible ways, and a number were killed.

The final toll of the Chinese invasion was devastating: Over 1.2 million Tibetans were eventually killed, one-fifth of the entire population, and over 6,000 monasteries and nunneries were destroyed.

After the devastation of the Red Guards that came in the 1960s, the 1980s brought some return of religious freedom. The monasteries — not completely devastated, including Drepung — began to reopen under stringent Chinese regulation. The damage, however, was already done. Tibetan Buddhism, which relied on a strong oral tradition, had lost many of its elder monks to either death or exile. Lama Tenzin Tashi, while still relatively young, was now one of the senior monks. He was asked by Abbot Lobsang Gyaltso to assume the post of second in command, which he accepted.

One thing from his past that had never left was his love for reading, and Tenzin began to gather books. This time, though, they had to be smuggled in through the black market, and he carefully kept them hidden away in a secret basement at Drepung. He affectionately named it The Forbidden Library, remembering the name Gyen la gave to his first collection of books. As his friendship with his English-fluent abbot deepened, Tenzin shared his secret, and they enjoyed many hours of reading together.

After his agreement with Matthew Johnston, Tenzin had taken great pains to obtain Oklahoma and American history texts, which he had practically memorized. Some day, he sensed, he might need them.

ཨོམཉིཔདྨེཧཱུྃ ཨོམཉིཔདྨེཧཱུྃ ཨོམཉིཔདྨེཧཱུྃ

He roused from his thoughts as the jeep screeched to a halt in front of Drepung. He pulled his pack out of the vehicle, thanked the driver and headed to the office of his abbot. He still had no idea what he was going to say, but knew his thoughts were completely transparent to his old friend, so there was no point in not telling the truth. The hard part would be deciding the best way to do just that.

The door was open as he walked up, and Lobsang smiled in recognition. "Come in, old friend! This is a most pleasant surprise. I hadn't expected you back so soon. I had just moments ago happened to glance out my window and saw you step out of the jeep. I assume you had an enlightening trip?"

Tenzin replied, "Very much so."

Lobsang said, "It's such a beautiful day. What do you say we go outside and have a chat?" He rose, and the two monks walked outside to their favorite place for private conversation, the open courtyard. They both sat on the ground, and Lobsang patiently waited for Tenzin to speak first.

"How much do you need to know?" Tenzin said.

Lobsang smiled his most comforting smile. "Truthfully, very little. In fact, why don't you let me tell you what happened."

Tenzin raised his eyebrows in surprise.

"First of all, I'm going to guess that our young friend, Dawa, knew more than he let on. Secondly, if that is indeed true, and I think it is, I expect at some point in time he made an effort to kill you to get that which he wanted."

Tenzin stared, open-mouthed.

"Next, I'm guessing that since you are here, and Dawa is not with you, you were the victor in your battle. Knowing you as I know you, he was killed accidentally. And finally," he smiled when he said this, "you were able to accomplish your mission successfully, and sometime in the coming years you will want to make a trip to the United States of America to a place called Oklahoma. While the trip over the Himalayas is difficult, it is not impossible. Tell me, dear friend, am I correct?"

Tenzin was mute with astonishment. Finally he managed, "Lobsang, my friend and abbot, I am completely baffled at how you know all of this. Are you a visionary able to read the past and perhaps the future as well?"

Lobsang laughed heartily. "Not at all, my brother. As you know, for many years I have been an avid fan of the English writer, Agatha Christie. From our collection in The Forbidden Library, I have read most of her mystery novels and very much enjoy her main investigators, Hercule Poirot and Miss Marple. Through their intuition and powers of observation, they were able to, as the Americans say, put two and two together. Do you want to know more?"

"Oh, yes!"

"From the very beginning I knew of your agreement to find the next incarnation of Matthew Johnston, as you know. And I also was aware it involved an almost unthinkable amount of wealth. I knew your motivations were altruistic, but I also was sure that money of this amount would be coveted by those of lesser will.

"When Dawa begged me to allow him to go with you on the trip to Drak Yerpa, I suspected that he somehow knew. Then, of course, when you asked to go to Yamdrok-tso, I felt you should not go alone, and I approached him to accompany you. When he accepted, I saw that his enthusiasm was far greater than it should have been. Meanwhile, I watched his devotion to his knife — hours of sharpening and handling it. No one performs any such task for so long unless there is a purpose behind it.

"I perhaps should have said something to you, but I simply wasn't certain enough to voice my thoughts or to find someone different to travel with you. Now, it seems, I should have done both. Anyway, old friend, I knew you were quite intuitive yourself, and I suspected you already might have some idea."

Tenzin shook his head in dismay.

Lobsang continued, "I saw your pack when you left that morning, and it seemed fuller than I might have guessed it should have been, so I suspected you had your treasure with you and planned to hide it at Yamdrok-tso. Now, of course, your bag is not so packed, even more so than I would have thought for the food you might have eaten. From this, I know your mission must have been satisfied. You have hidden the treasure, and since you have returned earlier than planned, you did not need the full three months to discover the location of the next incarnation of Matthew Johnston.

"And since he was from Oklahoma, it is likely he has chosen to reincarnate there — and that is where you must travel. You must first confirm his location, and secondly, you must bring him back when he is of age to claim his fortune. Tenzin, are all my presumptions correct, or am I a dawdling old fool?"

"You are no fool."

"Then I must know a few things. Will Dawa's body be discovered?"

"No," Tenzin said.

"Good," said Lobsang. "I do not recommend that you report yourself to the police. You and I both know you did not kill Dawa intentionally. Correct?"

Tenzin nodded.

"Rather, I would like to believe that he inadvertently killed himself. You have certainly done nothing wrong." He nodded, as if that closed the subject. "Now," he added, "we both are aware that Dawa was an orphan, so there will be no family that will ask questions. Dawa was a loner among his monk brothers, so if we say he decided to quit the monastery and leave the country, it would be accepted as true. Which, in actuality, it is.

"Now then — one thing I have intuitively read, my friend, is that you have a very deep purpose to fill in this lifetime. This cannot be accomplished while behind the bars of a Chinese gulag or being put to death. Soon enough, I will make the great transition. In the papers to be read at my death, I have recommended that you assume the role of abbot of Drepung. We need your strength to continue our fight for survival of not only our religion but also of our people. I must know now. Will you accept this charge?"

Tenzin was honored beyond words. Tears dripped down his face as he simply said, "Yes."

"Excellent, my friend," said Lobsang joyfully. "Now I think it's time we put all of this discussion behind us and have a nice, hot cup of yak butter tea. I have a pot especially made for us by our fellow monk, Dorje Dondrub, the best cook in all of Tibet."

"Lobsang," Tenzin said, "I cannot thank you enough."

"There is no need for thanks," Lobsang said as he looked on Tenzin as a father would look on a son. He affectionately gripped his shoulder. They then rose and walked back into the monastery.

ཨོཾ་མ་ཎི་པདྨེ་ཧཱུྃ་ ཨོཾ་མ་ཎི་པདྨེ་ཧཱུྃ་ ཨོཾ་མ་ཎི་པདྨེ་ཧཱུྃ་

A month after Tenzin had returned from Yamdrok-tso, much to his surprise, he discovered a letter from Pema Dorgye. Of course, he fondly remembered Lhamu Adhe.

In truth, that little one saved my life.

He also saw wrenching feelings of betrayal rise again in front of him. He let them pass through his consciousness. He remembered the wise words of Carl Jung, "What you resist persists."

He quickly opened the letter and read:

July 9, 1992

Dear Brother Monk,

Now it has been around three weeks since we met walking around Yamdrok-tso. I am back at home with Lhamu Adhe, and, of course, my mother and two sisters. Our grocery business is doing well, though there will never be a lot of extra money.

I think Lhamu misses you. Every time an ochre colored robe passes in front of her, she looks closely at the monk's face. I know that she is only a few months old, but I am sure she is disappointed when she realizes it is not you.

The main reason I write this letter to you is to apologize for not telling you about the monk that paid me to watch you. Can you find it in your heart to forgive me? I never knew and never asked his name. For me, 500 yuan is a lot of money, and I could not turn it down.

As you and I grew to know each other, I knew that I could never betray you. I decided to tell you everything when we ended our walk, but was unable to do so when I saw him come up behind you. I was terrified and ran away as quickly as possible. Truthfully I had nothing to inform him about anyway, but I am afraid that he will return for the money. Do you know what happened to him? Is there a chance that he will come back? I am frightened. There was something dark and evil about him, even though he is a monk.

I also want to thank you for all the wisdom you shared with me. Sometimes it's easy to look at one's glass as half empty, rather than half full. Truly I am most blessed. I have a healthy baby. I have a mother and sisters who love me, and I am well and have enough to eat. Does one really need any more than that? Well, I still hope for a husband, though it will take a special man to want to be with a woman who has a little baby. I will be patient. I have a feeling I will know him when I see him.

Brother Monk, I have a few requests to make of you. First of all, I would like to be your friend. Good friends are very hard to come by, as I am sure you know.

I hope you are able to accept my offer. Most importantly, I would like to ask you to be little Lhamu's godfather. I travel to Lhasa every three months or so to get supplies for our shop, and on those times you will be able to see her. I smile when I think of how you looked at each other when you held her, and I know that you both are connected at a very deep level. Perhaps you have known each other in a previous life? Who can tell?

Whether or not you chose to write back, I do wish you the best in your life. I am a better person since I met you.

Sincerely,
Pema Dorgye

July 20, 1992

Dear Pema Dorgye,

I was very pleased to receive the letter from you a few days ago. We have been very busy here at Drepung, and the rains of the monsoon have slowed our work more than a little.

I see that you have asked me for forgiveness. If it is necessary for you to hear those words, then, of course, I forgive you. But there has been no wrong committed. As a hired spy, you were simply doing what you were paid to do. You did not harm me in any way.

Now I want to address your concerns. Let me assure you, you will never see that monk again. He has left the monastery, and I'm certain he will never be back. He has moved into another life. You and Lhamu will never be harmed in any way by him. I don't believe, though, that your perceptions of this young monk are correct. He had a beautiful spirit and performed his duties quite well. He simply, as is possible with all of us, allowed himself to be seduced by the illusions of this world. There is no blame in that. And I'm sure he will learn from his experiences.

I accept both of your offers! Your hand of friendship is warmly received, and I happily welcome the idea of being Lhamu Adhe's godfather. Please be aware that, as a poor monk, I have nothing to offer her financially, but I will hold her in my prayers daily. She is a beautiful soul, and I will cherish her presence in my life. I would be delighted to meet with both of you when you visit Lhasa. It is not a long walk for me. It will give me great pleasure to share tea with a friend and to spend moments with my goddaughter.

I hear your concerns about the disadvantages you present to a man. Let me assure you that anyone who could have you as a wife and Lhamu Adhe as a child would be very blessed. I think you are wise to be patient. This sort of thing has a way of taking care of itself. It needs no prodding.

I also send the both of you blessings for long and prosperous lives. Please remember that there is no time as precious as now. Before you know it, your baby will be an adult, living her own life, and this is as it should be.

Stay in the present moment.

Warmly,
Lama Tenzin Tashi

He sat quietly after he had written the letter. Much had happened over the past years. He had accepted the job of finding the incarnation of Matthew Johnston. He had, as far as he could tell by the visions he had seen, located it. Dawa Dorje was dead, ensnared by an overwhelming desire for the attractions of wealth. He was now a godfather to a beautiful infant and friend to her mother. In the years to come he would travel over the treacherous mountain passes to Claremore, Oklahoma, in the United States of America, and assuming all went well, would repeat the adventure much later. At some time in the future, he would become the abbot of Drepung. He prayed, though, that his friend would remain in that position for many more years.

For the time being, he had nothing to do but perform his duties as a senior member of the monastic community and spend as much time as possible meditating. The Chinese would continue to present difficulties, but that was something he could not control. Truly, they were his teachers and absolutely necessary for his spiritual unfolding.

How can one advance without tribulations?

He sighed as he pulled the weathered picture of Matthew Johnston out of the top drawer of his desk. He had faithfully kept it in his possession; now it was no longer necessary. Tenzin looked briefly at it before he placed it into the flame of the burning candle on his desk. As he saw it reduced to ashes, he thought:

Matthew Johnston, you have changed forms, just as the burning twig.

He smiled when he thought of seeing the world outside of Tibet. It was something many of his colleagues would never have the opportunity to do.

The United States of America.

Is it really a Land of Opportunity?

Soon he would discover for himself.

Deep inside this aging monk was still an adventurous little boy, Sampa Dhondup, one who loved dancing in the meadows, exploring the mountains of Batang and seeking out the unknown.

Sampa will always be a part of me.

With that comforting thought, he began to listen to his breath and followed it in and out as he was taught by Gyen la. Soon he would be unaware of the external world and conscious of only the inner. But he knew that, for the greatest growth, he must experience both.

He breathed again and silently entered the inner sanctum of peace.

Book Three

WADE
JOSHUA
ADAMS

"In the present circumstances, no one can afford to assume that someone else will solve their problems. Every individual has a responsibility to help guide our global family in the right direction. Good wishes are not sufficient; we must become actively engaged."

—Dalai Lama
from *The Path to Tranquility: Daily Wisdom*

Chapter 1

October 26, 1996, Claremore, Oklahoma

W ade Joshua Adams was not a happy boy. He sulked around the playground of Claremont Elementary School during recess, staying mostly to himself. One would have thought, given his sixth birthday was today and his mother was throwing a big party for him this evening, he would be in a better mood. His teacher in his first grade class, Mrs. Miller, even had the class sing "Happy Birthday" to him — without any noticeable improvement in his disposition.

Later on, his little brother Todd, now in kindergarten, seeing his funk, did all sorts of things to try to cheer him up. He made faces, tickled him right at that sensitive spot just below the armpit and even let him beat him in a game of tetherball. Not that losing to his brother was a big surprise — Wade was a master of the sport.

The only person who could consistently beat Wade was Todd's fellow kindergartner, Sonali Baber. What she lacked in size, she made up in agility and sheer smarts. Just when Wade would think that she was going for a block, she would move back and expertly strike his highly angled shots. And once she gained control of the ball, there was no stopping her. Wade could only best her part of the time, as he did today during the second recess. This was usually cause for celebration — but not today.

After his puzzled brother and friends decided it was best to just leave him alone, Wade wandered over to the northwest part of the playground and sat on the ground with his back against the corner of the fence. No, nothing could cheer him up; his birthday always reminded him that his father was not around to celebrate with him. Not that he remembered that much about him; his dad had died when Wade was only four years old.

ཨོཾ་མ་ཎི་པདྨེ་ཧཱུྃ་ ཨོཾ་མ་ཎི་པདྨེ་ཧཱུྃ་ ཨོཾ་མ་ཎི་པདྨེ་ཧཱུྃ་

Josh Adams had been an oilman and was on the road almost constantly. While working a rig in McPherson, Kansas, he was close to a large pipe being hoisted from the ground. It rocked out of position, came loose from its supports and crushed him underneath. He had died instantly.

Wade still recalled the ominous ringing of the phone in the middle of the night; in fact, it was one of the few memories he had from those days. His mother, Abby Stanton-Adams, was a veterinarian, and late night calls were not at all unusual. But this one was different — Wade remembered it had a dark, scary feel to it.

As his brother slept soundly, Wade crawled from his bed in his footed Sesame Street pajamas to investigate. As he rounded the corner into the living room, he heard an audible gasp and found his mother, phone to her ear, sitting on the floor, talking as she wept.

"My God, when did it happen?"

She listened . . .

"Did he suffer? Oh, I see —"

She listened . . .

"Hell, no, I don't have a funeral home picked out! He was only twenty-seven years old! Do you think I was expecting this?" She sobbed, then held back the tears. "I'm sorry. I know these are questions you have to ask." Looking up, she discovered Wade, holding his comfort blanket, leaning against the wall, eyes as large as saucers. "Excuse me. I'll have to get back with you. What is your number?"

She listened . . . and scribbled on a nearby note pad.

Then she hung up the phone and pulled Wade close to her, saying, "Your daddy is gone. Oh, baby, your daddy is gone!"

The days that followed were nearly a complete blur, though he did remember several things: He recalled the near constant crying of his mother. He also recollected walking with his brother, one on each side of his mother, holding her hand. As they passed in front of his father's open casket, he heard the voice of a well-meaning uncle saying, "Your father has just gone to sleep. He'll wake up again when Jesus comes."

Wade recalled thinking:

He's dead, and he'll never wake up.

Then came the sense of loneliness and knowing his father would never come home again.

Their house was on Cherokee Street, close to the railroad tracks, and when the train went by at night he listened to the lonely whistle and the rumbling as it ran the tracks. Many times when his father was alive he would come into Wade's bedroom to tuck him in. He would sit on the edge of his bed, and they would hear the train. Then it was a comforting sound, but no more.

He so missed his father's smile and warm hugs. He loved the happy expression on his mother's face as she leaped into his arms when his dad returned from work. His father was often covered with grease, but it made no difference to her.

Wade loved the way his father's pipe hung from his mouth, and the fragrant aroma it produced. When he thought of his father, oftentimes he could still smell it.

ༀམཎིཔདྨེཧཱུྃ ༀམཎིཔདྨེཧཱུྃ ༀམཎིཔདྨེཧཱུྃ

Moving back against the fence, Wade put his hand to his head and wiped his brown hair from his forehead. His piercing blue eyes gazed at the clouds floating in the sky. It was fall in Oklahoma, and the air was crisp and clean. Soon the class bell would ring, and he would have to return to class — but he was suddenly aware of something behind him.

Wade slowly turned his head, and there was an older man with a shaved head. He was wearing a brownish red robe, and he beamed a radiant smile at Wade.

The man's hands were pointing upwards and pressed together against his chest. His joyful smile deepened, and slowly he bowed to the astonished youth. "Greetings, little one," he said as he rose up. Now erect, his sparkling eyes connected with Wade's.

Wade heard the ringing of the school bell and glanced toward the playground. His fellow students had begun to head back to class. He rubbed his eyes and turned back around. The mysterious man was no longer there. Wade stood and looked in all directions, and no one was to be found.

Am I imagining things?

He dusted off his jeans and walked slowly to class. Every few seconds he would turn and look around, still seeing nothing but streets, a car or two, and a residential neighborhood.

Okay, either I am going crazy or some wacko is stalking me.

He grinned to himself.

Probably I am going crazy.

Looking ahead, he saw his two best friends, his brother Todd and Sonali, waiting for him.

"Hey, guys," Wade asked, "did you see anyone standing behind the fence while I was sitting there? A bald guy wearing a red robe?"

They looked at each other and shrugged their shoulders. Sonali made a circular motion with her right index finger on the side of her head to show she thought Wade had gone completely nutty.

"Just thought I'd ask," Wade said. "Let's get back to class before we're late. I don't want to get a tardy slip."

With Todd taking his left hand and Sonali his right, they giggled — and swinging their arms together, they ran back into the school.

And all the bad memories were forgotten.

ཨོཾ་མ་ཎི་པདྨེ་ཧཱུྃ ཨོཾ་མ་ཎི་པདྨེ་ཧཱུྃ ཨོཾ་མ་ཎི་པདྨེ་ཧཱུྃ

Lama Tenzin Tashi continued to smile as he walked away from the elementary school. He was certain he was the first Tibetan monk to ever set foot in this town, evidenced by the stares from the passing cars. A few blocks away waited a taxi, which would return him to the Tulsa airport. From there, he would fly back to India and would make the more hazardous journey again — across the Himalayas into Tibet.

Now, though, his dark inner voice returned. The guilt of the choices he had made became more and more intense. No, it was more than just guilt; it was shame. He realized that, as a younger monk, he had allowed his pride to get the upper hand. He had somehow believed he could change the world and feed the starving millions. Besides that, there was also the death of Dawa, which happened because he had chosen to undertake this task.

He could only guess what the 14th Dalai Lama would think of what he had done. He wondered how his old hermit teacher, Geshe Choden Nyima, would judge his actions. He bowed his head in disgust with himself. But it was too late to turn back. Right or wrong was no longer pertinent. He had identified and with certainty had found the incarnation. As per his agreement, when the child reached the prescribed age he would find him again and hopefully convince him to fly to Tibet. There he would give him the portion of the fortune that was his and his alone.

How available are the memories of past lifetimes? Can I prove to the boy and his family beyond any shadow of a doubt the truth of my claim?

He pulled out his old picture of a very young Dalai Lama, tucked into the inside pocket of his robe. As he touched it he could still sense the presence of Gyen la imbedded within. This gave him great comfort.

He smiled in spite of himself.

Chapter 2

December 28, 2009, Claremore, Oklahoma

T he snowy hill of the Will Rogers Memorial beckoned to three college students who were home from Oklahoma State University for their Christmas break. In the early afternoon Wade and Todd Adams, along with Sonali Baber, drove up in a white Honda CRV into the parking lot of the Memorial. Wade jumped from the driver's side and opened the rear door. Out bounded two very excited dogs, one a black-and-white rat terrier and the other a yellow Lab. Simultaneously Sonali bounced out from the passenger side and Todd from the back seat.

Wade yelled out, "Sunshine, Zoe, stay close!" Hearing their names, both dogs obediently ran to his side, allowing him to attach leashes to their collars. "Good dogs!" he said.

Wade pulled doggie treats from his pocket and gave one to each. He looked down at the happy face of Sunshine, the rat terrier. She had been his pet for over five years, and never had he seen such a happy dog. The minute he laid eyes on her as a puppy, he knew there was something unique about her. And she seemed to feel the same way about him, having leaped excitedly into his arms from the litter of puppies.

Sonali took the other leash from Wade and bent over to hug her Lab. She missed Zoe more than anyone could know and planned next fall to take her back to OSU with her. She had found her at the Claremore Animal Shelter, and while she was initially skittish, with Sonali's patient love she became as happy as a young dog could be.

Todd pulled their sleds out of the back of the CRV. He also grabbed a football and tucked it under his right arm. A short walk led them to the slope that gently fell away from the Memorial. Here, away from the risk of traffic, Wade and Sonali released their dogs from their leashes. They romped and nipped at not only each other but also the snow, as if they had never seen it before.

Todd and Sonali quickly jumped on their sleds and took off at breakneck speed down the hill. Sunshine and Zoe ran after them, just like they were chasing two human sized bones. Sure enough, toward the bottom, Todd and Sonali crashed into each other, rolling off their sleds into the snow.

Wade watched as they rose and started flinging snowballs at each other. Sonali, whose family roots were from India, was tiny compared to the athletic Todd, but she hit him with three snowballs before he knew what had happened. Wade smiled. His brother was no doubt his best friend, and Sonali was his true love.

How could I be happier?

Wade sat down on his sled and looked up at the majestic statue of Will Rogers riding atop his faithful horse, Soapsuds. A number of bright red male cardinals sat on Will's head. They looked as if they were expecting a ride.

It's great to be back home.

He was a sophomore, following in his mother's footsteps and majoring in veterinary medicine. Wade loved animals — being with and caring for them just came naturally. He planned on going to vet school at OSU, where his mother had attended. Wade was pleased when, the following year, Todd and Sonali had also chosen to enroll there.

Wade smiled as he watched Todd take another snowball to the head. Todd had developed into quite an athlete in high school, playing quarterback for the Claremore Zebras, though now he was an outstanding freshman quarterback at OSU. When Todd entered college he opted not to move into the athletic dorm and chose instead to room with Wade at his apartment. They were more than just brothers; they were buddies.

Wade was no slouch in athletics, either, though his strength was in wrestling. While he was undefeated his senior year and won the state championship, for college he chose to focus on academics. He knew his GPA had to be high to have a chance at vet school.

Wade gazed at Sonali as she continued to pound Todd mercilessly with snowballs. Sunshine and Zoe had finally exhausted themselves, and both sat to the side, tongues hanging out with happy looks on their faces. They seemed to be enjoying the pummeling Todd was getting.

"Wade!" Todd yelled at the top of his lungs. "Come down and protect me from this crazy woman! I'm getting —" Just then he was interrupted as a large snowball struck him right in the mouth and knocked him to the ground.

Sonali laughed heartily. "You'd better get down here, Wade," she said. "I think our hot-shot OSU quarterback needs your protection."

"I think you're right." Wade hopped on his sled and headed down the hill. As soon as he arrived at the bottom, he was met by a shower of snowballs that could only be described as a barrage. Like his brother, once he stood he was quickly bowled over.

Todd laughed so hard he could barely catch his breath.

Wade thought quickly. *It is time for desperate action.* His only hope was to get a hold of her. After all, she wasn't over five feet tall, and if she weighed more than 100 pounds he would be surprised.

He stood, taking a snowball in the face, and charged in the direction it came from. He was hit again and again. He heard Todd's laughter become nearly hysterical. Wade thought: *Does she ever miss?*

Running as quickly as he could, Wade was able to get a glimpse of a figure that was elusively darting from side to side. At last he was able to grab one of her tiny feet and pull her to the ground with him. It was like grabbing a slippery eel. Wade felt her relax, and she twisted around to face him. Her long dark hair was dusted with sparkling snowflakes.

"I was hoping you would catch me," she said mischievously as the white landscape reflected in her dark eyes. She kissed him softly on the lips. "Wade Adams, I love you."

"Sonali Baber, I love you, too."

"You know what?" she said.

"What?"

"You'd look a lot better with a little more white on your face." With that, she smashed a large snowball right up his nose and into his eyes. She jumped out of his grasp, then ran over and plopped down beside the dogs, who happily clamored around her.

Wade wiped the snow from his face and gazed at her, a beautiful young lady — he hoped some day she would be his wife. What had started as a close friendship in grade school had developed into a romance after she started attending college. He well remembered the moment.

ༀ་མ་ཚི་པ་ཌྲེ་ཧཱུྃ ༀ་མ་ཚི་པ་ཌྲེ་ཧཱུྃ ༀ་མ་ཚི་པ་ཌྲེ་ཧཱུྃ

It was late October when Wade and Sonali took a long, quiet walk around the OSU campus. It was a beautiful autumn day, and they were surrounded by the browns, oranges and reds of falling leaves. They eventually wandered to a local pizza hangout and enjoyed their favorite: mushroom and black olive. On the way back, they stopped at Theta Pond, sat on one of the benches overlooking the water and watched the ducks paddle by. They had saved some pizza crust, which they broke apart and tossed into the water. Soon there was a swarm of ducks at their feet, fighting among themselves for the morsels of bread. When their supply was exhausted the teeming mass of ducks began to disperse.

Before Wade even consciously knew it, he had faced Sonali and had taken her hands in his. He looked at them for a long time, pondering the minutest details. Her fingernails were closely trimmed and clear polish covered them. He gazed at the lines in her palms and felt the calluses at the tips of her fingers, reminding him that not only was she quite a good violinist, but she also enjoyed working with her hands. These were not the hands of a dainty female who cringed at the thought of breaking a nail; rather, they were those of someone who would be comfortable digging in the earth or hammering a nail. Since she was the daughter of two physicians and was herself a pre-med major, one would have guessed that her parents would have brought her up to be self-sufficient. Yes, there was no doubt about it, Sonali was a strong woman.

He followed her toned arms up from her hands. Then he looked closely at her neck, her face and her eyes, which were expectantly gazing directly at him, tears building at the outside corners. As he looked into her deep brown eyes, he discovered a familiarity that made him start.

Must be all those years we have known each other.

Then he released her hands and gently brushed the moisture away from her face. She smiled, and he smiled back. No words were spoken. They did not need to be.

ༀ་མ་ཚི་པ་ཌྲེ་ཧཱུྃ ༀ་མ་ཚི་པ་ཌྲེ་ཧཱུྃ ༀ་མ་ཚི་པ་ཌྲེ་ཧཱུྃ

Recovering from his reverie, Wade said, "Okay, Sonali, there's no doubt that you are tougher than Todd and me combined."

Sonali grinned at his acknowledgment and continued to rub the heads of the most-happy canines.

Todd nodded his agreement. He picked up the football. "Hey Wade, go out for a pass."

"You've got to be kidding? In this weather?"

"Why not?"

"Well, okay."

Todd said, "Fly pattern, with a hook thirty yards down the field." He barked out, "Hut! Hut!" Once Todd began backpedaling, Wade streaked down the snow-covered field and did a perfect hook pattern. He clung to the ball as it struck him in the chest.

"Touchdown, OSU!" yelled Sonali.

Wade jumped up and down, as if he were celebrating in the end zone. He flipped the ball back to Todd and said, "Okay, Todd, let's see if you're a real man or just a wiener. Deep post forty yards down the field."

"Hut! Hut! Hut!" Todd again backpedaled and waited as Wade slogged across the snowy ground. Just before he made his cut, Todd threw the ball, which sailed far over his head.

Wade bent over, trying to catch his breath, his warm exhalations fogging the air. "Just as I thought, you're a wiener. God, why did I have to have a brother with such a rubber arm. I was wide open! It would have been an easy touchdown."

Todd said, "Give me a brother who could run a decent pattern, and it would have been a touchdown."

"Oh, yeah?"

"Yeah."

With that Wade barreled into Todd, and the wrestling match was on. Soon Sonali joined the fracas, and Sunshine and Zoe barked excitedly. When they finally wore themselves out, they all lay on their backs in the snow, fighting off the dogs who thought they all should be licked in the face.

After some rest, Wade said, "Let's head over to our house for something hot to drink. Mom will be expecting us. Besides that, it's starting to get really cold." The sky had become cloudy, and there was a deepening chill in the air. Sunshine and Zoe both barked their approval, and they headed to the Adams' home for anything that smacked of being warm.

ཨོམ་ཚེ་པ་རྗེ་ཧྲི ཨོམ་ཚེ་པ་རྗེ་ཧྲི ཨོམ་ཚེ་པ་རྗེ་ཧྲི

Wade and Todd could immediately tell that something was different when they pulled into their driveway. Perhaps it was the fact that there were more lights on than they would have expected. Their mother was definitely an environmentalist, and she did not waste electricity. The sky was beginning to darken, and not only were the front porch lights on but also most of the ones in the living area.

After putting the dogs into the heated garage, the three piled onto the front porch. "Mom, we're home!" Wade called out as he cracked open the door. They burst into the entryway, feeling the cozy warm air.

They heard their mother from around the corner. "Boys, Sonali, we have a guest. Come on in. I want you to meet him."

When they entered the living room, Wade, Todd and Sonali stopped dead in their tracks. Abby Stanton-Adams was sipping a cup of tea, sitting in a chair across from a wrinkled, smiling old man with a shaved head. He was dressed in the ochre robes of a Tibetan monk and also held a cup in his hand.

"Wade, Todd, Sonali, I would like to introduce you to Lama Tenzin Tashi, a Buddhist monk, who is here all the way from Tibet."

Wade stared with disbelief.

Could it be?

He shook his head. This was an older version of the man he saw at the Claremont Elementary School when he was six years old. The memory of his face had been imprinted on his young mind.

What is he doing here?

The old man put his cup of tea back in its saucer, sat it on the end table and stood somewhat unsteadily. His smile extended from ear to ear. He placed his hands together in front of him in a praying position and bowed deeply at the waist.

Sonali understood immediately and mimicked the actions of the monk. She glared at Wade and Todd, who took the cue and responded in kind.

Abby smiled at their clumsiness and said, "Go ahead and take off your coats and have a seat. I believe this man has a most interesting tale to share with us. First, let me get you something hot to drink. Anyone care for hot chocolate?"

The three yelled, "Yes!"

Abby smiled as she left the room.

Wade glanced uncomfortably at the monk, who had a radiant smile that seemed to never leave his face.

In a few moments Abby reappeared with a tray containing five mugs of hot chocolate with tiny marshmallows floating on the foamy tops. Wade, Todd and Sonali each grabbed one.

"Lama Tenzin Tashi?" Abby asked. "Have you ever had hot chocolate?"

"No," he said, curiously studying the remaining cups.

"Would you like to try one?"

"Of course. One should be willing to try new things, even when you are as old as I am." Abby then lifted the tray to him, and he removed one of the leftover mugs.

Abby took the last one and sat back in her chair.

They all watched him as he cautiously sipped the concoction and chuckled when the pleased look came over his face.

"I think this could be better than yak butter tea!" he said after he dabbed his mouth with a paper napkin. His insides warmed, the aged monk sighed in satisfaction.

They all sat together, silently sipping the hot beverage. When they had nearly finished, Abby spoke. "I suppose you are all curious about how our guest came to be here. The truth is I'm wondering the same thing. When he knocked on our door this afternoon and introduced himself, my first reaction was to lock the door and call the police. But as I'm sure you all will agree, after my initial shock, it was clear that there was something gentle and safe about him — and curiosity replaced my fear. After all, what in heaven's name is a Tibetan monk doing here in Claremore, Oklahoma, the heart of the Bible Belt? Not only that, but what is he doing here at our home? Of course, I invited him in for hot tea. We had just sat down, and the kindly lama was just about to explain himself, when the three of you arrived. I'm ready to hear what he has to say. What about you?"

Wide-eyed and interested, all three nodded.

"Well, sir, go right ahead. I think it is unanimous."

Lama Tenzin Tashi placed his mug back on the tray, and his seemingly endless smile vanished into a somber countenance. He looked at his rapt audience and began. "First, let me tell you a bit about me. As you know, my name is Lama Tenzin Tashi, but it was not always that. I was born with the name Sampa Dhondup in the little village of Batang in what used to be eastern Tibet. At the age of ten, I became a member of the monastic community at Chöde Gaden Pendeling Monastery, and my name was formally changed to what it is today. Some years later, I made the long trek to Drepung Monastery. Currently I am the abbot there, replacing the most wise and beloved abbot, Lobsang Gyaltso, who died just last year. Not only was he my superior, he was my best friend." The old man's eyes welled up with tears.

Wade felt sympathy for him and reached over and touched his shoulder.

Nodding his appreciation for the kind gesture, Tenzin wiped his eyes and continued. "In February of nineteen ninety, a most unusual event occurred. An American, a Mr. Matthew Walker Johnston, arranged a meeting with my abbot. The venerable one asked me to attend with him. The man, as we discovered, had terminal cancer. Not only that, he was extremely wealthy. He made a most interesting request of us." He paused for a moment. "Before I go any further, may I ask you if any of you believe in reincarnation?"

Abby glanced at her sons before she spoke. "I was raised in a Congregational Church, and I have been taught to be not only open minded but also discerning. I have tried to bring up my boys in the same way. I can't speak for them, but for myself, I have wondered if that were a possibility. If you believe there is a part of us that survives death, then it doesn't make sense that we sit in heaven for eternity, strumming harps and singing 'Kum Ba Yah.' It feels right that we would have further opportunities to grow and learn. And as I'm sure you know," she said, winking at her sons, "I've got plenty to work on."

Wade and Todd smiled at her, though they wisely decided to remain silent.

Sonali then spoke up. "My parents are Buddhists. As they have taught me, reincarnation is not just a belief, it is a reality."

Tenzin turned to Wade and Todd. "What about you? What do you believe?"

Wade looked puzzled. "To tell you the truth, I haven't given it much thought. It seems to me that if I lived in other lifetimes, I would have some memory of it."

Todd remained silent, obviously skeptical.

Tenzin nodded and continued. "The request that Matthew Walker Johnston made of us was that we find his next incarnation and give him back his fortune. For our services we would receive a substantial donation. At that time, the amount to be given to the incarnation was worth around two hundred and fifty million American dollars in precious gemstones. It is undoubtedly worth considerably more now."

Sonali gasped out loud. "No way! This is a joke, right?"

"This is not a joke," Tenzin said. "Of course, the venerable abbot Lobsang Gyaltso refused, and the meeting was ended. I must confess, though, that I was the weaker of us and thought of all of those I could help with the donation he would make. Some days later we reached an agreement, and as you in Oklahoma might say, we 'shook on it.'" Tenzin looked at his listeners. There was dead silence.

The three youths were transfixed. Abby had paled, with a thin sheen of sweat beading up on her forehead.

"Some months later, on October eighteenth, nineteen ninety, Matthew Walker Johnston died in Tibet. Over the next few years, I began an intensive search for his incarnation. Finally, during periods of meditation while circumambulating around the sacred lake, Yamdrok-tso, visions were given to me of his next birth. I discovered, beyond any reasonable doubt, who that is.

"To be certain, I paid a visit to Claremore, Oklahoma, in October, 1996 and positively identified him. At that time I retained the services of a private investigator so that, even if he and his family moved away, he could be located."

At that moment, Tenzin turned his full attention to Wade and smiled. "Wade Joshua Adams, you are the reincarnation of Matthew Walker Johnston, and I have come to take you to Tibet, where you can claim your fortune to do with what you will."

Suddenly a loud *thud* was heard along with the breaking of glass. Wade's mother had passed out, her half-empty mug of hot chocolate smashed into small pieces on the floor.

ཨོཾ་མ་ཎི་པདྨེ་ཧཱུྂ་ ཨོཾ་མ་ཎི་པདྨེ་ཧཱུྂ་ ཨོཾ་མ་ཎི་པདྨེ་ཧཱུྂ་

When Abby came to, she was lying on the couch, being sponged by Sonali with a cool washcloth. Todd had swept up the broken glass and was mopping the floor dry. Wade was sitting beside his mother, holding her hand, a look of concern on his face. As her eyes opened, he said, "Mom, are you all right?"

"Of course, I'm not all right!" she said angrily as she quickly sat up. "Some lunatic is claiming my son is the reincarnation of an extremely wealthy man, someone I've never heard of before. Not only that, he wants to take him to Timbuktu to get his fortune. How would you feel?"

Tenzin, who had not moved from his chair, looked at her patiently. "I certainly understand your feelings. In my country such a thing is readily accepted as truth. In your Western culture, however, such ideas must seem like nonsense."

Abby blurted out, "First of all, there's no way you can know how I'm feeling right now. And secondly, you're right, this seems totally insane. I consider myself a reasonable person, but this is too ridiculous even to consider."

Tenzin nodded in acknowledgment and continued. "In the search for the rebirth of the Dalai Lama, there are a series of tests the search committee performs to prove beyond any doubt the child being examined is indeed the reincarnation. Once those evaluations are satisfactorily completed, the family accepts the decision of the monks. Here, the opposite seems to be true. While I am certain Wade is the reincarnation of Matthew Johnston, I must somehow prove this not only to him but also to you."

Tenzin paused, looked at the floor and measured carefully his next words. Looking up at last, he said, "I had concern this might be the reaction I would get. I promised, though, to a dying man over nineteen years ago that I would do all I could to convince you of the truth. For now, it is getting late in the day, and I would like to return tomorrow morning for further discussions.

"Before I leave, though, I would like to do one last thing." As he spoke, he pulled a tarnished Tibetan singing bowl from his robe. He smiled with the memories it brought. "Please close your eyes," he said as he did the same. He then rotated a now-splintered wooden dowel on the outside edge of the bowl, which produced an oscillating sound. Even after he pulled the dowel away, the ringing continued to resonate. It seemed to relax everyone present. Tenzin had hoped for such.

When the sound diminished, he said, "I am staying at a hotel in downtown Claremore, and, with your permission, I will return in the morning at nine a.m. I have with me objects from the incarnation of Matthew Johnston. Do you have, how do you say it, a CD player?"

"Yes," said Todd.

Tenzin continued, "Please have it here tomorrow. It is possible Wade will somehow recognize one or more of his previous possessions. We will soon see." With that, he bowed and headed for the door.

Before the door closed behind him, a blast of cold air made the remaining four shiver.

Chapter 3

December 29, 2009, Claremore, Oklahoma

I t was a frantic scene at the Adams' home.

Abby appeared not to have slept a wink. Her brown hair was tousled, and there were dark circles under her blue eyes. She had cancelled her clinic day and was bustling around trying to put things in order. She was happy to see Sonali, who had arrived early so she could pitch in and help. While Sonali didn't look particularly tired, a look of concern was written all over her pretty face.

Wade and Todd had talked late into the night and were slow in getting themselves together. However, remembering the lama's request, Todd had positioned their CD player on the coffee table in front of the sofa. At 8:58 a.m. their frenzied activity was completed, and they were on deck and ready. Two minutes later, the doorbell rang.

Wade, wearing a warm up suit and sneakers, jumped up as if shot from a gun. "I'll answer it," he said and went to the door. He looked through the peephole.

Standing outside in the frigid morning was Lama Tenzin Tashi, wearing a short black rainproof jacket and boots — obviously his nod to the weather, and he carried a small brown satchel at his side.

Despite the winter wear, Wade couldn't imagine what was keeping the man from turning into a human icicle. He flung open the door and said, "Come in before you freeze to death."

Tenzin smiled and said, "Thank you." He limped into the living room where the others sat waiting on the edge of their seats — expectantly. "Good morning," he said brightly.

Abby pushed herself from the sofa and stepped forward to hug the aged lama. "Please forgive me for my behavior last night. I'm afraid that I overreacted."

Tenzin accepted her hug, then removed his coat and said, "There is no need for apology. You are a concerned mother who is worried about her son. This is completely normal."

Abby was pleased this gentle man had not been offended. "Coffee or tea?" she asked.

"Tea," said Tenzin. "A warming cup would do well by me."

Wade, Todd and Sonali then greeted the lama and settled him into a comfortable chair, so that he might be center stage. They took their places across from him on the sofa.

Abby poured from the tea pot on the coffee table and handed a cup and saucer to Tenzin, saying, "Some people like cream with tea." She lifted a small pitcher, questioning.

Tenzin declined the cream, sipped the tea, then said, "Now to the matter at hand. As Matthew Johnston was preparing to die, I asked him for three objects that might help jog the memory of his next incarnation. The ones he gave me are in this bag. Have any of you ever meditated before?"

"No," they all said in unison.

Tenzin fondly recalled his first lessons from Gyen la. "I will ask all of you to sit up straight and close your eyes. Now place your hands on your knees." Seeing that they were closely following his instructions, he continued. "Now concentrate on your breath as it moves in and out and listen carefully. Let the music enter your being." He pulled a CD from his bag, leaned over the coffee table and placed it in the player; he then carefully selected the appropriate track.

The music of a slow movement of a string quartet filled the air. Tenzin himself closed his eyes and focused. After Matthew Johnston's death, he spent more than a few times listening to this amazing composition. He had never heard more beautiful music.

He floated with the tones as they moved up and down the scale. He remembered Matthew Johnston had experienced romantic feelings with this music, but for him the experience was quite different, making him think of dying, with the ebb and flow of emotions one might have. The slowing at the end of the movement seemed to represent the gradual cessation of the breath.

He opened his eyes and looked at his beginning meditators. Todd had opened his eyes and was staring at the floor. Wade and his mother seemed to be listening intently, while tears of joy were streaming down Sonali's face. When the movement ended, Tenzin ejected the CD, placed it back into its cover and returned it to his bag.

"Sonali," he said, "you seem to be the one most affected by this music. What are you feeling?"

"That is the string quartet by Joseph Haydn, Opus 76, Number Five, the second movement," she said. "I am always moved by this music. I'm afraid that is where the feeling comes from, nothing more."

"Wade?" he said.

"I don't know what is real or what is my active imagination," the young man said. "All I can tell you is that it seemed familiar, even though I don't recall having heard it before." After a pause, he grinned and said, "This lifetime, at least."

Tenzin nodded his understanding. "Any other comments?" he asked.

"Yes," Todd said. "This is a bunch of malarkey. Wade, I've had enough. Wanna leave with me?"

Wade looked at his brother. "Todd, I want to hear him out. I don't think it will take too much longer."

Todd crossed his arms and nodded, though obviously irritated with the whole process.

"Your brother is right," Tenzin said to Todd. "This will not take too long. Let me get item number two." Next he pulled out a small black jewelry box. He handed it to Wade.

Wade paused for a moment then opened it. Sitting in the mounting was a five-pointed golden star, with a smaller silver one in the middle of it; the medal hung from a ribbon with red, white and blue stripes. His mother leaned over his shoulder and said, "Wade, that's a Silver Star. It's a medal given for heroism in time of war."

Wade broke out into a cold sweat, and he felt like he was about to explode. Before he could stop himself, he angrily picked it out of the case and threw it against the wall. It clinked on the tile floor. "I am not a hero," he yelled as he clenched his fists.

Sonali and Wade's astonished family stared as he jumped up and went across the room to pick up the medal and flung it against the wall a second time. Then he flopped back in the sofa, painful tears dripping down his face. He covered his eyes with his hands.

What is going on here?

Tenzin studied Wade compassionately.

Abby leaned over and consoled him. Sonali did the same, and Todd's apathy suddenly disappeared as he stood and squeezed his shoulder. "Brother, what happened?"

Wade stammered, "I . . . I don't know. I felt rage . . . like I have . . . never felt . . . before. Get that thing away . . . I can't bear to have it around me."

Todd got up and picked the medal off the floor, replaced it in the box and handed it back to Tenzin.

After a few minutes, Tenzin said, "Wade, Matthew Johnston had warned me that he felt very negative about this medal, but I had no idea your reaction would be this severe. If you would like, we can delay seeing the third item until tomorrow."

Wade said, "Sir, if it's all the same to you, I would like to see it now."

"Are you sure?"

"Yes."

"Very well, then. Before you view it, I want to make you aware that Matthew Johnston had an even stronger reaction to this object. Are you certain you are ready?"

Wade waited grimly, his loved ones surrounding him, all touching him in one way or another. "Yes, I am ready."

Lama Tenzin Tashi pulled a white jewelry box from the bag. He presented it to Wade with a look of concern.

Wade took the box and slowly opened it up. When he saw the object, he felt a sudden convulsion of emotion, and tears again poured from his eyes. A vision opened up before him — a beautiful Japanese woman with long shining hair. He could almost feel her as she reached out and touched his face. There was a familiar texture to her skin, and her scent created a sense of intimacy.

Just as rapidly as it appeared, the vision faded. Wade shook his head and glanced at his mother. Her eyes were misty, and she had a worried look on her face. Todd also appeared troubled and gripped his shoulder even harder. Sonali was as pale as a ghost.

Before them was a gold ring with an arrangement of diamonds on the front face in the shape of an open lotus.

"Enough!" Wade screamed, turning his head away.

Abby first looked at her son and then at the lama. "Do you mind coming back tomorrow morning?"

"Of course," Tenzin said. "I will be back at nine."

Tenzin accepted the return of the ring, packed it away in his satchel, donned his coat and took his leave as quietly as he had arrived.

ཨོཾ་མ་ཎི་པདྨེ་ཧཱུྃ ཨོཾ་མ་ཎི་པདྨེ་ཧཱུྃ ཨོཾ་མ་ཎི་པདྨེ་ཧཱུྃ

The following morning the aged lama rang the doorbell of the Adams' household.

While waiting for them to answer, Tenzin let his mind wander to his upcoming trip across the Himalayas. Of course, he would not attempt such a journey during the middle of winter. That would be far too cold for his aging bones. He would stay in India for the winter and make the crossing sometime in late April. There was still plenty of money left in his account at the Bank of India, so perhaps he could treat himself to a nice warm hotel room there as he had done here.

He grimaced with the thought of doing the arduous trip again. After all, he was almost 70 years old, and he could daily feel the aches and pains of aging. Both of his knees and hips had become arthritic, and he certainly didn't have the stamina of his younger years. Besides that, he began to notice a feeling of shortness of breath along with swelling of his legs. He could only guess at what the problem was, but his studies led him to believe he was starting to experience heart failure. When he returned home he would see a doctor, but he knew that he was seriously ill.

"Good morning, Lama Tenzin Tashi," said Abby as she answered the door. "Do you mind if I just call you Tenzin?"

The lama smiled at her. "I would be delighted. Do you mind if I call you — Abby?"

"Not at all," she said. "Please come in. We have been looking forward to talking with you." As he entered, Wade, Todd and Sonali were sitting on the sofa as before, expectantly waiting. Tenzin happily saw, on the tray beside his chair, a mug of hot chocolate with marshmallows floating on the top. He sat and took a few sips.

"Ah," he said. He closed his eyes for a moment, smacked his lips, and fully savored again this new delight.

Tenzin returned his cup to the tray, moved forward in his chair and looked at Wade. "It is time to make a decision. Are you willing to travel to Tibet and claim the fortune that is yours?"

Wade sat up and looked directly at the monk. "The answer is — maybe."

Tenzin was not surprised by his response. He warmly said, "Speak from your heart."

Wade said, "We have been discussing this since yesterday, and I hope you understand our discomfort. You make an incredible claim — I am the reincarnation of a wealthy man who died in 1990. When I was six years old you came all the way from Tibet to spy on me and to confirm your visions. Finally, and even more amazingly, now you want me to fly to Tibet to take possession of an alleged fortune. Honestly — this sounds like some sort of con game."

Tenzin glanced over at Wade's mother and saw a look of pride on her face.

"All this said," Wade continued, "I'm certain that the reactions I had to at least two of the three objects yesterday were absolutely real, and it made me wonder whether there was a possibility that at least some of what you claim is true.

"So," he said with some hesitation, "I want to go to Tibet and discover the truth for myself. While I have no reason to doubt you, I feel uncomfortable going halfway around the world alone. These are my conditions. First of all, I want Sonali and Todd to go with me." Todd nodded, his eyes narrowed in thought. Wade felt Sonali squeeze his shoulder. "Secondly, as we are all students at Oklahoma State University, we must delay such a trip until the end of this May, when the school semester is completed. Third, we are not a wealthy family." He glanced at his mother, who pursed her lips a tiny bit. "So, the expenses of this travel have to be borne by you."

The monk looked carefully at Wade, then at his mother. "Abby," he softly said, "what are your feelings in this matter?"

"Tenzin, I've never been out of the United States, and someday I would love to travel to other places around the world. But as we discussed yesterday, this is his decision and his adventure. I will not be going to Tibet."

"Very well, then," said Tenzin. "Wade, those many years ago, as I made plans with Matthew Johnston, we anticipated your concerns and felt you would not want to make such a trip by yourself. After yesterday I was fairly certain that there would be three making this trip." He handed an envelope to him. As Wade looked inside and saw a tight stack of one-hundred-dollar bills, Tenzin said, "I think you will find adequate funds to arrange your travel and for expenses while you are there. It is far too cold for travel at this time of year anyway, so May or June will be fine. I will need you to fly to Lhasa and plan to be there for about two weeks. Also, in the envelope is the e-mail address of a contact in India. He will help you arrange the details of your flights and hotel, as well as your visas, and he will relay the information covertly to me. I will meet you at your lodging in Lhasa at a time to be determined in the future.

"You will stay in that city for some days to acclimate to the altitude. We will then travel to a most sacred place, a location I will share with you later. There we will spend time in meditation before we unearth the gemstones. While I could simply place them in your possession, it is my intuition this preparation will be a most important key to the success of your journey. I strongly suggest you spend some time over the next five months in meditation. Do you have any questions?"

The four were silent.

Tenzin beamed a smile at them. "If anything comes to mind, I will be available for contact sometime in the middle of May." He stood to leave, bowed deeply and slipped into his warm coat.

As he reached the door, he turned and said, "Let me assure you. I am not crazy. It just seems that way." He laughed out loud and entered the blustery, winter day, confident that all had gone well.

Chapter 4

May 29, 2010, Drepung Monastery, Tibet

Lama Tenzin Tashi sat in deep meditation. Now, at seventy years of age, all those years of practice had borne fruit. The restlessness of the mind was nearly a thing of the past, and he had explored universes within. Today he had been sitting for ten hours and could have gone much longer.

As he brought his waking consciousness back, he again became aware of the discomfort of his body. The arthritic pain had gotten worse, and it was growing more and more difficult to walk. These days he used a cane to help keep his balance, and he walked with an unsteady stoop. He smiled as he remembered those days when his physical body was his ally and not his antagonist. As he uncrossed his legs, he began to think back to the recent past.

ཨོཾ་མ་ཎི་པདྨེ་ཧཱུྃ་ ཨོཾ་མ་ཎི་པདྨེ་ཧཱུྃ་ ཨོཾ་མ་ཎི་པདྨེ་ཧཱུྃ་

The trip over the Himalayas this past April was the worst of the four he had made. Not only was it unseasonably cold, but the Chinese had discovered his usual route in and out of the country and had effectively closed it off. It now required a circuitous trek that was longer and more precarious. That, added to his arthritis and his worsening difficulty breathing, made for a miserable journey. He knew it was the last such trip that he would make. His time away from his home country was over. His last days would all be spent in Tibet.

When he finally made it back to Drepung he discovered his second in command, Yeshe Tsering, had covered quite well for his prolonged absence and the Chinese were none the wiser. The authorities thought of him as a doting old fool, and when Yeshe explained to them he had to be gone for a lengthy period to take care of family matters, no questions were asked. After all, what risk to them did a feeble, decrepit old man present?

Once he had gotten back into his routine, he had made a long-overdue visit to a physician in Lhasa. He remembered the appointment all too well. The young Chinese doctor was respectful as he examined him. "Venerable abbot, how long have you been short of breath?" he asked.

"Six months, maybe longer."

The doctor shook his head. "You have fluid in your chest at the bases of your lungs. Also, you have the sounds of a narrowed aortic valve. Your heart has to work very hard to force blood into your body." He cleared his throat. "You have congestive heart failure."

Tenzin nodded. It was as he had thought.

"The chest X-ray shows your heart is severely enlarged." A flash of discomfort went across the physician's face.

Here comes the bad news.

"Sir, I'm afraid you do not have long to live. I will prescribe digoxin and diuretics, but the damage is already too severe."

"How long do I have?"

"One to two months. At most, three. I will leave your prescriptions at the desk. They will improve your symptoms but will not increase the length of your life." With that the physician awkwardly bolted from the room.

As he walked from the clinic, Lama Tenzin Tashi realized that he faced a most interesting conundrum. He was not afraid to die. In fact, with the gradually increasing pain he was experiencing, he looked at death with some degree of anticipation. The problem was what to do with the fortune in gemstones that was his?

Of course, he would keep nothing for himself, but it would take some time to covertly sell the jewels and distribute the funds. He hoped to see the happy faces of those who had once been hungry, now contented and burping with satisfaction. He desired as much as anything to provide medical care to the indigent.

Think of the hospitals I could build.

He chuckled to himself.

Desire still lives within me.

Hopefully he would live long enough to see the results of his efforts, but the timing was close.

Far too close for comfort.

ཨོཾམཎིཔདྨེཧཱུྃ ཨོཾམཎིཔདྨེཧཱུྃ ཨོཾམཎིཔདྨེཧཱུྃ

Tenzin roused himself from his thoughts. He was long overdue for some routine administrative duties his position required. He walked over and looked at his calendar. Of course, the picture accompanying the month of May was of Chairman Mao. He was required to keep it on his desk. If he removed the calendar, it would be noticed.

I live in a glass house.

He studied the dates. Tomorrow afternoon, on a flight from Beijing, the three young Americans would be arriving at the airport. Today they must be en route from Los Angeles. In the coming weeks, his promise made almost twenty years ago would be completed. Soon his earthly existence would end. He sighed.

Where has the time, no — where has my life gone?

Tomorrow evening he would be greeting Wade, Todd and Sonali at their hotel in Lhasa. He had no small amount of concern. He remembered the strong reactions Wade and Sonali had when they were confronted with the objects from the past. Tibet, being an innately spiritual place, would likely accentuate, rather than dampen, their experiences.

It would be a most interesting time.

ཨོཾམཎིཔདྨེཧཱུྃ ཨོཾམཎིཔདྨེཧཱུྃ ཨོཾམཎིཔདྨེཧཱུྃ

May 30, 2010, en route to Lhasa

Wade Adams sat in a window seat on the Air China flight from Beijing to Lhasa. They had left early that morning and expected to be at their destination in a few more hours, though they still had to stop over at Chengdu. Next to him sat Sonali, who appeared to be sleeping, her right arm intertwined with his.

To her left sat Todd in an aisle seat. He looked exhausted from all of the travel, and his usually neatly combed blonde hair was now in complete disarray. That, however, didn't keep him from flirting with the flight attendant, who checked on their row a bit more than one normally would have expected.

It had been a whirlwind experience since the visit of the monk in December. But at long last they were headed to Lhasa, the home of the Potala, the residence of Dalai Lamas for centuries and centuries.

But thoughts of doubt began to assault Wade's mind. He worried about dragging his love and his brother into this. He felt no small amount of responsibility for their safety.

Is the monk a charlatan who will hold us for ransom in some isolated cave in Tibet?

He pictured the three of them tied and gagged, being fed bread and water, and undergoing torture to learn their secrets — whatever they might be.

He looked over at Sonali as she slept.

If anything happened to her, I would never forgive myself.

Wade then took a few moments to practice the meditation technique the monk had taught them. He took some slow, deep breaths. As he looked inside himself, he became aware that he trusted the monk. Not only that, if the lama's outlandish claims were indeed true, he wondered what he would do with over 250 million dollars. Part of him wanted to live a life of luxury and provide that same sort of existence to those he loved. He thought of his mother who had worked so hard to make ends meet. Every so often a voice would whisper the idea of using the funds to help those less fortunate. He tried not to listen too hard.

After all, isn't this my fortune?

He smiled as he remembered cartoons where there was an angel and a devil floating above the head of the character, trying to sway him to their point of view. He closed his eyes and in time fell asleep.

Sonali came awake just as Wade began to nap. As the plane took them deeper into Asia, she began thinking of her family origins in India. Her mother and father had both been raised in the city of Bangalore in southern India and met while completing medical school. They finished their residencies while in India, her father a cardiologist and her mother a pediatrician. They returned to their birth place after finishing their training and hoped to raise a family there. As Bangalore developed into the "Silicon Valley of India," and their once-comfortable home town became a frantic beehive of activity, they decided to relocate. When they visited Oklahoma, and eventually Claremore, they found friendly people, a low cost of living and a leisurely pace. It all added up, and they happily moved. Sonali had been born at St. John's Hospital in Tulsa and was followed by a brother, Asim, and a sister, Indira.

She began to think about the emotions she felt with the objects shown by the monk. While she loved the Haydn quartet fragment that was played, she had no compelling visceral reaction. All present knew, though, that she reacted strongly to the showing of the golden ring with diamonds shaped in the form of a lotus. At that moment the ring somehow transported itself to her left ring finger, and she saw herself looking at it. She rotated her finger to see the diamonds sparkle in the light. She then, in her mind's eye, glimpsed the face of someone who was quite familiar, yet not someone she knew. He had thick, dark hair and was strikingly handsome.

What no one seemed to appreciate was her reaction to the Silver Star. While Wade reacted angrily to it, her immediate feeling was that of death — no, not just death — intense, nearly out-of-her-mind rage. When Wade threw it against the wall the second time, she had to fight back the urge to leap from the sofa and stomp on it.

She was glad to be going with her loved one on this trip, but at the same time she was afraid of what she might discover. If indeed the memories of past lives were blanketed by the protective amnesia of death, would she be capable of handling the truth should it be made known to her?

She closed her eyes and again drifted off.

Todd attempted to straighten his disarranged hair as he looked around for the flight attendant. Not seeing her, he began to think about the upcoming time in Lhasa. He knew what his role was, and that was to keep an eye on things. As he thought about it, he repeatedly popped his clenched right fist into the palm of his left hand. He had never backed away from a fight and didn't intend to this time. Wade and Sonali might allow themselves to meditate into La-La Land, but he would stay alert and ready.

After all, what's a brother for?

The plane prepared to land at the gateway city of Chengdu. Soon they would fly to The Forbidden City.

Lhasa.

Chapter 5

May 30, 2010, Lhasa, Tibet

The three Oklahoma travelers took turns looking out the window of their airplane as it weaved its way between majestic snow-capped mountains, eventually finding the runway of the Lhasa Gonggar Airport. The cold sterility of concrete, steel and glass greeted them as they came down the ramp into the terminal.

After they had picked out their luggage and walked outside, the chill of the airport was washed away by the radiant smile of a Tibetan who wore a sign around his neck that read, "Wade, Todd and Sonali Adams." As they approached, they saw he wore a crumpled brown canvas hat and a lime green shirt with black pants. He said, "Tashi delek. This means, 'Welcome and good luck.' My name is Goba Choephel, and I will be your guide." He then placed a white silk *khata*, a Tibetan scarf, around each of their necks.

Todd asked, "What does this mean?"

"This is a Tibetan tradition. The scarf symbolizes goodwill, purity and compassion."

Sonali pointed to the sign on Goba's chest and said, "Wow, it's great to already be a member of the family." She smiled as she nudged Wade with her elbow. "Can I start off by giving you a list of honey-dos?"

Wade laughed. "Sure, as long as you don't mind having dinner ready for me when I come home from work. Oh, while you're at it, could you rub my shoulders?"

Sonali glared at him for a moment then broke into a smile.

Goba then directed them to an old, battered, green and white Toyota Land Cruiser. As they sputtered away from the airport, they forgot the fatigue of travel and found themselves entranced by the barren mountain surroundings; the brilliant blue sky seemed to softly kiss the glistening peaks. Before they knew it, they had arrived at the outskirts of Lhasa. Cement block buildings identical to the ones they had seen in Beijing crowded the sides of the highway.

"Are you sure we're not in China?" Wade asked sarcastically.

Goba spoke quietly, as if he were afraid some outsider might be listening. "This is only a part of the gradual destroying of our Tibetan culture by the Chinese. Many of our traditional buildings have been removed and replaced by those of Chinese design.

"Besides that, since the nineteen eighties, China has been recruiting their people to live in Tibet. They gave them incentives to move — higher pay, housing and tax exemptions. In May of two thousand and six, the Qingzang Railway was completed, directly connecting China with Tibet. In the past our beautiful high mountains helped keep our country isolated. The railroad changed everything, and now the Chinese can flood into our homeland without obstacles. They are like a pack of hungry rats who have invaded a kitchen full of food." He paused and swallowed. "We Tibetans have become a minority in our own country."

"Why doesn't the world help you?" Wade wondered aloud.

Goba said, "China has rapidly become one of the world's great powers and holds over one trillion dollars in United States debt. Most governments, including yours, are afraid to cross them."

The three Americans shook their heads.

Soon a mammoth white and ochre structure rose to the left of the highway. The Potala loomed over one of the world's highest cities. The view was breathtaking.

"Oh, my God," gasped Wade. "I've seen pictures, but never imagined anything like this."

Sonali nodded and said, "Oh, yes! Let's check into our hotel — then walk back and take a closer look."

Todd reminded them, "Remember, we're at almost twelve thousand feet in elevation. We need to take it easy."

"Come on, Todd! We're in one of the most amazing cities in the world," said Sonali. "You can sit in the room and twiddle your thumbs if you want. Wade and I are going to check this place out."

"Don't worry, Sonali," Todd said, "I can keep up with you."

"Are you sure about that?"

"I'm sure," said Todd with a smirk. "The question is: Can you keep up with me?"

ཨོཾ་མ་ཎི་པདྨེ་ཧཱུྃ་ ཨོཾ་མ་ཎི་པདྨེ་ཧཱུྃ་ ཨོཾ་མ་ཎི་པདྨེ་ཧཱུྃ་

Before long, they arrived at the entry to the Kyichu Hotel. They were practically invited inside by the attractive glass doors framed in brass and brightly colored Tibetan designs over the entrance way. After checking in, they carried — yes, there were no elevators — their luggage up the creaking wooden stairs with matching banisters to their two-bedroom accommodations on the fourth floor. They all paused at the third level.

Todd was in a cold sweat, gasping for breath.

"Don't you have any guts, tough guy?" Sonali said as she dashed up the final flight of stairs.

A musty smell greeted them as they opened the door to their room. Large windows faced them, revealing a panoramic view of the city. Wade walked over and cracked open several of them, filling the room with fresh air.

In this main bedroom there were two sagging twin beds covered with brightly colored quilts. Night stands stood adjacent to each of the beds. Four scuffed wooden chairs were set against the windows. To their right was a tiny bathroom, and to the left was the entry to a smaller bedroom.

They took a few moments to rest before they left the hotel. A short walk led them back to the Potala. As they moved closer, they saw thousands of Tibetans walking clockwise around the holy place.

"Let's join them," said Wade.

Nodding their agreement, the three merged with the throng. Many were carrying prayer beads and chanting continuously, producing a low-pitched hypnotic murmur. There were long rows of prayer wheels placed adjacent to the walkway, which the Tibetans spun with their hands as they passed by.

"Why do they spin them? It makes no sense at all," Todd said.

Sonali explained, "On most of them you will see on the outside the Sanskrit words, om mani padme hum. Also, on the inside is a paper scroll with that same phrase written repeatedly. It is their belief that with each rotation of the wheel, it is as if one recites it many times, giving the practitioner an added measure of merit. It is even more powerful if one focuses the mind on the mantra as well." As she gazed at the devout crowd, she added, "Their passion to their spiritual practice is as deep as any I have ever seen. We Americans could learn a thing or two from them."

Todd felt something bump against his legs. Looking down, he saw a ragged beggar with no legs who had rolled up next to him on a low wooden platform. He lifted his hands in the air, pleading.

"Beat it!" Todd said to the man as he waved him off. He kicked the platform, jarring the disabled man and almost knocking him off onto the street. Suddenly the area around them was hushed.

An embarrassed Sonali and Wade stared at Todd.

Todd explained, "I'm not giving my money to some guy off the street. There are panhandlers just like him on street corners in America. They can work for their money just like I do." Todd was hot around the collar, somehow failing to remember that his mother gave him money every month when he was at school.

Sonali pulled a one-yuan note from her pocket. She sadly saw a picture of Chairman Mao on it. She bent over and handed the money to the beggar.

A smile crossed his tired face.

Todd shook his head and walked away.

Sonali said to Wade, "I know we shouldn't encourage dependence, but sometimes you have to listen to your heart. I would rather give money to a thousand who are not truly in need rather than miss the one who really needs our help."

Wade nodded and checked his watch as they hurried after Todd. They had to return to their hotel. The lama would soon be there.

ༀ་མ་ཎི་པདྨེ་ཧཱུྃ་ ༀ་མ་ཎི་པདྨེ་ཧཱུྃ་ ༀ་མ་ཎི་པདྨེ་ཧཱུྃ་

Promptly at 6:00 p.m., a knock was heard at the door, and all three rushed to answer it.

Standing before them was Lama Tenzin Tashi, leaning breathlessly on a wooden cane. He smiled. "Now that you are in my home country," he paused to catch his breath, "I must greet you in the Tibetan way. Tashi delek."

"Tashi delek," they all responded as he entered.

Wade was stunned at how much the monk had aged since they last saw him. *How long ago was it? Only five months?*

It was hard to believe. He had lost more than a little weight, and his face was skeletal. His step was slower, his stoop more pronounced and his lips carried a bluish hue.

Wade glanced down at Tenzin's legs; they were swollen at least twice their previous size.

Having caught his breath, the lama managed, "I trust you find your accommodations here acceptable?"

"Yes, sir," Sonali said. She pulled out a chair. "Please sit down and rest."

"Thank you, young lady. There was a time I could have danced up those stairs, but not now. I am afraid that old age is catching up with me."

The three then arranged chairs in front of him and sat down. The dull murmur of street noise seeped into the room.

Tenzin removed a small canteen from his backpack and gingerly took a few sips. "They tell me I need to restrict my fluids, but it seems I'm thirsty all the time." He took a last shallow drink of water, closed the canteen then shoved it back in his pack.

"Again, welcome to Tibet," he finally said. "I am happy that all three of you made it here safely. After I returned from our last visit, I imagined myself in your position, and discovered it would take a great amount of courage to make such a trip. I congratulate all of you." His eyes shone brightly.

"First, I am sure you are aware that you have just arrived at a very high altitude, and to give you time to acclimate, you will stay in this city for three days. There are many wonderful sights your guide will take you to in this ancient place. I would take you myself, but my health does not allow me.

"Now, it's time, as you Americans say, to get down to business. I must first ask you to keep what I am about to say completely confidential. Because of the wealth that we are talking about, there will be those who are willing to kill to obtain it." He paused for a moment, and a look of pain crossed his wrinkled face. "Please, please, tell no one here, not even Goba. Are we in agreement?"

Wade and Sonali whispered, "Yes."

Todd folded his arms and stared straight ahead.

"After three days here in Lhasa, your guide and I will take you to one of the four sacred lakes of Tibet, Yamdrok-tso. It is now a much safer trip; the road was paved some years back. By the shore of this lake, at a location known only to me, the treasure is hidden.

"While there, we will be staying at an old friend's home in the town of Nangartse, along with her husband, my goddaughter and godson. At the holy lake we will sit in meditation. When the time is right, we will dig up the gemstones and return to Lhasa."

Wade raised his hand and, after the monk's acknowledgement, said, "Why do we have to meditate at all? Most of us have practiced as you have asked." He looked over at Todd who was purposely looking away. "I know you said back in Oklahoma that this was important, but I still don't get it. Why we don't dig them up immediately and high-tail it back home."

"High-tail?" the monk asked.

"Rush," said Todd.

Tenzin said, "I know it must be confusing to you. I believe in my heart that this is more than just a trip to uncover the gemstones, and that you all have information locked inside yourselves that the waters of most holy Yamdrok-tso would help you discover. My sense is that she wants to assist you, just as she did for me some eighteen years ago.

"Still, I want to be as democratic as your wonderful country is. After all, you are from the United States of America. We will take a vote. Who wants the fortune to be dug up immediately upon our arrival at Yamdrok-tso?"

Todd glanced back and forth at the others, then meekly lifted his right hand.

"Who would like to spend some time in meditation before we unearth the treasure?"

Wade and Sonali both quickly raised their hands.

Todd shook his head.

"Ah-ha!" the monk beamed. "The will of the people is honored! For my coming incarnation, I would like to be born in your country. The freedoms I have experienced over my life have been severely limited, and next time I would like to have more choices. But I have wandered from the topic at hand.

"After we recover the gems, we will high-tail it —" he paused and winked at them "— back to Lhasa. We will change your flights to the earliest ones available and return you to your home. Also, for reasons which I will explain in a moment, we will re-route you back through India. The sooner, the better. While Tibet is one of the safest places in the world, I wouldn't want to risk a robbery. Many are suffering under the Chinese, and my countrymen are now doing things they would not have done in the past. Let's not give them a temptation that would be difficult for them to handle." He took a deep breath. "Trust me, I understand such things."

Todd appeared confused. "If these so-called gemstones actually exist, how do we get them through customs?"

Tenzin said, "Your question is an excellent one. Before your visit, I asked this very same question to a . . . well . . . book smuggler . . ." He stopped, cleared his throat and saw in his mind the large collection in The Forbidden Library. "Not about smuggling jewels, of course. I proposed to him you desired to smuggle tiny engravings of the Dalai Lama out of Tibet." Tenzin shrugged his shoulders. "Sometimes it is necessary not to be completely truthful."

He continued. "He has left these instructions so that you might safely conceal your fortune and get it out of Tibet and into India." He handed Wade an envelope. "Memorize this information, then destroy it. As my source said, 'Remember, they are not looking for stones, they are looking for weapons.'

"In India you will need further assistance." Tenzin then handed Wade a second sealed letter. "This is a letter of introduction to a Mr. Vara Vyas, a fine man I have met at the Bank of India in New Delhi." Tenzin then looked at Wade and spoke slowly for emphasis. "Unlike many, he can be trusted. This I am certain of. I am sure he will be happy to assist you." Tenzin then studied them carefully. He was pleased with what he saw. "Do you have any further questions?"

The silence revealed their answer.

"Very well, then. I will see you on the morning of the second day of June. As an old teacher, Geshe Choden Nyima, once told me, 'Expect the unexpected.' I believe that is a saying in your country as well. I agree with that, but would like to add one last thought." He hesitated. "We are all approaching a pivotal place. We have come together for a specific reason and purpose. That much I am sure of. The understandings we receive over the coming days will be weighted, and how we respond to them will be critical to the remaining years of our lives — how ever long or short that might be." With that, Tenzin stood up and moved to the door.

With a nod of the head and a slight bow to them all, he departed, quietly closing the door behind him.

ཨོམ་ཎི་པདྨེ་ཧཱུྃ   ཨོམ་ཎི་པདྨེ་ཧཱུྃ   ཨོམ་ཎི་པདྨེ་ཧཱུྃ

Even though it was late in the evening, Tenzin felt the desire to visit the foremost religious structure in all of Tibet, the Jokhang Temple. He felt his breath become labored as he quickened his pace. He knew the doors closed shortly and hoped to spend a few moments in meditation.

As he approached the temple, he was saddened; groups of Chinese soldiers were patrolling the area. Meanwhile, there were more surveillance cameras than ever before at all the major intersections, slowly rotating back and forth, watching the tiniest movement. Chinese snipers sat on the tallest buildings, peering at the crowd with binoculars. He was reminded of the book he had read years ago, *1984*.

George Orwell was right. There is a Big Brother, and he is Chinese.

As he reached the entrance to the temple, he prostrated three times and walked into the smoky atmosphere. The soft glow of thousands of candles illuminated the chamber. He sat down and felt the sacred energy. He sadly knew the abbot now in charge of this blessed shrine was a Chinese puppet. He also was aware that Tibetan Buddhism in his country was slowly dying. Even His Holiness, the Dalai Lama, had said he would consider foregoing rebirth in Tibet to keep China from controlling his reincarnation. Tenzin felt abandoned. He grimly reflected on the new holiday they now had in Tibet, Serf Liberation Day, on every March 28th. This was the date the Chinese had dissolved the Tibetan government and established the Tibet Autonomous Region under their rule.

Given the horrific consequences of the Chinese occupation, a better name might be Tibetan Enslavement Day. He shook his head as he recalled the so-called "testimonials" of those who said life was much better under Chinese rule.

Suddenly he heard a ringing noise and looked up to see a Chinese tourist answering her cell phone followed by a loud conversation. Then another cell phone, followed by a third, and finally a fourth. He felt anger building inside him.

They have not stopped desecrating our most holy place — and never will. To them it is still a pig sty.

Surprising those around him and even himself, a lifetime of repressed anger violently erupted to the surface. He had kept his promise to Sangye Phuntsog all this years, but no longer.

He threw his cane against the wall, stood up as erect as he was able and screamed:

"Get out of here! Get out now!"

He raised up his hands, clenching his fists in rage. Those in the temple withdrew to the safety of darkened corners.

"Look what you've done to us. You've taken everything away! We have nothing left. Not even our dignity!" He began to strike his chest with his fists, and fell to his knees, sobbing uncontrollably.

Hearing the uproar, a Chinese soldier entered the temple with a raised pistol and put the muzzle against his head. Tenzin heard the click of the hammer being pulled back. Tears streamed from his eyes as he thought:

Not yet . . . please . . . not yet . . .

The soldier lowered his weapon and walked away.

Soon Tenzin felt calm hands upon his shoulders. "Venerable abbot?" He looked up and saw the kindly face of a young monk from his own Drepung Monastery, still unscarred by the ravages of time and circumstance. Tenzin wondered if he had once looked like that. He hoped he had. "Venerable abbot? Let's go back to our monastery." He lifted Tenzin from the floor, handed him his cane and slowly they walked outside.

The tears continued to flow from the old man's eyes. He would never again return to the Jokhang. He knew beyond any doubt that he would take his last breath before the next opportunity arose.

He inhaled deeply of the thick smoke from the yak butter candles, knowing it would be for the final time.

Chapter 6

June 2, 2010, Lhasa, Tibet

W ade, Todd and Sonali waited impatiently at the front of the Kyichu Hotel. Soon enough a familiar Land Cruiser pulled before them and honked. It belched a cloud of black exhaust, and the engine sounded as if it were about to explode. In the driver's seat was Goba, the aged lama sitting beside him.

Wade opened the rear door, and the three piled in. All had experienced some altitude sickness in the previous days. Wade and Todd had some mild headaches, but Sonali had the worst of it, and in the wee hours they could hear her retching in the bathroom. She was not one to complain, though, and their daily sightseeing tours of Lhasa continued. This morning she seemed to be fully recovered.

With a screech the vehicle pulled away and headed toward the west. As they passed the Potala, they noted that the crowds of people had not diminished. Tenzin felt pride in his aging chest.

The drive to Yamdrok-tso was in nearly complete silence. As they passed through the small towns, the architecture was more typically Tibetan, with homes made of wood, rock, earth and cement, constructed on elevated south-facing locations. On many, the skull of a yak hung above the doorway.

Todd pointed and asked, "Hey, Goba, why is that placed over the entrances?"

"This is a remnant of the Bon religion, the one that preceded Buddhism here in Tibet," he said. "They are there as a guardian for the home and protect the occupants from evil spirits."

"Maybe we should take one home to protect us from the Sooners," Todd said with a smile.

Tenzin looked confused, but Sonali and Wade both heartily laughed, remembering their arch rival — the University of Oklahoma.

Finally after curving up and up, they crested over the final hill and gasped at the stunning beauty of Yamdrok-tso with its nearly infinite number of shades of turquoise.

Tenzin was appalled at how much lower the water level was since he was last here. The gradual draining of the lake to supply hydroelectric power was taking its toll.

When she dies, a part of Tibet dies.

Tenzin studied the landscape closely. Soon he spotted the location across the lake where the gemstones were buried. A brief pang of fear hit him.

What if someone has discovered them?

He knew he would feel much better when the gems were actually in their possession. He also was aware that at this higher altitude he was experiencing much more difficulty breathing.

Soon they entered the town of Nangartse and arrived in front of a modest white rectangular home. As they exited the vehicle, two excited teenagers greeted them; they rushed to Tenzin, bear-hugging him before he could take one step. "Uncle Tenzin! Uncle Tenzin!" they yelled. "We've missed you!"

He tearfully held and kissed them on their foreheads. It had been almost a year since their last visit, as his extended travels to the United States had taken away opportunities to see them.

He looked into the dark eyes of Lhamu Adhe, the one who had stolen his heart some eighteen years ago. As he studied her face, he realized that she had begun to look more and more like her mother. And, of course, there was Jughuma Passang, her younger half-brother, who came into the world around two years after his sister. With his impish grin and near-frantic energy, he looked like trouble waiting to happen.

Tenzin remembered that shortly after his and Pema's circumambulation those many years ago, she had met her husband-to-be, a humble Tibetan farmer named Champa Phurbu. A year after they were married they were blessed with Jughuma's birth. Of course, Tenzin was asked to be his godfather too, which he readily accepted. Each time they made a visit to Lhasa he would meet with them and bounce the two giggling youngsters on his knee as any grandfather would. While he had great love for both, Lhamu Adhe would always have a special place in his heart.

Pema and Champa quickly emerged from the house, and Tenzin heard a loud gasp. He saw Pema had her hand over her mouth. "My dear lama," she said, "what has happened to you? Let us get you inside." She and Champa put their arms around him, and with the steadying help of his cane assisted him up the stairs and through the front door into the living area.

They led him to a comfortable though somewhat threadbare sofa. After he was seated, his godchildren plopped down beside him, getting as close to him as they possibly could. The three Americans followed behind, carrying their luggage. They put their suitcases against the wall and sat in some wooden chairs across from the sofa. Pema and Champa also squeezed onto the couch next to their children. While Pema and Champa wore traditional Tibetan wear, both of their children were in jeans and tee shirts.

Wade studied the room. In the same area was a breakfast nook with a small kitchen. A large picture of the Buddha looked over the group, smiling in approval.

After they were all seated and had a few moments to rest, Tenzin spoke. "My dear friends, I would like to introduce you to the three Americans who are visiting our country." Pointing, he said, "This is Wade and Todd Adams, and that is Sonali Baber. Our hosts are Champa Phurbu, Pema Dhargye, Lhamu Adhe and Jughuma Passang." All seemed to understand except Champa, who was not fluent in English.

Sonali said, "Thank you for allowing us to stay in your home." She added, "How do you know the lama?"

Pema said, "Brother Monk and I met many years ago while doing a spiritual walk around the lake. He is the godfather to our children."

Wade saw Lhamu and Jughuma nod and smile.

"What is the purpose of your journey to our country?" Pema said.

Tenzin interrupted, "They will be staying here for some days of meditation. They have heard much about our sacred lake."

Wade, Todd and Sonali glanced at each other, reminded of the need for secrecy. Sonali said, "We have heard that there are visions here."

Pema said, "Indeed there are. There are answers in those waters to those who seek them. What you see may not be what you desire, but they are what they are."

Tenzin looked closely at his old friend. The only real appreciable change he could discern was some graying of her hair at the temples. He smiled. She was still a beautiful woman.

"Pema, if you would be so kind to show our guests to their rooms, I would like to have a word with you."

"Of course." With that, the three Americans hoisted their suitcases, and she led them from the living area and down a narrow hall. Wade and Todd shared a bedroom, while Sonali's space looked more like a closet with a tiny pallet squeezed onto the floor. They all set their luggage in the hallway and lay down in their beds to rest.

Pema returned to sit on the chair opposite Tenzin. She urged the children to follow their father to a chore outside. "What is it?" she asked.

Tenzin looked at the woman who had become one of his closest friends over the years. "Pema, there are some things that you need to know. And, of course, as I suspect you have already discerned, there is some knowledge I must keep from you. I ask for your understanding."

"Old friend, I completely trust your wisdom in this matter."

Tenzin decided to just come out with it. "Pema, I am dying."

She covered her mouth, murmuring, "No . . ."

"I found out just this past May, and I had hoped I had longer to live than was predicted. But now it is clear that it will be sooner rather than later. I felt I needed to tell you in person."

Pema rose and sat herself beside him; she placed her head on his shoulder, crying softly now, already in mourning.

He slipped his arm around her and patted her on the head. "There, there. I am an old man, and the fact I made it this long is no small miracle. I do have a favor to ask of you."

"Anything, dear friend," she sobbed.

"Pema, I think it is possible that I will die while I am here. I can sense the end of this incarnation is near. If that happens, it is my hope that you will take care of this shell that is my body. I would like to have a traditional Tibetan sky burial. Could you have it taken to Drigung Til?"

"Of course, Brother Monk, of course."

"There is something I would like you to have. This was given to me by my teacher, Geshe Choden Nyima." He then pulled his precious Tibetan singing bowl from his robe. "Would you like me to play it for you?"

Overcome with emotion, she was unable to speak. She simply nodded.

He took a familiar wooden dowel and began to rotate it around the outside rim. A modulating tone was produced, filling every inch of the room. Unexpectedly he suddenly found himself outside of his body. He saw the tone enter Pema's forehead and go down her spine to a yellow whirling vortex at the level of her solar plexus. There the spinning of the chakra increased, and the yellow light became brighter.

Ah, the healing power of the bowl is still there.

But the tone did not enter him.

Nothing can heal me now.

The vision lasted but a moment, and he found himself again comforting his dearest of friends. When the ringing ceased, he handed her the bowl, which she held close to her side.

"Pema, I have one more request to make of you," he said.

"Anything," she said as she wiped the tears from her eyes.

"Please give this to Lhamu Adhe after my death." With that, he again reached into the inside of his robe and produced a yellowed picture of a very young Dalai Lama.

He placed it in the palm of her hand and closed her fingers around it.

Chapter 7

At the crack of dawn, the monk and the three Americans were out of bed and ready to experience the holy waters of Yamdrok-tso. Pema was up with them and prepared cups of hot yak butter tea. Tenzin enjoyed watching the varied reactions of his guests. Wade and Sonali took to the beverage quite readily, though Todd wrinkled his nose in disgust.

Pema said, "Either you love it or you hate it, and I can tell who hates it." She smiled at Todd who left his full cup on the table.

Pema then put together a hearty breakfast of fried eggs and buttered barley rolls. The Americans cleaned their plates, but Tenzin was too nauseated to eat. He glanced up to find Pema looking at him with sorrow. She rose from the table and gathered the sack lunches of cheese sandwiches and chips she had prepared the previous evening. As Tenzin put his food in his pack, he saw at the bottom not only his trusty canteen but also his pick ax, the same one he had used all those years ago.

"It is time to go," Tenzin announced to the Americans, and they all rose from the table and bustled out the door. As Tenzin took up his cane, a tearful Pema embraced him.

"Goodbye, Brother Monk," she said.

"Goodbye, Pema," Tenzin said, holding her close — how he cared for her. He reluctantly released her and stumbled toward the door. To his surprise, Lhamu Adhe waited there.

"Uncle Tenzin," she said, grasping his hands. "Where are you going?"

"I am going to the lake."

"No," she said, "you are going away. I will pray for you."

"And I for you. Goodbye, Lhamu." He released her hands, kissed her forehead and embraced her. He felt her warm tears drop onto his neck.

I will miss her.

Tenzin then walked out the door. As he struggled down the steps to join the Americans, he looked back; Pema and Lhamu stood on the doorstep — waving.

They know, just as I know.

ཨོཾ་ཨཱཿཧྲཱིཿ ཨོཾ་ཨཱཿཧྲཱིཿ ཨོཾ་ཨཱཿཧྲཱིཿ

As the group slowly walked along the shore of the sacred lake, the sun began to peek over the tops of the mountains. Tenzin watched as the colors shifted in the clouds with the changing position of the sun. He was entranced.

We should look at every sunrise as if it is our last.

He nodded to himself, knowing this was his final one.

Even though the walk was fairly level, his breath became more and more labored, and he began to have tightness in his chest. He looked at his hands; the nail beds were turning a dusky blue color.

After a while they approached an array of rocks on the shoreline suitable for sitting in meditation. Tenzin was glad to have the chance to rest.

Across the lake, he could again see the site where the precious gems were buried. He thought of Dawa and how the young monk was seduced by the Enchantress of Wealth. He couldn't help but wonder what effect she would have on these three. He could only pray that they would be stronger than Dawa had been.

"We will sit here for a short meditation," the old monk said. After they had a chance to take a drink, he continued, "As I have told you, Yamdrok-tso is the place where I had the visions that eventually led to finding Wade. Also, I have sensed a benevolent nature in this lake. It is my hope that, along with the treasure, each of you will gain greater understanding and insight. Trust the feelings and thoughts you have. They are most likely accurate. Do you have any questions before we start?"

Todd said, "Yes. Why should we believe any of this garbage?"

Wade and Sonali gasped.

Tenzin only smiled. "Todd, I understand your skepticism. Even the Buddha asked that no one should believe anything unless they come by that knowledge through personal experience. Be patient a little longer, and perhaps you will get an answer to your own question."

Todd's face was filled with anger. "This is the biggest bunch of crap I've ever seen. I will be on the lookout, so don't try anything funny."

Tenzin's smile only deepened. "Let us begin. As you remember, you learned how to listen to your breath while we were in Claremore. We will do the same thing here, but this time we will have the energy of the lake to assist us. First of all, find a comfortable position, put your hands on your knees and close your eyes. Focus on your breath as it enters and leaves your chest. Keep your attention there and see what comes to you." Before he shut his eyes, he glanced at them.

Wade and Sonali had closed their eyes and appeared relaxed, but Todd was carefully surveying the surroundings.

Tenzin's breathing had finally slowed enough that he was able to begin his own meditation. It felt comfortable to be back at this place. He fondly remembered meeting Pema and Lhamu those years ago, and the many blessings that had transpired because of that rendezvous.

How dear they are to me — how dear —

He began to relax and took some deep breaths, following them in and out. He felt the waters of the lake take him into her depths. As his meditation deepened, the pain and disability of his body left him. Before long, he saw, to his surprise, the lavender curtain fall in front of him. He hadn't seen it since he was last here, and its presence shocked him

The lake has something she wants to show me.

As if the curtain could read his thoughts, it began to rise, revealing an indistinct image of an old, white-bearded man sitting in front of a most familiar Tibetan cave. He was wearing the loincloth of a renunciant. As the picture cleared, Tenzin inhaled deeply.

Gyen la!

Geshe Choden Nyima smiled deeply at his former pupil. "Sampa, I have been waiting for you. Please come and sit with me."

Tenzin looked into the eyes of the one that he missed the most, his teacher, his guide and his friend. In his vision, he sat at his feet.

Gyen la's eyes sparkled as he said, "Beloved one, the time is quickly approaching when you will make the great transition. Before this happens, there are a few things you must know. First of all, I perceive you still have some guilt over the death of Dawa. Am I correct?"

"Yes, Gyen la."

"Sampa, because he was consumed by desire, truthfully, Dawa killed himself. You fought with all your strength because, if you had lost, not only would you have been unable to fulfill your promise to Matthew Johnston, but also two innocent souls would have been irreparably harmed. I have read your intent, and it was not to harm Dawa. Also, is it not true that you feel ashamed because you have been blasphemous by tracking the incarnation?"

"Yes."

"If you look deeply, you will be aware that helping others was your main reason for undertaking the task. While it was not proper to do so, there is no one who can fault your motivations. All things must be taken in context. Are you able to release these shames from your consciousness?"

Tenzin gulped. He realized shame had become such a constant companion that he had mistakenly allowed himself to believe it was part of him. It was time to let it go. "Yes, Gyen la."

"Very well, then," Geshe said, his beatific smile making the atmosphere seem warm. He then reached over and touched Tenzin on the forehead. A light body arose from Tenzin, just as it did those many years ago.

"Gyen la," he happily said, "my spiritual body is bright and sparkling, just as yours was when I saw it all those years ago."

"Sampa, look a little more closely," he urged.

Tenzin gazed deeper inside and saw a tiny black smudge sitting at the level of his heart. "Teacher, what is that?"

Gyen la said, "Sampa, that is your ego holding onto the desire to be recognized for the beneficial effects of your portion of the gemstones."

"But I want to use them for the good of others."

His old teacher shook his head. "Helping others is one thing, and personal acknowledgement is another. The gemstones are the boy's karma and his alone. You have been fooled to believe that, because of your agreement, they are yours." He looked upon him tenderly. "Sampa, if you are able to release them, then the last black speck will be dissolved. There will be nothing that will keep you from merging with the Clear Light of the Void."

"What if I am unable to let go of them?"

"Then you will be required to remain in the round of incarnation. It is your choice and yours alone."

Tenzin heard the words of his teacher and knew the truth of what he had said. But it had been a dream of his for many years, and he wasn't ready to release it. "Gyen la, I must have some time."

"Time is something you have very little of. Soon you will be leaving your body. You must quickly go to the site where the gemstones are buried. I will be there to help. Hurry now."

"Thank you, Gyen la."

Just as abruptly as the vision appeared, it regressed, and as Tenzin roused from his contemplation, he was struggling to breathe more than ever.

There is no time to spare.

Chapter 8

Tenzin and the three Americans sat cross-legged around the site where the treasure had been buried so many years ago. As far as Tenzin could tell, the ground had not been disturbed.

It had not been difficult to procure a yak-skin boat, and the crossing had gone well. Wade, Todd and Sonali took turns paddling and eating their lunches, and before long they had arrived on the opposite shore. Tenzin dared not eat; the simple task of swallowing and breathing at the same time was no longer possible. Even though Wade and Todd had assisted him, the short hike up the steep hill had nearly pushed him past his limit. It was getting harder to hang onto his consciousness. Worried looks gathered on the faces of his companions.

"The gemstones . . . are . . . near," said a gasping Tenzin. "But first . . . let us . . . focus . . . on our breath." He watched as the three, even Todd, first gazed at the surface of the smooth lake, then closed their eyes. As for himself, he knew he could no longer meditate. His attention had to be devoted entirely on moving air in and out of his aging chest.

ཨོཾ་མ་ཎི་པདྨེ་ཧཱུྃ ཨོཾ་མ་ཎི་པདྨེ་ཧཱུྃ ཨོཾ་མ་ཎི་པདྨེ་ཧཱུྃ

Todd found himself gazing at the water and felt his eyes closing. His mind began to wander then opened to a place he had never seen before. And he was strolling down a cobbled street in the cool of evening.

Was it London?

Yes, there was Big Ben — and he was wearing the finery of the wealthy; in his right hand was an ebony cane with a heavy brass ball attached. A beautifully dressed woman was hanging on his left arm.

"Hey, mate," he heard someone behind him say in a cockney accent, "'ow about some shillings for the poor? Me children 'aven't eaten in two days."

He looked back at a dirty, unshaven man who unsteadily held a dented tin cup outstretched to him. He smelled of cheap whiskey.

"What ye say, mate?" said the man.

Suddenly his anger erupted from inside him, and he began to strike the beggar with the brass end of his cane. Blood poured from gaping wounds on the man's head, and he fell to the ground, unconscious. Todd's female companion giggled, and he heard himself saying:

"Let that be a lesson for you, you worthless scum. You don't need to beg. You need to work, just like I do." With that, he gave him two hard kicks to his chest — just for good measure.

The image changed, and in the drunkard's place was a Tibetan beggar with no legs on a wooden platform. He rubbed his eyes, and the image disappeared.

The scene changed —

Todd, or such as he was, then saw himself in the uniform of a Marine. He heard bullets whizzing past his head and somehow recognized his brother Wade, who was standing next to him. Wade was wearing a different face and a different body, but he was Wade all the same. Suddenly there was chaos. He felt the point of a gun pressing against his head. He screamed to Wade for help, then there was darkness.

ཨོམཚིངྲེ༔ ཨོམཚིངྲེ༔ ཨོམཚིངྲེ༔

Sonali Baber looked intently at the water and slipped into a deep state of meditation. She saw herself as a young Japanese woman walking in the middle of a vaguely familiar city. Without warning there was a deafening roar, a blinding flash of light — then mayhem. She heard the wails of the dying.

She then saw a handsome, dark-haired man wearing the uniform of a United States Marine. As he turned to face her, she stared in astonishment. His eyes and the soul mirrored within were those of Wade. She knew him well. He was her true love.

Finally she saw herself heavy with their child, but she was not well. She delivered a beautiful baby, but as she reached for him, the little one stopped breathing.

ཨོཾ་ཨཱཿཧཱུྃ་ ཨོཾ་ཨཱཿཧཱུྃ་ ཨོཾ་ཨཱཿཧཱུྃ་

As Wade focused on his breath, his mind floated off the hillside into the cool embrace of the lake, and the world around him disappeared.

He saw himself as a little boy sitting on the front porch of a country home. He was picking tick after tick off the back of a scruffy black Lab mix. He loved the dog with all his heart. When the animal turned to face him, there was no mistaking it. The eyes of Sunshine emanated love up at him.

But who was he — the black Lab or Sunshine? Suddenly he understood. *They are one and the same.*

Then he saw a man lying on his back in a rocky crater, lifeless. He knew it was his brother, Todd, even though he wore a different countenance. The pain he felt was overwhelming, and somehow, in some way, he felt responsible.

Next he saw himself looking into the eyes of a beautiful woman. She was Japanese, with a definite fire mixed with the love in her eyes. But wait — who was she really? While she was physically Japanese, he was sure she was Sonali. As he faced her, he knew she was his true love. In the next moment he saw her pale, lifeless body. She was cradling a dead infant in her right arm; he was certain the child was theirs.

He quivered, though deep in meditation, and found himself ready to come back to waking consciousness. He had seen enough, but the vision wasn't ready to let him go.

Deeper into his mind he went — he discovered himself sitting on the grass in the middle of a field in a football stadium. The stands were crammed full, and they all seemed to be staring at him.

Wade was suddenly aware of a calming presence sitting beside him. He appeared to be an aged Tibetan man who was wearing a loincloth. He had long flowing white hair and a white beard.

Wade said, "Who are you?"

"My name is Geshe Choden Nyima. I am here to assist you."

Looking at the stands, Wade asked, "Tell me who those people are."

Kindly he said, "Do not be alarmed. They are merely symbols of missteps you have made in your past lifetime."

Wade was shocked. "What am I to do?"

Geshe smiled. "I would like to share a story with you. In ancient times there was a devastating war. A brave man was leading his warriors from battle when they were ambushed. They were hopelessly outnumbered and all of his men were killed. He was knocked unconscious and left for dead. When he came to, he saw all of his lifeless comrades and went into a rage. He walked into a nearby village of his enemy and found a group of children playing. Before they could react, he attacked, killing all four. As he walked away he heard the shrieks of their mothers.

"As the years went by, he began to feel the shame of this crime. He felt he was going insane. He saw over and over again the terrified faces of the children as he killed them. One night, after an evening of heavy drinking, he stumbled down a darkened street and found an old man sitting in meditation. The man opened his eyes and said, 'There is one who has the answers you seek. He lives on a mountaintop in a simple cave. Take that trail,' he said, pointing to a narrow path, 'and you will find him.' The aged one then vanished into thin air.

"The next morning he awoke and started up the trail. Many days and nights later, when he had reached a point of near starvation, he dragged himself through a snowy blizzard to the mouth of a cave. He lost consciousness, but when he awoke he was sitting next to a crackling fire, and he had been covered with blankets. Somehow his stomach felt full. The same man he had seen in the village sat before him.

"The soldier said, 'Oh, wise one, how do I escape hell?'

"The sage smiled. 'I see that you have killed four innocent children, and you know now that was not the right thing to do. But if you look deeply, you know that there are many children in your enemy's country who are starving. The way out of hell is this: Find four children who would not live without food and feed them. Attend them until they are able to care for themselves. When you do this the ones you killed will smile at you, knowing that, through them, others were saved.'"

Geshe waited a few moments for his words to sink in. "So you see, Wade, by helping others, there is always a way to compensate for any missteps you have made. You have been given an amazing opportunity — and with it, a great responsibility. Don't let it slip away from you."

"I won't. Trust me, I won't," Wade promised.

Geshe said, "You are as bright as an old pupil I used to have." He wistfully smiled, then faded and disappeared.

ཨོཾམཎིཔདྨེཧཱུྃ ཨོཾམཎིཔདྨེཧཱུྃ ཨོཾམཎིཔདྨེཧཱུྃ

Wade, Todd and Sonali all opened their eyes simultaneously. There would be much to talk about later, but for the moment they focused their attention on the old monk, who was struggling to breathe.

Tenzin could barely speak. He reached into his pack and pulled out his pick ax. "Wade . . . dig here." He pointed to the area around which they were sitting.

Wade took the ax and swung it time and time again into the stony soil. After a few minutes of back breaking labor, Todd said, "Hey, Wade, let me take a turn."

Before Wade could respond, Tenzin sputtered out, "No . . . he must do this . . . himself."

As the hole deepened, Tenzin said, "Wade . . . you are close . . . now use your hands . . . we must not damage . . . the jewels."

Wade nodded, put aside the ax, and after pulling aside some jagged rocks, came upon a piece of frayed burlap. Reaching in, he pulled out a sack which had badly decayed. The inner plastic bag, though, was still intact.

Wade sat on the ground beside Todd and Sonali, and opened it. Inside they saw the bag was filled with objects wrapped in paper. Wade pulled a few from the top and peeled them open. They gasped as the light struck the gemstones. The colors were breathtaking. Wade then re-covered them and returned them to the bag.

Tenzin said, "Smaller bag . . . at the bottom."

"Oh, yes," Wade said. "That must be your portion." He pulled it from the sack. "Here, take it." He placed it in Tenzin's lap.

Tenzin carefully studied the bag and watched the tide of feelings as they moved back and forth through his being. After a brief pause, he handed it back to a puzzled Wade. Suddenly his breathing was easy, and there was a soft glow of light that illuminated his face and the top of his head. His eyes were newly bright and alert. "No, young one. This fortune, all of it, is for you and you alone. In a past life you obtained this wealth, and only you can decide what to do with it. I release it to you, its rightful owner."

Tenzin beamed a smile that warmed the three Americans.

"My friends, in a few moments I will be leaving this world. I am beginning to hear the voice of one who awaits me. When you return to Nangartse, please notify Pema of my death. She will make preparations to dispose of my body." He then reached in his pack and produced two small packages wrapped in brown paper. He handed one to Wade and another to Sonali. "These are for you. Open them when you return home."

Tenzin gazed out over the lake.

"A few final words for all of you. It is my intuition that you have just been given glimpses of your past lives and the interconnections you have shared. Is this correct?"

Wade looked first at Sonali and saw palpable warmth in her eyes. He then glanced over at Todd, who nodded. Wade said, "I think I can speak for all of us, and the answer is — yes."

"Very well, then. I'm sure you know it is rare to be aware of people and events you have shared past lives with. There is a reason for that. Can you guess what that is?"

Sonali answered quickly, "Because they aren't that important."

"Precisely," said Tenzin. "We all have the cloud of forgetfulness placed on the events of previous incarnations, simply because the most important thing is the here and now. In this most unique situation, the sacred Yamdrok-tso felt it was necessary to give you a brief vision of your past associations. Now, though, let the information you have been given fade into the recesses of your mind. Live the present moment. That's all you have. The past is over, and the future is yet to be."

Wade's eyes misted with tears. "Tenzin, we can't thank you enough." Wade placed his hand on his shoulder. "If not the gems, what will be your reward for all the work you have done?"

Tenzin smiled one last time, and his eyes twinkled in the Tibetan sun. "Nirvana, my son . . . nirvana . . ." He looked to the sky, and absolute rapture radiated from his face. "Gyen la . . . Gyen la . . . I am ready."

Tenzin took a final shallow breath, his head fell forward and he became unresponsive. He stayed, though, in the lotus position, and the gentle smile remained.

ཨོཾ་མ་ཎི་པདྨེ་ཧཱུྃ ཨོཾ་མ་ཎི་པདྨེ་ཧཱུྃ ཨོཾ་མ་ཎི་པདྨེ་ཧཱུྃ

Wade quietly sat with his love and brother on the Tibetan hillside overlooking Yamdrok-tso. They felt no rush to leave this sacred place. They were not distracted by the body of Tenzin, sitting peacefully among them.

Wade then realized he had missed a golden opportunity. With all the clamor of the past days, he had never asked Tenzin about Matthew Walker Johnston. There was much that he would have enjoyed knowing. He sighed and looked over at Sonali and Todd. They were both sitting quietly with their eyes closed.

Wade picked up the smaller bag of gems the monk had handed him and prepared to place it back into the larger one. As he opened the mouth of the sack, he discovered an envelope inside which he had not noticed before. He pulled it from the bag, broke open the seal and unfolded a yellowed sheet of paper covered in hard-to-decipher cursive. He began to silently read:

September 26, 1990

To my next incarnation,

My name is Matthew Walker Johnston. I am a native of Davidson, Oklahoma. I was born on May 27, 1926, and am soon to die.

To write this note requires a huge leap of faith. One must believe two things: First, that reincarnation really does happen, and second, that the good lama is actually capable of tracking me to my next lifetime. Personally, I think that both are a long shot, but just in case they are true, I wanted to write this note to you. Perhaps you would like to know more about me, perhaps you would not, but I think that I can offer you some perspectives from my life which you might find valuable.

To be blunt: I blew it. I was raised by the most loving mother and father that one could ask for, and I had two brothers and two sisters. We were all close, not only because we were family, but also by necessity. We struggled together during the hardest of times: the Great Depression, the Dust Bowl and eventually World War II. I don't need to go into detail here, but it is important for you to know that, in spite of the wonderful upbringing that I was given, I let the difficult events of my life drag me to the lowest imaginable places. My life became hell, and I took a lot of others with me. I will die a lonely, miserable old man. So, let's get down to the nitty-gritty.

I have allowed my life to be wasted. If Lama Tenzin Tashi (I'm guessing you have met?) were here, he would say that I have created a lot of bad karma. So, what are we to do? I'm afraid that we are in this pickle together, so here's my advice. First of all, whatever happens in your life, no matter how bad it seems, keep your chin up. If you let it drag you down and keep you there, then you are in deep shit. Truthfully that means you are feeling sorry for yourself, and, trust me, I know all about that. Second, make every moment count. In this way you won't have any regrets when the most wonderful of times eventually fade into the past. AND THEY WILL — IT'S GUARANTEED. Third, I can only assume that since you are reading this note you have the financial sum of my life sitting before you. Those gems are pretty dazzling, aren't they? Enjoy looking at them, but don't get too attached. You have a lot of work to do to make up for all the karma (crap) that I have created. I'd like to think this wealth gives you a greater chance to make up for my failures. Feed the hungry, treat disease and alleviate the suffering of others. In other words, just do all the good you can. If you go about this the right way, I think that we've got a good chance to come out of this about break even or maybe, good Lord willing and the creek don't rise (Do they still say this in Oklahoma?), a little ahead.

I'm counting on you more than you could ever know. And one more thing: If you run across a woman that is beautiful, smart and feisty, grab her! With any luck at all, she may be the one that I loved with all my heart. I would give anything to have time with her again, and if there really is a God, maybe I (you) will.

Matthew Walker Johnston
Lhasa, Tibet

Wade felt his eyes fill with tears. This was a letter written to him and him alone. It would remain his secret.

He reread the last sentence before he put the note away.

Yes, there is a God.

Chapter 9

June 3, 2010, Yamdrok-tso

ust as Todd and Sonali also roused from their meditation, the three Americans heard the scraping of rock and a grief stricken Pema appeared with her two children. Lhamu began sobbing and rushed to hug the dead lama. Jughuma stood at his mother's side.

Wade said, "He passed away a short time ago. We were just coming to get you. How did you know?"

Pema cracked a slight smile. "The dear lama and Lhamu were connected spiritually. She let me know the moment he took his last breath."

After all the three travelers had seen and experienced, none were surprised by this.

Pema continued, "I asked in town which direction you had taken and discovered you had rented a boat. When I saw it on the opposite shoreline, it was not hard to find you. Before I left, I told your guide of the lama's death, and he is waiting for you at my home. Tenzin had informed me that once you completed your mission, you would want to leave Nangartse as soon as possible. Is this still true?"

"Yes," Wade said.

She glanced at the sun. "Even though it's getting late in the day, you could still make it into Lhasa tonight. When I have finished here, I will telephone the Kyichu Hotel to expect you. But enough idle talk. I have work to do. Safe travels back to America, young ones. May you be blessed by your visit." She wiped the tears from her eyes. "Before you leave, may I ask one small thing of you?"

"Of course," Wade said.

"Please, pray for us, for Tibet. Please . . . please . . ."

Then Pema turned away and began weeping. She and a tearful Jughuma joined Lhamu beside the old lama.

Wade, Todd and Sonali stood for a moment looking at Tenzin, as if engraving him in their memories, then turned and walked down the hill to their boat. Just as they began their crossing, they heard the sonorous tone of a Tibetan singing bowl ringing from the hillside. It was played over and over again, echoing across the lake, bidding them farewell. Wade felt it enter into the middle of his forehead and go down his spine. He smiled.

I think I'm starting to imagine things.

ཨོཾ་མ་ཎི་པདྨེ་ཧཱུྃ ཨོཾ་མ་ཎི་པདྨེ་ཧཱུྃ ཨོཾ་མ་ཎི་པདྨེ་ཧཱུྃ

Saddened by the death of Tenzin, Goba — accompanied by the exhausted Americans in the back seat — drove on. The sky was beginning to darken and in a few hours they would be safely back in their hotel. Goba said, "Do you still wish to leave Lhasa tomorrow?"

"Yes," said Wade.

"Then I will go ahead and change your flight schedule. Are you sure that you would not like to stay in our city for a little longer? There is much you have not seen."

Wade said, "No, it is time for us to go. As I'm sure the lama told you, we want to return via a different route. When would the soonest flight to New Delhi be available?"

Todd interrupted, "We can't leave Lhasa until tomorrow afternoon."

"Why?" said Wade.

Todd cleared his throat. "Let's just say that I have some unfinished business to take care of."

Wade and Sonali looked at him questioningly.

Goba said, "Tomorrow afternoon it will be. For New Delhi, you will have to be routed through Kathmandu, Nepal. Get some rest, and I will let you know when we arrive back at your hotel."

ཨོཾ་མ་ཎི་པདྨེ་ཧཱུྃ ཨོཾ་མ་ཎི་པདྨེ་ཧཱུྃ ཨོཾ་མ་ཎི་པདྨེ་ཧཱུྃ

Early the next morning Wade felt himself being shaken. "Wade," Todd said. "Wade, wake up."

"What is it?" Under Wade's pillow were the gems. He had not slept well.

If anyone knew what I have . . .

"I've got something I need to take care of. Want to come with me?"

Wade said, "Sorry, I can't leave the jewels. It's just too risky."

Todd said, "I understand. I'll be back in about an hour, okay?"

Wade said, "What's going on?"

"Let's just say that God is giving me another chance." With that, Todd pulled the door closed. He heard Wade click on the lock.

After a short stop at the front desk of the hotel, Todd set out at a brisk pace in the chilly morning air. A few minutes later he found himself in front of the Potala. Even at this early hour, there were many circumambulating and chanting. Todd pulled a thick wad of one-yuan notes from his pocket. Soon he was mingling with the people and passing out money to each and every beggar.

Todd studied the crowd, and before too long he found the same disabled man they had seen several days ago. When the beggar recognized Todd, he began to wheel away.

"Stop," Todd said, motioning to him. Todd raced up and bent down beside him on his knees, so that they were face to face. The beggar's filled with fear.

Todd said, "I know you can't understand a word I'm saying, but there is something I need to share with you. I have been given two chances before to help you, and I have failed both times. The third try is a charm." He then pulled ten 100-yuan notes from his pocket and handed it to the astonished cripple. The beggar stuffed it quickly into his pocket, gave Todd an unexpected hug and excitedly wheeled away.

Todd knew that he had given him the equivalent of around one-hundred and fifty U.S. dollars. That plus the other money he had passed out had nearly depleted his share of the more than adequate pocket money Tenzin had so generously provided to each of them. He didn't care; he felt as if a huge weight had been lifted from his shoulders. Funny, until now, he didn't even know it was there. Never mind, this experience had given him an idea — not just any run-of-the-mill idea, but a great one.

ཨོཾ་མ་ཎི་པདྨེ་ཧཱུྃ་ ཨོཾ་མ་ཎི་པདྨེ་ཧཱུྃ་ ཨོཾ་མ་ཎི་པདྨེ་ཧཱུྃ་

Todd softly knocked on the door to their hotel room. "Hey, Wade, it's me."

Wade nervously cracked it only a little before letting him in. Todd said as he entered, "Is Sonali up yet?"

Wade closed and locked the door. "No, but we'll need to wake her soon. We've got to get things together to go to the airport. Goba will be here before too much longer. By the way, what've you been up to?"

Todd said, "I'll fill you and Sonali in on the flight. But Wade, before you get her up, I'd like to talk with you. We haven't had a chance to go over what happened during our meditation at Yamdrok."

Wade said, "You're right — what did you experience?"

Todd said, "Well, there's really not much to say; I've forgotten nearly everything I saw during the meditation. All that I'm left with is a strong sense that we have been through some serious shit together in a past life."

Wade said, "I'm like you; I can only remember bits and pieces, and I agree — I have the same feeling. But, as Tenzin said, it's doesn't really matter. All I can say is that I'm glad we chose to hang together *this* lifetime. And —" Wade smiled to himself as he spoke, "good Lord willing and the creek don't rise, we should have many more years left. At least, I hope we do."

Todd said, "Me too." They slapped each other on the back and started gathering their belongings. Soon they would wake Sonali, have breakfast and head back to home-sweet-home, Claremore, Oklahoma.

But first, Kathmandu, then New Delhi.

Chapter 10

June 5, 2010, New Delhi, India

I t was late at night, and the three Americans found themselves in the middle of a throng of people at the Indira Gandhi International Airport in New Delhi. With the immense wealth they had on them, they were more than a little nervous. Everyone who stepped in their path looked like a thief who might rob them of their precious cargo. While they had made it through customs at Kathmandu and New Delhi without any trouble, Wade wasn't looking forward to the rest of the trip. The stress of getting the gems into India had been bad enough.

They waited what seemed like forever for their luggage, and it was only when they were in a cab and heading to their hotel did they relax a little. Goba had recommended and made reservations for them at a cozy hotel not too far from the main branch of the Bank of India where Vara Vyas worked. And there was another problem: Tomorrow was Sunday. Would he be willing to meet them?

Once in their room, Wade punched out the first of two phone numbers Tenzin had written on the outside of the envelope intended for Vara Vyas. After four or five tries, he finally connected. It rang a few times, then a half-asleep voice answered and spoke some words in an Indian dialect.

Wade said, "Do you speak English?"

"Of course I do," the voice said. "I speak more languages than you have shoes. How many do you have?"

"What?"

"Pairs of shoes?"

"Four."

"I speak many more languages than that. At last count, it was nine. Who are you?"

"My name is Wade Adams. Are you Mr. Vyas?"

"Yes. What do you want?"

"I have a letter from Lama Tenzin Tashi. He asked me to deliver it to you."

There was a long pause. Wade began to wonder if Mr. Vyas had hung up on him.

Finally Wade heard him speak again. "I must see this letter as soon as possible. Can you meet me at my bank tomorrow morning at nine?

"You do realize tomorrow is Sunday, don't you?"

"Of course I know what day it is. I will meet you at the front entrance. I am a Trust officer. Security will let us in. I will see you in the morning. And my first name is Vara. Please call me that. We are friends already."

With that, Wade heard a loud click.

The weary travelers ordered room service. After they had eaten, they removed the gems from where they had been hidden in the nooks and crannies of their clothes and carry-on bags, and secured them back into the plastic sack. Wade again tucked the bag under his pillow.

It would be another restless night, his mind busy guarding the gems and imagining what an encounter with this officer from the Bank of India might be like.

ཨོཾ་མཎི་པདྨེ་ཧཱུྃ ཨོཾ་མཎི་པདྨེ་ཧཱུྃ ཨོཾ་མཎི་པདྨེ་ཧཱུྃ

Sunday morning found Wade, Todd and Sonali arriving at 9:20 a.m. They would've been at the bank in plenty of time but were caught in a brake-squealing, tire-screeching traffic jam. Carrying the fortune with them was bad enough; their nerves were stretched to the limit.

They had brought their luggage with them to the bank, since Wade had the feeling Mr. Vyas might just send them packing. They'd agreed to head straight for the airport should that occur — and then worry about what to do.

Waiting for them at the impressive marble and glass entrance was an Indian man who couldn't have weighed more than 120 pounds soaking wet. He looked to be in his 50s, and his closely trimmed black hair was streaked with grey. He wore white sneakers with navy Dockers slacks. A thin blue and yellow paisley tie — it might have been a remnant of times long gone — graced the front of his well starched and ironed blue striped shirt. "I am glad to see you. I might guess that you have also been victims of our poor transportation system. I was late myself." He frenetically shook all of their hands. "My name is Vara Vyas. Tell me your names."

Wade spoke for them. "I'm Wade, the one who talked with you last night. This is my brother, Todd, and this is Sonali."

"Greetings!" he said. Vara Vyas then led them through the front door, showed his ID to the armed guards, and they walked inside to an elevator. After they entered, he pressed the button for the third floor. When they exited he led them down a spacious marble-floored hallway to an office. There was no name on the door, and when he opened it, here was a tiny room with a cluttered desk. Behind it was a large framed photograph — it was Vara Vyas with an arm around a Tibetan monk's shoulder. The three looked more closely. It was Tenzin! His picture made Wade realize how much he had grown to care for the old monk and already how much he missed him.

The three also saw on his desk a picture of Vara Vyas as a much younger man with, as he said "— my beautiful wife and daughter."

Vyas pulled up chairs for them, indicated they should sit, then settled himself behind his desk — which looked as if it might have participated in the decline and fall of the Roman Empire.

He studied them intently. Then, out of the middle of nowhere, he hopped to his feet and said, "Just last week I was in Dallas, Texas, on business, and I bought this cowboy hat." He pulled down a dark brown cowboy hat perched atop a coat rack and placed it on his head. "See, I look just like a cowboy, don't you agree? Just like a cowboy."

Nothing could've been farther from the truth, but all three smiled and nodded their heads. This man was definitely a character, and they all found themselves relaxing.

He pulled the hat off his head, dropped it back atop the coat rack and settled himself again at his desk chair. "Now, tell me, how is my very special friend Tenzin doing?"

Wade gulped. "You don't know?"

"Know what?"

"He died several days ago."

"I had no idea. Please excuse me." Whereupon he jumped to his sneakered feet and bolted from the room.

When he returned a few minutes later, he was wiping his eyes and blowing his nose into a large white handkerchief. "Please forgive me. I became devastated.

Tenzin and I were . . . so many years . . . good friends. I knew he was ill, but I never expected . . ."

"We're so sorry," Sonali said.

"I'm sorry too," Vara said. "He was a wonderful man. We met when he made his first trip to America. Some years before that a man named Matthew Johnston set up a rather large account with us and asked me to make the good lama a signatory. This Mr. Johnston was apparently quite well connected, as a few days later I had a copy of the monk's ID along with his signature. Communications were difficult because of his location in Tibet, but I treasured the moments I spent with him when he was making his trips to, where was it . . . Oklahoma?"

Todd said, "We are from Oklahoma."

"So, he was visiting you?"

Wade said, "Well, yes, in a way. Would you like to see the letter now that he gave to us for you?"

"Oh, of course. Forgive me. I have a tendency to wander from the topic at hand. I would love to see it."

Wade produced the envelope.

Vara Vyas opened it and scanned the letter. "Ah, I see. He is requesting me to transfer the funds from his account over to you. That will not be a problem. Do you know how much money is in it?"

Wade shrugged his shoulders.

"It seems that Mr. Johnston wanted to be sure the monk had plenty of money for his needs. There are around $100,000 American dollars left."

Todd said, "You've got to be kidding."

"Do I look like one to play a joke? Of course I'm not kidding. Now the letter says that you may have work for me. Can you tell me what that is?"

Wade pulled from his backpack a plastic bag and set it on his desk. Vara looked at it for a moment, then pulled it open. After he unwrapped one, then another and finally a third, he exclaimed, "Dear me!" He jumped like a rocket from his desk and rushed to the door of his office and clicked on the lock. After he sat back down, he studied the jewels for a few more moments, then asked, "Are the rest in this sack also gemstones?"

"Yes," said Wade.

Vara replaced the jewels and resealed the bag. He motioned toward a safe set in the wall beside his desk. "May I?"

"Of course," said Wade.

With that he carefully set the bag inside, closed the door and turned the lock.

"No one has this combination except for me," he said. He turned back to Wade. "Rare, very rare. But I'm no expert. How did you get them?"

"Let's just say that they have been mine for longer than you could ever imagine, and they need to be confidentially sold. Do you know anyone who can give me a fair price?"

Vara nodded. "What is your time line?"

"As soon as possible."

"Very well, then. I can have someone here immediately. Please come back today at four p.m. By the way, do you have a place to stay tonight?"

"No," said Wade.

"Any who knew the lama are friends of mine. Would you honor me by being guests at my home?"

Wade smiled their acceptance.

Vyas picked up the phone and spoke a few undecipherable words. Then he said to them, "My assistant, Mr. Chohan, will show you around our city. If you will wait for him at the front of the bank, I have business to attend to. You may leave your suitcases here if you like." With that, he ushered them out of his office, in and out of the elevator, and to the front door.

ཨོམ་ཨིན་ངྲེ་ཧཱུྃ་ ཨོམ་ཨིན་ངྲེ་ཧཱུྃ་ ཨོམ་ཨིན་ངྲེ་ཧཱུྃ་

Mr. Chohan arrived momentarily and drove them around in a new black Mercedes on a short tour of the city. He seemed to be a younger version of his boss, wearing white sneakers and a narrow tie, which was poorly matched to his striped shirt.

They visited a couple of museums, though the highlight of the afternoon was a sweetmeat shop. There they gorged on delicious Indian delicacies and sipped on hot chai tea.

ཨོམ་ཨིན་ངྲེ་ཧཱུྃ་ ཨོམ་ཨིན་ངྲེ་ཧཱུྃ་ ཨོམ་ཨིན་ངྲེ་ཧཱུྃ་

Back in Vara Vyas' office they waited for him to arrive.

Vara came in and solemnly rearranged his tie as he sat at his desk. "Well," he said, "even though it is Sunday, when I told my sources a small bit about what you had, they were more than anxious to make a bid." He produced four crisp pieces of paper with figures on them. "Look at all of them carefully," he said as he handed them to Wade. "Perhaps we could do better, but if you need a quick liquidation, this one offer is the best."

Wade picked out the sheet. Todd and Sonali leaned over and stared with him.
$2,000,000,000.00

Vara said, "In case that is too many zeros for you, you should know that is two billion American dollars."

Sonali screamed out loud, and Wade and Todd clutched their heads in disbelief. Vara smiled. "Is that a yes?"

Wade merely nodded his head. He was speechless.

ཨོཾ་མ་ཎི་པདྨེ་ཧཱུྃ ཨོཾ་མ་ཎི་པདྨེ་ཧཱུྃ ཨོཾ་མ་ཎི་པདྨེ་ཧཱུྃ

After giving them some time to recover, Vara said, "I will have the funds for the full amount in the morning. If you don't mind me asking, how do you plan to use such a large sum of money? I will be willing to advise, if you like."

Wade said, "Sir, we discussed this very thing on the plane from Kathmandu. All of us have different ideas, and I'll let Sonali and Todd speak for themselves. For starters, I am a pre-vet student, and I see a lot of suffering of dogs and cats due to animal overpopulation. I would like to set up worldwide spaying clinics with fees to be paid on a sliding scale. With vet volunteers, its operation could be self-sustaining, and, in time, we could effectively end euthanasia for population control.

"I also see one of the biggest problems in the world is the lack of uncontaminated water. Clean water would prevent any number of health issues, and I would like to begin a project to provide this for the world. It probably would take longer than my lifetime, but you have to start somewhere."

Vara nodded his head and turned to Sonali.

She said, "I am a premedical student, and many cannot afford basic healthcare. Besides that, one of the world's greatest problems is the HIV epidemic. When I finish medical school, and eventually complete my fellowship in Infectious Diseases, I would like to open clinics in the poorest countries. I want to provide patient education, not only for prevention, but also for treatment of HIV.

"Besides that I am interested in human rights — especially those of women. I would like to be involved with the promotion of equality and provide safe havens for those who have been abused."

The three then turned to Todd.

Todd said, "I have decided that while I'm at OSU, besides playing football, I want to get an M.B.A. You remember, Wade and Sonali, the disabled man at the Potala? The one I found later and gave the money to?" Wade and Sonali both nodded. "Just think what could happen if such men could be trained in a job and could fend for themselves. So, I would like to start schools that provide basic job skills at no cost. Along with that, I want to organize banks to provide interest-free micro-loans to those who want to make a go of it. Why give a fish to someone when you can give them a net?" He smiled, and the others smiled back.

Wade had never been prouder of his brother. All of Todd's rather amazing athletic accomplishments paled in comparison to Todd's new goals.

Vara looked seriously at the three of them. "I want to help you. I am certain that you can and will change the world for the better. For now, even without touching the principal on the money from the gems, at the tiny amount of one-percent interest, you'd earn around twenty million dollars yearly. With your per-mission, I will deposit all of your funds in a confidential Swiss account and set up a trust so that, when you are ready, your funds will be available. Do you need any money for expenses right now?"

Wade looked at Sonali and his brother. Their looks told all. Wade said, "No, we want to use it all to help others. Also, please deposit the money left for me by Tenzin. We've got enough to get by."

Vara said, "I am pleased to be of service to you. There is no reason that your dreams cannot become a reality."

Wade thought:

Matthew Johnston would be proud.

Not only that:

Tenzin would be proud.

In his mind's eye, he could see the old monk smiling at the three of them. Wade smiled back.

ༀམཎིཔདྨེཧཱུྃ ༀམཎིཔདྨེཧཱུྃ ༀམཎིཔདྨེཧཱུྃ

Sonali and Wade sat on the couch in a lavish living room at the home of Vara Vyas. They had, earlier in the evening, a most wonderful home-cooked Indian meal and were stuffed to the gills. Vara and his wife had stepped outside, and Todd was taking a garden stroll with their daughter, Sameena.

Everything had been arranged. Their flights to the United States had been set for the morning. Also, Wade had received confirmation of the Swiss account for the MWJ Foundation. Yes, it was all going smoothly.

Just then Todd and Sameena appeared through the French doors to the living room. They said their good nights, and she disappeared down the hall. Wade rubbed his eyes.

Did I see them kiss each other?

He looked over at Sonali — the shocked look on her face indicated she had seen the same thing.

As Todd sat on the chair across from them, he seemed dazed and glassy eyed.

Wade said, "Are you okay?"

Todd said, "Wade, I know this sounds crazy, but there is something, well, extraordinary about Sameena."

Sonali said, "What do you mean, Todd?"

Todd said, "There's something about her. Looking into her eyes, it seemed like I've known her before."

Wade and Sonali smiled and exchanged knowing glances.

They both knew exactly what he meant.

ཨོཾམ་ཎི་པདྨེ་ཧཱུྃ ཨོཾམ་ཎི་པདྨེ་ཧཱུྃ ཨོཾམ་ཎི་པདྨེ་ཧཱུྃ

Sonali looked over at a sleeping Wade.

Is there any way I could love this man any more?

She thought not.

Todd was also napping. It had been a whirlwind twenty-four hours. They were at last en route to the good old U. S. of A.

Wade opened his eyes. "Hi, love."

"Hi, love," she said in return.

Wade said, "You know, we haven't had a chance to talk since our time at Yamdrok. Do you mind sharing with me what you discovered in your meditations there?"

"You first," she said.

He looked around, and saw no one else seemed to be paying attention. He whispered, "Well, there's no doubt that Todd and I were connected in a past life. Also, in my meditation I was given some information that my past life, well," he paused, looking for the right words, "wasn't exactly stellar. It seems I've got a lot of catching up to do. Now the most important part is what I experienced concerning you and me."

"Oh?" she said, trying to sound indifferent.

"Yes," said Wade. "While those memories are fading fast, there is one thing I am certain of, and that is — we have been deeply in love in a past life. Now what do you remember?"

Sonali smiled. "Wade, I remember being madly in love with you, but I'm also remembering less and less."

Wade reached over and wrapped his arms around her. He whispered in her ear. "The most important message for me is that we are being given the gift of sharing our love again," Wade said. "I love you, Sonali."

"Wade, I love you more and more each day. I could even say more and more each lifetime." They both chuckled.

Wade took a few deep breaths. "Sonali, I know that this isn't the right time or place, but I can't wait any longer. I want to know if you will marry me. It would be a rush, but we could have the ceremony sometime in August before we go back to school. I don't want to delay another second. It's time for us to spend our lives together." He nervously looked at her, waiting for an answer.

Sonali moved her hand to her chin, as if she were thinking. "Hmmm," she said, "I suppose I do have one condition."

Wade's heart stopped. "And what would that be?"

"I want a tetherball pole in our backyard, and we have to play at least once a day, even if it's snowing. Winner gets a foot rub. Deal?"

"Deal," said Wade.

"Well, then, unless I can think of more conditions, and I suppose I can't at the present, the answer is Y—E—S, YES!"

They then threw their arms around each other, and as they hugged and kissed, for those with eyes to see, a faint, glowing, pulsatile orb began to materialize over their heads. There was a presence inside it, watching carefully and silently rejoicing.

Will I be called Rinji again? I wonder.

The presence glowed brighter for a brief period, then faded and disappeared.

Chapter 11

July 25, 2010, Claremore, Oklahoma

It was a hot, steamy Sunday afternoon, and Wade, Todd and Sonali decided to take a walk around beautiful Claremore Lake. With them were two panting dogs, Sunshine and Zoe, who romped and played in spite of the heat. A light, cool breeze danced off the lake and into their faces, turning what could have been a miserable stroll into a pleasant one. Wade and Sonali walked hand in hand, and, of course, Todd carried a football with him. Every so often one of them would run out for a pass, much to Todd's delight.

Wade smiled to himself. Their wedding plans did not catch their parents by surprise, and the date was happily set for Saturday, August 7th at ten in the morning. Of course, Todd was to be Wade's best man, while Indira, Sonali's sister, was chosen to be her maid of honor.

They had stayed in close contact with Vara Vyas, and on occasion Wade, Todd and Sonali would sit and discuss their future plans. All of them believed they could make the world a better place.

Why not?

As he thought of Vara, Wade said, "Hey, Todd, how's Sameena doing?"

Todd grinned as only Todd could. "Great! We chat through the Internet nearly every night. Looks like she and her parents will be visiting during fall break."

Sonali said, "That comes as a big surprise!"

Todd turned a light shade of red.

Suddenly a rabbit jumped from the bushes, and Sunshine sped after it. Zoe sat with her tongue hanging out. She had done enough chasing for the day.

Wade yelled, "I'll be back," and took off. After he caught up with her, he sat on the grass and stroked her head. "You know, Sunshine, I think we have been buddies before. Last time you were black and a lot bigger. I don't know what your name was then. Could it have been Blackie? I may have been into French words and called you — Noir."

Sunshine looked blissfully at her master. She wasn't concerned at all about the past. She was happy just to be sharing this time with him.

Wade kissed her on the head. "You want to come to OSU and live with Sonali and Zoe?" She barked excitedly. "I thought that you would. Come on, let's go back." They walked back to find Sonali and Todd sitting on the bank by the lake. Wade sat down beside them.

Zoe, like any self-respecting Lab, was swimming in the water, her eye on a group of ducks. Sunshine jumped in after her. The birds swam away from the eager dogs as fast as their legs could paddle.

"Hey, get a load of this," said Todd. Wade and Sonali looked in the direction he was pointing. A shirtless man wearing white drawstring pants was sitting in a lotus posture about twenty yards away. He was beneath the shade of a tree next to the water. "Are we still in Tibet? Let's go check it out."

They waited until the dogs swam back to shore, then the three rose and walked closer. Wade studied him closely and felt goose bumps rise on his forearms.

He looks familiar.

He appeared to be Arabic, with flowing tightly curled black hair, which was tied back behind his neck with a dark beaded tassel. He had his eyes closed, and he had a soft smile on his face. Curiosity drew the three closer, and when they came within ten feet, he opened his dark eyes and turned his head to face them.

"It's great to see you again," he said.

The three exchanged glances. "Where do we know you from?" Wade asked.

"From a land far, far away, but at the same time, as close as your breath," he mysteriously answered. "May I ask you a question?" Without waiting for a response, he added, "Would you like to skip stones?"

"Sure," Wade said. Sonali and Todd also nodded and began searching the bank for suitable rocks.

"You go first. I have to warn you. I have been practicing."

Todd found a perfectly shaped flat stone, and said, "Here goes nothing." He pulled his arm back and flung the flat surface parallel to the water. "One — two

— three — four — five. Let's see you beat that!"

Sonali said, "I'll go next." Using all the force available in her slender form, she tossed the rock onto the water. One — two — three — four — five — six! Ah-ha! I beat you, Todd." She smiled and strutted along the shoreline.

The stranger laughed heartily.

Wade grinned; this was something he was really good at. No one could beat him, of that he was confident. He found an ideal stone; it cradled in his hand perfectly. He snapped his wrist and let the rock fly. "One — two — three — four — five — six — seven!" He jumped up and down and yelled as if he might be a boxer who had just won a big prize fight.

For the first time, the stranger began to look a little nervous, and perspiration beaded on his forehead. He slowly rose from his sitting position, collected himself and took his time in selecting a rock. He stared at one for well over a minute and carefully placed it into his right hand. He looked even longer at the water, as if he were a golfer attempting a difficult putt. Finally he pulled his arm back and flung the rock. He counted out loud, "One — two — three — four — five — six — seven — eight — nine!" He immediately screamed at the top of his lungs, fell to his knees, then rose and danced along the shoreline. When he finally stopped he bent down on one knee and did a repetitive fist pump, yelling, "OOOH . . . OOOH . . . OOOH."

Wade, Sonali and Todd all laughed at his reaction.

Now he said, "You have to understand. I've been waiting a long time for this moment. Longer than you can imagine." Abruptly, he stood and added, "I must go. I will look forward to seeing all of you again."

"What do you mean?" Todd said.

"Someday you'll find out — someday." He looked at them and smiled.

After those words, he turned his back on them and walked toward the water. He gradually became more and more transparent, and when he reached the water's edge he was no longer visible.

ཨོཾ་མ་ཎི་པདྨེ་ཧཱུྃ་ ཨོཾ་མ་ཎི་པདྨེ་ཧཱུྃ་ ཨོཾ་མ་ཎི་པདྨེ་ཧཱུྃ་

Todd had taken his departure; he was off to Stillwater for a football meeting. But Wade and Sonali lingered by the tree where the man had sat, pausing in the wonder of it all. The many unbelievable events that had occurred since the monk visited them in December were beginning to seem more and more like a dream, something that had seemed real in the moment but with time becoming vaporous and ethereal.

Sonali glanced at the two dogs sleeping nearby. She then looked at Wade and said, "I've got my box here that the monk gave me. Did you bring yours?"

"I did."

"Let's open them now," said Sonali. "You first."

Wade pulled the small container covered in brown paper from his pocket. When he peeled the paper off and saw the black jewelry box, he knew immediately what it was. He opened it and again saw the Silver Star. He quickly snapped the lid shut. His reaction to it had mellowed somewhat, but he still wanted it away from him. "What should I do?" he asked.

Sonali nodded toward the lake.

"Good idea," he said, and without hesitation heaved it as far away from him as he could. Wade turned away before it hit the water. He did not want to see where it landed.

"Wow, that feels better," Wade said. He looked at Sonali. "Now it's your turn."

She unbuttoned the front pocket of her blouse and removed the little package within. She tore off the paper, and when she popped open the enclosed white jewelry box, she discovered the golden ring with diamonds on the front arranged in the shape of a lotus.

She removed the ring from its container and gradually rotated it around. It sparkled as the evening sun reflected through it. "Wade," she said, "as gorgeous as this ring is, it is part of the past, just as that medal was. As Tenzin told us, it is important to release the past, so that the present moment might be fully appreciated. Do you agree?"

Wade did not hesitate. "I do."

Sonali said, "I'm ready now. Are you?"

"Yes," he said.

With that, Sonali took one last look at the ring and threw it high into the air. It made a faint plopping sound as it hit the deep water. The concentric waves created by the ring spread out farther and farther until they lightly touched the shore next to them.

Fireflies began to dance as dusk arrived, and the two lovers sat and snuggled on their blanket by the lake.

"Wade," Sonali murmured, "do you know what a haiku is?"

"Isn't it a Japanese poem?"

"Yes," Sonali said. "Well, I have a surprise for you. We studied them in World Literature, and I have written one for us. Are you ready to hear it?"

Wade nodded.

Sonali said:

> Tibetan mountains
> Rolling Oklahoma hills
> We walk together

Wade let the feeling of the poetry embrace him. How could he love this woman more than he already did? There were no words to describe his feelings. He pulled her close to him.

As the stars began to become visible in the darkening sky, Wade said, "Hey, look, there's Orion, my favorite constellation."

Sonali said, "No, that can't be, because it's *my* favorite constellation."

Wade said, "How about if we share?"

Sonali wrinkled up her nose, as if seriously considering his offer, and finally said, "Well — okay — for you."

They laughed together.

As the night deepened, they lay on their backs and watched the array of stars as they moved across the night sky. The peaceful sound of cicadas surrounded them.

Acknowledgments

The four year process to research and write this book would not have been possible without a number of helpers. First of all, I want to thank my circle of friends, who not only offered their support but also their inspiration as this book was constructed. I am especially indebted to Chris Corbett, whose fresh ideas were most appreciated when I was at places of gridlock. Another who deserves special mention is Dr. Joe Westerheide, a Marine veteran of the Vietnam War. He assisted me in grasping the ins and outs of military life, and his deep spirituality greatly added to my understanding of some of the more challenging metaphysical concepts presented in this writing.

I also owe a great deal to my aunts and uncles, who shared many details of their lives in Oklahoma during the 1930s and 1940s. The history of that time is one of the most interesting in our country's brief existence, and the verbal relaying of information dwarfs the sometimes sterile descriptions found in history books. My father, Donald Gene Conrad, a native of Davidson, Oklahoma, is a proud veteran of U.S. Army in the Korean War, and also provided counsel concerning the armed forces. My mother, Patricia Sue Sutherland Conrad, was born and raised in Claremore, Oklahoma, and she shared many details from that historical area, which added greatly to the richness of this novel.

There is no question that this book could not have been completed without the cooperation of Gen Tsesum Tashi, an elder Tibetan monk who is currently in exile in Dharamsala, India. I came to know him when I became his sponsor many years ago. He provided details of Tibetan life that could not be found in any references, and, over the years, he has become one of my dearest friends.

Many thanks as well to my editors, Betty Wright and Betsy Lampe, who spent countless hours poring over the text with me. There was much labor required to put this work in an acceptable form, and they offered much time and energy in that regard.

There is no doubt, though, that I owe the greatest thanks to my wife, Sheridan. Not only did she provide the illustrations for this book, but she also inspired and encouraged me through this undertaking. The research required for this book was enormous, and during times of fatigue, she was the catalyst that consistently pointed me onward.

The true heroes of this book are the Tibetan people. The decades of suffering and hardship they have suffered at the hands of the Chinese government are among the worst chapters in the history of humankind. In support of their plight, I heartily recommend donations to the International Campaign for Tibet (ICT) at SaveTibet.org.

About the Author

Gary D. Conrad is a native Oklahoman who lives with his wife, Sheridan, and their dogs, Zoe and Inky, in Edmond, Oklahoma. His interests include Tibetan rights, meditation, the music of Joseph Haydn, organic gardening and wilderness hiking. He received his undergraduate diploma from Oklahoma State University, his M.D. degree from the University of Oklahoma, and since 1978 has been a practitioner of emergency medicine. He has also completed the fellowship in integrative medicine at the University of Arizona.

Accompanied by his wife, he made an expedition to Tibet and Japan in 2008 to gather first-hand information for *The Lhasa Trilogy*.

If you would like to contact him, he may be reached at his web site, GaryDConrad.com, where you will find some of the author's photographs from the starkly beautiful country of Tibet and news of his upcoming books.